Praise for Jessica Auerbach's previous suspense thriller, *Sleep, Baby, Sleep*

"This gripping story of a young mother searching for her kidnapped baby could have been lifted from recent headlines. . . . Told with edgy intensity."

— *Publishers Weekly*

"Her best work yet, well written and engrossing."

— *Library Journal*

By Jessica Auerbach:

PAINTING ON GLASS
WINTER WIFE
SLEEP, BABY, SLEEP*
CATCH YOUR BREATH*

*Published by Fawcett Books

CATCH YOUR BREATH

Jessica Auerbach

FAWCETT GOLD MEDAL • NEW YORK

A Fawcett Gold Medal Book
Published by Ballantine Books
Copyright © 1996 by Jessica Auerbach

All rights reserved under International and Pan-American Copyright Conventions. Published in the United States by Ballantine Books, a division of Random House, Inc., New York, and distributed in Canada by Random House of Canada Limited, Toronto.

http://www.randomhouse.com

Library of Congress Catalog Card Number: 96-91027

ISBN 0-449-15043-7

This edition published by arrangement with G. P. Putnam's Sons.

Manufactured in the United States of America

First Ballantine Books Edition: July 1997

10 9 8 7 6 5 4 3 2 1

For Sarah and Liz

CHAPTER ONE

ROSIE HEARS THE NOISE, BUT IT IS WAY FAR off, wandering around in the back of a very sweet dream, so she turns over and makes it go away for a while. And then the noise rolls up at her again from out of the dream, like a rumble or a growl; odd, but familiar. Then, as sudden as a lightning flash, she knows exactly what it is: It's her two-year-old, and he's struggling to breathe.

Please no, not again, she thinks as she grapples with the sheet and comforter, trying to untangle herself from the bed. She stumbles across the narrow hallway to Jason's room, scoops him up out of his crib, and she sees that, yes, it's like the last two times, with the gasping and with his breathing gone all screwy. Rosie flips on the light and sees her child's brown eyes big with terror, begging her for help. She holds him against herself, too tightly, maybe, but she can't help it; it's like he's going to slip right through her arms if she doesn't. She tries to remember what the doctor told her to do if it happened again, but she comes up blank. "Jason, honey," she pleads while she rocks him, but his breathing still comes in little twists that get cut off as soon as they begin. Rosie carries him into her room because she's going to have to get dressed and drive him to the hospital—she can't go in this see-through thing she's wearing—but as she tries to lower Jason down onto her bed for a minute, he clutches at the fabric of her nightgown and the gasping becomes more labored. She can't do it. She can't put

1

him down. What if she were to let him go and he stopped breathing altogether?

Call Quinn, she tells herself, because with the two of them here, they'll be able to deal with it. One of them will hold Jason and one will drive, and it'll be fine.

As she lifts the telephone receiver, she realizes that she's never coded Quinn's number into the memory. They're separated now, trying to be independent of each other, trying to stay further apart than one telephone digit. Pushing the first three numbers, the exchange, which she knows has got to be the same as hers, she figures the rest will come to her, but her fingers only hover, spiderlike, over the number pad. She must have put it in her address book, she thinks, and hangs up the phone. Before she can even find the book of numbers, she has to throw half the contents of her night table out onto the floor, but yes, she has written Quinn into it. Her fingers shake as she pushes at the buttons that'll connect her to him.

And then he doesn't answer. Jason's body feels rigid against her chest, like he's trying to resist whatever it is that's torturing him. She puts her cheek down on the baby's head. "Hurry up," she growls into the phone, and then she hears Quinn's voice, deep with sleep, saying hello. "Quinn, Jason's having a little trouble breathing," she says, minimizing, trying to sound calm so as not to make Jason any more frightened than he already is, but she knows she's doing a lousy job of it, feels the way her voice explodes as it hits the word *breathing*.

"What?" he asks.

"He's not breathing right, Quinn. You've got to come over here."

"Like croup?" he asks, much more alert sounding now.

"Maybe. Maybe it's like that," she reassures herself, for she has remembered the time Quinn is talking about, when Jason, only a tiny infant, had a terrible cold and almost stopped breathing. Maybe it was like that, maybe he had a cold now.

"You need to turn on the shower," Quinn says. "Make it hot, then take him into the bathroom so he can breathe the steam."

Yes, she remembered all that. She tosses the receiver down onto the bed, then carries her two-year-old into the bathroom.

She holds Jason against her hip while she reaches her hand into the shower to turn the hot water on full blast, just like Quinn said, and then she sits down on the floor, leaning up against the tub. She's crying now, because she's started to think about Jason dying and she can't bear it, losing him, she couldn't possibly live without him. She strokes his head and back and tells him that she loves him and everything's going to be all right, but she knows it's not. This is the third time this has happened and something is really wrong with her child. She's got the door closed to keep the steam contained, and that's why she doesn't hear Quinn when he comes to the front door and finds it bolted from the inside. She doesn't know that he has already ripped through the screening of the storm door and she doesn't hear him pounding both fists high against the wooden door. She doesn't hear him shouting her name into the night.

QUINN KNOWS ALL HIS NEIGHBORS ARE asleep, but that's just too damn bad. As soon as he realizes that Rosie's never going to hear him, he's at Louisa and Arnie's door, one house down, banging with both hands here, too, and ringing the bell for all it's worth till the front hall lights come on and Arnie opens the door to him.

Quinn doesn't explain much, just says Jason's sick, and Arnie has a fleeting moment of indecision about helping out— Quinn seems so out of control and Arnie knows there's been marital trouble, so it's possible Quinn's just on a rampage, one of those insane jealousy things, and that he's really gunning for Rosie. But then Arnie realizes Quinn's asking him only to call the police, so it's got to be all right. What we need is the police no matter what's wrong, Arnie tells himself as he lifts the receiver.

By the time the police get Rosie's door smashed in, the paramedics have arrived. They follow Quinn upstairs at a run and discover she's locked the bathroom as well. Quinn is expecting this second obstacle because he knows Rosie always pushes in the little brass button whenever she pulls the door closed behind her, even if she's just washing her hands or checking out her hair in the mirror. This time, though, Rosie hears

3

Quinn's fists against this hollow door, but she's badly startled by the commotion because she's been listening to the strangely syncopated rhythms of Jason's breathing, and because the hot fog and the sound of the water have wrapped around her so thoroughly, she's forgotten that Quinn should have been here long ago. She rises, stiff from sitting on the tile floor, and when she opens the door, she's surprised to see a whole group of people arrayed before her. "Give Jason to them," Quinn orders, and Rosie extends her arms slightly but finds it difficult to slide her own away, even when an emergency worker has his hands around Jason.

They lay her baby down in the hallway, where there is carpeting, and two men and a woman bend over him, so her small child seems to disappear altogether beneath them. He'd been very quiet for a while before they arrived, breathing a little better, almost sleeping, maybe, Rosie had thought, but now he calls out—for her, she thinks—and she hears the choked, frightened syllables and hears the way the breath doesn't fill him up properly, and she circles her arms around herself so she can stand the sound and sight of what is happening. Quinn has knelt down over Jason along with the paramedics, and Rosie starts to bend, too, in order to join them. She's only partway down when her head goes woozy, maybe from all the steam, and she starts to lose her balance. Somebody reaches for her and guides her over to her room, to her bed, but she can't stand being so far away and starts to get up. "Hey, relax, Quinn's with him," her guardian says, pushing gently back down on her shoulder. She sees it's Ben Lesser, a police officer, one of Quinn's coworkers. Ben tells her to take some deep breaths, and she does, and she sees color come back into the room, though she hadn't even noticed it had left. Ben is holding her hand and sitting next to her. "Relax," he says, and he's wearing such an overblown smile, Rosie's sure he's hiding something from her. She grips his hand, almost clawing at it.

"Jason's okay," Ben tells her. "He's doing fine. You want me to go check again?" She nods. It gets quieter suddenly and she realizes the water in the shower has abruptly stopped. Someone has finally thought to turn it off.

When Ben returns, he tells her that Jason's just fine, that they've given him an injection and his breathing's a little shallow, but he's doing okay. He says the emergency people think they should take him up to the hospital just to make sure, only because it doesn't seem like croup to them. So, just to make sure, he says again, leaving the thought hanging unfinished. And he smiles again, too. Everything about him looks exaggerated—the ends of his black hair seem sharpened and the bristles of beard just beneath the skin make Rosie think of a wire brush.

"Why can't we take him in the car?" Rosie asks. "Then I can hold him, be with him."

"It's better to let somebody who's not involved do the driving," Ben says. "But you'll be right next to him," he assures her. She's thinking that the ambulance might frighten Jason. She knows that if they're even thinking about an ambulance that Jason must be in serious trouble and realizes that mostly she's the one who's scared now. Ben says he'll go make sure there's room for her in the ambulance.

By now she's sitting up, suddenly conscious that her nightgown barely covers her. She makes her way over to her bureau and gets her aqua sweats out of the bottom drawer. She pulls the pants on over her gown, vaguely aware that she'll probably be uncomfortable later with that extra layer of clothing inside her waistband.

Ben sticks his head through the doorway. "If you want to go in the ambulance with Jason, you have to hurry," he warns her.

"Where's Quinn?" she asks.

"He's going, too," Ben tells her, and he motions toward the hall, the obvious place, and Rosie moves in that direction, pulling on her sweatshirt as she goes.

"What's wrong with him?" she asks when she sees they've lifted her child onto a stretcher. Her voice is a quavery attempt that is lost in the paramedics' strident instructions to one another. She wants to talk to Quinn, but he's already started down the stairs just behind Jason.

By the time Rosie gets to the top of the stairs, she sees they're already out the door, and the steep look of the stairs makes her head go dizzy. She feels like she can't hold to a center, that pieces of her might break off, vital pieces will fly away, and that what will be left won't be enough to help Jason. Her body shivers and even her teeth chatter. A police officer takes hold of her arm and, though it feels to her as though her feet can't move at all, she somehow gets down the whole flight of stairs, out the splintered front door, and into the open belly of the ambulance.

CHAPTER TWO

NOBODY TELLS THEM ANYTHING. THEY'RE just left there in a waiting room. Nobody tells them anything except that the doctors will talk to them just as soon as they're free. And Quinn won't come near her. He hasn't said a word to her since they left the house. She doesn't even know where they've taken Jason. "He could be in surgery for all we know," Rosie says when Quinn's pacing brings him within range of her voice.

"They'd tell us that, wouldn't they?" he asks, looking thoroughly shocked.

"We signed that release—it said they could do anything."

"We need to talk to somebody," he declares, then strides off to the nurses' station.

She's right behind him, wanting to hear, wanting to stand next to him, but the nurse (who looks like she's about thirteen) hands him off to another nurse, who tells him he has to wait for the shift supervisor. This woman, the one who purportedly is in charge of this segment of the world, is nowhere to be seen. Rosie takes a few steps back and finds support against the wall. "If she's the supervisor, then why the hell isn't she supervising?" Quinn wants to know.

"She's just stepped into the ladies' room, sir," the nurse says, and Rosie knows the woman has recognized the rage of the man who stands before her, and that she will choose her words carefully from now on. "Give her one minute, sir," she says with measured deliberateness, a clear warning to back off.

Now he is pacing a shorter distance, the length of the nurses' station. Rosie counts his steps and tries not to keep looking down the hall to where the restrooms are. When the supervisor does appear, smoothing her white uniform over her hips, Quinn heads her off only a few steps from where she emerges. After the woman has made her way behind the station and checked a clipboard and a computer screen, Rosie hears her say, "I have no information right now." She goes on to say that Quinn will definitely be the first to know of any news, as though there is a contest being waged and he should be delighted to be in this honored, first-place position. "I know this is difficult, but please, try to be patient," the nurse suggests. Quinn turns his back on the woman and Rosie watches him walk off to a far corner of the floor, where he steps out a small, closed circle.

It's taking too long, Rosie thinks, and she can imagine it all in her head, doctors and nurses standing over Jason's still body, choosing up among themselves who will have to deliver the tragic news. Now she no longer wants to be here when the phone rings in the nurses' station. She doesn't want one of those women in white to know her fate before she does or to pronounce the finality of her sentence aloud into the air that smells so thoroughly of cleaning products. She moves off into the waiting area, tracing a walking tour around the chairs and couch, and after a while Quinn's circle opens wider, and their paths weave back and forth over each other's till a nurse offers them coffee, which they both refuse. They want what they want: news of Jason. And only moments after that, while their anger churns in an ugly mix with their fear, a man in mint green scrubs comes down the hall toward them, asking if they are the Sloans.

"Yes," Quinn says, his voice no more than a whisper, and she can feel his heart, along with hers, tighten for the terrible, wounding blow he thinks he is about to receive.

"I'm Dr. Grady," the man says, holding out his right hand. "Nice to meet you. Jason's doing just grand. He's a strong boy, and he's going to be bouncing off the walls just like any other terrible two by tomorrow." He puts a hand on each of their shoulders, and she feels herself crumple a little, wishes they could move even closer, the three of them, put their arms around one another. She needs holding now, even though the news is good. "What we need to do," the doctor continues, "is to go over a few things, make sure we've got a complete history, now that we're over the crisis."

He guides them back over toward the blue vinyl couch and she hears Quinn begin to laugh, to babble, to talk of his fear, his overreaction. Rosie still can't take a full breath and she knows it's because she doesn't really believe what the doctor has said. "Are you sure he's all right?" she asks, interrupting whatever it was he was saying.

"He's all right," Dr. Grady says, and now he pats her knee. He is sitting opposite them, on a table, actually, a solid, Formica-covered cube, in front of their couch.

"I want to see him," she says.

"Of course. In five minutes you'll be able to go down to his room. But let's get through this history business first."

Dr. Grady has brought a clipboard over to the waiting area and he begins to run through the information that Quinn gave the paramedics back at the house. "Let's see," he says. "Mr. Sloan, you told the paramedics that Jason is twenty-four months old, in general excellent health, no known allergies, no medications, no serious illnesses, no major surgeries, no previous breathing difficulties other than an infant attack of croup." He looks up at the two of them. Quinn is nodding. She has to tell now. "Has he been exposed to anybody with similar symptoms?" Quinn shakes his head but looks at Rosie for confirmation.

"No," she tells the doctor.

"Any exposure to people with illnesses, or to chemicals or toxins, anything like that?"

"No," they both respond.

"Any travel outside the U.S.?"

"No," Rosie says. She needs to tell. "There was another attack," she says.

"The croup thing," Quinn clarifies, nodding toward the physician. "But that's not the same, right?"

The doctor begins to answer and Rosie says, "No, not that, not the croup," though she is aware that she's begun shaking—she doesn't know why she hasn't told Quinn about this before and she's not sure why she said *another* attack, rather than *two other* attacks, which would certainly be the more accurate way of saying it. "Twice." She forces the word out. "I brought him to the emergency room the first time. The second time I took him to the doctor's office because it was daytime, office hours."

"When, Rosie?" Quinn snaps at her.

"Two weeks ago, no, maybe three, I'm not sure. I brought him here. To the emergency room, I mean." It's the doctor she's talking to, because she can't actually bring herself to look at Quinn.

Grady takes out a pen and begins making notes. "I'll get the record sent up from downstairs. "Was it a similar onset and symptoms?"

"Yes."

"Both times?"

"Yes."

Quinn has stood. "We're separated," he tells the doctor. "I didn't know about this."

"Was he given any medication either time?" he asks, directing his question to Rosie.

She doesn't answer because she feels scared all over again. Of course she should have told them about medication before any other treatment was given. She should have given them Jason's doctor's name, too.

"He had medication," she tells Dr. Grady now. "And I know you should have had that information, but it was just Benadryl the first time, just a simple antihistamine, over-the-counter stuff. Then the other doctor started him on another antihistamine and theophylline."

"When was his last dose of each?"

"Bedtime. Eight o'clock."

"You know, Rosie, they asked me about this, back at the

house, and I should have had this information." The tension is visible in his lips, audible in the sound of the long, narrow intake of breath.

"Yes," Grady says. "You two need to have closer communication about Jason, obviously. Much closer." Quinn's lower jaw moves around, seeking, but not finding, a resting spot.

"Is my son in danger from this other medication?"

"No, no," the physician says, rising. "All we've given him is a follow-up injection to the adrenaline the EMTs gave him. There's total compatibility, no issues of drug interactions, nothing to worry about. In the future, of course, Mrs. Sloan, you have to be very, very careful that such information is shared between both parents so that it can be given to any medical personnel. Drug interactions can sometimes be worse than the presenting condition. Some medical procedures interfere with medication, too. Do you understand what I'm saying and how important this is to your son's health?"

"Yes," she hisses back at him, and hates that he's treating her like a naughty child. Rosie doesn't have to be told she's behaved badly. She's a physician's daughter, so she knows, through a full lifetime of experience, that a thorough, accurate history can sometimes be more important than a physical examination. Her chest feels tight and her breathing is surely as shallow as Jason's.

"Give me about five minutes to make sure he's settled comfortably and then you can see him. I'll buzz the nurses' station, and they'll let you know we're ready for you." And then he walks away, leaving them together in the empty waiting area.

Quinn waits till the doctor has entered the elevator, then he leans down toward his wife, who is still seated on the couch. "Why did you keep that information from me?"

"I don't know," she says, "but it's over now, okay? He's all right, and we should take it from there."

"Really? You mind telling me what happened to your fabulous medical knowledge all of a sudden?"

"This doesn't have anything to do with medical knowledge, Quinn."

"No? You don't know that a doctor should always be told

what medications a person is on before starting treatment? I seem to remember you're the one who made me tell the dentist I took Tylenol before he cleaned my teeth."

"It was an extraction you were having, Quinn, not a routine cleaning, and it was aspirin, which interferes with clotting. There's a world of difference. Don't exaggerate. And anyway, what's your point?"

"That you of all people should know better." He speaks each word as though it has a bitter taste upon his tongue.

"All right, Quinn, but they didn't ask me, they asked you."

"How could I give them that information if you didn't even tell me my child was on medication?" Not surprisingly, the bulky table doesn't move under the sharp blow he delivers to it with his fist.

"Quinn," she says quietly, aware that the nurses must be getting their thrills from watching them fight, "I should have given that information and now I'm sorry. Can we just move on from here? Look, when we go in to see Jason we should be unified and supportive, not tearing at each other this way."

"Why lie to him?"

She clamps her teeth together so hard it hurts. "Because he's two years old, Quinn. He's still a baby. Our baby. And he needs us."

Quinn stands and walks a few steps away. She watches his back rise.

Rosie sees one of the nurses heading toward them. "You can see your son now," she says as she approaches them. "Fourth floor, room 417."

"Thank you," Rosie says. By the time she retrieves her purse from the other end of the couch, Quinn is by the elevator, holding the door open and motioning impatiently for her to hurry.

JASON IS ASLEEP AND LOOKING LIKE ONE OF those chubby-cheeked holy infants of Renaissance painting. Rosie leans over to kiss him and to listen to the sound of his breathing. The rhythm is perfectly even, but it seems too loud, much too pronounced. "What's that rasp?" she asks Quinn.

Her husband bows his head lower, so close to Jason he obscures him from Rosie's view. "I don't hear anything."

"He's not right," she protests, and grabs for the call button, which swings on a cord over Jason's head.

"Rosie, don't," he admonishes her, and moves to wrest the mechanism from her, but she jerks it toward herself and presses it firmly with her thumb.

"It's just like Abby," she wails at him. "I'm not standing by this time, letting him die."

"It's not like with Abby," he says quietly. "He's stabilized. He's fine."

"How do you know?" she snaps at him. And when the nurse has barely made it through the doorway, Rosie proclaims, "His breathing's still off."

"He's fine," the nurse tells her when she has leaned over the child, pausing there with a faraway look in her pale eyes. Her plastic pin says she is Betty Adams, R.N. "He's just exhausted."

"Maybe I should take him home tonight," Rosie muses aloud.

"Now, honey, he's going to get the best possible care here, you know that," the R.N. says as she straightens the blanket, then straightens her beige hair. No, I don't, Rosie thinks. "You've been up all night with this child and you're going to help him most if you get yourself home and get some decent sleep."

"She's right," Quinn says. "I'll call a cab and take you home so you can rest."

"Don't you condescend to me, too, Quinn. You're just as tired as I am."

"Hey, I know that," he says. "We're both exhausted. We should both go home."

"I'm staying," she insists, and asks the nurse if she can spend the rest of the night in the room.

"You can," she says, "but I'll tell you from long experience that it's not in the family's best interest. You won't sleep and

13

you won't be in any shape to take care of him tomorrow." The woman adjusts her hair again and Rosie realizes it's a wig. She's an older woman, closing in on retirement age.

"I'll decide what's in my family's best interest," Rosie growls back.

"Rosie," Quinn pleads with her, "you're not going to be able to take care of him tomorrow if you're wiped out."

"So what are you suggesting? That we just leave him here? Have him wake up alone and be completely terrified?" A sob rises up from behind the curtained cell next to Jason's.

"Please keep your voices down," Nurse Adams requests.

"I'm staying," Rosie says, her voice whispery but defiant.

"Okay, I'll come back in the morning and take him over to my place."

"You don't need to. I'll take him home." She knows she should be letting him share the burden of Jason's care, but she can't concede that point. She wouldn't be able to concede anything right now, she thinks. Maybe it's the fatigue or the separation, she's not sure, but she feels like she has to be the one in charge. Absolutely, absolutely.

A steady, sad whimper of a song is coming from the next cubicle. "You really must go out in the hall," the nurse warns them. Quinn has already headed for the door, and for a brief second Rosie thinks about kicking the nurse, or pulling at the wig, but is instantly jolted by her own imaginings. What am I doing? she asks herself almost as soon as the violent image has taken form. She follows Quinn out into the hall.

"I'm sorry," she says when she catches up to him. "I'm definitely losing it. You're right—one of us should stay and one of us should take him in the morning." They nod to each other and in their exhaustion almost forget to assign the tasks, one to the other. In the end, Quinn stays and it is a difficult, sad tug for her, leaving Jason, but she knows she's of little use without sleep, and Quinn, from long years on strange police shifts, has learned to operate at high efficiency on very low power.

"This is silly, because there's no way on earth that I'm actually going to sleep," she says to him when she leaves, but in the cab going home, she falls asleep in each of the small breathing spaces the cabby leaves in his monologue about Bradford's corrupt city government. When the cab pulls up in front of her house, she sees the damaged front door and suffers a wave of panic. I can't deal with any more problems, she thinks. If Quinn were here, she tells herself as she touches a finger to the split wood of the door, he'd figure out some way to fix it to get us through the night safely. Or at least he'd be here, a large body on the side of the bed closest to the door with a length of two-by-four on the floor next to him, a service revolver atop the armoire. Standing outside the door, she eyes it from different angles to see just how visible her vulnerability is to someone passing by on the street. She considers draping a sheet over the door, feels a light thrill at the brilliance of her own idea, then realizes it would only call more attention to the house.

When it is clear that there is no real solution at this hour of the night, she leaves the partially shattered door as closed as she can and climbs the stairs to her bed. When she checks that the stereo and VCR are still there and convinces herself that there hasn't been a break-in in her absence, she picks up the pile of things she threw to the floor earlier in the night and puts it all back in her night table. Then she lies down for a moment, just to take stock, letting it sink in for the first time, really, that Jason is fine, that the crisis is past, and she sleeps well on into the day.

CHAPTER THREE

SHE DOESN'T REALLY KNOW WHY SHE DIDN'T tell Quinn about Jason's trip to the emergency room. Probably because by the time she actually got Jason to the hospital he was perfectly fine. What exactly would she have said? I took Jay to the hospital because I thought he was sick, but he wasn't? What would have been the point of that other than to make herself sound stupid?

Jason's recovery had been pretty miraculous. It reminded her of what her father used to call The Laying On of Eyes. With certain patients, he said, symptoms disappeared when the doctor walked into the examining room. In Jason's case, he was cured when she'd pulled into the parking lot at the hospital. Though of course being only two years old, he wouldn't have known where he was, so she didn't really think it was the same phenomenon at all. Whatever was wrong with him had simply run its course by that time.

It was almost embarrassing to show up with a kid in emergency and have him be squirming out of her arms because he wanted to get down and explore the place. He smiled at the receptionist and flirted with the nurse by catching her eye and then burying his head in his mother's chest. Rosie found herself almost wishing he'd just lie back and act lethargic or gasp once or twice just to prove she wasn't making it all up. The doctor couldn't even get Jason to lie still because the child was so interested in all the shiny things in the examining room. Rosie was so defensive: she felt like she had to make it sound like Jason had been at death's door the whole way over in the car.

Of course Rosie had been scared out of her mind back in the kitchen, otherwise she wouldn't have brought him to the hospital at all. She almost passed out when she heard him gasping—gulping, really—for air. And the way he'd stared at her, those big brown eyes looking up at her, begging her to save him, to explain to him why he couldn't get any air, had turned her inside out. But it'd paralyzed her, too. She'd just stared back at him, listening to the sound of her own heartbeat, immobilized for the longest time. Then she'd reached down and scooped him up into her arms, and from then on it was all instinct, no thought at all. She crooked her finger into his mouth, in case he was choking on a toy or something he'd picked up off the kitchen floor. When she brought her finger out looking brown and syrupy, she'd really panicked. God, it looked so much like blood. That's when she'd clicked off the oven and grabbed her keys off the counter. She didn't even stop to get her license.

She strapped him into the car seat, but then as soon as they were moving she was kicking herself for not thinking to move the seat into the front with her so she could touch him, reassure him, at least see him while she was driving. He was still gulping then, and she was thinking she was going to have to pull over and do mouth-to-mouth. She was trying not to look at what was drying on her hands because she knew, if he was hemorrhaging, there wasn't going to be much she could do for him.

At the traffic light at North Street, she turned around and looked at him, really scared of what she was going to see back there, and she realized he wasn't gulping anymore, that he was looking around, and when he looked at her, he gave her a smile—not much of one, it was true, but she knew he was telling her he was back, that he was breathing again and on top of whatever he'd been fighting. His cheeks were so red, they looked almost burned. And then she saw he was still clutching the big stainless mixing spoon she'd given him loaded up with chocolate, only it'd been licked shiny clean. She looked at her hands then and realized it was chocolate that she'd scooped from his mouth and knew he was probably having an allergic reaction to it. And it was chocolate that *she'd* given him to eat. Pure, melted semisweet chocolate. A dose that would have made anybody with the slightest tendency toward allergy break out in full battle symptoms. So maybe that was part of why she didn't tell Quinn.

She knew what he'd have said: "You're the one who had the fit when I let him have a chocolate chip cookie." And he'd have been right. She was well aware that kids could have chocolate allergies. Severe ones. Respiratory reactions. So she had no excuse. She hadn't told him because she was afraid he'd say Jason should be with him from now on.

She'd been making one of her mother's recipes, and when her mother made it, back when Rosie was a kid, she'd always handed the chocolate-filled spoon on down to her. A ritual; part of the whole process of how the cake got made. She remembered how she felt when she handed the spoon to Jason, like she was acting for her mother, connecting the three generations.

So she hadn't told Quinn, because Jason was fine, perfectly fine. She could have turned around in the hospital lot and not gone to the ER at all and that would have been an entirely reasonable way to handle it. She was actually being pretty hypercautious having him checked out, but with losing Abby, she couldn't take chances with breathing stuff. Not that a two-year-old could actually die of SIDS. But anyway, every tiny thing that ever happened in Jason's life didn't always have to be reported back to Quinn, did it?

The emergency room doctor, a thirtyish, comfortably rounded man, confirmed Rosie's diagnosis about chocolate being the probable cause. Jason's symptoms—the reddened cheeks, the reduced air passage—were typical of an allergic response. "Just don't give him any more chocolate for a few years," he'd warned her, though he said that chances were Jason would eventually outgrow the allergy. "What you gave him today probably wasn't just a tiny taste. Am I wrong about that?" She'd shaken her head then, feeling small and silly, pointing to the spoon in Jay's hand.

"Phew," he'd said. "That would've done it. If you hadn't so seriously overdosed him this time, he might never have shown a reaction." And then he'd taken a pen from the pocket of his white coat and started drawing on the paper of the examining table. "See," he said, "when we start children on new foods, we start with small amounts." His hand shaped a sideways V like a musical crescendo over and over on the paper, but the pen left no ink marks on the glossy paper. "Anyway," he said, slipping the ballpoint back into his pocket, "increase slowly over time in order to test out the tolerance. And avoid foods like chocolate altogether, if you can, because they don't exactly contribute to nutritional health. It's just common sense, really," he added. Rosie kept her eyes down on the markings on the white paper so she wouldn't start telling him she knew all this, that she was a doctor's daughter, that she'd read everything there was to read about nutritional sequencing for infants and toddlers. None of that exactly jived with handing a mixing spoon full of chocolate over to a two-year-old, so it seemed prudent to keep her silence.

By then she was already thinking, I can't let Quinn know. Because she'd just handed that spoon to poor Jason, said, "Special treat, sweetheart," and then he'd smiled up at her, looking almost quizzical, like he was asking, what do I do with it? "Well, you know what to do with it, don't you, big stuff?" she'd said. "You put a spoon in your mouth, don't you?"

And then he'd opened his lips, unsure still, maybe because it was so oversized for his little mouth, and she had to laugh at how suspicious he seemed. His pink tongue came out, twisting a short distance over the brown surface, then back into his mouth. That look of surprise on his beautiful face, the lips curled outward in clear appreciation, the smile that she could eat up in a second, and the tongue again, no hesitation this time. What a face he had under those deep brown curls, she had thought, and leaned down to kiss his chubby cheek even as he kissed at the spoon. "Good boy," she said to him, thinking that

19

would hold him for a while, and then went back to finishing her cake and getting it ready for the oven.

And she would have let him lick the bowl, too, if he hadn't started gasping.

But thank God, he'd been better, totally recovered by the time she got him to the hospital. The doctor had given him a small dose of Benadryl (though, personally, she didn't see the point, the acute reaction was past, but he said because Jason's cheeks were still inflamed, the histaminic reaction was still ongoing, so it was better to be safe than sorry). If she hadn't panicked back at the house but had figured out it was the chocolate before she went leaping into the car, she could have given Jay a dose of Benadryl herself and that would have been the end of it.

The ER doctor suggested that she take Jason in to see an allergist so he could be completely checked out. Just to be sure. "It's almost certain that you've simply overloaded his system, but sometimes a reaction like this can be an early warning signal of a more general allergic disposition in a child." She asked for the name of an allergist with a subspecialty in pediatrics or at least somebody with good rapport with kids, and the emergency room physician wrote a name and telephone number out for her.

At the time, her main goal had been getting the hell out of the hospital so she didn't have to hear any more nasty comments about what a bad mother she was or implications about her lack of common sense. Good doctors do not condescend, her father had always said. Well, this one was young, she thought, and he still had a hell of a lot to learn. Looking back, though, it was clear the doctor was right about one thing. It *was* an early warning of some really bad stuff to come.

CHAPTER FOUR

AT FIRST QUINN HAD REFUSED TO GO TO A marriage counselor with Rosie. He said he wasn't talking about his marriage to a stranger. "Then talk to me about it," she had practically begged him.

"What's to talk about?" he asked her.

"That you never talk to me anymore. That right now you can sit there and say there isn't anything to talk about."

He shrugged. Poked at something, perhaps a crumb, on the table. He twisted his chair a little more away.

Rosie had taken lately to toughing it out, returning silence for silence, but that wasn't getting them anywhere. She'd also tried gentling him: "What, Quinn? You look so out of it, what's on your mind?" Those questions, he seemed not to hear at all. The counseling was the only other thing she could think of. What she suspected was that Quinn was in love, or at least involved in some way, with someone else. But she couldn't bring herself to ask him that.

"I want out," she said, and the words were cold and startling to her.

He moved his hand over his neck like he was trying to ease his own swallow. "Don't do that to Jason," he said after a few moments.

She felt the absence of the two of them in his response. Like he was admitting it: their part of the marriage was dead. Only Jason was left. Like the remainder in a division problem. "Do you honestly think this is a good situation for Jason, Quinn? Won't it better for him to see us each be happy apart instead of so unhappy together?"

"Will you be happy if we're apart?" he asked her, seeming to twist something that she couldn't see between his hands.

"Yes. And I think it'll be better for Jason." She expected a response. She could even visualize it. Quinn rising to his full height out of the chair, gesturing desperately, hands outstretched, grasping, resisting. Instead he tilted his head slightly, considered a moment, and nodded slightly.

"I want to be the one to stay here," she said. "I don't want to move Jason." He turned sharply toward her with a penetrating stare that made her shiver. "You need to find an apartment," she persevered through the glare.

"You're the one who wants out," he reminded her. "And besides," he continued, scraping a fingernail along a raised grain marking on the table, "who said Jason stays with you?" And then he'd pushed back his chair, opened the back door, and left.

So of course she dropped the matter immediately. She didn't know what else she could really do in the face of such a threat. She was terrified that Quinn would draw up battle lines and hurl Jason headlong into the fray.

She went into counseling on her own. Zoe, her therapist, was quick to point out that their sessions couldn't be called marriage counseling if both husband and wife weren't in attendance. She warned Rosie not to start thinking that the relationship could be pieced back together from such incomplete patchwork. They would work on strategies to bring Quinn into the counseling, she suggested, and if they were successful, then they could begin to move on from there.

Rosie imagined that Quinn came to the sessions and that they sat together in the same awkward silence that they shared at her kitchen table. She heard herself ask her husband: Are you having an affair? Then she saw Zoe lean toward him so as to hear every word. But Rosie didn't stay with the image long enough to hear the answer.

Rosie opted for yet another approach with Quinn. She told

him she'd begun the counseling and that he was welcome any time. She gave him the times of the next two appointments. He said, "Did you ever think that maybe there's nothing to say?"

She waited for her tears to begin, for the cruelly bitter words to take effect, but nothing happened. She realized this now, finally: she believed him. There was nothing left to say.

SHE MOVED TO THE GUEST ROOM. AFTER ALL, they hadn't made love in over a year now. Zoe said it made no sense to share a bed if there was no intercourse—sexual or otherwise—between them. "Accustom yourself to physical distance," the therapist urged.

A week later she complained to Zoe about the new sleeping arrangement. "It doesn't help. It's not working at all."

"What was it you were expecting would happen?" Zoe inquired.

Rosie couldn't say. She stumbled and stuttered but drew no coherent picture with her words.

"Did you think that if you moved across the hall he'd come running to you?"

Rosie saw it now: Quinn kneeling alongside the guest room bed, his hands held together in front of him as though he ardently beseeched her. She blushed to think how wrong she'd been.

"You're still waiting for a miracle," Zoe told her. "All this arrangement is supposed to do is help the two of you begin the gradual process of pulling further away. In as amicable a way as possible," she added. "That's what Jason needs right now."

Then Rosie took one more step. She packed her bags. Not everything, mind you, just enough for two weeks for herself and Jason. She loaded all of it except for one suitcase into the car, then waited in the front hall for Quinn to come home from work. She might have departed before he came home and left a note on the kitchen table or taped one up on the bathroom mirror explaining her absence. She preferred, however, to stand in the front hall, the remaining suitcase at her feet while Jason wound up a toy mouse and sent it scurrying all over the wood floor of the hallway. She had imagined the scene, with clear blocks of color—Jason's red shirt, her taupe clothing, the black suitcase—in sharp contrast, one against the other, the words they would speak, dark echoes in the vast uncarpeted space. She thought Quinn would remember the look and sound of it, too. It was important that he remember it. She might even have entertained the thought that he would be haunted by it.

"I'm going," she said when he opened the front door wide enough to see the full tableau. Framed in the doorway, he looked huge to her. There were funny shadows all over his face—bristles of beard starting to show, weird dark hollows under his eyes, and even his short dark hair seemed more a reflection or reference than it did honest-to-goodness hair. Her own small-limbed body felt oddly delicate and she almost had to shake it off, take on a different, larger, firmer self, to make it all work. She explained that she'd be visiting friends and handed him an itinerary complete with phone numbers. She saw that Jason had made his way over to his father and now hugged him around the knees. Quinn lifted his son and kissed him. For a moment she thought he was going to refuse to relinquish the child, and she was furious with herself for preferring her staged event over a simple note, but then Quinn put Jason down. Rosie took her child's hand, picked up the remaining suitcase with her free hand, stepped around Quinn, and went out the door. As Zoe had instructed, Rosie made no reference to what would happen after the two weeks were up.

By the time Quinn called Rosie to say he would be willing to go into marriage counseling with her, she had started to enjoy being away. She knew she wasn't fully on her own, living with friends as she was, but she could now imagine her way through to independence, and she liked what she saw. She was almost disappointed that she would have to go back and try again.

QUINN WAS LATE TO THERAPY EVERY TIME and, not surprisingly, he spoke very little. What he did say, he directed at Zoe. The therapist wanted them to speak of the beginnings of their relationship, but it was almost more than either of them could bear, remembering the silliness of who they once had been. By the end of the sessions, they'd edged away from each other so often, their chairs were turned nearly back to back.

Zoe suggested they talk about why they couldn't look at each other. Rosie started to offer her analysis, but Zoe stopped her. "You're doing almost all the talking. Let's hear from Quinn as to why he thinks you can't look at each other. Quinn?" Zoe prompted.

"Because we don't *want* to look at each other," he said, the words petulant; a child's response to an adult's insensitive inquiry.

"But what I'm really asking is *why* you don't want to, Quinn."

"Because it's over." And then husband and wife tried once again to edge their chairs away from one another, but they'd gone as far as they could in that direction, and any further turning would bring them slightly closer together. So neither of them moved.

"Do you want to talk about the anger, say, the source of the anger?" Zoe inquired.

After some time passed, Rosie tried sending her voice into the void. "I'm angry that he doesn't speak to me."

"Quinn?" Zoe did her prompt again.

Quinn leaned back and Rosie could hear his breaths deepen. "We need to face the fact that it was always wrong. We got married to shock our parents. We were doomed from the start," he said solemnly.

Zoe gave them assignments to do at home. They were to make a list of things they liked about each other, and then a list of things they liked to do in their leisure time, and one time, a list of their likes and dislikes. They were supposed to compare their lists and see which things they had both written down. Jason was the only entry that ever appeared on lists they'd both written. "This is such crap. It's so unreal," Quinn said.

"So what's real, Quinn?" Rosie asked.

"What's real? Death."

"Death?"

"Yes. My work is real. Seeing a teenager kill two of his

friends by driving drunk is real. Seeing that guy the landlord blew away because his rent was late, ditto. Or having a baby burn up in a car, with the mother screaming to save her, I think that's pretty real, too. Remember all that stuff?"

"Yes, Quinn, I remember, you're quite the soldier, but don't change the subject. It doesn't have anything to do with what we're talking about, does it? We're talking about our therapy."

"All right, so then let's talk about where the hell you found this therapist."

"She comes highly recommended and she's got great credentials," Rosie said.

"So of course it can't possibly matter that she's a bad therapist?"

"She isn't."

"*I* could ask better questions than she does."

"Ask, then," she suggested.

He looked down and Rosie thought, now it'll happen. He'll start talking. This is where Zoe has been leading us, to this moment. His eyes were turned downward, and she could hear the unevenness of his breathing. He had something to say to her, she thought—or was that mere wishful longing? "Poor Jason," he said, and raised his eyes toward the ceiling.

"What do you mean?" she asked, trying to make more words come from him, trawling for meaning, casting her net one more time.

"Because we're splitting, Rosie. Because it's all over."

AFTER THAT, HE SPOKE EVEN LESS IN THEIR sessions, and when he did, his words were invariably shouted. "This is what it's come to," Rosie complained to the therapist. "It's either total silence or a shouting match in our house now. And Jason's the one taking the brunt of it," she added, scanning Quinn's face to see if she had gotten a rise from him by evoking his child's name.

"I never raise my voice in front of Jason," Quinn retorted, his volume forcing her words back down.

"Oh, yes, you do," Rosie growled back, though she knew he was actually right—he didn't shout when Jason was around. That was when he went most thoroughly silent. The urge to contradict him, though, had become too powerful to control.

"This marriage was and is a mistake," Quinn pronounced. "Let's get on with the next step."

Zoe said it wasn't helpful to think of relationships in terms of mistakes.

"You're the one who said you didn't think we'd be happier apart," Rosie addressed Quinn, completely ignoring Zoe's remark.

"That was a long time ago." And Rosie could feel him shut down again, as though there were a click in his voice, the flipping of a switch to the off position.

"Think of the marriage as something that happened to you because you were young. It isn't anybody's fault. There's no blame here. Neither of you is evil."

"Enough already, Zoe," Quinn said.

"We weren't really in love with each other," Rosie said quietly, and knew it was the summation.

Quinn said, "This is my last session. If we're split, we're split."

And Rosie asked, "Are you having an affair, Quinn?"

There was a silence first, before he answered. "No," he said. His voice sounded definite. But Rosie knew about lies and verbal overcompensation.

They sat enmeshed in their silence once again. "A woman I work with . . . ," he said, drifting from the sentence.

"I knew," she said.

"Not an affair—"

"I knew," she repeated.

"It's not, let me finish."

"Quinn, you offered *me* no words and no sex. There's an obvious explanation, isn't there?"

"Why is everything so damn obvious to you?" he shouted at her, rising from his chair.

"*Are* you having an affair?" Zoe asked him.

"No."

"But you were," Rosie said, deciding it.

He turned abruptly toward her. "No." And then, to Zoe, "Are we done here or not today?"

Rosie could heard the sound of his ragged breath moving in and out. She'd been right. She'd known, she told herself.

Quinn didn't come to Zoe's office again. Without him there, Rosie and Zoe had to work out the terms of the separation by themselves. Zoe said Quinn probably wouldn't agree to anything Rosie asked for now, that was a given, but maybe he'd at least come back to a session in order to work out compromises he found tolerable.

Rosie presented the terms: "You move out. Jason stays with me, but he visits you as often as you like once you have an apartment, so long as I have decent notice. Like twenty-four hours, say, and I don't already have plans that involve him. The other part is I get a job again and you do your own housework, you don't pay somebody to do it."

"Fine," he said, catching her by surprise.

She said she could explain the thinking behind it, and he didn't say anything like, Sure, go ahead, but she went ahead anyway. She said Zoe thought that because they had married so young, they'd had a sort of arrested development compared with the average adult couple. They'd gone from living at home to living together without ever living alone. "Zoe says I need to get a job so I'm not so dependent on you for money and for fixing things in the house, and you need to be in an apartment and taking care of yourself, not dependent on me for putting food in your refrigerator and on your table and washing your clothes and all that."

"Okay," Quinn said. His lack of resistance—he didn't even bad-mouth Zoe—made tears rise into her eyes.

The next afternoon, when Quinn was loading his bags into the car—he would stay at a motel till he found an apartment—her stomach was doing flip-flops of fear. But by the time she had dinner ready for herself and Jason, she heard the phrase "fresh start" let loose in her head, and right away, she began to feel better.

Jason asked where Quinn was, and Rosie explained, once again, about how Daddy was going to have his own special house for a while, and Jason would get to go see it soon. Her time with Jason at the dinner table that evening had a lightness to it, as though they'd both been released from the pull of gravity and floated together weightlessly through their meal. She didn't have to stare at a silent husband across the table, or try to figure out strategies to make him look at her. She smiled at her baby and laughed at his efforts with peas as he lifted them one at a time onto his spoon. She was going to like being on her own, finally. Praise the Lord and sound the trumpets, she said to herself as she cleared dishes from the table. At least if there was silence now, it would be her very own.

CHAPTER FIVE

ROSIE CAN'T BELIEVE SHE'S CRYING IN A doctor's office. And not just crying, either; she's turned into such mush, she can't even talk. Dr. Linder has just told her that Jason's condition may be an atypical form of asthma. "It's this naming of it," she says, though the words are fairly mangled by her sobs.

"Yes," the doctor says quietly. She finds the simple response oddly comforting, though she wouldn't have been able to explain why. Maybe it's because he doesn't cut off her distress by urging her to get hold of herself so he can continue on with his medical explanations. He says nothing more but only waits while Rosie takes time and space to explore the depth of her wound.

"It seemed like just the chocolate. I mean, I hoped it was that, an allergy, not a whole disease," she says.

And again he says, "Yes."

She tries the word out again inside her head: *asthma*. She doesn't even know if she can spell it. What she does know is that she won't be able to seek comfort in such phrases as *breathing difficulties*, *respiratory distress*, *allergic reaction*, or *episode* anymore. All euphemisms are to be left in the box at the door from now on, thank you. Now she must admit to— and in some sense, actually commit to—the idea of a long-term illness for Jason. She strokes Jason's soft hair, and the baby turns toward her, moving his hands up over his mother's shoulders and over the surface of her face. Her tears begin anew. She finds herself stuck on this phrase: "The beginning of the end." It won't stop slipping into her brain, rearing itself in her consciousness. Dr. Linder says she must embrace optimism, so she tries to push the phrase down, wrestle it into defeat, but it keeps resurfacing.

Dr. Linder takes a small box of tissues out of his desk and hands it to her. "I'm sorry," she says. "It's not like you didn't mention this as a possibility right from the beginning."

"And remember, I'm still not saying that's the definitive diagnosis because Jason lacks the full complement of standard markings for the disease. But asthma, like any illness, is going to have its variants, especially in a child as young as Jason. What I'm really saying is that we should upgrade our way of thinking about asthma, say, from it being a *possibility* to it being a *probable possibility*. That way we're less likely to be taken by surprise by what happens next." He has stood up and moved out from behind his desk. "But right now," he tells the two of them, "I'm going to give this big kid another dinosaur." He reaches down for the toddler who barely hesitates before he raises both hands to Linder. While doctor and child sit together on the floor and scrounge in a cabinet drawer across the room, Rosie blows her nose and runs her hands through her thick brown hair in a vague attempt at reorganization.

A few moments later, Jason rushes back toward her in that headlong toddler way so that he can show off a magenta brontosaurus. This is the fourth such creature—one for each visit to this office—that Dr. Linder has let Jason choose out. The toy is at least three times the size of typical handouts at doctors' and dentists' offices for, as Linder has already explained, he doesn't give out anything small enough to fit into a toddler's mouth. Jason holds the creature out to his mother, showing off its remarkable arched neck. "Red," he pronounces, almost sure.

"It's very beautiful," she tells him. Jason lets the animal light on his mother's open palm for a second, then he lifts it away so he can continue to study its long flexible neck.

"The head's safe," Linder tells her, touching a finger to the vibrant pink, peanut-sized cranium. "It can't be bitten off." She nods, and he adds, "I've tried it."

"Tried biting it?" she asks, surprised.

"Strange and embarrassing as that is to admit, yes. I figured that was the only way to be sure. There was a case about two years ago of a child being given a small toy as a reward for getting an injection and then on the trip home in the car"—Linder stops midsentence, then adds in a more hushed tone—"the child expired."

"Oh, God," Rosie says, imagining a child who looked just like Jason limp in his car seat and a mother who looked just like her leaning in from the car door, thinking to lift her sleeping son from his seat and finding him totally unresponsive. *Expired.* A word that Jason, who has made his way over to the windowsill so that Bronty can promenade across it in style, would not grasp, as has obviously been Linder's intent. She looks over toward her own real, living child and feels an almost cleansing sense of relief that she still has him and that the only thing that's wrong with him is asthma, not sudden death through asphyxiation. She wonders if this was part of Linder's intent in telling the story about the other child. Did he mean to make her feel lucky that she had asthma, not death, to deal with?

"Tell me if I'm wrong," she begins to ask Linder, still troubled by this other child, this now deceased one, "but don't doctors study child development? Don't they know about oral fixations?"

"Sure they do, but in most offices the party favor–type stuff gets handled by a receptionist. She orders it out of a catalog and she's the one who hands it out to the kids. And she's going to want the baby to have one if the big brother does, I promise you. But what good is all our accumulated scientific knowledge that we use to save children if we're going to kill or injure them with plastic toys?"

Jason has returned to his mother's side and he starts to try to entwine Bronty's neck around her arm. Rosie likes this doctor. He looks at the whole picture; the whole child. And he's not trying to impress his patients with flash. His office, in fact, is somewhat lackluster, even shabby compared to other professional offices that Rosie has been in over the last few years. There is neither nursing nor billing staff here, but only Marcy, who apparently acts as receptionist, secretary, and occasional doctor's aide. The mismatched chairs of the waiting room look like the chance gatherings from several weekend country tag sales. The examination table in the inner office is dark, distressed wood and aged brown leather. Poised over that table is a goose-neck lamp that is so archaic, Linder has to use two hands to bend its resistant metal coil to the right height. The place, however, is clean and the walls bear fresh-enough paint.

There is really nothing flashy about Greg Linder himself, either, unless you count the glints of red that appear in his brown hair when he bends his head under the light of the goose-neck lamp. He wears his hair on the long side so that it brushes his shirt collar, but Rosie thinks it more than likely that this is the result not of deliberate cultivation of a neo-sixties style, but mere neglect. It wouldn't surprise her to arrive one day and find he'd remembered to get himself to a barber and to see him with very short hair, which then, in time, would find its way back down the length of his neck.

"Let me just go over the new medication with you," he says, handing Rosie a bottle. She pushes down on the childproof cap, opens it, and as he'd instructed her with the last medication he'd prescribed for Jason, pours a small quantity of the viscous stuff into the cap. She brings the purple-pink liquid close enough to breathe in the sweet grapy smell. "Don't forget to open it before you leave the pharmacy," he reminds her. He believes in checks and balances, he'd said at Jason's first appointment, and to that end, he keeps duplicate versions of all the medications he prescribes so that when his patients arrive at the prescription counter they'll know whether they're getting what the doctor actually ordered. People, including pharmacists, get distracted and make mistakes, he says, so would it be so surprising if two labels got inadvertently switched? Rosie wonders why no other doctor she's consulted has ever thought to do this for his patients, given that the consequences of such a mistake could be life-threatening. She knows her father would have applauded the idea.

Linder suggests a meeting that doesn't include Jason so they can spend a full hour going over the basics of living with the illness. He reminds Rosie that Quinn will need to have this information as well. "Up front, not sprung on him after he makes mistakes with Jason's care." Rosie has told him about the fiasco at the hospital with the glitches in the reporting of Jason's medical history. It makes her uneasy—embarrassed, really—to have him refer to it again. "Quinn can either come to this meeting, or if he prefers, I can have a separate meeting with him, or you can just fill him in."

"I'm kind of new at this," she says. "I don't know what Quinn will want to do. We don't exactly have a set policy yet."

"Yes," he says, just as he did when she broke down over Jason's diagnosis, giving her space with this pain as well.

When Rosie is ready to leave, Marcy sets up the next two appointments—one for Jason's recheck in a week, and the other for her consultation with Linder, only a few days hence. "He does his consults last thing at the end of the day," Marcy tells her, "so it can be here, or at The Coffee Stop in the building next door. He's a caffeine fanatic," she adds, "but it's up to you whether you like pastry with your medical information or if you'd rather avoid the temptation of their dessert case." The receptionist rolls her eyes at the thought.

"The Coffee Stop's fine," Rosie says. "I'm so stressed I can eat anything I want and I only lose weight."

"I am *so* jealous," the receptionist says, clasping a hand to her heart in mock despair.

WHEN ROSIE SHOWS UP ALONE FOR HER CONsultation with Linder, he tells her he's not surprised that Quinn isn't there. He says he rarely gets two parents to show when there's an existing marital problem and that the offer for Quinn to have a solo meeting is still on. He says he'll call Quinn if she thinks that's best, but Rosie says no, she knows she's only making it worse by avoiding talking to him. She'll fill Quinn in, she assures Linder. The next time they talk.

Linder orders a double dark roast coffee for himself and drinks it black. Rosie orders a latte with a shot of chocolate, and after a brief initial demure, orders a piece of white chocolate mousse cake. The doctor's examination coat and the stethoscope are gone now, of course. Linder is wearing a sports coat, and his blue oxford cloth button-down shirt is open at the collar. If she had to guess at his age, she'd say early thirties; not terribly old, as doctors go, but old enough. Linder hands her a bunch of pamphlets that explain how to rid your home of allergens. There are so many possibilities that could be the source of Jason's problems—dust, mold, foods, plants, animals—it looks to her as though the monitoring and cleaning required to protect Jason from these noxious substances will be very extensive. "I thought I was going to start looking for a job," she says, "but I don't know if I can do both; work and do all this stuff with the asthma."

"I'd hold off on the job hunt for a while," he advises.

"Can't we test him to narrow it down and find out what causes the problem?"

"No," he says firmly. "With an older child, I'd probably opt for testing, but with a child as young as Jason I rarely do comprehensive testing. It's stressful and frightening and it's just going to make him fear my office. And anyway, with asthma, even an atypical case like this, you don't necessarily see substance-specific responses. A child might get an attack from something as benign and uncontrollable as a sudden change in room temperature, or a gust of strong wind. Even laughing can bring it on in some kids. So I think we ought to do some of these environmental changes, see how they work, and hold off on testing," he concludes.

Rosie finds the picture of the dust mite, magnified a zillion times that creeps across the cover of one of her pamphlets, completely repulsive. It has a pointy head and feet and rigid hairlike projections coming off random locations on its globular body. "These things are walking around on Jason?" she asks. "Going up his nose?"

"They're mostly walking around his mattress and pillow," he says. "It's actually their droppings that are going up

35

his nose." She makes a disgusted face at him. "They haven't singled him out, you know," the doctor points out. "You're breathing just as much of it as he is. It's just that *his* body works overtime rejecting the stuff and yours doesn't." Rosie tells him she doesn't feel any better about the mite dung for having been told it's all over her, too.

Linder has also brought information about all the different medications that are used to treat allergies and asthma and he underlines the one Jason is currently taking and writes in the dosage. He gives her journal articles about the treatment of children with asthma-like breathing disorders and a series of blank charts that she can use for tracking Jason's medication, his reactions, and his symptoms. He tells her that careful monitoring is what will keep Jason healthy. "I can't stress too strongly how important it is to give the medication exactly as directed," he tells her. "Even if you don't see any symptoms. Because we can't pin Jason's situation down firmly, we can't know exactly where it might go next."

"How bad can it get?"

"Oh, it runs a huge range. I've seen cardiac involvement, and, worst case, an episode can lead to arrest, but that's very, very unusual. The important thing is to be aware, that's all. Protect *before* things go that far."

Rosie feels her own heart pause in terror at the prospect he has named. She wants to say, "Cardiac arrest? You mean like where they put paddles on the chest and shock them back?" And, "Did you ever see a child die from this?" But Linder has passed on to other information and she tells herself, It can't be that bad or that important if he has just mentioned it in passing. She runs her fingertips over one of the papers as though she might absorb information directly into her body that way. She wants to know it all now, so she'll be prepared *before* anything bad can happen. And then she is able to breathe again, her heart joins in once more, and she listens to Linder talk about the bibliography he has for her. He annotates this page with asterisks. The best book, he tells her, circling the title, is out of print, but he'll lend her his copy for a week if she would like.

Dr. Linder gathers all the material he's brought with him off the green marble tabletop and slips it into a glossy red folder. There is a sticker on the front with his name, address, and telephone number, and the number of the hospital and the poison control center. "That ought to keep you busy for a few evenings," he comments as he hands it to her. He calls the waitress over and orders another double cup of dark roast and a second latte for Rosie. "Any questions?" he asks when the waitress has moved away.

"A cardiac problem?" she asks him.

"Rare," he says, shaking his head as though, she thinks, denying he'd ever mentioned it.

"With no warning?"

"No, no, no. You only see that when the caretakers aren't doing good monitoring or the child isn't brought in when he has symptoms. That's not going to be happening in Jason's case—I know that and you know that. This isn't something for you to be worrying about, okay?" She nods. "Anything else?" he asks.

"No," she says. "I'll read this stuff, then I'll probably have questions."

"I suspect you will. But you're okay with everything for now? No questions about things we've gone over before, office procedure, any of that?"

She smiles, then asks something she's been wondering about ever since she first went into his office. "Where'd you get that examining table, the leather-topped one?" she asks.

"Hey, let me change gears here," he says, laughing. Then he tells her he bought it from a retiring physician. "Before that," he says, "I rented a high-tech examining table from a medical supply house. But I've had my eye out for an antique one like that since the day I got out of medical school."

"My father had one like that, though that's about a hundred years ago."

"Mine, too," he says. "That's why I went for it. He had the most wonderful, elegant office, all leather and fine woods. But that was back when he still had money. Eventually he sold it all off."

"Your father's a doctor, too, then?" Rosie has already told

Linder that her father was a physician. She's always sure to make this connection clear in a first visit to any medical facility because as her father used to say, it puts a doctor "more on his toes" if he knows you have access to medical knowledge.

"My father was a doctor," he confirms, and she nods.

"Well, then," she says, "we're almost related."

"Or from the same tribe, anyway."

"People don't realize, but it *is* like that, a special culture, isn't it?"

"It's interesting you put it that way because I've always thought of doctors' families as having a kind of subculture."

"Well, anyway, I like your examining table. All the antique stuff you have. It's comforting, I guess."

He laughs. "For you, maybe. For those patients who aren't members of our tribe, beat-up examination tables probably make them worry about whether my training is as hopelessly outdated as my furniture."

"I doubt it," she says. "Once they're talking to you, they'll feel the difference, don't you think? You spend the extra time with your patients. Nobody does that anymore. Doctors are always checking their watches. I'm so used to talking fast when I go to the doctor's, I had trouble actually slowing down in your office."

"Thanks for your kind words," he says. "Maybe I should limit my practice to families of physicians."

"Older physicians," she points out. "The ones who go back as far as the antiques." He nods. "And speaking of watches," she says, looking at hers, "I have to pick Jason up at Quinn's." They both stand then, she gathering the materials he's given her, and he reaching for the restaurant check. "Thanks," he says again, but his eyes and the set of his mouth make her think he has something else he wants to say, and she waits, but he only smiles, and it's a smile that goes more sideways than up, moving tentatively, and she recognizes a shyness hiding behind his professional expertise she had altogether missed before. She likes it, this unexpected hesitation, this other unasked question, whatever it is, and she smiles back, completely forgetting to offer to pay for her own coffee and cake.

Get a grip, she tells herself when she's back in her car. He's Jason's doctor. And he's probably got a wife and three kids, besides.

ROSIE IS SURPRISED WHEN GREG LINDER calls her at home a few days later. "Listen," he says, "is this off the wall?"

"What?" she asks him.

"I've been thinking about the coffee, how comfortable it was. I mean, the talking with you. And I think this probably *is* off the wall, but I did enjoy that, and I've been thinking about it, and I don't know, I really don't want to jeopardize our medical relationship, because your son is a major concern to me and the last thing I would want is to have Jason suffer for this schoolboyish thing I'm about to do, but . . ." She hears him inhale, then exhale. "Would you maybe want to have coffee with me again, but nonbusiness, nonmedical this time?"

Rosie has to laugh with how good it is to hear someone talk to her, to make an effort to get into her space, not close down against her. She has been thinking about him, too, or no, she's been thinking about how many days it was till Jason's next appointment, but she's been telling herself that it's because she wants more feedback about her child. "Are you married?" she asks him, and immediately regrets it because it sounds so predatory.

"Divorced," he says. "A long time ago. So what do you think?"

"Was there maybe a yes-or-no question back there somewhere?"

"I think it's a 'yes' question," he says, then quickly adds, "No, I didn't mean that. That sounded manipulative, didn't it? It's a yes-or-no question, but you should feel free to say no for whatever reason, because you can, you absolutely can. I mean, this is definitely a weird situation. I have never asked the mother of a patient out before."

"Tell you what," she says. "can you just ask me that question again without all that other stuff because I don't think I exactly remember what the question is anymore."

"I think the question is, Do you want to have coffee again sometime?"

"Sure, why not," she says, and she realizes she's smiling. "The Coffee Stop again?"

"That's fine," he says, and she can hear in the briskness of his answer his surprise at how little she fought him on this. "Or, no," he says. "Wait a minute. Maybe we should make it dinner."

"How about we compromise on lunch?" she proposes, feeling a need to participate more directly in the terms. And it is agreed that it will be Wednesday at noon.

When she hangs up, she realizes she has actually made a date. And then this occurs to her: she has never before ever in the history of the world had a date with anyone except Quinn. That thought gives her a shiver that raises the hairs straight upright along her arms, and she tries pushing them back down with her hand. She paces the room, saying to herself, What have I done? Then she tries to remember him, to picture him again, and she sees the red highlights of his hair, that smile at the end of their meeting, and the light-colored hairs on her forearms rise again. And she likes the sensation very much.

CHAPTER SIX

ROSIE ARRIVES FIRST, THOUGH SHE ISN'T early. She's feeling jittery about this whole thing, about whether they'll have anything to say to each other without all those photocopies and pamphlets in front of them. And she doesn't like what she's wearing—it's too planned. She's completely overdressed. Not for the occasion, but for who she is. She never wears skirts. It's like she's in costume for a 1950s version of "Rosie Goes on a Date." She's even taken the scissors to her own hair, clipping at the longish dark strands that tease down her neck below her otherwise short haircut. She should never have cut them. Now it's just a haircut. Before it was offbeat, slightly tough. She might as well have donned white gloves and a hat. She peeks through the windows of Bentley's, the small restaurant he's suggested for lunch, and though several tables are occupied, he's not there. Now she doesn't know what to do. What she'd really like to do is go home and change her clothes.

Maybe he isn't coming. Maybe he forgot, or maybe he got tied up with a patient. The restaurant isn't far enough from his office for heavy traffic to be the explanation. But she's not going to go into Bentley's and sit there all by herself feeling like a complete ass watching recognition dawn on everybody's faces as they each figure out she's been jilted.

She waits outside. And she tries not to pace. She glances through the window again, shading her view this time with a hand to her forehead, but surprise, he's still not in there. After twenty minutes she's not jittery anymore, just plain enraged. Even if he shows up now, she figures, she's going to be so hostile it'll be a complete disaster between them. She debates about just walking away, taking long strides across the street to her car and getting the hell out of here, but decides she won't be so thoughtless as he has been. She will leave a message with the restaurant, saying that she has come and gone. She checks her watch. The message will emphasize that she has waited thirty Very Long minutes.

She enters Bentley's and a perky waitress dressed in the same blue-and-yellow fabric that covers the tables and who can't seem to keep her upper body still asks her if by any chance she's Mrs. Sloan. When she says she is, the girl tells her that Dr. Linder has called and left a message for her that he'll be a little late. "A little?" she retorts, but the waitress has slid away to deliver two plates of sandwiches to a nearby table.

A hand settles on her shoulder, startling her. "I'm here," he says from behind her, and when she turns her head toward him, he starts talking in that tumultuous way he did on the telephone. "I am *so* sorry. I should never have made this for lunch because I know, I know, I can never get out on time. I know that about me and I could almost have predicted this, making you stand here and wait. Why didn't you sit down? You should have sat down." By now she's turned to face him and she's close enough to see that his eyes are green, really green, and she doesn't think she's ever seen that color eyes before. "Did you just get here, too, maybe?" he continues. "I mean, you were right by the door."

"Actually, I was just leaving."

"Oh," he says, and then blows a long breath out through pursed lips. "I deserve this. I don't know what to say."

The waitress has returned to them, menus held against her chest. "You want that one by the window?" she asks, oblivious to the convoluted negotiations they've been undertaking.

He looks at Rosie, his eyebrows raised.

She turns back toward the waitress. "That one's fine," she says. The angry tightness is shifting, unwinding from where it has repeatedly wrapped around and over itself. In fact, she feels oddly like laughing. At him and at herself. At how they both want this to happen. She wants that table by the window. Or any table. So long as he's going to keep on talking that way, breathlessly, eager to tell her things.

"You look lovely," he says as they're pulling the chairs out from the table. And she blushes. *Blushes:* she can't believe it. She starts to say thank you and the words twist out of her control, sounding as much like a giggle as language.

He asks her if she's nervous and she laughs again and has to fight the urge to clap her hand over her mouth. She shrugs and she takes a look at his eyes again. Still green over here, in different light. And it isn't because he's wearing green—he's got on a charcoal black herringbone jacket and a white shirt and his tie is a red-and-black print—no green tones anywhere.

"Well, *I'm* nervous," he tells her. "But that's probably obvious, isn't it?" She smiles. She's not sure she wants to chance speaking for another couple of minutes. It might come out again as a giggle, or a gasp, or as pure choking. She's not going to take the risk till forced into it, she thinks. She hadn't thought about *his* nerves, but actually, all this frantic talk—on the telephone and now—is such a contrast to the way he is in his office and the way he was at The Coffee Stop. In those settings he's very spare of words. Of course he's nervous. "I haven't done anything like this—dated—in a really long time," he says. "In fact, I don't even know if they still call it that. Is there some other more politically correct term that's replaced 'dating'?"

"Not that I know of," she says, and is relieved that the words aren't transformed into idiotic noise bits this time. "But I'm hardly an expert," she adds.

"Well, yes, you've been married a long time, haven't you?"

"Eight years. But you said you're divorced a long time?" she asks, hearing the incompleteness of the question, wondering herself what it is she's asking.

"But not doing much dating," he says. "I tried once or twice, but then I did this same thing, showing up late, only worse, I suppose, canceling because of emergencies, and it didn't go over too well. I honestly am not good at making time work right, I don't think. And, of course, the medical practice is so unpredictable in its demands. I once set up a whole 'Day in the Country Adventure' thing with a woman. You know, antiquing, gourmet picnic lunch, a boat ride down the river, dinner at an inn, and one of my kids went into arrest and I had to call it off ten minutes before we were supposed to meet. And then I didn't call her back for—I don't know—a couple of days, I guess. And when I did, she told me there wasn't any point to rescheduling anything because I obviously lived for my practice and no wonder I was divorced, and I was going to end up a very lonely, pathetic person, et cetera, et cetera, all of which she was probably right about. Anyway, you better take my late arrival as fair warning. I do this, and you might as well know now, up front."

"I guess I could try showing up a half hour late. That might get us into sync," she suggests.

"Good adaptive behavior," he comments, nodding. "Let's try that."

"Provided I don't actually tell you I'm doing it."

"I've already forgotten you said it," he assures her, reaching for the bread basket, then lifting the flap of blue-and-yellow napkin, offering the contents to her.

While Rosie spreads butter across a piece of raisin bread she considers how in these few sentences they've both made definite reference to future meetings. It seems bold, almost aggressive, that they've colluded this way, imagining themselves into the future. Is this what people do now?

She knows for certain that she's right about one thing: they both want this.

The waitress has come and stood by their table expectantly twice already, and this third time while she hovers over them Linder says, "Yes, let's be good children, Rosie, and make our selections." Neither of them has looked at the menu, but now they both begin scanning.

The waitress shifts her feet impatiently. "There's the special soup and half sandwich," she suggests.

"That all right with you?" the doctor asks Rosie.

"Sure."

"Two of those specials," Greg tells the waitress, and they hand over their menus.

When the young woman has moved away from their table, Linder leans toward Rosie and whispers, "Did she tell us what the soup is?" And Rosie shakes her head. "What about the sandwich?" he asks.

"Beats me," she says, and they laugh together at themselves, and she likes the sound of it—the gentle, unembarrassed silliness of them mixing together. But then he stops laughing, and he's staring at her and she doesn't know what to do, what to say. His eyes catch hold of hers, but his look is so intense, she has to slip out of it, sideways, a little, turning her head as though she's scanning the restaurant, evaluating it, while she tries to will her pulse rate back to something steady and slow.

"Why did you become a doctor?" she asks him, breaking through the skin of what had felt, so briefly there, like a spell.

He smiles at her. "I didn't think there were any other choices. I grew up with it, like you. I figured it was the way to go. But it didn't work that way for you, I guess."

"No," she says, shaking her head. "When I was little, of course, I wanted to be what he was. Maybe even *be* him. But the reality was that I hated math and science and I was lousy at them. The kinds of things I did like—photography, pastry baking—my father thought of as frivolous. He told me they'd make great hobbies for a doctor."

"As if doctors have time for hobbies."

"Right. He certainly didn't. I guess if he'd had a son, it would have been different. All he had was just me and my older sister." She ponders for a moment whether what she's just claimed is true—if she'd had a brother, would she have gone some entirely different route, bypassing Quinn altogether?

"Your sister didn't become a doctor either?"

"No. Beth made it clear right from when she was little that there was no way that was going to happen. She'd cover her ears or gag when he started talking about symptoms or surgical procedures. It used to pain me that she was so rude to him, but

45

looking back, I can see it was just necessary honesty for her emotional survival."

"Is she still rude?" he asks.

"Very," she says, smiling.

"But you were the good daughter and didn't do any of that back-talk stuff, right?"

"Right. Because I knew I was his only hope. I didn't want him to be sad, so I figured I'd do it for him, become a doctor, if that's what he really wanted."

"And you went into full competition for the Martyred Daughter of the Year prize."

She shrugs. "I guess I thought Vestal Virgins were cool. Honor and sacrifice seemed as good a way as any to go."

The waitress places a platter with steaming French onion soup and a prosciutto sandwich in front of each of them. Rosie picks up her spoon and uses it to break through the cheese-and-toast crust that covers her soup. When she brings the spoon to her lips and discovers how very scalding the liquid is, she decides to let it cool down and continues with her story. "Seriously, I really felt like I had no choice but to do the doctor bit. He talked about me going to medical school—even back when I was only seven or eight—as though it were a given. And it wasn't just any medical school, actually, it was Johns Hopkins—'The best training ground for a physician that exists anywhere in the world.' " Greg laughs. He's sipping gingerly at his soup. "Where'd you go to med school?" she asks him.

"No place special. University of Oklahoma."

"According to my father, you shouldn't have bothered," Rosie says. " 'Go to Hopkins, or forget it,' he used to say. 'Exceed your reach.' "

" 'Go for the gold.' "

" 'Strive for the blue ribbon.' "

" 'Dare the impossible.' " Their voices alternate the echoes of childhood in overachieving households.

"I tried to be a science major in college, but I had no talent for it. It was a constant struggle for me just to stay alive in most of my classes. Then I tried working in a hospital doing non-medical things—mostly fetching stuff for patients—I hated that. Not the fetching part of it, but the patients. I couldn't stand being with sick people. I was constantly on the verge of gagging or passing out. Finally there was enough evidence for *me*, at least, to realize that I'd gotten trapped into something truly weird with my father and that I needed to get out. But even then I put off telling him because I was afraid he was going to be disappointed and reject me. I wanted *him* to see that it was a terrible mistake without me having to say it. I wanted him to see how I was barely making it in science and urge me to quit and stop with the self-sacrifice bit."

Greg shakes his head, though he's smiling at her. "I don't think the fathers of Vestals ever do rescue them. I think they're consumed with pride and honor at being allowed to give up their daughters to the cause. At least I don't remember anything to the contrary about that from my high school Latin classes." He pauses for a moment. "Did you, by any chance, tell him you hated the hospital?"

"Oh, yeah. It wasn't like he didn't have plenty of information about how I felt. He told me I had to learn to deal with discomfort in order to be a good doctor. I had to conquer my tendency to faint and I had to buckle down and concentrate more in school so I could pull my grades up. I tried. I cried a lot, and I stuck with it a while longer, but I despised all of it. And then I met Quinn and I instantly knew he was going to be my ticket back to reality." She pauses for a moment, tries the soup again, and finds it tolerable. "You know," she says after a few spoonfuls, "all this sounds terribly clear-headed, like I calculated and planned it all out deliberately, choosing some unacceptable guy to goad him, but I don't think it was like that. I wasn't consciously thinking about having my father conclude, Oh, if she likes this worthless person, then she obviously won't be good Johns Hopkins material. At the time, I honestly thought I was madly attracted to Quinn."

"Hindsight is a wonderful tool."

"And therapy," she adds.

"That'll certainly do it. So what was so terrible about Quinn? He wasn't in pre-med or something?"

She laughs. "No, he definitely wasn't pre-med. I met him at

a bar when I was home on vacation. He was living at home, working two crummy jobs, and taking a two-year course at the community college, shame, shame," she says with a look of mock horror on her face. "He wasn't even going for a real bachelor's degree. And his chosen field was law enforcement. He wanted to be a cop." She laughs. "Let me tell you, it was all the absolutely most wrong stuff to try to get by my parents." Rosie's finding that onion soup, with its strands of cheese that attach mouth to bowl, is much too complicated to eat while conversing. She pushes the soup off to one side and Greg does the same, though she sees that he's consumed most of his.

"So they hated him?"

"Well, they never said that. My father would just say things like, 'How come if he's interested in the law he doesn't do it the right way and go to law school?' He'd say it like that, The Law, and it sounded so hallowed, part of me would secretly wish that Quinn was going to law school, but to my father I'd say something more like, 'Because he likes blue uniforms.' "

"Ah, no more the Vestal Virgin, then. Enter the provocateur."

"I guess so," she says. "Once I told him it was because Quinn wasn't smart enough to do college-level work and I could actually see my father shudder. It would have been as if I said I didn't want to be a doctor but I wanted to be a lab technician or a nurse's aide. My parents had contempt for that level of achievement and ambition. Or lack of ambition, rather."

"Did they ever try to actively interfere, to forbid you to see him?"

"Oh, absolutely not," she says, shaking her head. "They prided themselves on being open-minded and liberal about everything. So they were in a real bind: What were they going to object to, that he was working class? Because that's what I think was really at the heart of it. Lord knows, liberals aren't supposed to care about class, right? So they let Quinn come and go through the house and they were superficially polite to him, but I knew they couldn't stand him. They'd barely speak to him, and when they did, I could see the pain all pinched up into their faces. My mother always seemed to need to clean and straighten after he left a room. But they didn't even bad-mouth him to me. And then I got myself pregnant." She picks up her sandwich and bites off the prosciutto and sprouts that hang out beyond the bread.

"Ah," Greg says. "This is a very elaborate plot indeed." He shakes his head. "Now, don't take this as a personal criticism here, Rosie, but along the way, didn't it ever occur to you that just telling your father that you didn't want to go to medical school would actually have been easier on everybody in the long run?"

She nods, chewing her mini-bite. "I told you, I didn't think of it consciously as something I was doing to that end. At the time I felt like I couldn't keep away from Quinn. He was very sexy. And we didn't try to get pregnant; we just weren't very good at preventing it. Like I said, it's only hindsight that lets me see what I was really doing."

"So let me guess what happened next. Daddy still didn't understand that you didn't want to go to medical school, did he?"

"No, he didn't give up that easily. He arranged an abortion through a friend of his."

"Which you had, not actually preferring self-immolation or other Vestal-style acts of self-sacrifice."

"Wrong," she says, shaking her head vigorously. "That's when Quinn and I got married. I came home from my hotshot college and I enrolled along with him at the local place and we rented a room in a house that had a picket fence and a front stoop where I could sit out on summer evenings and look pregnant and working class."

"No kidding," he says, then asks, "but the baby . . . ? I didn't know you had an older child."

Her fingers have pressed down suddenly into the thick bread, flattening it into a strange, skewed shape. She puts it back down on her plate. "She died at two months. Sudden infant death."

"Oh, no," Greg says, reaching for her hand.

Rosie looks toward the ceiling, catching the tears before they let loose, letting her fingers move through his. "Sorry for the tears," she says after a moment. He shakes his head. He slides his fingers down the length of her palm, then back up again. Both of them follow the gentle motion with their eyes.

"Jason's not going to do that to you, you know, disappear in his sleep. That happens only in the first year. And almost exclusively in the first five months."

"I know all that. I know it and I still overreact."

"Personally, I don't think you overreact."

"When Jay was first born, Quinn didn't sleep at all, I don't think. It was like he was waiting for it to happen again. I wasn't much better." Linder nods. "And I don't think he ever believed me," she says in little more than a whisper.

"Who, Quinn?" he asks, leaning toward her words, folding his hand around hers once more.

"My father."

"About . . . ?"

"The cause of Abby's death." She looks directly at him. She shakes her head hard, like she's shaking something off herself. "It made me even crazier, the way my father made us go over it again and again." She breathes deeply. "He called in experts, consultants. He had his own pathologist do a second autopsy. It went on for months. It went on longer than my baby lived. The police left us alone long before he did." She shakes her head at the memory. "You know, this may sound really awful, but in a weird way, I was almost glad when Jason had breathing difficulties. It was like I was a little vindicated, you know what I mean? Like this was the evidence that Quinn and I have babies with breathing problems. I could finally say, 'So there' to my father. Only neither of my parents is alive anymore, so they'll never know."

"SIDS is so vague, parents always feel they're being blamed. It's universal, believe me."

"I know." She's ready to change the subject. She leans back, sliding her hand away from his. "So, that's the story of my rebellious marriage," she finishes crisply, and with a smile.

"Ah, yes, blessed rebellion," he says. "The stuff that probably half the marriages in America are made of, I'll bet."

"You think so?"

"Absolutely."

"Were you in that half of America?"

"No," he says emphatically. "I'm part of the other half. I bent over backward to please them."

"So maybe that makes us some kind of matched set, you know what I mean?"

"Not really," he says. "You want to explain that one?"

She feels like a jerk for saying it that way, making it sound like she's hinting that they'd make a good couple. God, he must think she's on the prowl with her man-grabbing pincers fully extended. "I didn't put that quite right," she manages to say, placing the words carefully into the embarrassed silence they now share. "I meant to say that you and I seem to represent two different sides of the parent-child conflict."

"Only it's not really ever so one-sided as that. It's not that you're with them or against them. Isn't it that you're always torn between doing things their way and not doing them their way?"

"Yes. Definitely," she declares, nodding deeply. "Even now that I'm married and have my own family and my father's not even alive anymore I still find myself slipping back into doing things his way. But I hate that. Every time I have to make a decision, I have to go over how he'd do it. Like with all this stuff with Jay. I keep asking myself, would he get a second opinion? Would he use this drug? I play conversations about it with him through my head all the time. I'm always arguing with him. His way versus mine. I'm fighting him, but I'm fighting me, too, thinking maybe he's right."

"Now that's prime therapy stuff."

"That's for sure." He's right, she probably should have talked more about this with Zoe. About her mother, too, and what he did to her. "You know, when my mother was ill," she says to Greg, "my father had her make this hideously long trip out to Minnesota in the middle of winter so she could be evaluated by the 'Best.'" Rosie wiggles two fingers of each hand to shape out quotation marks as she speaks the last word.

"And to hear the same thing she heard out here, I'll bet."

"Pretty much. And then when she got back here, she had to

have the very absolutely best doctor, the best setting, for her treatment, so they traveled eighty miles, three, four times a week. It wore her out. Personally, I think it just killed her faster."

"It's so hard to stand by through that kind of thing when you're on the sidelines."

"Of course I should have told him, I should have said, Don't do this to her, don't make her take that long drive. Sometimes she'd have to stay in a motel, she'd be so tired. It made me nuts that she was spending some of her last days in crappy motels and a car so the alleged best doctor on earth could pour chemicals into her."

"But you never said anything? Never objected?"

"No, of course I didn't. Because I thought he might be right. I was terrified he might be right. What did I know? He was the expert. Like you said, hindsight is wonderful." She shrugs and looks at him. "This is boring, isn't it?"

"Oh, no," he says. "We're a matched set on this one, just like you said. All this speaks directly to who I am: the screwed-up son of a father."

He holds his hand out again toward her, an offer, she is sure, of himself, of the wounded stories, that he, too, will have to tell. He closes his hand around hers, suddenly, eagerly, then shuts his eyes for a moment. It is a few minutes later—she has no idea how much time has actually passed—that they smile and let one another go again. He checks his watch and says, "Damn. Now I've done it. I'm going to be late for my afternoon appointments."

"You haven't finished eating," she points out. He's taken only a few bites out of his sandwich.

"I'll be okay," he says, motioning to their waitress for a check. He starts to rise, then sits again. "This is ridiculous, cutting things off this way, partway through our meal. My patients can wait a little while," he says, sitting again. "Maybe they should all learn that the doctor has interests other than medicine." She feels herself blush again, only this time she doesn't try to hide it because she just doesn't care.

CHAPTER SEVEN

HERE IS HOW IT ALL SHAKES DOWN, ROSIE thinks. There are actually two completely separate relationships. There's Greg and Rosie who go out to lunch in cozy places and who occasionally touch and who could be lovers (she's sure of this, though first she'd have to agree to dinner, which she hasn't so far, but thinks she will, next invite). And then there's Dr. Linder and Jason Sloan and his mother, Rosie Sloan, who meet in an office and discuss medications and symptoms across the distance of a great wide desk. It's an odd, arbitrary separation, she knows. It isn't as though Jason disappears out of her life while she has lunch at a restaurant, but she feels a need, in that setting, to keep him silent.

She knows it's a strange way to divide up her life.

And lately, she's in the office more than she is out with this man socially because Jason isn't getting better. In fact, he's worse. Rosie's thinking maybe they should stop seeing each other till Jason's better, and maybe he's thinking that, too, because he hasn't suggested that they get together for almost a week now. She thinks it's because both of them know Jason's troubles aren't going to be kept so easily at bay anymore. Yes, she thinks, it'd be better to wait till Jay's stabilized again.

They've never discussed this division and they certainly have never set guidelines or rules about what constitutes fair grounds for conversation. But one thing has occurred to her—Dr. Linder gets his share of talk about dust mites and vacuuming and wheezing and antihistamines with any number of mothers in any given day in his office. She remembers what he said in that first telephone call: "I have never asked the mother of a patient out before." To her, the meaning is crystal clear: she cannot be the mother of his patient if they are going to date.

It'll work out, she tells herself. They'll back off the Greg and Rosie stuff for another week or two, give Jason some time to improve, and they'll be okay again.

But she *is* the mother of a patient, that's the real rub. Come on, Jason, she urges him in silence as she watches him finally sleeping comfortably after another emergency visit to the office. Get yourself in gear and cut out the wheezing already. Dr. Linder has had to change doses every time they've been to the office lately. Rosie covers her child with the new blanket that's made out of a brand new revolutionary fabric that no one's ever been known to be allergic to. *Yet,* she thinks. No one's been allergic to it yet. Because Jason's getting worse, she wonders how these manufacturers can be so all-fired sure these new products are allergy free for absolutely everybody. But, of course, she hasn't bought the new vacuum cleaner yet, the one that's got the super filter that really gets rid of mites and doesn't just blow them around the way hers does. Tomorrow she'll talk to Quinn about some money to do it.

This business of trying to keep the house dust free is a royal pain. Jason's room has had to be stripped of almost everything that isn't a hard surface and then what still remains has to be covered in plastic. The stuffed animals had to go. The lovely handmade quilt with his name and birth date embroidered on it had to be stored away. It seems to her that it is all the comfort that must go.

"Why is this happening?" she asks him in the office. She means these new episodes of coughing and difficulty breathing.

"Because we haven't found the ideal level of medication," he says. "Because asthma has unpredictable aspects."

"What about the tests?" she asks him. She's been thinking about how her father would have handled this. He'd have pushed to get as much information as possible. He'd have definitely gone ahead with them.

"You'll still have unanswered questions."

"But something has to be done, doesn't it?"

"You can set it up with Marcy," he tells her.

She has filled in all the spaces on the charts. She's given the medication exactly on time. Although perhaps when Quinn had him, he didn't. "It's because we're separated," she says. "We're not unified or something."

"That may be part of it," he says, "but we'll work it out. You and Quinn have to talk more, maybe, but you don't have to get back together to get Jason stabilized again." She wonders, is this a step beyond patient-doctor advice? Is this Greg or Dr. Linder speaking? Maybe he's wrong—as a doctor—maybe she *should* get back together with Quinn, she thinks, the thought a flame inside her head, like one of Jason's asthmatic flares, sudden and debilitating.

"This is a hard thing to deal with," he says. "For everybody involved." That's Greg speaking, now, she's sure of it. He means for him, too. He's having trouble crossing over, having her as a patient and as a potential lover. She thinks maybe she should ask him to recommend another doctor, but consistent care is important with these chronic conditions, she knows that. She couldn't do that to her child simply because she wanted her love life to be better.

And another thing; it has occurred to her that ever since Jason's disorder has been diagnosed and labeled, everything has gotten a lot worse. There didn't used to be wheezing, really, and now there is almost daily. It's as though the disease has been summoned up in full force, challenged, as it were, to behave in a fashion that is true to its name.

As Linder has said, it's probably because she's now more aware, that's all. She hears the wheezing and identifies it as such. Before, it was just toddler breathing. Leftover cold symptoms. It didn't have a name that implied a disease. Yes, she can believe that she's more aware of it and that it might have been going on and been ignored for months. For his whole life, maybe.

She feels agitated almost all the time. Here is what it really comes down to: the Greg-Rosie part is over, isn't it? She might as well have dreamed it.

Shall I go back to Quinn, then? she will ask Linder. Shake him up, make him see, she has choices. And then she's thinking, this isn't how it's done. I am too eager and that very eagerness has undoubtedly already scared him away. Back off, she warns herself. Stay cool, she counsels. Now, if only she will listen to herself.

SHE HAS MADE A LIST OF ALL THAT SHE NEEDS to tell Quinn. This time, she will give him a copy of the medication and symptoms charts when he picks Jason up. She will tell him how important it is that they both fill in the spaces and that they work together as a team in order to keep Jason from having any more attacks. Today. She has given Quinn all the medication, even the one Linder has prescribed for extreme emergencies, when she can't get help fast enough—the Just In Case Meds, the doctor calls them. Rosie has also told Quinn that Linder wants to do the skin tests. "How much do they cost?" he asked.

"Quinn, this is your child's health. How can you ask questions like that? Anyway, your insurance will pay for part of it."

She will ask him if he has cleaned out the room in which Jason sleeps. Whether he vacuums the requisite number of times (even if Jason isn't there, she'll tell him. We have to keep the air clean in preparation for when he is there). She will ask, Are you sure you'll hear him if he wakes with difficulty in the night? This is the part that bothers her the most. She imagines Quinn sleeping soundly through Jason's struggles. Maybe she will suggest that Jason not have overnights anymore with Quinn till he stops having flares.

Rosie waits till Jason is in bed, till the quiet, even track of his breathing tells her he is sleeping comfortably, and then she dials Quinn's number.

"Hello," a woman's voice greets her. Rosie is startled, and says nothing for a moment. The greeting is repeated, and then, "Did you want Quinn?"

"Yes," Rosie says. And then silently to herself. "Who else could I possibly want?"

She hears the voice again, at a distance now. "Quinn, phone for you."

It is several more moments till he comes to the phone, and Rosie has time to consider the possible advantages of crashing the receiver back down before it is handed off to him, but she hangs on. "Hello?" he says, and his voice is full of question, perhaps slightly confrontational, and certainly not greeting at all.

"Who the hell was that?" Rosie asks, not bothering to identify herself.

There's a pause then, in which she knows he is formulating his response. "A friend," he finally tells her.

"Uh-huh," she says, which is her way of telling him that's not enough explanation. But he asks after Jason's health and makes no more mention of the woman who answered his telephone.

Rosie tries to find her way back to her preset agenda—how they must be more vigilant with Jason, how Quinn needs to prepare his apartment for his son's visit, but her sentences are jagged, her concentration all skewed toward this woman's voice calling Quinn from out of another room. Quinn doesn't protest any of Rosie's requests for increased vigilance, though he also doesn't register much enthusiasm for the task. But this isn't surprising, Rosie knows. He hasn't been enthusiastic about anything for a long time, and certainly house cleaning wouldn't be the place she'd expect him to suddenly find a new life's interest. "By the way," she says to him after they agree on the specifics of the following day's visitation, "I'm sort of dating this doctor. Jason's allergist, actually. A nice guy," she adds, trying to make it sound as offhanded as possible.

"Good," he says. And she cannot read his reaction in the space of that little word. She hadn't meant to tell him, and wouldn't have, but for the voice of his "friend" at the other end of the line.

When she hangs up, she realizes she's absolutely furious with him. What colossal nerve, she thinks, to refer to a woman

57

who feels she can take the liberty of answering his telephone as "a friend." And Quinn knew Rosie was going to call around this time to talk about Jason's visitation, so maybe he told this woman to answer the phone because maybe he hoped Rosie would make this discovery in just this way. Was he being deliberately cruel? Deliberately provocative? It hasn't even been that long since they're separated, only a couple of months, so when exactly did all this happen? And it's late already, well into the evening, so was this woman staying there overnight? Damn him, she thinks, and she feels suddenly so wrenchingly lonely she can't bear it. She goes to the bedroom, opens his closet, and sees, for the first time, how much he has taken. Only ten or twelve hangers still bear clothing. There are a few pairs of off-season slacks in there and some older, ragged shirts he never wears anymore, and two of the outdated police uniforms, but otherwise, nearly all of it is gone.

ROSIE HAS MOVED THE GUEST BED MATTRESS into Jason's room. This is where she sleeps now. She's covered it in plastic, of course, and she has to lift it every day to vacuum underneath. She's bought the new vacuum, courtesy of a check from Quinn, but he did ask her when she expected to find a job as he handed the money over.

"Quinn," she said to him, "by the time I get finished with all the anti-allergic stuff I have to do in this house every day, I barely have enough energy to tie Jason's shoes, let alone start job hunting. I'm hardly sleeping, either. I lie there afraid to sleep. I just listen to his breathing all night." They're standing just outside her front door. The one the police split, though it's fixed now.

"You shouldn't be sleeping in his room," Quinn says.

"I'm making my own decisions now, thank you," she retorts. "And by the way, I've taken him out of day care, so you don't have to pick him up there on Thursday. He'll be with me." She's got hold of the doorknob behind her. It's too chilly to be having this conversation out here.

"What'd you do that for?"

"You mean take him out?"

"Yeah, that's exactly what I mean."

"Because that place is filthy."

"They must have a cleaning service."

"Well, maybe they do, but there's dust in all the corners, on the shelves, and all over the heating ducts. Check it out yourself if you don't believe me. You know what those commercial services are like—they run a dust mop down the center of the room and can't be bothered with edges or corners or anything above shoulder level. Those mops probably bring in more mites than they take out. And there's stuffed animals and dolls and dress-up clothes—all the stuff he's not supposed to have—and those cots and blankets that have been there for a hundred years gathering dust. I can't justify bringing him in there every day so long as he's still having problems, not when there's so much obviously wrong in there. And remember, I only put him in there so I could look for a job."

"So what's he doing instead?"

She moves away from the door and crosses her arms over her chest in an abortive attempt at keeping warm. "He's with me. We're doing stuff, don't worry about it. But I obviously can't just pick up and go job hunting when I have him home full time."

"Rosie, this is wrong. He likes that place. He likes being in day care." Quinn's shifting around, up one step, down two, up one again. She wishes he'd just stand still.

"He likes chocolate, too, Quinn," she says. "Are you going to feed it to him?"

"That's your job, not mine," he says, and she wants to push him right off the steps. "When we split up, Rosie, one of the conditions that *your* therapist set up was that you were going to get a job."

"Listen, when we split, we didn't know about the asthma. We couldn't anticipate all this. You don't want me to leave him now, do you?" He goes down one step, then seems to be looking at a defect in the concrete step, pushing at it with the front of his shoe. "We've got to be flexible about those original rules," she says. "Anyway, when he's stabilized, I'll be able to look for work. This is temporary." She closes her eyes knowing that this is when he'll turn on his heels and go back down to his car, but a few seconds later when she opens them, he's still there.

"You seem so angry lately," he says. "Is it because of Diana?"

"Diana," Rosie says, releasing the name slowly into the chilly air. "You mean your 'friend'?" she asks, setting the noun off as though it were encased in elaborate gilded curlicues.

Now he runs his shoe over the edge of a step, then says, "Don't be unreasonable, Rosie. You're dating, too."

"I know what I'm doing."

"And you think I don't?"

She shrugs. "I think maybe you're confused. Is she a friend or something more? Do you know?" She starts rubbing her upper arms, trying to keep warm.

"We're getting a divorce. This is what happens when people get divorced."

She swallows hard because for a moment, the way her cheeks have started to ache, she thinks she might start crying, but it passes. She's okay now, just chilled. "Do you talk to her?" she asks him.

He starts to point a finger at her, to begin a sentence, to explain and justify and defend and pontificate, but it never happens. The hand goes down and he turns, just as always, and he walks away from her. "Does your Diana like silence?" she shouts after him, but he is already in his car, the windows drawn up tight, and he doesn't even turn his head toward her.

CHAPTER
EIGHT

Rosie's standing at the picture window between the drapes and the glass, watching the road for Quinn. He's not really late, but she's just wanting to see Jason again. He's been gone since the evening before and she gets restless being all by herself in the house.

When the car pulls up she goes right out to the street. Quinn's already lifting the toddler out of the car seat by the time she gets there. "There was much more wheezing this time," Quinn says as he hands Jason over to his mother. Quinn's speaking slowly, as though she might have difficulty understanding him otherwise. Or maybe he's just having more trouble speaking. Maybe the vocal cords are getting rusted over, Rosie thinks, and can't help laughing to herself.

Rosie rests her cheek against her son's soft face. "Did you have a good time, baby?" she asks him, and he nods and smiles at her. Jason reaches a hand toward each parent and his fingers graze over their chests for a few moments, tracing out abstract messages that Rosie is certain are about love and separation. Her heart aches for wanting to make it easier for him, and she kisses the little fingertips of his right hand, one after the other, and he giggles at the sensation.

"What'd you do with your dad?" she asks, but he only lowers his head to her shoulder and snuggles against her. Rosie hears the catch in his breathing, the slightly labored quality. "How long has he been sounding like this?" she asks.

Quinn shakes his head. "Most of the day. No energy either. He wanted to be held the last couple of hours." He reaches back into the car, lifts the medication charts off the passenger seat, and hands them to her. "I think we should get a second opinion," he says with even more deliberation than before.

"Are you talking about a second *medical* opinion?" He nods. "Why?"

"Because he's not getting better and he doesn't seem like himself."

"He's probably tired. Did you feed him?"

"Of course I fed him." He pushes the words out through his lips so she can almost read them as they travel the distance between them.

"What did you give him?" Quinn never took any initiative in feeding Jason when they'd all lived together. She's had to give him lists of his favorite foods.

"He had pastina and chicken stars. Stuff he likes."

"Well, it's eight o'clock. He's probably just tired. I'll go put him down." She means this to be a sign-off, a form of good-bye, but Quinn strides behind her, and on into the house.

"What if you put him to bed and then we could talk," he suggests.

She wants to say a hundred different things like, Cat give you back your tongue? Or, I didn't know you could talk, but she simply agrees to the suggestion. "Make yourself some coffee and you can scrounge around for food if you want," she tells him. Quinn says he's already eaten.

Rosie carries Jason upstairs and undresses him. She sits on the floor and he stands next to her, leaning against her, his arms draped around the sides of her neck as though he can't hold himself up otherwise. In the past when he's gotten really tired, he's sometimes become almost hyper, moving faster and faster, as if being still for even a second might cause him to fall instantly asleep.

"You're my sweet monkey," she says to him while she snaps up his sleeper. She puts him into his crib and then goes across the room to his bookshelf, but she's thinking more about what Quinn really wants than choosing Jason's bedtime story.

Why is he hanging around downstairs like this, waiting to talk after enduring silences for such a long time? Does he want to come back or to negotiate new terms? She's almost afraid to think of it, and especially to think of what she'll say about Greg if he asks about him. She does know one thing: she needs to be as vague as possible about him so she doesn't back herself into a rigid position.

Rosie goes into her bedroom, where she now keeps Jason's collection of picture books, dust-catchers that they are. She scans the shelves for one that Jason likes, finds *Good Night Moon*, and carries it back to her child's room. Jason is in exactly the position she left him, and his eyes are closed. The side of the crib is still lowered—he's old enough now to scale even a raised side, so it is permanently kept down so that his entry and exit height are closer to the floor. She leans in and kisses his warm lips. She can barely hear the wheeze now.

Quinn turns the TV off as soon as she walks into the family room. "He scared me today," he tells her. "He didn't have any spirit, you know what I mean?"

"Maybe you just wore him out. What did you do with him?"

Quinn shrugs his shoulders. "Not all that much. I took him over to the zoo and took him on that little train ride they have."

"The zoo?" She can't believe it. "Don't you think it might be from breathing in all that animal hair?"

"He's got to do something, Rosie. He can't sit around in a bare room all day."

"But a zoo, Quinn?"

"Rosie, the world isn't stripped bare." He's stood up now. "Where do *you* take him?" She's starting to answer when he asks, "A hospital ward? That's the only place I can think of that might be clean enough according to the standards you've laid down. And I'll tell you something else; Diana was very allergic as a kid and she says her symptoms were much better controlled than his, and that was twenty years ago. Before your so-called modern science came along."

"Oh, so that's what this is about? Diana?" Rosie takes in a deep breath and walks away from him, back toward the kitchen.

"No, Rosie," he says, following after her. "This is about Jason. And about us trying to help him. Diana knows something about this and she says the quality of his respiration is getting worse, not better."

Rosie turns suddenly back toward him. "Wait a minute. Is she with him when you have him? Is that how she knows all this? This 'quality of respiration' business?" Quinn doesn't answer. "On this trip to the zoo, Quinn, was she there?"

"Yes, she was there. What of it?"

"Quinn, it's totally inappropriate for her to be there." She's ready to pound a fist against his stupid chest.

"Why? She likes him."

Rosie imagines this woman holding Jason as they walk through the zoo, cooing at him in idiotic baby talk, no less, about the different animals. "Quinn, did it ever occur to you that you're putting Jason in a very difficult emotional situation?"

"No," he says flatly.

"Think about it for ten seconds, maybe, Quinn, and you'll see what I'm talking about. She probably scares the hell out of him. He's two years old, Quinn. He thinks you're asking him to choose between us, between her and me. Did you see how when I was holding him he reached out one hand toward each of us? It's like he's trying to make sense of it, like he's asking us, 'Are you two still my parents?' 'Who's that other woman?' Did you see the way he almost caved in against me, like his ordeal was finally over?" She holds her hand, fingers spread wide, against her chest.

"Don't make more out of it than it is, Rosie. There's no *ordeal* going on here."

"No? He's a baby, Quinn. He doesn't understand. He thinks she's a new mommy. Maybe when he's with her he thinks he'll never see me again. No wonder he's depressed."

Quinn rolls his eyes and she thinks he's going to bolt right then, but he doesn't. "I've explained to him that she's a friend. And by the way, that's a completely accurate description. Jason can understand that concept. He likes her. It's not like he cringes around her. He goes to her, he sits on her lap. He likes her."

"He's depressed, you said."

"No, that's your word, not mine. He just seems to be exhausted. And he has these allergy symptoms."

"It's not allergy, Quinn, it's asthma. I don't know what your friend had, but if it was allergies, it's completely different. And anyway, it's absolutely none of her business. As far as I'm concerned, Jason's visits are with *you*, not with you and this friend of yours. Because, frankly, I'm very worried about what exactly her agenda is."

"What do you mean 'agenda'?"

"I mean, maybe she wants to be Jason's mommy and your wifey and that's what all this is about."

"Jesus, Rosie, it's not like that."

"Don't be naive," she tells him. "You believe what you want to believe, but I don't want her there when Jason's with you. And I don't want her things in your apartment, either, when he's there. It isn't fair to him, and he should come first."

"Don't overreact like this, Rosie."

"I'm not overreacting at all, Quinn. You're the one who said he was so much worse today. You want another opinion? Then let's go back to the therapist together." Quinn says nothing, which doesn't surprise Rosie one bit. She can see he's seething. She can hear it in his short, tight breaths. And then, just like always, Quinn turns and leaves. No summing up, no closing salutation. Just out the door. Slamming it behind him.

Rosie follows him, then bangs on the door with her fist as though it is his house, his territory, that lies on the other side. Of course there were no new terms, no discussion of Greg. There was nothing. And then her hand hurts so much, she stops pounding on the new wood, and brings her injured hand up to her lips.

CHAPTER NINE

THERE IS ONE MORE VERY BAD TIME BEFORE things turn strange and topsy-turvy. Before Quinn singsongs his way through a chorus of I-told-you-so, and before the state says they know what it means to nurture and care for a child, and that Rosie does not. There is one more flare, or episode, or attack, or, as Rosie thinks of it, one more Vision of the End.

And this time, Rosie doesn't call Quinn.

This time, she is right there, sleeping, or rather, trying to sleep, on a mattress next to Jason's crib when she hears the sharp sound of her toddler's struggle, his lungs emptying but failing to refill, and she feels the fear—his and hers—mixed so hot together that it seeps up around them both and draws breath from her, too, nearly paralyzing her as she watches him, sitting in his crib, struggling to hold on to his life.

She has the portable phone right at her side, just for this very moment, planning for it, yes. She presses the single number that will connect her to her sister, even as she rises up from her mattress to go to her child. "Beth," Rosie tries to say into the mouthpiece when her sister offers a soft, sleepy hello, but no sound comes out. Rosie thinks she will never make herself known, but Beth instantly speaks her name, and somehow Rosie is able to make it clear that there is some kind of terrible problem. Beth tells her sister she will be right there.

This time, thankfully, Rosie knows exactly what to do because she's gone over it with Linder. She dials his answering service and reports Jay's symptoms using the numerical ranking system Linder has taught her for rating wheezing, coughing, and breathing ratio. This time her voice doesn't fail her, and she speaks the numbers distinctly. There is no scale by which she can report the level of her fear and despair, or the utter panic she sees in Jason's dark eyes and in the clenching of his miniature fists. When the doctor calls back, which he does in about two minutes, he tells Rosie to wrap Jason in a blanket, and to bring him to his office immediately. He says she can try the inhaler, but that he doesn't think it'll do any good. That last phrase makes her chest feel as though it's been tightened yet one more notch, and he must hear the labored sound of her breathing because he tells her, "Please, Rosie, stay calm for the baby's sake."

This time, she doesn't bother to change into clothes. She concentrates on Jason, on wrapping him, on reassuring him, on finding the chambered device, though she cannot load it without putting him down—which she won't do—so she cannot make use of it until they are in the car. She goes downstairs to wait for Beth, rocking Jay, watching through the window, standing under the drape again, scanning the deserted street for a car, then realizing she shouldn't even have drapes, she should have pulled them down and given them away, but because they were new and expensive, she'd kept them, making gods of money and decorating while her child gasped for breath. And now here she is, bringing this sick child right into the midst of them, enveloping him in their inner folds, the side she hasn't even vacuumed, shrouding him in dust, she thinks, and she moves out from behind them as quickly as she can.

She doesn't even have a robe on. She goes to the front closet and pulls a jacket from its hanger. She'll toss it in the car, put it on once Jason is in his car seat. And then she remembers there is no car seat in Beth's car, she'll have to hold him, which is horribly dangerous; no way is she going to do that. She'll have Beth get it out of her car, or no, that's absurd, time is too precious right now. She remembers the story Linder told her of the child choking on the toy in her car seat. No, she's going to hold him so she can feel his breathing. So she'll know, instantly, if she has to push her own air into his mouth and lungs. She has opened the front door so she can see out to the street and she remembers that cold air can sometimes make asthma worse, so she pulls the blanket up over the back of Jason's head and she holds him so that his face is toward the house, toward the warmer air. He's stiffening the way he did that other time when they had to take him to the hospital. And then, thank God, Beth's car screeches around the corner and pulls into the driveway. It isn't till Rosie's actually hustling him down the concrete stairs that she realizes she has nothing on her feet.

When they arrive at the professional building, Linder is already there and he has prepared a syringe of epinephrine. In the car Rosie had managed to fill the chamber inhaler, but, as predicted, it hadn't worked. Jason has never understood that he must breathe in the medication. "One, two, three, Jay," she tried coaxing him, but then ended up blowing it all over his face.

"It doesn't usually work with the little ones," Linder says. "Even for the ones who can do it when they're not having a flare; when they're in trouble, the last thing they want is something in or even near their mouths." He's stroking Jason's back while Rosie holds him in her arms and she can feel the baby's rigidity begin to ease even though no medication has been administered yet. Linder brings his face close to Jason's and he speaks to him in a whisper, telling him that he's going to give him a shot and that it will help him. Jason barely flinches as the needle enters his flesh or when the plunger forces the drug into his body. Rosie is dizzy with sadness seeing him accept this pain so easily; knowing that he's already learned that a shot can bring relief and that this brief hurt is vastly preferable to what he is suffering. After a few moments, Rosie feels her child's hand moving around her neck, the fingers no longer closed into hard fists. She rests her cheek on his soft damp hair and feels his little hand pat, pat, pat across her arm, as though she's the one in need of comfort. Linder pulls a chair over for Rosie, then one for Beth and one for himself, and the three of them sit, waiting through the changes, the easing of his breathing and the softening of the frightened eyes. There is marked twitching in Jason's limbs, which she has learned is normal with this drug. Linder touches Jason's hand or cheek from time to time, perhaps to judge something about his skin or muscle tone or temperature, perhaps just to connect, Rosie can't be sure which.

"He's not going to have to go to the hospital," Linder says after a while. "We caught it in time." He has his hand on her shoulder and she reaches for it in an almost ravenous way, needing to hold tight to him, to make him understand how he has saved not just Jason, but herself as well.

"Thank you," she whispers, her fingers slipping between his. "It happened so fast this time," she says, and begins to cry as soon as she starts to speak the words. His hand tightens around hers.

"You probably slept through the early buildup," he says.

It hadn't felt like she'd been sleeping, but she supposes he must be right. He has told her that she should be sleeping in her own bed so that she can at least be comfortable and rested. He says she is just as likely to sleep through early symptoms in the same room as in another because if she's sleep-deprived she'll fall into occasional very deep sleep cycles to compensate. He's told her to get an intercom so that she can both sleep in her own bed *and* hear Jason, but she hasn't wanted to ask Quinn for yet more additional money.

"You can get a simple portable monitor that'll pick up his cries. One of my patients told me she found one at Costco for under thirty dollars. Quinn's not going to begrudge you that kind of money, is he?"

"You obviously don't know Quinn," Beth interjects.

"No actually, I don't. We've never met."

"I didn't think so," Beth says, laughing.

Rosie's laughing, too, but Beth is right; dealing with Quinn over money has become a decidedly unpleasant affair.

It is nearly an hour that they sit there in the quiet of very early morning. Linder hasn't lit the office to the bright daytime level she's used to here. There is only one light on, and it is down at the other end of the room. Where they sit, there is a dusky, restful feel to things. Jason is asleep now and his breathing has returned to something like it had been when Quinn first brought him home, a gentle wheeze, nothing more.

"He'll be okay," Linder says. He has given Rosie towels to wrap around her feet and some elastic bands to secure them. "I don't want to wreck your towels," she says, trying to hand them back. "The car's parked right outside the door, it's no big deal."

"You shouldn't risk getting chilled. You need to stay healthy for Jason. And as for wrecking them, I keep them here for just this use. You can't imagine how many people show up here barefoot in the middle of the night," he says, shaking his head just contemplating it. "I've considered running a sideline business—you know, inexpensive casual shoes, disposable, even, that sort of thing." He smiles at her, and she feels his eyes soften into something more like what they are when the two of them meet outside this office, and for a moment, she wants to lean across the distance between them and lay her head against his chest, but Beth is here. She feels herself start to sway, not even necessarily toward him, just away from herself, uncentering, drifting, and then the phone rings, startling them both.

There is another emergency. Another family with a very ill child. He looks at his watch when he hangs up the phone. "No more sleep for me," he says, and raises his hands in a gesture of surrender.

By the time Linder has done a final check on her sleeping child and Rosie has swaddled her feet and rewrapped Jason in his blanket, the doctor's next emergency has arrived. As they pass each other in the outer office, Rosie sees how she herself must have looked an hour or so earlier, thoroughly bedraggled and frantic. Rosie remembers seeing this family, the Moores, at Great Pond, the town swimming area. She thinks the mother's name is Megan, though she's forgotten the father's and the little girl's names. The child is about a year older than Jason, and she looks striking, with a head of soft red curls—or she does when she's not gasping for breath. Rosie didn't know their daughter had asthma, but then, why would she? How many people had actually seen Jason have an attack? Rosie tries to remember if this other child might be in the older class at Jason's day-care center, if maybe she, too, has gotten some heavy-duty exposure in that setting. "Oh," the woman says, when she sees Rosie, "you've got it, too? Asthma, I mean?"

"Yes," Rosie acknowledges. "But he's fine now." She smiles, hoping to ease this family's fears. And then Megan and her husband's eyes are fully on Linder as he emerges from his inner office, and they move swiftly past Rosie and on into the examining room with the doctor.

"Did I thank Dr. Linder?" Rosie asks her sister once they're in the car and heading toward home.

"Of course you did. As soon as Jay started to breathe right again you got into Fifty Ways to Say I Thank You."

"But what about when we left? Did I thank him then?"

"Yes, you did, and I thanked him, too. In fact, it was all I could do to keep from leaping into his arms when Jay started calming down and breathing again. I'll tell you, that ride over was sheer hell. I was so scared, listening to that poor baby struggling for his life, I don't honestly know how I managed to get us there."

Beth reaches a hand over and pats her sister's arm. "Don't worry about the doctor, Rosie. He knows how grateful you are. It was written all over your face. And besides, you did thank him. I promise you, it's okay." Rosie nods. "He's the big secret, isn't he? The one you said you're *sort* of seeing?" Beth asks.

Rosie's been reluctant, almost superstitiously so, to say much about him because it's been so tenuous, so ill defined. She hasn't wanted to frighten away the little that there was by speaking of it. But of course she has mentioned that there might be someone, unnamed, undescribed. Tune in tomorrow, she's told her sister, who complained bitterly at being given mere wisps of information. Rosie sighs deeply now, thinking about how it'd be better to keep it all quiet awhile longer.

"I knew it," Beth said. "Good choice, little sissy. He's very good looking."

"You think so?" Rosie asks, despite her resolve to say nothing.

"Definitely. I like the contrast with Quinn, if you don't mind me saying."

"That's okay, you can say whatever you want." Beth has never been a big Quinn booster.

"I mean, he has all that nice hair. I think the way people choose to wear their hair is very important. A man who keeps his hair that long is probably very sensual."

"Spare me your generalizations," Rosie says.

"Well, think about it. He could wear his hair as short as he wanted, shave his head, even, and nobody would blink. Men can do that. But he keeps it long, so he must like the feel of it on his neck or something, and I say that means he's a sensual type."

"Or maybe he's just lazy and hasn't found time to get it cut."

"Uh-uh. Long hair takes more time to wash and dry and get to look right, so it's not laziness. I'm telling you, stop fighting it. You know I'm right. Look at how he touched Jason all the time, reassuring him nonverbally. He's into touch. He's human and warm and all that good stuff. Maybe you're so used to the emptiness of life with the short-haired automaton that you can't see it anymore." Rosie looks down at Jason, still sleeping in her lap. She doesn't like Beth to bad-mouth Quinn in the child's presence, but he's certainly oblivious to it right now. "And you're crazy about him," Beth declares.

"Don't say that," Rosie complains, and she wonders if she's blushing—though what would it matter? It's probably too dark for Beth to see.

"It's so obvious that you are. *And* it's *so* mutual."

"Is it?" Rosie asks, a breathiness filling up the words.

"See? You wouldn't ask that, you wouldn't care, if you weren't in love with him."

"I'm not in love."

"In lust, then."

"Stop it." Rosie slaps lightly at her sister's arm.

Beth laughs. "You two wanted to touch so badly, I couldn't stand it. I haven't seen anything like that since high school. People don't *long* anymore; they jump into bed and that's it.

Myself, I'm a great fan of longing. I'm sorry it's passed out of the romantic vocabulary."

"What'd you think of him?"

"I just told you that." Then they both laugh. "You're definitely goofy in love." Rosie shakes her head. "De-ni-al," Beth intones. "Deep, deep, denial. You really want to know what I think?" Rosie shrugs. She's not looking at her sister, she's got her eyes on the road. "I think," Beth says without waiting to be urged to continue, "that if you two would only just get together already, you wouldn't have to go out barefoot in the night anymore to deal with Jason's medical problems."

"I don't know. I don't know if there's anything really happening." Beth guffaws and twists the steering wheel left and right so the car seems to be confused as to where it's supposed to go. "Watch it, Beth, Jason's not in a car seat," Rosie warns her, though she's not really worried because the car never strays from its lane. "See, the problem is, he's busy with his practice all the time. You saw how full time, round the clock it is. There's no time for us to get together. So far it's just been a couple of lunches. I think it may never work. It may never go beyond longing."

"You need to up the ante, sister. Screw this lunch business, that's for a ladies' afternoon out. Invite him for dinner. *Do* something, my dear. Somebody needs to be happy, and why not you?" Beth hasn't been happy in a long time, Rosie knows. Her husband left her two years ago for the woman he was ride-sharing with to work. "And I'll be happy to sleep with him if you decide you don't want to."

"You weren't asked," Rosie is quick to say.

"Yeah, but under the right circumstances, I might be able to wrangle an invitation. But wait a minute, were *you* asked?"

"None of your business."

"Ooooh. Over lunch? He asked over lunch?"

Rosie laughs. "I told you nothing's happening."

"Well, work on it, please. Give me something to fantasize about at least."

"God, I'm so tired," Rosie says when they pull up in front of her house and she has to figure out how to gather enough energy to get herself and Jason on into the house, especially with these ridiculous shoe-towels on her feet.

"Yeah, me too," Beth says. "And I have to tell you, I was real big time scared seeing Jason like that."

"He's okay," Rosie says, and she lets Beth lift Jason from her arms and carry him to the house.

"I don't have anybody to get home to, so I'm staying," Beth proclaims when they reach the front door. Rosie never locked it, so now they're able to simply push the door open, walk straight in, and on up the stairs.

"You don't have to," Rosie says quietly to her sister's back as she carries the baby back to his crib.

"You go to bed," Beth instructs her little sister.

It isn't till Rosie has lifted the covers and slipped into bed that she remembers that she sleeps now in Jason's room. She decides to lie there just for a couple of minutes to relax a little in the wide comfortable space before she gets up. But her mind drifts, silent and swift as a river, over to sleep's side.

CHAPTER TEN

NEXT MORNING, ROSIE CALLS QUINN AT HIS office, but very early, when she knows he's not likely to be there. She leaves a message on his machine. It's cowardly, she knows, but she just doesn't want to be called to task for every move she makes anymore. The message is brief: "Quinn, Jason had a difficult night. I'm taking him to the doctor this afternoon so we need to reschedule your time with him. Call me."

"How bad was he?" Quinn asks when he calls back. As usual, he hasn't said hello nor identified himself, though of course Rosie knows who it is.

"Not too bad," Rosie says. She's decided to downplay the events so that Quinn doesn't get too crazed. "Just bad enough to make me a little concerned." She listens to his breathing, tries to figure out if they breathe at the same rate.

"Why are you waiting till this afternoon to take him in?" he finally asks.

She'd actually hoped to be able to skip Quinn past the night visit to the doctor, but it doesn't look like that's going to happen. "This is just a recheck, Quinn. I brought him in last night. But just to the office, not the hospital." Dead air again and she can't think of what to say next that won't make things worse. "Is tomorrow okay for your visit?" she asks finally.

"Something's got to be done," he says.

"Quinn, Jason has asthma. I'm sorry that he does, it breaks

my heart, but it's a fact of his life and ours. Now, given that terrible fact, I'm doing what needs to be done."

"I disagree." His response comes back surprisingly quickly.

"Obviously. So maybe you want to go to Dr. Linder's and talk to him. I'll set up an appointment for the three of us to meet. Would that make you happy?" She's instantly sorry that she phrased it that way. She knows it sounded mocking, that "happy" bit.

"The score's stacked two to one against me."

"Let's not get paranoid here, Quinn."

"You two are involved, right?" Now it's her turn to pull the silent treatment on him. "The friendly triangle concept doesn't appeal to me," he informs her.

"Then go see him alone, okay? Go confront him. Maybe ask him what his intentions are toward me, because personally, I think that's what you really want to know, Quinn. In fact, you want his number? I've got it right here." She's started rummaging in the drawer for her address book.

"No, I don't want to meet him."

"Fine. At least we've got that straight now. Do you want to see your son tomorrow or not?"

"You know what I want?"

"No, what?"

"I want to be kept informed about my child's health. I don't care if it's the middle of the night."

"Fine," she retorts. "And where can I reach you in the middle of the night?"

"You know my number," he says, each word a hard crystal of anger. "I'll pick my son up at four o'clock tomorrow," he says just before he hangs up.

IT IS THE NEXT MORNING THAT ROSIE GETS A phone call that sounds like it's for one of those fund-raisers where they hit you up by playing on your emotions. The caller's voice has the upbeat enthusiasm of the telephone solicitor. "Is this Mrs. Sloan?" the voice sings out.

"Yeah?" Rosie says, a bit snappishly, as she does with such calls.

"This is May Donovan and I'm calling from the Department of Children and Families."

Rosie thinks she knows what this one's going to be about—buying tickets to something—a circus, more than likely—for underprivileged kids. People are always trying to get her to buy tickets to a circus, but as far as she knows there hasn't been a circus in Connecticut in a tent since the Hartford circus fire in 1944. Why would anyone want to go to a circus if it weren't in a tent?

"Mrs. Sloan, I'm going to need to verify your address. Are you at twenty—"

"I don't give out my address on the phone, and I'm not interested in buying anything at all right now," Rosie says, cutting the woman off. "I'm on a fixed income these days." Rosie doesn't wait for a response before she hangs up.

The phone rings again and it's May Donovan once more. "Mrs. Sloan," she says, "I'm not selling anything. I'm with DCF, which is a state agency that is responsible for the health, safety, and welfare of children. I have some information for you and I just wanted to verify that you're the same Rosie Sloan I'm looking for."

"What information?" Rosie's taken aback and slightly embarrassed because maybe it's not a money hit. Those types don't usually call back.

"Can you verify that you're at twenty-six Clark Lane?"

"Yes. Is this about asthma?"

"In a way," the woman says slowly. There's more a sense of sobriety to her now, less of overflowing optimism. "Can you verify that you have a child named Jason?"

"Yes," Rosie says, while her mind goes off in all crazy directions, trying to figure out what this could be about. She knows Jason is upstairs napping; this can't be about him being kidnapped or in an accident or anything like that.

"Mrs. Sloan, there's no easy way for me to tell you this, so I'll get right to it. Our agency has received a complaint about Jason's well-being and I'm going to need to come over to check on him. I'd like to set up an appointment with you."

"He's fine," Rosie says, but she's fumbling badly through the words.

"Is eleven-thirty this morning all right with you?"

Rosie feels like she did when she was eleven years old and she boarded the wrong bus. She doesn't know where she's heading, and she doesn't recognize the landscape that's slipping by outside her window. "What does the complaint say?"

"I can go over that with you when I get there."

"No," Rosie says, refocusing. "What's the complaint? And who made it?"

"Briefly, it concerns neglect."

"Neglect? I'm with him twenty-four hours a day. I sleep in his room."

"A lot of complaints are unfounded, Mrs. Sloan, so you really owe it to yourself to clear this up as soon as possible. That's why I've moved my own schedule around so that I could be there at eleven-thirty, if that's all right with you."

Oh, save me from what's good for me and from all your kindnesses, Rosie thinks. "Who complained?"

"I can't tell you that."

"Oh, right. You get an anonymous phone call and you shift your whole schedule around to check it out?"

"It wasn't an anonymous call. The person gave his or her name and number, but I'm not allowed to give that information out to you."

"This is crazy," Rosie complains. "Don't I have a right to know my accuser?"

"Nobody has accused you of anything. Someone has asked *us*, our agency, to check into the welfare of a minor, that's all. We'll come out, see that your child is safe, and that'll be the end of it."

"That's just semantics. Somebody's accusing me of neglect and I want to know who it is."

"Let's clear it up first," the social worker suggests. "Let's establish that there isn't any problem."

"And the caller? Does the caller have any responsibility or does he just get his thrills off this and that's it?"

"We deal with the caller once we establish that the child is safe. Can we get together and talk about this?"

"Yes," Rosie says. "Eleven-thirty." She's already begun straightening things around her as they talk. She's loaded the breakfast dishes into the dishwasher, wiped the counter, and put the cereal boxes back in the cabinet by the time she hangs up. She's thinking, too, about whether to pull those dust-collecting drapes down.

MAY DONOVAN IS NOT SO YOUNG AS SHE sounded on the phone—she appears to be in her early thirties and she tells Rosie she's been working for DCF for more than "eight long years." She wears a suit that is either brand new or extremely well cared for and properly dry cleaned. And very au courant. Brand new, Rosie decides. And worn with the right silk blouse—feminine, but not demure or seductive. Maybe it comes from a special catalog called *Soft Office Wear*.

Ms. Donovan makes a fuss over Jason and gets down on the floor with him to look at his dinosaur collection even though her skirt barely gets to her knees when she's standing. She doesn't seem to fear runs in her stockings or scrapes along the sides of her leather shoes, maybe because she's immune to all those ills, for when she stands up, she's perfect again. She doesn't even readjust or smooth out. She just is.

What is she doing in this low-paying job? Rosie wonders. Her wool gabardine must have cost the equivalent of a week's salary, the shoes and silk, another week's.

"Do you have children?" Rosie asks her, having already caught sight of the ring set on the woman's finger, supporting a diamond that is as large as any Rosie has ever seen up close.

"We're still in the planning stage about family," the social worker says in that smiley, sticky way she has. Right, Rosie thinks. She's one of those people who believes that mothers need to be "mature" before they're capable of parenting. Rosie considers saying that she has never had a diamond and doesn't miss it, but she catches herself. The last thing she wants to do right now is play poor cousin to someone who is investigating her.

The woman wants to see where Jason sleeps. Once they're actually standing in the room and the social worker is scanning its emptiness, Rosie realizes how much it looks like a prison cell. Especially with the mattress on the floor. Rosie's thinking about news stories she's seen where they find children chained to radiators in bare rooms and she glances over at the young woman to see if maybe she's thinking the same thing, but her expression is unreadable.

"I had to take down the curtains and get rid of the rug because of the asthma," Rosie tries to explain, and her words strike the walls and ricochet from one hard surface to another, explosive noises in the open space. Ms. Donovan takes notes on what she sees and on what Rosie says. She carries a clipboard and she flips through her sheets from time to time, nodding to herself. She asks Rosie if it would be all right for them to go down to the kitchen again. Rosie leads the way back downstairs, though she has the sense that she's being pushed from behind and isn't leading at all. As they pass by the front door, Rosie considers bolting through it, Jason in her arms, but she continues on, obediently. Her feet feel exactly as they did when they were wrapped in Dr. Linder's towels, bulky and unfamiliar, so that it is a challenge to place their shapes upon the floor in a way that gives firm footing.

When they are seated again at the table, Jason next to them on the floor with his collection of oversized Legos and dinosaurs, the social worker asks questions about Jason's development, his current illness and its onset, symptoms, and treatment. Several times Rosie asks to be told the exact nature of the complaint, but the young woman only smiles at her with each request and shakes her head. One time the investigator seems to bare her teeth when questioned, but oddly, she's smiling still. Rosie decides to stop asking.

"Do you recall what medical tests he's had?" Ms. Donovan asks.

"What does all this have to do with a complaint of neglect?"

"I'm just trying to verify that he's getting good medical care."

"Is that the nature of the complaint, his medical care?" Rosie asks, and she knows now that it's Quinn who has contacted the agency. When the social worker becomes vague and elusive on this point, Rosie's even more sure. She tries to explain to the woman that Quinn's just into a power trip and that this has nothing to do with neglect. "This is a private battle," Rosie says. "Quinn wants to be in control of the medical decisions and he's really just using your agency to get his way. Like a spoiled child," she adds. Ms. Donovan isn't writing any of this down. Rosie's face is hot with anger.

"Tell me something—am I actually required to tell you absolutely anything you want to know about? Because that doesn't make sense to me. This feels like a violation of my basic right to privacy."

"I'm asking on behalf of the state," Ms. Donovan counters.

"And that's supposed to make it okay? The government violates civil rights on a daily basis. Somebody has to object and hold the line."

"These are just routine questions," May insists, and smiles. "Think of it this way: I'm trying to paint a picture of Jason's world for others to look at. I try to get as many details as I can while I'm here so that when I go back to my office I'm sure to put all the right details into the picture."

Rosie doesn't believe her. This is silly talk designed to soothe. DCF is looking for something very specific and Rosie can feel it. May Donovan has come here with some fixed idea about Jason's care that she's hoping Rosie will confirm. She's even offered to provide advice about child care, which Rosie has said she doesn't feel she needs, thank you very much. Rosie thinks maybe she should have called a lawyer the minute May Donovan contacted her. Yes, that's what she should have done, and she's kicking herself now for letting this woman into her house. She's probably said all the wrong things and made herself totally vulnerable. "Isn't that enough info?" Rosie asks, and she's surprised when May agrees and slips her pen back into her purse. Why has she given in to me so easily? Rosie asks herself. And then for a few minutes, all she can think about is asking Ms. Donovan how many suits she owns.

When the social worker is at the door, Rosie doesn't want to let her just walk out with things so horribly unresolved. "There's no neglect, is there," Rosie says, trying to sound confident, to make it impossible for the woman to do anything but agree, but Rosie's voice fails her, cracking over the words.

"I still have to talk to Dr. Linder," the social worker says, and Rosie notices the woman is avoiding looking straight at her.

"You're checking to see if I'm lying?" Rosie asks. Rosie has truthfully answered all the questions put to her, though with a little exaggeration as to her own attentiveness to her child and to the supposed eagerness with which she has sought out and destroyed dust mites and other allergens in her home. But she would have lied—and easily, too—if doing so would have meant protecting Jason and herself from the further meddling interference of the state and Quinn.

"We try to verify all our information," the woman tells her.

"Like I said." There is a pause then, while each of them seems to wait for the other to reach for the doorknob. "When will I . . . ?" Rosie starts to ask, but can't think how to phrase what she needs to know. Perhaps it would be something like, When can I stop being scared of you?

"Soon," the woman tells her, and Rosie wonders what question the social worker thinks she's answering. She's become so self-conscious in front of this woman, she's not even sure she's holding Jason in a state-approved way now, and she shifts him from hip to shoulder, though he's too big for that, and back again, waiting for May to smile upon one of the arrangements, though this doesn't happen. Jason complains after several of these variations, pushes against Rosie's chest, and asks to be put down.

"Will you be in touch with me?" Rosie asks her investigator.

"Oh, yes," May says, the old enthusiasm of the phone solicitor back again. Rosie thinks that means she's found something, that May Donovan is anticipating that in a few minutes she'll be able to report something exciting to her supervisor. Rosie watches the woman walk toward her car, leading with her hips; not swinging them, but gliding easily and comfortably, through space. Rosie's legs are shaking.

CHAPTER ELEVEN

"**W**HY ARE THEY DOING THIS TO ME?" Rosie asks Linder. She called him as soon as May Donovan was out of her house and he's squeezed her in between patients. She's got Jason with her, otherwise she might be throwing herself at his knees or just crumpling into a heap on the floor, she's not sure what, but she feels completely out of control. As it is, Linder has to tell her to sit down to make her stop pacing back and forth in front of his desk.

Linder shakes his head. "By law, the Department of Children and Families has no choice but to investigate once they receive a complaint."

"I'm going to kill my husband. My ex," she corrects herself. "He's the one who's siccing them on me. What if they decide there *is* neglect, what if they try to . . ." She stops. She can't finish the sentence with "take Jason away from me," not with the child sitting right there, taking it all in. And she shouldn't be talking about Quinn this way, either, she knows that. Even if he is a bastard.

"Once they come to talk to me and I confirm that you've done all the right things, that'll be the end of it."

"This is so unfair."

"Rosie, listen to me," he says, leaning across the desk. His voice is softer now, so soft, in fact, she has to lean toward him to hear what he has to say. "The worst thing you can do right now is to start thinking of yourself as a victim. Self-pity looks a whole lot like distraction and disorientation. If you get into that, they'll start questioning your competency. You've done everything correctly. We've got documentation to prove that you were on top of the problems from day one. This woman, this—what's her name?"

"May Donovan," Rosie fills in.

"Yes, Donovan. Don't let her think she's rattled you or that you're bothered by her investigation, because in the simplistic world that she moves in, that means she's touched a nerve and that she's closing in on some major truth. All her warning lights will start flashing."

Rosie closes her eyes and moans. When she looks up again, she asks him, "What if I already did the wrong thing?" Rosie's holding Jason on her lap and she circles her arms more closely around him as she speaks.

"Rosie, most of these complaints are brought by the other parent in a divorce. The agency knows that as well as you and I do. The problem is, even though they know most of these complaints have no merit, they still have to investigate them because that's the way the law reads. One or two of those hundreds of cases does have merit. Your job is to make them see yours isn't one of those. Don't question your own motives in front of them and don't act like you're sorry or regretful about anything you've done on Jason's behalf. Or anything you haven't done. Don't say anything like, 'I don't know, maybe I should have had him checked out when he coughed that time when he was two months old.' You know what I mean?" She nods. "You did everything you should have. You went above and beyond, in fact. And I'll tell them that and you'll be fine."

"The social worker—or whatever she is—wouldn't confirm that it was Quinn who made the complaint."

Linder tips his head slightly sideways and shrugs. "You asked her if it was Quinn?"

"Yeah."

"I don't know who else it could be, do you?" Rosie shakes her head. Linder sits back in his chair. "It doesn't take much for people to get into this when their nerves are exposed already from a split-up."

"What should I do about him?"

"Quinn, you mean?"

"Yes. Should I confront him, tell him I know, or should I ignore it?"

Linder smiles. "It hadn't occurred to me that you might be able to ignore it. I just figured you'd put it to him straight on."

"Well, I guess the truth is there's probably no way on earth that I could ignore it. I guess I just want you to tell me that I'm not going to make things worse by going to him with what I know."

"I don't think you will. I would think that the more you talk, the better this is going to be." For a few moments neither of them speaks. Rosie's thinking about the two of them—herself and Greg—getting together again. She's hoping he'll mention it, first. "Your breathing's more level than when you first came in," Linder notes finally. "How are you feeling?"

"I'm calmer. Almost okay, I think. But my stomach's racing."

He comes out from behind his desk, reaches down for her hand, and starts taking her pulse. His thumb is pressed lightly into the soft hollow of her wrist. For a couple of seconds she feels like she can't breathe, and then her pulse starts dancing so fast against his hold that it's embarrassing. She's watching his face, looking for his reaction, but his eyes are following the second hand of his watch. "Good," he says, after a while, then pats her hand a couple of times before letting go. "Tell yourself the investigation's not going anywhere, nothing's going to happen."

"Yeah," she says. "I'll be okay." She can still feel the heat of his thumb in that soft place.

"Try breathing, too," he suggests, smiling at her. "It's good for the heart rate. You know: oxygen. All that good stuff." He looks at Jason then, and asks, "And how are you, big kid?"

"Sauros?" Jason asks, stretching out his arm toward the doctor, palm and fingers spread wide to receive an offering.

"Of course," Linder says, lifting the child from his mother's lap. He leads him over to the cabinet that holds the dinosaurs. Jason's so excited, he's doing the toddler march-in-place routine, lifting one foot, then the other, again and again, unable to stand still while Linder pulls the box out. Rosie wants it simple again, too, Jason-style: you hold out your hand, you ask, you get. Should she say, Lunch again? She could say it as soon as he crosses back to this side of the room. Or she could raise the ante, as Beth suggested. Dinner at my place?

"Let's set up an appointment for Jason for next week," he says, moving behind his desk. Rosie nods and takes her child's hand.

CHAPTER TWELVE

BETH SAYS SHE DIDN'T THINK QUINN HAD IT in him to be so clever, getting at Rosie in this roundabout way. "There's more to the man than we had thought," she says as she puts a tuna salad sandwich, a can of iced tea, a plastic spoon, and a straw down on the kitchen table. She's come over to take care of Jason while Rosie goes hunting up Quinn.

"Maybe I should call him, make sure he's going to be there, because if he's not, I'll be making you waste your whole lunch hour over here for nothing," Rosie says.

"No, you're not going to call him and give him warning that you're on his case." She's folding up her canvas lunch bag. "I told you, surprise is everything with something like this." She pops the tab on her tea. "The last thing you want to do is give him time to work out some slick explanation. And definitely don't worry about me. I'm thrilled to death to be able to dine with my beautiful nephew. Ain't I, Jay," she says, lifting him from Rosie's arms, kissing him, and blowing his hair up off his forehead so he laughs and rubs his hand rapidly where her breath has tickled his skin. "Time for you to put on riot gear, sister," Beth advises.

When Rosie pulls up in front of the big white Victorian structure that houses the police department she doesn't get out of the car right away. She doesn't even shut off the ignition because she's thinking about turning around and leaving. This was an incredibly stupid idea, coming here, she tells herself.

She knows all the other guys are going to be straining their ears to hear what's going on between her and Quinn. But to hell with those other cops. She's just going to have to go in there, and she switches off the car. She'll keep her voice way down so the others can't hear it and she'll say the words slow and hard, up close by his face, so he'll get every syllable. *You bastard.* Beth says that'll be enough, that those two words will touch off his guilt, and she won't even have to mention the investigation. Beth says she *shouldn't* mention the investigation. She says Quinn will know what Rosie's talking about, and if he's caught off guard like that, he'll give himself away, blurt out something about it while he tries to defend himself from her name-calling.

Rosie's hands are shaking when she turns the big brass knob to open the front door of the police station. Why on earth this town still has this old building on a hill to house its police, she doesn't know. Unless you knew what it was, you could ride around for hours trying to find the station. Heaven help the person who actually needs police help, she thinks.

Inside, the place is no longer the gracious old mansion it appears to be from outside. A dividing wall has been added at the front end of what was once an elegant entryway. The wall is solid, white, and stark, the vast expanse of it broken only by a door to the rest of the station, and by a piece of glass about the size of a bedroom window. Bulletproof glass, Quinn has told her. She walks up to the window, rounds her back, and lowers her face so that her mouth is poised right in front of the round speaking grid. The uniformed officer behind the window is turned away from her, and he's speaking into a tiny telephone receiver that juts off a head-band he wears. She pushes the ring-for-service button embedded in the wall next to the glass and is wondering whether the wall is bulletproof as well when the officer swivels his chair back toward her. It's Quinn. "What are you doing here?" she asks him, forgetting the opening accusatory phrase she rehearsed.

"Filling in," he says. She knows Quinn hates phone work or desk work of any kind. "I can't talk to you now," he says. The phone's ringing. He's pressing one finger against the earpiece of his headphone and he's speaking into the mouthpiece.

"You bastard," she says, but she doesn't think he's heard. He certainly doesn't act like he's heard. He's telling whoever's on the line with him that the squad car will be there in five minutes. "Don't touch anything," he says into the plastic receiver. "Go outside now, Mrs. Trent, and wait for the officers there." Then he's listening to the caller. "No, I don't think they're still in the house, but there's no point taking any chances. I think you might walk down to the end of the access way, wave the squad car down, ma'am, and that way you'll be sure they know which drive is yours." Rosie sees him push a button on the console, and she knows the call is over.

"Quinn," she says sharply, but she doesn't have her mouth anywhere near the opening, so he isn't likely to have heard that, either.

"Is there something wrong with Jason?" he asks her.

"I don't know, is there?"

He looks puzzled. "We're doing riddles now?"

"What do you want from me, Quinn? Why are you doing this to me?"

He stares at her, then shakes his head like he's seen something strange. "I'm trying to answer phone calls. I'm not doing anything to you."

"You're making a few phone calls out, too, aren't you?" She's pressing her mouth practically up into the metal opening now and her head is at a very uncomfortable angle.

The phone rings again. "Eastleigh Police Department," he says, then she sees him consult a calendar, run a fingertip down the Saturday column. "Saturday the twentieth," he says. "Nine A.M. to five P.M."

"What's your goal in this?" she asks him when he's disconnected this call. He doesn't answer. He slides his jaw forward for a second, switching into some meaner version of himself for a second, some volatile mix she's unused to, but then it's gone, and he's only Quinn again. If we were at home, Rosie thinks, he'd be bolting out the door by now. "Don't play dumb with me, Quinn." He turns slightly away from her, toward the telephone equipment. She sees his finger hover over the telephone, hoping for another call, hoping for a way out. "Call them off, Quinn."

"Call who off, Rosie?" He's turned back to face her and he's got both hands on the desk, like he's just about to push himself up and toward her. "What the hell's going on?"

"Call off DCF."

His dark eyebrows draw down toward the middle of his brow. "What are you talking about?"

"Department of Children and Families. You filed a complaint with them."

Now he opens his eyes wider, then shakes his head. "No way. What kind of complaint? Did they say I did? Because if they did, they're lying, plain and simple."

"You know they don't say. *I* know," she says, pointing at her chest. "I know you called. Because you want custody."

"Jesus, Rosie, I don't want to take him away from you." The phone rings again, loud and jarring. "Damn," Quinn says. He presses a finger against the earpiece. "Eastleigh Police Department. Yes, sir. What's the address? Any injuries? How many cars? And your name, sir? One moment, please." He pushes a button, dispatches a car and an ambulance to Route Seven at Highview. Another button. "They're on their way, sir," he says, completing the call. "We shouldn't be doing this now," he says, looking at his wife.

"Yes, we should." She almost bangs her hand against the glass, but stops herself, before her fist is raised high enough for him to see.

"What's the alleged complaint?"

"You tell me."

She sees him push another button. "Matt, can you take the horn for five minutes for me? Yeah. Local emergency," he says, and Rosie wonders if this is standard code for a family dispute.

Rosie turns away, walks across the hall to the front door. She doesn't want to look at Matthew Sharp when he comes up to the desk. He'll be trying to read the problem off her face so he can speculate on it for the rest of the cops as soon as she's gone.

* * *

WHEN QUINN COMES OUT INTO THE HALL-way a couple of minutes later, he heads straight for the door. "What's the complaint?" he asks again, as soon as they're outside.

"Neglect," she says.

He shakes his head, takes a pack of cigarettes from his pocket, and pulls one out.

"Since when did you start smoking again?" she asks, lifting the pack from his hand.

"Since I don't know." He lights up.

"You're the abuser," she says. "You know how dangerous smoke is for an asthmatic?"

"I don't smoke when I'm with him."

"If you smoke in that apartment, the particles are still there when he comes to visit."

"I'm not an idiot, Rosie. I know all this stuff. I don't smoke in the apartment." He breathes in smoke, holds it for a moment, then blows it out. "What are they talking about, neglect?"

"The woman who came to the house wouldn't say."

"Somebody came to the house?"

"Yes."

He shakes his head. "They're taking it seriously, then. They're thinking about removing him."

"I know that," she says. "What did you expect?"

"It's not me, Rosie," he says, tossing the partially finished cigarette to the pavement and crushing it with his foot. "I don't want Jay taken away from you. Why would I do that?"

"I don't know why. Because you want to prove I'm a bad mother. Because you think he should have another doctor. You've been bugging me about that for weeks now."

She can see he's looking at the crushed cigarette. He pokes it with his foot. She hands him the pack and he takes out another. "You know," he says, "I don't care if Jason sees another doctor." He points the unlit cigarette at her.

"Then what the hell was all that about?"

"I don't know." He stares at her for a moment and she looks away. He works the cigarette back into the pack. "I guess maybe it was about you. About you and him. The doctor. Like you said."

"You mean because I'm dating him? You mean a jealousy thing?" Quinn shrugs. "But what about you? You're dating somebody," she says, her voice edgy with accusation.

"I don't know, Rosie. I know it's not rational. I just don't like it. When I thought about you being with somebody, I felt . . ." He glances at her. "I don't know how to describe it. I didn't like the way it felt." He's talking to the landscape, gesturing across the hill as though he were describing it.

"And then you made the complaint, so you could get me away from Greg Linder?"

Now he's facing her straight on, his eyes coming at her in a way she hasn't seen in ages. "No." He holds up both hands in front of him. "I didn't do that."

His response is so simple, so lacking in defense, she believes him. Maybe because he's exposed himself about Linder, talking about his jealousy. He takes a few steps back, leans up against the station house, like he needs to, like he needs a physical support.

"Somebody called them," she points out.

"Not me," he reiterates. He slips the pack of cigarettes back into his pocket.

She walks along the bottom edge of the stairs, thinking about it. "Okay," she concedes. "It isn't you, but it's somebody. Can they put somebody on it?" she asks, gesturing toward the station house. "Can they find out who *did* call?"

"The police can't investigate this. Filing a complaint with a state agency is completely legal."

"But this is harassment or something, isn't it, because it's not true."

He shakes his head. "No. Maybe if the person did it repeatedly it would be, but chances are, DCF wouldn't continue to investigate after the first time, anyway."

"So what do I do?" She can hear the need in her own voice.

"Wait it out, I think. The state won't find any neglect." He looks at her for a second, his eyes narrowed down. "What about the day care?"

"What do you mean?"

"Could somebody at his old school want to get back at you for pulling him out?"

She thinks for a minute. "Well, I guess so. I guess somebody there could be crazy, right? It wouldn't even mean being very crazy, would it, just angry and frustrated and overzealous, maybe. Though there is a waiting list at the school, so you wouldn't think they'd even blink twice to lose somebody. And suppose it is somebody there, what do I do about it?"

He shrugs and pushes back his sleeve so he can see his watch. "I've been out here too long," he says, and turns back toward the building.

"Quinn," she complains, but he's gone already, back into the Victorian mansion.

CHAPTER
THIRTEEN

THE NEXT TIME, MAY DONOVAN COMES WITH-
out her clipboard. And she doesn't call beforehand, either.
Bitch, Rosie thinks when she opens the front door and sees her
standing there, smiling. She looks around quickly: what evidence is there that will make this woman scream neglect? The
vacuum cleaner is sitting in the middle of the living room.
Maybe Ms. Donovan will go back to her office and write down
that Rosie still hadn't gotten the dust mites out of the carpet at
one in the afternoon. And what else am I doing wrong? she
wonders. What are the rules? she'd like to ask. Tell me how I
can win this round? Please tell me.

"I was just passing by and I thought I'd stop in," May
chimes.

Oh, right. Of course. Like we're friends or something.
"Why do you need to stop by?" Rosie asks her, unable to mask
her fury.

"To see Jason," she says, and Rosie's thinking, How can this
woman be so stupid as to think I'm so stupid that I could
believe any of this, that she could actually have an attachment
to Jason after staring at him once? And she looks at how May's
dressed, a different suit this time, a different silk blouse, the
same screaming diamond.

Rosie shifts her child to her left side. "I was in the middle of
getting the dust mites vacuumed," she explains. "You want to
hold him while I finish?" Rosie says, handing Jason over. It

wouldn't be so terrible, she thought, if Jay were to mess up that lovely ecru silk with his clutching hands, maybe even a little drool. The baby looks back at his mother, puzzled, but May's cooing to him and he's listening, suspicious, but listening, though he's also still checking over his shoulder for her. Rosie picks up the wand of the vacuum, pushes the toggle switch with her foot, and starts moving the power attachment over the part of the carpet that she hasn't finished till she's made those smooth lines appear over the whole surface. Now May Donovan will have no doubt that she's vacuumed the whole thing, she thinks as she turns off the machine. "So," Rosie asks, tugging at the cord, getting the automatic rewinder to suck it back inward, "what two places are you between that you happened to be passing by here?" May doesn't really have time to answer before Rosie says, "Aren't you supposed to be at work?" She can almost see May starting to form the words *I am at work* but catching the phrase before she unmasks herself. After all, this is supposed to be some kind of social call. Jay reaches a hand toward Rosie and she lifts him from the social worker's arms.

This visit is shorter than the last one, Rosie notes, for she's noting everything, trying to figure out where she might stand with this woman. What does it mean that she's not staying as long this time? "I'll see you soon," May says breezily as she prepares to leave.

"What are my rights?" Rosie asks her, and May looks genuinely puzzled for a moment.

"What do you mean?"

"I mean, can I say no, you can't come back?"

"People don't, usually."

Rosie's thinking she's going to say something more, but that's it. *People don't* is all she has to tell Rosie. For Ms. Donovan, it's that simple.

As soon as the door is closed between them, Rosie regrets her belligerence. I should have said, Just kidding, of course you can come back. I love having you here. The woman will make use of her resistance, she knows. She picks up Jason and holds him tight, rocking him, rocking her own sad self, as well.

Something has to be done about this, Rosie thinks during the third visit of the social worker. She's decided she will give nothing more to this woman. She won't fall into those silences the caseworker leaves after Rosie answers her questions by rattling on and on, telling too much. In fact, she will say absolutely as little as possible. Let her do her stupid little play routine with Jason, trying to make Rosie feel worthless because she interacts with him so beautifully or something. And so Rosie watches the two of them. After a while, she gets up and leaves the room. She doesn't want Ms. Donovan to see her tears.

After that, there is just one final telephone call from May Donovan of Children and Families. Rosie's not sure what the woman is talking about when she calls. She says Rosie has to make an appearance on the fourteenth and asks her if that date is convenient. Before Rosie can answer, May says that Jason's been assigned a lawyer, and that she should write his name down. Rosie lifts one of Jason's oversized crayons from his pile. Jason gets up from the floor, where he's been drawing a series of nearly circular shapes across sheets of recycled drawing paper and watches Rosie's hand loop purple letters across another piece of paper. She still hasn't asked Ms. Donovan what she means by "appearance." The crayon snaps in two before she's finished writing. "Where do I have to go?" she asks.

"Bradford," Ms. Donovan says, a lilt of surprise in her voice, as if to say, Everybody knows that.

"Where in Bradford?" Rosie snaps at her.

"White Street. I'm not sure of the courthouse address. It's down near the college, but across the street."

"The courthouse?" Rosie asks, and she has to put a hand to her temple because suddenly she's got this sharp pain attacking her right there.

"I didn't say that?"

"No, you didn't say that. I have to go to court? Is there a charge against me?"

"Well, neglect, like we talked about—"

Rosie cuts her off: "We didn't talk about it. You didn't tell me anything, remember? You didn't tell me who called you and you didn't tell me what they were charging."

"Well, actually, that part, the complaint part, doesn't matter anymore because this hearing comes out of our investigation. We filed for a hearing based on our findings."

"What do you mean 'we'? And what findings?"

"The state, Mrs. Sloan. I suggest you get in touch with your lawyer. He'll handle it all for you."

"This name you gave me?" Rosie asks, looking at the paper, seeing she hasn't written anything she can actually read.

"No, that's Jason's lawyer. The state appoints a lawyer to protect the child's interests in cases like this. Your lawyer will want to contact him, too, I'm sure. If you can't afford a lawyer, the court will assign you one."

"I can afford a lawyer," Rosie says, though she has no idea if that's true.

"You'll be getting this same information in the mail, probably tomorrow or the next day. I just wanted you to know as soon as possible. As a courtesy. So you could start in on your end right away. Also, to see if you had any questions."

"I have many, many questions."

"People always do," May comments.

Rosie steadies herself and tries to grab hold of just one of the questions that's racing through her brain right now. "What's going to happen?"

"Well, the state presents its findings, then you get to respond. Or your lawyer does, actually. Then the judge makes a decision. It's really a lot like *People's Court* on TV."

"That's not what I meant," Rosie says. "I know what happens in a courtroom. I mean, where is this headed? Are you trying to take Jason from me?"

"Don't think of it that way, Mrs. Sloan. We're trying to do what's right for Jason and right for you."

"Spare me," Rosie says, and she doesn't care how that sounds. "Just tell me—if the judge agrees with your findings, what happens to Jason?"

"Mrs. Sloan, these are questions for your lawyer, not me."

"You know the answer," Rosie says, shouting the words into

the phone. Jason's in the room, has been this whole time, sitting on the kitchen floor, drawing his circles, and now he's rushed to her legs, holding on. What has she said? What has he heard? "I'm sorry," she whispers to her child, leaning down, stroking his head.

"All right, then," May Donovan says, accepting the apology, seemingly, and she hangs up before Rosie can explain it wasn't meant for her.

"THE WELL-DRESSED MORON DIDN'T EVEN SAY she was sorry," Rosie tells Quinn when she's describing her conversation with May Donovan. She has dropped Jason off at Quinn's apartment.

"That's because she isn't sorry."

"I know that, but people say it, don't they, to ease somebody else's pain, to show they're human, which obviously she isn't."

"Rosie, she's doing her job. I don't apologize to people when I arrest them."

"Never?" she asks him. And she's wondering why she's having this fight with him. But she can't stop it: she wants to understand. "Don't you ever think you might have the wrong person when you're doing an arrest?"

"If I'm the arresting officer, I'm pretty damn certain, otherwise I don't make the arrest. Given that, there's no room for sympathy."

"Well, I don't think that obnoxious, rule-driven social worker should be able to pass judgment on something this important."

"The judge is the one who decides."

"Quinn, did you ever arrest somebody who wasn't guilty?" He doesn't answer.

"Tell me. Did you ever make a mistake like that?"

"Yes," he says, and she sees him lift his eyes upward. "I've made all kinds of mistakes."

Rosie see that Quinn is drifting, just as he used to back home, moving in on something inside his head. He's taken that plunge into vagueness, into *all* the mistakes in the world, past, present, and future, perhaps. And then he looks at her as though he's about to say something more, to clarify without being asked, and she knows, as surely as if he has spoken the words aloud, what the mistake is. It is the same one she has never named to him: We should never have married. And she has to turn her eyes away, clear her head.

CHAPTER
FOURTEEN

ROSIE DOESN'T KNOW ANY LAWYERS EXCEPT the one they used when they bought their house. A real estate lawyer obviously will not do.

So what Rosie does is, she calls her father's old lawyer. "It's a child's rights case," she says, hoping to be vague.

"I'm not sure what you mean by that." Edgar Morrison's voice is deeply resonant. She looks for a volume control on her phone, but there is none. "How about we go for a little more specificity?" he asks her.

"Okay," she says.

"So, can you be a little more specific about the case?" he asks again after a space of time.

"Oh," she says, reconciled to the fact that she must say more. "I'm being charged with neglect." And then: "It's not true."

"Oh," he says, his voice a delayed echo of hers. "I don't know anybody personally in that field."

Rosie feels like he's just told her he won't even associate with attorneys who deal with these kinds of cases, let alone with the accused.

"I can check with the bar association and get some names for you, if you like, but it's not likely to be anyone I know well."

This, she could do herself, she thinks, but she says, "I'd appreciate that."

* * *

ROSIE LIKES THE LAWYER MR. MORRISON comes up with well enough. He works by himself out of a tiny office that probably costs almost nothing in the way of rent, and the neighborhood's reasonably safe. He's on the young side, which at first bothers her and makes her obsess much too long and hard on how much experience he has. Eventually she's forced to realize that young attorneys are the only ones who'd be so foolish as to take such cases—the older ones have all moved on to personal injury, business deals, and real estate, where the money flows regularly and freely. Ted Fisher, far removed from that arena, graciously offers her his sliding scale of fees so that they can struggle together. And perhaps he will be a good match in the courtroom for May Donovan. Perhaps he will understand how to deal with her better than an older lawyer would.

Attorney Fisher tells Rosie that he wants her to try to "depersonalize the case." "You've got to think of it as the state that's making the accusation, not this young woman, and put her completely out of your mind," he counsels. This doesn't really help Rosie relax. The state seems much too large, much too connected to resources to be something she could ever work her way around. Surely the state will be taking more legal expertise with them into the courtroom than she will.

Ted says Rosie is in a very good position because even if the court finds against her, which he very much doubts they will, they will almost certainly put Jason in Quinn's care, not the state's. "They always place with a parent when they can," Ted says, "and they'll bend over backward to keep a child out of foster care. Because you're separated, Quinn's the perfect choice for them." She's so relieved to hear this, she almost rises from her chair and leaves—as though it's over, decided, and Jason is safe. But that feeling lasts only a fleeting moment, for Ted continues questioning her, making her remember it has merely just begun.

Ted asks good questions that range over nearly the whole of Rosie's life, her marriage, and her first child's short existence. Rosie's impressed by the effort he's making to understand the

101

details of Jason's illness. He says he'll suggest Beth as another alternative caretaker for Jason—if she's willing, he adds, but Rosie assures him she would be. "If it has to come to that," Rosie says.

"And until we figure out exactly who filed the complaint, don't discuss Jason's illness or the charges with anyone. It could be someone at the daycare or even further out on the fringes of your life, like someone who knows someone who you confided in. Gossip travels too fast for you to take those kinds of chances."

Ted suggests that Rosie sign a waiver of her right to keep Zoe from testifying if the state chooses to call the marriage counselor as a witness. He says if she's got a good relationship with Zoe and she hasn't confessed some specific mistreatment of Jason to her, she'd be better off having the benefit of her testimony. Rosie says she'd told some fairly intimate things to Zoe about her marriage—would they have to come out?—and Ted says it'll be his job to block them if they do, so she signs. Ted also has her sign a medical release allowing him to request medical records from Dr. Linder. "Has the doctor ever criticized how you handled things with Jason?" he asks her.

"No. He's very supportive." She's wondering if she should mention anything about her relationship with Greg, but she's no longer sure how she ought to describe who they are to each other. "We're friends," she says finally, and she's hoping her face isn't going to burst into full flush.

"Good." He puts his pen down and looks at her. His lips are pressed together and he seems to be waiting for her to say more, but she can't figure out what—does he want her to elaborate on her relationship with Greg? "Now," he finally says, leaning toward her, "we get to the big question. Do you want to fight this charge?"

She's genuinely surprised by what he's asked—that's exactly why she's here. "Of course I want to fight it. They're wrong."

"There are other options."

"Such as?"

"Such as, you can agree now to let the state have temporary custody of Jason, which, in your case, as I told you, will probably mean that he'll be placed with Quinn or your sister. I'm sure they'll ask for an evaluation, more home visits, they'll want you to go to parenting classes, and there may be more things they'll require."

"If I agree, wouldn't I be saying I neglected him?"

"Well, you'd be saying you were letting them help you in this, that's all."

"That the state knows best, you mean?"

"Something like that."

"And they'd definitely take him from me, then, right?"

"Yes. Temporarily, anyway."

"And if I fight back, he might not be taken?"

"If you win, he won't. It's a gamble, of course."

"I'm taking the gamble," she says firmly. "I didn't neglect my child."

"We'll go at them full speed ahead, then," he says, and he smiles and pushes himself back in his chair.

"And how?" she asks him.

"Stop worrying," he advises. "That's my job." His intercom buzzes and he depresses the respond button. "Yes, Alice?" he says. Alice fields calls for Ted and two other people—a psychologist and an accountant—who are squeezed into the first floor of this house.

"Mr. and Mrs. Magnusen are here," the electronically enhanced voice announces.

"Tell them two minutes, would you, please?" He stands, clearly bringing the interview to a close. She rises much more slowly than he does. "Don't worry," he reiterates. She's heard this already. She wants more. Something else. She wants him to be just her attorney, not the Magnusens', not a whole slew of people who are pressing him for his attention, but he's taken her arm and has started to escort her to the door. "I'm going to call Quinn," he says. "He *was* the responding officer in that crash where the child died, wasn't he?"

"Yes, but . . ."

Ted silences her with a shake of his raised hand. "It's not a big deal, I just want to coach him on court strategy on that one."

"Why would *that* come up?" She can't believe people can't forget that incident already.

"Quinn may be granted full temporary custody. If the state decides to get nasty and to throw a roadblock up, they might drag it into the proceedings because a child died in that accident. A child not too far in age from Jason."

"Why does everybody remember that about it, but nobody remembers that Quinn saved the mother?" She can still see the oversized capital letters that the local newspaper used to set their headline: BABY DIES IN CAR WHILE OFFICER WATCHES. "He saved a woman and her unborn child. He did what he could before the car actually exploded."

"Of course, he did, Rosie. You and I both know that. But I'm talking about something different. I'm talking about the general perception of that case. The newspapers, the evening news, they all harped on how that woman was shouting, 'Save my baby.' What people remember is that nobody saved her baby."

"She was nine months pregnant," Rosie says, shaping out a huge belly in front of her. "Quinn thought it was that baby she was yelling about, the one she was carrying." She realizes she's yelling the words.

"I assure you, I don't place any blame on your husband. I just know what the public thinks: There was a call for help that was ignored by Quinn. If it comes up, he should have a clear-cut way to deal. He shouldn't get defensive. *You* shouldn't," he adds. She casts a cold stare at him for this remark, but she knows he's right, she's very defensive on this issue. "Of course I'll object if they bring it up at all, so it probably won't even be an issue."

"You know, the fact is . . ."

"Wait," Ted interrupts her. "I know people like to think of courtrooms as being governed by fact and statistics, but believe me, they're not. Fact's a big percentage of what goes into a verdict or ruling, but there's also theater and timing and emotion. If it were just fact, trials would take an hour, not weeks, the way they so often do. But look, I'm making too much of this. Forget I even said it. Go home and relax." Sure, she thinks. Fat chance of that.

He's reaching for the doorknob when he stops and looks at her. "One other thing," he says. "Are you and Quinn spending any time together these days?"

"Some. Since this happened—the charges, I mean—we keep in touch about what's going on."

"Well, don't do that anymore. And you might even want somebody else to be transporting Jason between the two of you."

"Why?"

"Because if the court thinks you two have ongoing contact, and they want Jason away from you, they may be less eager to have him be with Quinn. Limit the phone calls, too, to what might be necessary to make child-care arrangements."

"I was going to go over now to pick up Jason."

"Do you have somebody else who could do it?"

"My sister, usually, but not today. She's in New York."

"All right, do it this time, but don't go into the house. Stand back a few steps, even. Let the neighbors see you don't want contact with Quinn. I'll call Quinn and explain to him why we need a different arrangement. And I think he should have his own lawyer. Make it look like there's genuine conflict between you."

CHAPTER FIFTEEN

ROSIE DOES EXACTLY WHAT HER ATTORNEY has instructed her to do. After she rings the bell at Quinn's garden apartment, she walks partway back down the path toward the sidewalk and then waits for him to come to the door. At first he stands behind the storm door, peering through it, but then he pushes that open as well and comes all the way out of the dwelling. "Why are you all the way down there?" he asks her.

She explains that her lawyer will be calling him, about the need for an appearance of conflict. She tells him he's going to need to get his own attorney.

"I can't even hear half of what you're saying," he says, and starts walking toward her. She backs farther off, saying, "Don't come any closer, Quinn. We have to keep our distance from now on." She's even got one hand raised, as though she might push against him if he were to get too close. This last bit she's said loud enough so that if anyone in the nearby apartments happened to be listening, they'd have had very little trouble understanding her words. Behind her, on the sidewalk, a jogger slows almost to a stop, debating, she supposes, whether he should intervene in these domestic threats.

"I don't like this," Quinn says.

"Why not?"

"We're *not* in conflict. I hate playacting. I hate lawyers."

"We're doing it for Jason, Quinn." She walks toward him so

she can speak without being heard by the entire world. "The way it works is, if the judge thinks we don't want any contact with each other, he'll let you have Jason. If he decides to take him away from me," she adds in a whisper. Her throat is so thick with the words, she's barely able to give them voice. He puts his hands in his pockets and rolls slightly on his heels. He's looking at the ground. "It's to keep him out of foster care. My lawyer will tell you the same," Rosie says, and she's begging him. Now he's turned his face off to the side, like he's checking out the traffic level at the cross street. She hasn't been able to see his expression through any of this. "Please?" she asks him.

It's a long time before he speaks. "Okay," he finally says, but he's still not looking at her. "Maybe Bernie will do it." Bernie's on the force with Quinn and he's been through law school, nights. "I don't know if he's passed the bar yet."

"Thanks," she says, and the relief feels sweet as rain on a scorching July afternoon. "I should take Jay now. We shouldn't leave him alone in there for so long."

Quinn goes back into the house. Rosie steps up to the storm door and watches him walking toward the kitchen. It's several minutes before he reappears with Jason in his arms. Beyond the two of them, Rosie thinks she sees someone else, but there's a glare, a distortion of the glass. She's got her hand on the latch, ready to open it, to figure out who it is. The figure leans in her direction, and she sees her clearly then. A woman. Quinn's so-called friend, Diana, surely. Diana is looking toward her now, but then she quickly steps back, altogether disappearing into the kitchen, hiding. As Rosie starts to push the door open, Quinn is pulling it from the other side, coming back outside, though this time with Jason. The baby is holding out his arms to his mother. "Frahbabies," he says, his word for strawberries.

"I thought she wasn't supposed to be here," Rosie says, taking her child. Her words are etched with anger. Jason holds a strawberry out toward his mother's mouth. She turns her head slightly to avoid the wet fruit. "You said she wouldn't be here when Jason was here."

"You said that, Rosie, not me." He hands her the medical charts. "I had to give him one of the antihistamines at dinner. Can't you get that in liquid form? I hate having to grind that tablet."

"See, it's not even phony, is it, Quinn?"

"What?"

"The conflict. The division between us." She gestures toward him, toward herself. "It won't require any playacting on your part, I don't think. Certainly not on mine." She's backing away, putting the distance between them again, but then she heads back toward him. He's standing motionless in the doorway, the storm door resting against his shoulder. "What's her whole name?" she asks him, but he doesn't say anything.

"I have a right to know, Quinn. He's my child, and he's being cared for in part by her. I wouldn't hire a baby-sitter if I didn't know her last name, so you damn well better tell me what it is."

"Messerly," he says, though he's not looking at her.

She stands there a moment longer and Jason pushes the strawberry at her lips once more. "Come on, honey," she says to her child, and she turns back toward the street. She hears the storm door reengage, and then the heavy inner door meet its strike.

When she's buckling her child into his car seat, she kisses his cheeks, strokes down his messy hair. He's holding his strawberry with two fingers, drawing it in and out of his lips, sucking on it. "Eat it now, Jason, honey," she says. "Bite into it." His small white teeth break off a piece. "Good boy," she says. She wants the berry gone before she starts the car. It's got just the right size and firmness to block a two-year-old's windpipe. "Who gave you your frahbaby?" she asks him.

"Frahbaby," he says, looking at the remaining half, checking out the ragged edge his teeth have carved into it.

"Who gave it to you, sweetie?"

He looks at her and smiles and shrugs a little. "Did Daddy give it to you?" He shakes his head. "Did Diana give it to you, sweetpie?" He nods. "She should have cut it up first," she says.

"Next time tell her to cut the berries up for you. Say, 'Cut the berries, please.' Okay, sweetpie?" She's got tears in her eyes, hearing the foolish request she's making of the inarticulate child.

Jason's concentrating on where he's going to take his next bite. "Frahbabies," he says again.

CHAPTER
SIXTEEN

ROSIE HAS TROUBLE FINDING THE COURT-house. She has the street address, but the numbers seem to skip over exactly the one she wants. She pulls into a gas station and the attendant points across the street to a chain-link fence. "Back behind there," he says while he wipes his greasy hands on his overall bib.

Once she's pulled in, way past the fence, she sees it. It's one of several one-story government buildings that are huddled together on the blacktop. The second one sports a large blue sign that reads JUVENILE COURT.

Inside, she goes through a metal detector and sets off the alarm. She has to remove her watch, her keys, and hand her purse over to the sheriff's deputy and go back through the security device before he lets her into the waiting area. Solid-looking metal chairs ring the perimeter of the room. Most of the chairs are occupied, but she finds one, next to a young family. Most everyone, she realizes as she looks around, is part of such a family group, all of them looking as nervous as she feels.

By the time Quinn arrives, there are no chairs left. He paces, trying not to look at her, she knows. Rosie assumes that the courtroom must be in the back portion of the building, beyond the door through which all the men and women with briefcases are passing. She had expected high ceilings and marble flooring, not cinder block and linoleum.

Ted, who was supposed to meet her here so that they could confer before the proceeding, is late. Or at least he's nowhere around. Nor is Bernie, Quinn's lawyer. Perhaps they had already passed beyond the waiting room door before she arrived and they're seated, at this very moment, at a dark-grained refectory table, enjoying coffee and croissants and laughter with all the other attorneys. She could ask the sheriff seated at the other end of the room if he could tell her where her lawyer is, but if she gets up, she will certainly lose her seat. She stays where she is and continues to pull at her short skirt, fool-ishly hoping to get it to cover more of her than it does, envying the other women in the room who are wearing slacks or jeans.

The skirt is Ted's idea. A silk shirt, a suit, and dress pumps were what he told her to wear to the hearing.

May Donovan clothes, she'd thought. "I don't own stuff like that," she'd tried to explain to him.

"Do the best you can," he'd advised.

So she'd scrounged in her closet. She supposed these plain black heels were what he meant by that old-fashioned word, pumps. And she found she actually owned two decent shirts—neither of them genuine silk, but close enough, probably. Ted was going to have to settle for a skirt and cardigan sweater because she'd never owned a suit. She called him back when she was dressed. "This isn't me," she complained, eyeing her-self in the mirror. "I think it's a really bad idea for me to wear this because I don't feel comfortable. I feel like I'm in a cos-tume. And if I feel self-conscious, how am I going to be myself on the stand?"

"That judge is going to have a pile of reports in front of him that are slanted toward a negative view of you. When he peers out over his half glasses at you, we want him to see something really positive. I know this judge, Rosie. I know what he likes."

"Then he better like frumpy clothes, Ted. This is not impres-sive." She tries pulling more of the shirt out, blousing it over the waistband, but that looks, if anything, worse. "How does he feel about tears?"

"All things considered, he probably prefers witnesses who don't cry, I'd say." She imagines filling in a form marked No

Tears and having that absolutely determine her behavior. "You do your best, that's all," he adds.

Now, finally, she sees Ted come through the front door of the courthouse, right behind a round-faced man who looks vaguely familiar. The buzzer sounds as her attorney goes through the metal detector, but the deputy laughs and waves him on. He doesn't step into the waiting room area, but once he has made eye contact with Rosie, he motions with a tilt of his head for her to come with him through the inner door.

Someone taps her on the shoulder just as she approaches that doorway and she turns to see Greg Linder. "They subpoenaed me," he says.

"I'm sorry."

"No, no. It's not your fault," he protests. "You take care," he says as she moves to catch up with Ted.

"You look lovely," the lawyer says when they are side by side again. "Perfect." He pats her arm—the black cardigan—reassuringly. "How do you feel?"

"Awful. Like I'm in a play and they never gave me the script. Like I'm in a nightmare. My stomach's a complete mess," she says, laying a palm across her abdomen.

"There's no script, Rosie," he says, but he seems distracted, like he's giving her an automatic response, leaving the major part of his brain to work on something else. Maybe he's more scared than she is. Or maybe it's just that he's losing patience with her. What if he decides she's not worth his time? She knows there's no script. She knows all hell can break loose in there, that's why she's worried. "Just think positively," he tells her, and pats her arm again. "I'm looking for a room where we can talk," he explains as they start down hallway.

The hallway is filled with people gathered in loose bunches around whom Ted and Rosie must weave their path. Rosie can spot May Donovan down at the other end of the hall. As they pass each group, she hears tiny pieces of their conferences—an admonition, a denial, and even some raucous laughter, though that comes from a small pocket of men in dark suits—attorneys. A sheriff passes through, calling a name, just like the hostess at a restaurant. "I think this is going to have to do," Ted says, guiding her into the last opening on the hallway, a combination furnace and storage room. There are no chairs here. "Space is at a premium," Ted says, stating the obvious.

Her lawyer puts his briefcase down on the floor between his feet and reaches into it for a manila folder. She sees her last name scrawled large across the front. He starts shifting through papers. "You'll do fine," he says to his papers and to himself as much as to her.

"Can *we* ask the judge for anything?" Rosie inquires.

"Like what?" His eyebrows are drawn together in puzzlement.

"Like when Jason's with Quinn that the girlfriend can't be there."

Ted closes the file and draws in a deep breath. "It depends on your reason. The judge isn't going to do it just because you don't like somebody or you don't want your ex to have a love life."

People keep passing by the room, poking their heads in, looking for unoccupied space.

Rosie takes a moment to try to compose an argument. "She gives him food that's too big that he could choke on, that kind of thing. She just doesn't make good decisions about him. You know, age-appropriate and all that."

Ted looks at her squarely and shakes his head. "The judge isn't going to think of her as a threat to the child." He lifts a ballpoint pen from the leather briefcase, clicks the point down, and scribbles a note in the margin of a paper.

"It's not like we're talking about whether she should have *custody*, Rosie. What you're talking about, at least as far as the judge is concerned, is whether Quinn can choose his own friends or whether you get to choose them. Now I can tell you that not only does the judge not care about that, but it's going to reflect badly on you if you even raise it. You'll come across as petty. The judge will be much happier with you if you're generous toward Quinn." Ted closes his briefcase, clicking the two locks simultaneously.

Rosie feels confused, like the boundaries have all been

shifted right out from under her when she wasn't paying attention. "I thought you wanted Quinn and me to be in conflict. I thought that was part of your so-called script. I didn't even say hello to him out there," she says, gesturing behind her toward the waiting area.

"Yes," he says slowly, as though he's spelled, not spoken the word. "You can be angry with him, but not—never—vindictive."

"I'm not being vindictive," she says through closely held lips. He's lecturing her now. "I'm genuinely worried about Jason being with Diana."

"Concentrate on the real issues." He's back to scanning his papers, scribbling. "Speaking of which," he says, "there's a new wrinkle."

Rosie feels something lurch forward in her chest. "What?"

"They've raised the charge to abuse. They're talking about physical abuse, not just neglect, now."

It feels like something's crashing around inside her. Like a whole bunch of hard-edged metal objects have suddenly been tossed randomly around in her chest, cutting and bruising her from the inside. She's starting to sweat. "Why didn't you tell me?"

"Rosie, I've only just now been told myself."

A sheriff appears at the door. "Sloan?" he asks.

"That's us," Ted says.

"You ready?" the uniformed officer asks.

"All set."

"Well, that's everybody. Courtroom two," the sheriff says, and disappears.

When Rosie starts to walk toward the furnace room door, her head feels wavery, like she's stood up too fast, but she's been standing the whole time. She wants to clutch Ted's arm, but already he's walking slightly ahead of her and it's all she can do to keep upright in her slippery shoes. They go into the courtroom and for a second she thinks they must be in the wrong place: it's so small it could be a conference room. She'd expected rows and rows of seats but sees only a single line of gray metal chairs, perhaps

114

seven or eight of them, unevenly spaced along the rear wall. Ted steers her more forward, to a small table. Before them, a white-haired man of about fifty sits in his black robe. May Donovan is already seated with two men at a table identical to the one at which she sits. Quinn and Bernie, his lawyer, have taken seats in two of the metal chairs. Quinn lifts his eyebrows when she looks at him, but she doesn't acknowledge the possible greeting. She hates this sham.

Ted looks toward the other side of the room and Rosie follows his gaze. "That's the social worker," she whispers, tilting her head slightly in that direction.

"I figured," he says.

"Who are the others with her?"

"Members of the honorable state team. The heavy guy with the beard is Jason's lawyer. The one with the slim-cut suit is James Burden, state's attorney. Not evil, just eager," he says of him.

"Who's that?" Rosie asks when she sees a woman in a tailored blue silk dress enter with a steno pad. "Is she from the newspaper?"

"No. She's a court clerk. There's no press allowed here. Juvenile hearings are closed. Absolutely private. Now, relax," he admonishes her. The woman has moved toward the small desk in the front of the court.

"Do we have everyone here?" the judge asks suddenly, his voice jarring amid the whispers.

"Yes, Your Honor," Ted responds as he stands. "Attorney Theodore Fisher, representing Mrs. Sloan, seated to my left." The judge nods. The man in the slim-cut suit, James Burden, has risen and introduces himself as well.

"And I am Judge Mannon, for those of you who are new to my court. This is a hearing for an order of temporary custody, so I'd like to keep this brief and to the point," the judge instructs the attorneys, head slightly lowered so he can see them above his half lenses. "Is that understood?"

Both lawyers rise. "Yes, Your Honor," they say in unison.

"Good, good, good," Mannon says, smiling now. "I'm not really that hard to please, you both know that." He adjusts the drape of the sleeves of his robe. "Now, Mr. Burden, you may begin."

The assistant attorney general for the Department of Children and Families rises, leans forward, hands pressing down at the very edge of the table. He's not using notes, as far as Rosie can tell. "Your Honor, we're asking that the two-year-old minor child, Jason Sloan, be removed from his mother's care because of intentional and repeated physical abuse. You have documentation of the abuse as part of the DCF petition in front of you," the advocate informs the judge.

Judge Mannon lifts the packet of papers, examines the top page, then the next page after that, and he begins to make some notes on a pad. "And the father, where's he?" the judge asks. Rosie glances toward the other side of the room and sees Quinn start to rise, then stop as Bernie places a hand on his shoulder, keeping him in place.

"The parents are separated at present."

"How long?"

"Three months."

"You may proceed, Mr. Burden."

"Thank you, Your Honor. We believe that the mother Rose Sloan, has deliberately and repeatedly caused her son to become ill and thereby put him in grave danger and has also deliberately caused him to undergo medical procedures with the intent to cause pain and suffering."

Rosie feels like there's a charge of electricity moving through her, sending shock waves out in all directions through her limbs. She can't believe what she's hearing. "Hush, Rosie," Ted whispers, and she realizes she's breathing— gasping—so loudly that everybody must be able to hear her. She clasps her hands together in front of her. She has to grip them tightly to keep them still. To keep herself from flying apart. When she glances over toward Quinn, he and Bernie are conferring, heads down.

"Your Honor, Jason is a child who *appears* to be suffering from severe but intermittent breathing problems," Burden is saying. "He has required emergency treatment at least six times in as many weeks. All his breathing difficulties occur when he is with his mother. And all of them date from the time period *after* Mrs. Sloan separated from her husband. The State of Connecticut contends that Mrs. Sloan has caused each and every one of these potentially life-threatening crises. We believe she did this because she herself has an unusual psychological condition known as Munchausen's syndrome by proxy.

"Your Honor, people afflicted with this disorder are known to induce illnesses in their own children in order to gain sympathy for themselves. Mrs. Sloan's behavior fits the text-book description of this syndrome. Let me enumerate the correspondences." Burden lays one index finger perpendicularly across the other and lists his first point: "Mrs. Sloan is recently separated from her husband and is clearly—and successfully—using these crises to bring him back to her side." His index finger comes to rest now across two fingers of his other hand. "She has a thorough knowledge of medical procedures because her father was a physician." Index finger strikes three fingers. "But the most telling evidence against Mrs. Sloan is the fact that her first child died a mysterious death seven years ago. Your Honor, I intend to call several witnesses to support our petition to have Jason removed from her care."

"Just keep it brief and well focused, gentlemen."

Rosie is clutching Ted's wrist. He pushes his legal pad toward her, points at something he's written there. *Breathe*, it says.

The sheriff's deputy has gone to call a witness from the waiting room. When he returns, Rosie sees that he's brought her neighbor, gray-haired Arnie Porter, with him and he leads him to the witness stand. Mr. Porter? Rosie wonders. Does he have some issue with her? Is he the one who called in the state?

"Good morning, Mr. Porter," Attorney Burden greets him exuberantly, as though this were a social occasion.

"Good morning."

"Mr. Porter, can you please tell me what happened on the night of January fourteenth?"

Arnie nods. "My neighbor, Quinn Sloan," he says, pointing

toward him, "came over, very upset, to say his wife had locked him out and that the baby was sick. He wanted me to call the police."

"Did you do that, Mr. Porter?"

"Yes. He had me send paramedics, too."

"Then what happened?"

"Well," he says, "they came—sirens and everything—and they broke the Sloans' front door down. They they took the baby to the hospital in the ambulance."

"Thank you, Mr. Porter."

Mr. Porter sighs and starts to stand up, but the judge explains that Mr. Fisher will now question him.

"Sorry," the man says, reddening slightly.

"Mr. Porter," Ted asks from his position at the table, "did you see Mrs. Sloan trying to prevent the emergency staff from attending to her child?"

"Well, I wasn't in their house, so I couldn't see that one way or the other."

"But you saw that they were able to take the child to the hospital?"

"Yes."

"How long would you estimate they were inside the Sloan house?"

"Not long."

"Can you estimate the number of minutes?"

"Five, I guess. Maybe seven at most. No, more like five."

"Thank you," Ted says.

Burden sends the sheriff for another witness. When he enters the court she sees that it's the man whose round face she thought looked familiar out in the waiting area. The attorney addresses him as Dr. Meyers and asks him if he has ever examined Jason Sloan. When he says he has, Rosie remembers: this is the emergency room doctor. She didn't recognize him in his suit and tie. Burden goes over his credentials, then asks him to describe Jason's condition.

"He was stable by the time I examined him," Dr. Meyers says.

"Was he having breathing difficulties?"

"Not actually. The mother described breathing difficulties, but they had subsided by the time I examined him."

"Did he have any other symptoms?"

"Flushed face."

"What was your diagnosis?"

"Allergic reaction."

"And what was that diagnosis based on?"

"Primarily on the mother's description of symptoms, and it was consistent with the mild cough, respiratory congestion, and reddened cheeks."

Burden doesn't pace the court—there's not room for that sort of behavior. In fact, he stands nearly stock-still, though occasionally he runs his hand down his side, appreciating, perhaps, his own slender physique. "And did you reach any conclusion as to what might have caused the reaction which you observed and the mother described?"

"Yes. Chocolate."

"How did you determine that chocolate was the culprit?"

"The mother told me he'd had a large amount of chocolate just before the symptoms began."

"Did she tell you how the child got hold of that chocolate?"

"Yes. She said she gave it to him."

"She gave it to him?"

"That's what she said." He shrugs as he says it.

"What did she give him, a piece of a candy bar or something?"

"No, she said she gave him a spoon that was covered with melted chocolate. The child still had the spoon with him in the ER. It was one of those big mixing spoons." His index fingers trace an oversized teardrop shape as he speaks.

"So you saw the spoon that Mrs. Sloan used to administer the dose of chocolate?"

"Yes, sir."

"I didn't administer a dose," Rosie says under her breath to her attorney. He doesn't respond.

"Would you say, given the relative size of the spoon, that this was a small amount of chocolate, a moderate amount, or a massive amount?"

"Actually, given the size of the child—he's small for his age—I'd have to say massive. Based on body mass ratio, which is how we generally think when we determine drug dosage in children, I'd say massive."

Ted stands up. "I object, Your Honor. Chocolate is not a drug. It's a food."

"We don't have a jury here, Mr. Fisher, and I understand the distinction, thank you." Ted takes his seat again.

Burden turns back to his witness. "Was Mrs. Sloan surprised, Doctor, when you told her that the symptoms she'd observed might be from chocolate?"

"No. She's the one who told *me* she thought it was chocolate, and she said she knew she shouldn't have given it to him because severe respiratory reactions to chocolate can occur in children."

Rosie's shaking her head. "It was a mistake," she whispers to Ted. He writes her a note. *We'll discuss everything later*, it reads.

"Thank you, Dr. Meyers. I have no more questions."

"Mr. Fisher?" Judge Mannon says, and Ted steps toward the witness.

"Dr. Meyers, did you suggest to Mrs. Sloan that she should consult an allergist about Jason's health?"

"Yes."

"And why did you do that?"

"Because when a young child has a severe allergic reaction, it may mean he has general allergic tendencies, and that ought to be monitored, if possible."

"So then you're not saying Mrs. Sloan made up this illness; you're saying you thought her child did have a severe allergic reaction?"

"The mother described symptoms that would indicate he did."

"And you believed that he had?"

"Based on what she said, and the fiery cheeks, yes. And she said she was a physician's daughter. Family members generally give very reliable histories."

"Why is that?"

"Why are they so reliable?"

"Yes."

"Because they're privy to lots of information. They hear histories being taken on the phone all the time, so they begin to understand what's important and what's irrelevant for a doctor to know. They're familiar with the language of medicine."

"So family members in physicians' households tend to be more aware and more concerned about medical issues."

"Generally."

"Did Mrs. Sloan tell you what the circumstances were that led her to give Jason this chocolate?"

"She said she was baking. Is that what you mean?"

"Yes. So it was like a little treat, a way of sharing with him?"

"Yes, I guess so." And then he adds, "In her mind."

"But it wasn't her intent to cause an allergic reaction?"

"I don't think I know whether it was or not."

"Did she tell you how she felt about having given Jason so much chocolate, Doctor?"

"I think she said she felt stupid, something along those lines."

"So then it was an unintentional act on her part; an accident, correct?"

Burden leaps to his feet, objecting. "Your Honor, he's putting words in the doctor's mouth."

"Mr. Fisher," Mannon intones. "Ask a question I can allow."

Ted looks down at the yellow pad with his notes, then looks up again at the witness. "Dr. Meyers, you don't know for certain that it was her intent to injure her child, do you?"

"No."

"Dr. Meyers, you've testified that Mrs. Sloan gave her son a very large amount of chocolate, but you also testified that he appeared not to have very severe symptoms when you treated him. Is that correct?"

"Yes."

"Those two things seem to be contradictory to me, Doctor. I mean, either giving this chocolate put Jason in jeopardy or it didn't. Was he very sick from this chocolate?"

"Not when I actually examined him."

"So then she didn't really do him any harm, did she?"

"I have to take into account what she described to me, as well. She was describing a child in serious distress. And he did have some symptoms consistent with an earlier allergic response."

"I understand that. But the point is, when you examined him, he was virtually recovered, wasn't he?"

"Yes."

"No harm done, right?"

"No harm done right then, maybe, but from what I understand about the later episodes—"

Ted cuts him off. "We're not asking you to conjecture about anything else, Dr. Meyers."

The doctor nods. "Couldn't Mrs. Sloan have exaggerated the description of the symptoms, exaggerated, even, how much chocolate she gave her child, because she felt guilty for causing any reaction, even a small one, and because she was worried and wanted to make sure you took her complaint seriously?"

"Yes. Or because she wanted attention."

"That's not what I asked you. Could it be simply out of care and concern for her child?"

The doctor hesitates. "I suppose so."

"That's a yes, Doctor?"

"Yes."

"Thank you," Ted says to him, and returns to his seat.

"Anything more for this witness?" Judge Mannon asks Burden.

"No, Your Honor," the assistant attorney general says.

Burden will tear me to shreds, Rosie thinks, and her chest aches with each new attempt of her lungs to take in air. She can't go up on the witness stand. He'll thrust those questions at her, cutting off her answers, snipping and shaping what she says the way a child uses scissors on a magazine picture, cutting round and round and round, smaller and smaller, till only some tiny, unrecognizable portion remains.

It is May Donovan whom James Burden actually calls next.

The woman looks perfect as she walks to the stand. Her shoes, though even higher than Rosie's, slip not the slightest, but rather, they take control of all the space they choose to enter. Ms. Donovan's silk shirt drapes in graceful folds over her chest and shows out through the opening of her jacket as though it were designed specially for that one suit. Even the color of her hose is so obviously right—a soft gray that highlights the charcoal crepe wool suit and makes her long legs seem part of the whole costume. Clearly, that is how Ted had wanted Rosie to dress. Rosie feels a restlessness that is something almost like jealousy, for she knows Judge Mannon is bound to like May better than her. Perhaps, she thinks, he will even fall in love with her.

The state's attorney asks Ms. Donovan to detail her findings on the case, and the social worker consults her notes frequently while she testifies. Rosie hears herself being characterized as "extremely aggressive" in her approach to Jason's illness. May lingers over the description of Jason's bare room, using words like "barren" and "sterile." "A punishing environment, devoid of comfort," the woman says, and Rosie wonders how many years of testifying this way it took for Ms. Donovan to come up with such perfectly damning phrases. And this is not all. Ms. Donovan is now adding that "the mother took away the baby's blanket and pillow and all his stuffed animals. She took away all of the soft, cuddly objects. There weren't even any books in the room. Nothing."

"Was there anything else Mrs. Sloan said or did that set off any special concern for you?" Burden asks her.

"Well," Ms. Donovan begins, "she didn't seem all that anxious to care directly for him." Rosie looks at Ted and shakes her head.

"Can you give me an example of what you mean by that?"

"One time, she handed him to me the second I came in the door, as though she couldn't wait to be relieved of him. And then she started cleaning, doing housework, like she preferred that. Most mothers wouldn't do that."

Rosie's got her elbows off the table and now she rests her head in her hands. She's feeling sick to her stomach. I told you,

123

she's saying inside her head, I told you I was trying to get the dust mites up to please *you*, to make *you* happy. To make you *like* me. Why couldn't you have just told me what you wanted, then maybe I could have done it?

"Likewise, another time," May continues, "Mrs. Sloan left the room, left me with the child, like she was glad to be able to get away from him."

Rosie takes the pencil and writes these words for Ted: *Because I didn't want her to see me falling apart—crying.*

Burden presses her for more of what he calls "concerning behaviors." May explains how Rosie slept on the floor in her child's room. *So I could hear him*, Rosie wants to shout. It's all she can do not to raise her hand as though she were back in school, to wave it madly before the judge's view, to demand he call on her.

"She said it was so she could hear him if he had an attack, but she could have had a monitor in her bedroom and slept in her own room. Choosing to do it this way reinforces to an outsider how much she has to sacrifice and suffer with this illness. That's common in Munchausen's."

"Did she tell you why she didn't have a monitor?"

"She said it was too expensive."

"Did that seem to be a reasonable explanation?"

"Not really. The vinyl covering for the mattress and the new hypoallergenic blanket that she invested in so that she could sleep in that room probably far exceeded the cost of one of those little monitors."

Rosie wants Ted to object to all this. What right has this woman to pick her apart this way, to tell her, after the fact, how to live with this illness? But Ms. Social Worker is going on, full speed ahead, telling now how she offered Rosie information about asthma, only to have it be summarily rejected. How Rosie removed her child from day care, thereby "depriving him of all stimulation." "In cases like these," May says for about the hundredth time, "in cases of deliberate abuse, we see a strong resistance to giving and accepting information. When a parent simply lacks skills, we'll see an eagerness to learn, and that was entirely absent here. What I saw, repeatedly, was defensiveness and secretiveness. Moving him out of day care was part of that overall pattern—an attempt to keep him and what was happening to him from others. It also made her the only caregiver, and again, I think this was an attempt to collect more sympathy, a way to say, 'Look how difficult my job is, how I suffer with this child, with his illness, all by myself.' "

"In your opinion, who was this effort to get sympathy aimed at?"

"Primarily at her husband."

The day care was a dust trap, she scrawls across the legal pad in front of her, then pushes it over to Ted.

"And did anything Mrs. Sloan say particularly concern you?" Burden is asking while Rosie stares at the unchanged expression on Ted's face.

"I asked her what she found hardest about having a child with asthma and she said that people didn't take her seriously."

"Did she explain that in any further detail?" Burden's hand slides admiringly down his hip again. Maybe it was the phrasing of his question that pleased him, Rosie thought.

"Yes, she said people didn't understand how hard it was for a parent because outsiders usually see a perfectly healthy-looking child and secretly believe the parent is making up the illness or exaggerating it. She said she was relieved when Jason had really bad symptoms."

Rosie's stomach starts flipping over. She didn't mean it that way. This is an incredible reinterpretation of what she really said.

"And did she explain what she meant by that?"

"Yes. She said people only paid attention when he was really sick." The flawlessly attired woman reads from her notes: " 'Everybody goes into high gear in the acute phases.' "

"Did she specify which people she meant?"

May Donovan is nodding so vigorously, Rosie has to look away. This is really bad. Why does this woman hate her so much? "She mentioned her husband and the doctors. She said, 'It's the only time you get action out of anybody, when he's so sick he's almost dying.' "

She hadn't said that, it'd been something like that, maybe,

but May Donovan had twisted it, made it mean something different. And she couldn't have said "dying." She wouldn't have been able to use that word in reference to Jason, it would have been impossible.

"She said she was relieved when he was sickest?"

"Yes, sir."

Rosie grabs for the yellow pencil. *Relieved that he got GOOD CARE*, she writes. Ted looks down, reads it, and nods. And? she wants to ask him. Can't you get her for exaggerating and lying?

"Thank you, Ms. Donovan," Rosie hears Burden say.

"Ms. Donovan," Ted begins, taking his time over her name. "Did Mrs. Sloan say she was pleased with the care Jason got when he was ill?"

"Yes, I think she did."

"Isn't it possible that the relief she expressed to you was because he got such good care when he was at his sickest?"

"No," May snaps back at him. "She said she was relieved that he was sick. Relieved that her husband was paying attention to her, finally."

Rosie wants to cover her face but doesn't. She's trying to look blank. The way Ted does. The way he's told her to, but she feels the flush of anger across her face. And Ted's making everything worse, having this woman get angry, repeating her stupid accusation, saying it with more firmness, more hostility. She wants him to sit down already. Maybe she'll fire him.

"Are you familiar with the procedures for caring for a child at home with asthma?"

"Yes."

"Isn't part of the treatment to clear all dust-catching items from a child's bedroom?"

"Yes. But you can go to extremes."

"But, Ms. Donovan, isn't it proper medical procedure to remove the rug and curtains and books and stuffed animals?"

"I guess so."

"Have you visited Jason's day-care center?"

"No."

"Then you can't testify to the level of dust infestation there, can you?"

May's mouth looks pouty for a brief second. "No," she says. Ted pauses briefly, seems about to ask another question, then says, "Thank you, Ms. Donovan."

"DR. LINDER, CAN YOU TELL ME HOW YOU know Jason and Rosie Sloan?" Burden asks after Greg Linder has taken the stand.

"Jason is a patient of mine. Mrs. Sloan is his mother." He looks toward her when he says this.

"And what are you treating Jason for?"

"Non-specific asthma."

"By non-specific, you mean what, Doctor?"

"We don't know the exact cause. Which is common in asthma cases, especially at this age. At Jason's age. Two years. The symptoms are also less than typical." All his answers are sharp and crisp. Nervous, Rosie thinks, and he's trying to say as little as possible.

"How would you describe Mrs. Sloan's handling of her son's illness?"

"I'd say she's a very caring parent. She clearly places his comfort and health above all other issues." Linder shifts in the chair, looks toward Rosie again. This is going to work, she thinks. Burden is letting him have his say.

"Can you give me some examples of how she's manifested her concern?"

"She brings him in the instant he has symptoms. She keeps detailed records of his condition and medication. She's taken steps at home to reduce irritants which might increase his discomfort. Some of the changes she's made require a great deal of work on her part, like very frequent, very thorough vacuuming and laundering. And she's had to spend a lot of money to make some of the changes—buying special casings for all of Jason's bedding, for instance. She even bought casing for her own bedding, which is above and beyond the usual recommendations, but she thought it would be helpful. She purchased a new high-efficiency vacuum cleaner. She had the

127

carpeting removed from his bedroom. She also authorized a program of testing that's been quite costly."

"These extraordinary expenses—can you tell me who paid for them?"

"I wouldn't know."

"Can you tell me where your bills went? For those additional costly tests you mentioned, for instance."

Greg glances at Rosie, but only for a second. "I bill her husband."

"Would you know, Doctor, would such items as removal of carpeting, a vacuum cleaner, are those expenses typically covered by medical insurance?"

She watches Linder's tongue move across his lower lip. "No."

"Yes. Now, those tests you mentioned, Doctor. Can you tell me what they are?"

"A number of different things. We started with a series of skin tests."

"Can you describe those tests, how they're administered?"

"Portions of potential allergens are placed under the skin, first by pricking the skin, then by injecting a substance subcutaneously."

"Is this a painful procedure?"

"Uncomfortable, I'd say, not really painful."

"How about for a two-year-old?"

"Well, any process is more difficult for a child that age than for an adult because he wouldn't understand what's happening to him or how it will help him the way an adult would. Everything seems like torture to a two-year-old, I guess," he says, and smiles. "But I don't mean to say it's *particularly* painful," he adds quickly. "More like tedious."

"Can you define 'tedious,' Doctor?"

He resettles himself in the chair, as if he's looking for a better vantage point from which he can catch on to some new insight into how to explain things. "Well, for a toddler, just sitting for any length of time is difficult. For these tests, Jason had to sit on his mother's lap and have these procedures done all over his back. He was instructed not to move—which is, as I said, difficult for him, pain or no pain. Mrs. Sloan was very good with him, though. She talked to him and sang to him the whole time. Made a game out of the need to stop moving. She kept reminding him that at the end, there'd be a treat for him. She had a different treat for him each time."

"Each time? There was more than one day in which Jason had to endure these tests?"

Again Greg moves, reseating, finding another corner of the witness box. "We did three test sessions," he says flatly. Rosie realizes he's shutting down—he doesn't like the questions and she figures he's going to be very stingy with his answers from now on.

"There were three different sessions where this child had to sit absolutely still with his shirt off and have his back pricked and injected?"

"Three sessions," Linder says, as though he hasn't heard the details of the second half of the question.

"And itching, Doctor? Was there itching where a positive reaction occurred?"

"Yes."

"Were these tests absolutely necessary for the treatment of the child's difficulties?"

Linder waits a few seconds before he answers. "There are different opinions about allergy testing in pediatric asthmatic patients."

"I'm asking *your* opinion."

"I'm . . ." He stops and the courtroom is silent. The stenographer's fingers hover above the keys.

"Let me rephrase the question for you so you can give me a simple yes-or-no answer." The recorder's hands have dropped back down and move in their strange, syncopated rhythm, jumping from key to key. "Do you routinely administer such tests to two-year-olds, Doctor?"

"No. But because they're not routine doesn't—"

"Did you insist on these tests?"

"No."

"Did you urge Mrs. Sloan to do them?"

"No." He sighs with the effort of deflecting the question away.

"Why don't you normally do these tests?"

"They don't give very conclusive results for asthma, and with these very young children there's a question as to whether the discomfort outweighs the benefit." He looks away as he answers and raises a hand to his lips as though trying to silence himself.

"Then why were they done in Jason's case?"

He takes a bit longer to prepare this time. His hand comes down before he starts and when he does begin, his voice sounds as though he's feeling along the answer, making sure it's whole and sound, just as you feel along a wall in a darkened corridor when you're looking for the light switch, wary of encountering something else unseen, unknown. "When Jason wasn't getting better, Mrs. Sloan asked if I would consider the tests in order to get more information. She wanted to pin down the diagnosis more accurately."

"Did you tell her of the discomfort Jason would have?"

"In medicine, you always have to weigh discomfort against benefit."

"At an earlier date you had recommended against these tests, is that correct?"

"Yes."

"Did Mrs Sloan become more insistent that she wanted the tests done on her child?"

"Yes." He's no longer looking at Burden, but somewhere off left, toward the window. The lawyer is backing him into a corner, Rosie knows, making him say, as May Donovan did, that she's a manipulator. It wasn't like that, she wants to scream at all of them.

"Can you tell me why you completely reversed yourself on that point, Doctor, why you gave in to her requests for skin testing?"

"Objection, Your Honor," Ted says, rising. "Your Honor, Mr. Burden is leading the witness."

"I'll withdraw the question," the state's attorney says before the judge has a chance to respond. "Why did you change your treatment plan for Jason Sloan so that it included skin testing?"

Linder draws in a deep breath. "Asthma is a physical condition, but it's also one which affects an entire family. It has a very complicated emotional aspect to it because a family has to confront possible lifelong illness and learn to incorporate disease into its routine. Lots of times, parents have to try everything possible to bring relief to their child in order to feel comfortable with the disease."

"So then you did these tests for the comfort of the mother?"

He holds up his hand, palm outward in an effort to stop Burden's assault. "That's only part of it. I did these tests because, first, they *might* have turned up new, useful information about allergens, and second, because having the mother comfortable with the disorder, and confident that she's done everything she can, often helps the child, regardless of what concrete information is gained."

"So you're talking about a psychological effect?"

"Primarily."

"On the mother?"

"Yes. But I'm telling you that that's very important with asthma cases."

"How many different substances was Jason tested for?"

"I don't know the exact number in Jason's case. We usually run about forty."

"Did these tests show any specific allergic reactions in Jason?"

"A very mild reaction to dust mites and a reaction to ash pollen."

"Ash pollen?"

"Yes, sir."

"Where and when would a two-year-old typically come in contact with ash pollen?"

"In the woods in spring, I suppose."

"So there was a total of two out of forty positive responses?"

"Yes."

"One out of forty that actually might be found in the home?"

"Yes."

"Did this information allow you to treat Jason more effectively and cure his asthma?"

"Asthma isn't necessarily a response to a specific allergen. It's—"

"I need a yes or no here, Doctor. Did this information allow you to treat the child more effectively?"

Linder is silent for a moment, coldly staring at his inquisitor. "No," he finally says.

"Did you tell Mrs. Sloan ahead of time that this would be the case, that you were unlikely to be able to administer better treatment as a result of the tests?"

"Yes." He's turned his eyes downward, and he seems to be scratching something off the wood surface that rings him into his witness box.

"Dr. Linder, when Jason was brought to your office with severe symptoms, what treatment did he usually receive?"

"I administered epinephrine by injection. And a second follow-up injection approximately twenty minutes later. That's standard in severe asthma episodes."

"A painful procedure, I presume."

"Briefly painful and necessitated by the child's respiratory stress. Jason is a very bright child who seemed to accept this; to understand that it made him better."

"With each of these acute episodes of breathing problems, Doctor, was there an identifiable cause?"

"No. Asthma isn't like that. Medical treatment isn't as perfect as people would like it to be," he says, leaning forward so that these words hit the microphone more crisply than what he's said before.

"Can you tell me, Doctor, if Jason were deliberately exposed to certain things, like, for example, chocolate, might it have produced the respiratory stress you saw in your office, the stress which caused you to administer injections, proceed with painful tests, and recommend uncomfortable conditions at home for Jason?"

"Chocolate might do it, but she didn't—"

"Dr. Linder, are you familiar with a syndrome known as Munchausen's syndrome by proxy, or factitious disorder by proxy, as it's also known?" Greg closes his eyes for a second. "Have you heard of it, Doctor?" Greg glances toward Rosie, then turns away, shaking his head slightly. He seems to have turned entirely inward. "Dr. Linder?" Burden prompts.

"I've heard of it."

"Can you tell me if Mrs. Sloan appears to have this syndrome?"

"I'm not a psychiatrist, I'm an allergist. I don't consider myself qualified to make such a judgment."

"But you're aware, are you not, that Munchausen's is characterized by an overzealous concern for a child's health?"

"Yes, but frankly, I don't even know if it's recognized by the APA as a disorder. It strikes me as one of these things manufactured by the press."

Burden walks back to the prosecutors' table and picks up a book. "Dr. Linder, this is the *Diagnostic and Statistical Manual of Mental Disorders*, which is published by the American Psychiatric Association—the APA you just referred to. Are you familiar with this reference work?"

"Yes."

"Let me read to you what it says here about this disorder: 'The essential feature is the deliberate production or feigning of physical symptoms in another person who is under the individual's care. Typically the victim is a young child and the perpetrator is the child's mother. Cases are often characterized by an atypical clinical course in the victim and inconsistent laboratory test results.' Isn't this *exactly* what you've been describing, Doctor, a child with atypical symptoms and testing that doesn't back up apparent symptoms?"

"Yes, but that could be true in a lot of asthma cases. That's why asthma is so difficult for families. And your basic premise is absurd: the symptoms weren't produced by the mother."

"Allow me to go on: 'Life stressors, especially marital conflict, may trigger the behavior.' Mrs. Sloan is separated from her husband, is she not?"

"Yes, but so are a lot of people."

"All those acute health problems developed in Jason *after* the separation, didn't they?"

"Yes." He moves his shoulders sharply left, then right, as though he's testing the confines of the witness box and Burden's power over him. He wants to run just as much as she does, Rosie knows.

"And one more item here." He points dramatically to the open page. "The perpetrators 'commonly have considerable experience in health-related areas and seem to thrive in a medical environment.' Mrs. Sloan is a physician's daughter and as Dr. Meyers, the emergency room physician, has already testified, quite expert with the language of medicine, isn't she?"

"Yes, but—"

"*Yes* is a perfectly sufficient answer. Thank you, Doctor." He puts the book back down, pauses, hand still on the volume. The gesture makes Rosie think of oaths on Bibles. Is he doing that deliberately? "In your opinion, does Mrs. Sloan's pattern of behavior with her child fit this description?"

"No. I told you, she's a caring mother. She'd lost one child already, so that had to be on her mind all the time. Her goal was protecting Jason from something similar. She didn't cause any of those episodes except that first one."

"All right, Doctor, forget that sentence I read to you about the mother causing the illness. All the other descriptives apply, don't they?"

Greg's eyes go to Rosie's for just an instant, then dart so fast about the room, she can't tell where they're going to light. She's stopped breathing, waiting for his answer.

"Yes, but—"

"Thank you, Dr. Linder, that will be all."

Greg looks startled. Lost. Rosie's shaking and she can't believe Burden's backed him—and her—against the wall this way.

"Attorney Fisher," the judge says.

Ted takes several moments to flip through his pages of notes, then he rises but doesn't step from behind the table. "Dr. Linder, the acute attacks of breathing problems that brought Jason to your office could have had a variety of causes, couldn't they?"

"Yes."

"Thank you. That's all for now."

"Nothing further, Your Honor," Burden says.

"You may step down, Doctor," Mannon instructs Greg Linder.

Rosie has a million things she wants to say to Ted, starting with, That's it? That's all you're asking him? but she knows it's not going to make any difference. Ted's not going to ask more questions just because *she* wants him to. Ted pushes his legal pad toward her, and he's pointing at something he's written across the top. *No harm done*, it says. She wants to crumple up his stupid notes and throw them at him, but then Burden calls another witness, and she doesn't have the time for temper fits. It's Zoe he's calling. Rosie's marriage counselor.

Zoe's wearing slacks. Clearly, nobody coached her about sacrificing herself to the judge's sexist predilections. And poor Zoe is obviously nervous. More than nervous: scared. Her voice cracks as she speaks her name into the microphone. Her address is inaudible. Judge Mannon makes her repeat the information. Rosie hears her voice waver through the list of her credentials as though a strong wind were behind it, making it swell and falter unnaturally.

Burden asks Zoe to tell the court what Rosie has told her about Jason's illness.

"Anything she told me is protected by the therapist-client relationship," she says, and her voice is surer now, almost clear in its delivery.

"Ms. Upton, Mrs. Sloan has waived her right to privacy on this matter, so you may answer all questions put to you here today."

"Even things she said in therapy?"

"Yes, ma'am." Zoe nods. "Now, can you tell me how you think Mrs. Sloan was handling her child's illness?"

"She was handling it very well. It's always difficult for a parent when a child is critically ill." She looks at Rosie when she finishes saying this and Rosie nods slightly, enough for Zoe to see she appreciates her support and her attempt to protect her.

"Did she say that Jason was critically ill?"

"Yes. I understood that he had very severe symptoms."

"Could you tell me when Mrs. Sloan seemed to be under the most stress?"

"At the beginning. The beginning of the illness, I mean. The beginning of the separation. The first time or two Jason got so sick."

"After that she appeared to be under less stress?"

"Yes. When she finally got the diagnosis, she seemed much calmer."

"She was calmer when she found out her child had a disease?" Burden asks, stopping in his tracks as he approaches the stand, stroking his side again, glorying in his cleverness.

"Because it was definite, finally."

"Was she still stressed by the episodes after the diagnosis was made?"

"Not quite as much."

"Ms. Upton, would you say Mrs. Sloan was calmer right after one of Jason's medical episodes than she was before it?"

"Yes."

"Almost as though she might have been anticipating something difficult, and then relieved that it was over?"

"I suppose you could describe it that way." Her voice has cracked its way through this sentence, again, though she'd been doing pretty well for a while before that. Zoe has a tissue in her hand and she runs it over her lips, now. Rosie's never seen the woman like this. Zoe's always been the one in control.

"Did Mr. and Mrs. Sloan set up certain conditions of their separation and discuss them with you?"

"Yes."

"Why did they set up those conditions?"

"I recommended it as a way to foster independence for each of them. Mr. and Mrs. Sloan have been together all their adult life. I thought they should establish some personal strength apart from each other before they went on to deal with their shared problems."

"They agreed to these conditions freely?"

"Yes."

"What conditions were on Mr. Sloan's side?"

"That he do his own housework, cooking, shopping, and not hire anyone for those things."

"Did he abide by that?"

"I believe he did."

"And Mrs. Sloan's corresponding condition?"

"That she get a job."

"Has Mrs. Sloan, to your knowledge, ever held a job?"

"Yes, I think she worked for the local paper doing layout, but she lost that job when they were bought by an out-of-town conglomerate."

"And when did she lose that job?"

"I'm not sure, but I think it was several years ago. Before Jason was born, I know that."

"And did she tell you how she felt about going back to work?"

"She said she was nervous about it because of being out of the market so long. Layout was the only thing she'd ever done, and she said there isn't much call for that anymore with computers taking over."

"How did she feel about jobs in other fields?"

Zoe shrugs. "Well, she didn't have training. She was nervous, as I said."

"Did Mrs. Sloan fulfill the conditions of the separation and get a job?"

"No, but that was because there was Jason's illness. Circumstances changed."

"Mr. Sloan took his agreed upon step toward independence, whereas Mrs. Sloan didn't, is that correct?"

"Things changed." She holds one hand, open palmed, in his direction, as though begging for his understanding.

"Did Mrs. Sloan try to get a job?"

"No." Zoe breathes out a snort of protest. "I mean—" she starts to say.

But Burden cuts her off, saying, "Ms. Upton, to your knowledge, do Quinn Sloan and Rosie Sloan have contact with each other?"

"Yes. They confer about their son regularly."

"Is their separation amicable?"

"Yes." Zoe's answers are more like questions, as though she's not certain that she's giving the right response and wants Burden's assurance that she is.

"Would you expect them to be able to continue to have amicable contact in order to discuss Jason's welfare?"

"Oh yes," she says, with more sureness than her previous answers.

Attorney Burden says he has no more questions and Rosie's lawyer moves forward.

"Ms. Upton, isn't it natural for someone to feel a sense of relief upon finally getting a diagnosis; finally understanding what has been causing terrible symptoms?"

"Yes."

"Mr. and Mrs. Sloan are separated, aren't they?"

"Yes."

"And wouldn't you assume that any couple that separates has done so because they have irreconcilable conflicts?"

"Not irreconcilable, necessarily."

"Conflicts?"

"Yes."

"Thank you, Ms. Upton."

Ted strides back to the table with a real look of victory on his face. He smiles and winks at Rosie as he approaches his seat and she finds herself smiling back, feeling buoyed by his positive aspect. It's okay. It must be. He's winning, she thinks, though she can't see how or why, yet. Burden confuses everybody. It's all semantics, isn't it? Won't the judge see that?

Rosie is startled when Burden speaks her name aloud. She doesn't even know why he's done so till Ted whispers to her that she needs to step forward, to take the stand.

She forgets about the slippery bottomed shoes as she starts toward the front of the court and her left foot slides out behind her just as she comes round the corner of the table, but she's able to regain her balance right away. Then, just as she gets all the way to the stand, she realizes she doesn't have the black cardigan on over the pseudo-silk shirt anymore, that she took it off because she'd gotten so overheated. And of course, she's perspired mammoth stains into the shirt. She considers walking back—or sliding back, actually, that would be a more accurate description—but decides that would make her look even more absurd. It's too late, she tells herself, and steps up into the witness box. She thinks her blouse may have pulled out of the waistband in one spot, but it'll have to do, as is. She'll have to do.

Rosie's heart is beating so loudly she can actually hear it. Can anybody else? The judge is looking down toward her, over those glasses, just as Ted said he would. When Burden asks her to state her name and address for the record, she hangs her mouth open foolishly—soundlessly—before she is able to whisper it at him. She knows she has to do better than this. "This will take only a few minutes," he says, and she nods. "Mrs. Sloan, is Jason your firstborn child?"

"No," she says, but she can't really hear it over the unrelenting beat of her own heart. He's doing it. He's going to go after Abby. He's going to make her go over all of it again. Her hands clutch tightly at the arms of her chair.

"Mrs. Sloan," the judge says, "please speak directly into that microphone. I need to hear every single word you have to say."

Rosie pulls the gooseneck toward herself and the angry amplified sound her fingers make as they move across the surface surrounds her. "You had another child born to you and your husband, Quinn Sloan, before Jason?" Burden asks over the noise.

She leans forward and speaks into the mike. "Yes." The shrill roar of feedback fills the room suddenly and the attorney reaches for the mike. He fumbles with it for a short time and then the room is quiet again.

"What was that child's name, Mrs. Sloan?"

"Abigail." She whispers the word, but it sounds huge.

"Did Abigail die, Mrs. Sloan?"

"Yes."

"How old was she?"

"Two months."

"And what was the cause of death?"

"Sudden infant death syndrome. Respiratory failure." The

139

amplified words come back at her as though someone else is shouting them at her.

"But there was a second autopsy, wasn't there?"

"Yes."

"Your Honor, I ask to have these two autopsy reports admitted as evidence."

"Mr. Fisher?"

"No objection, Your Honor, those are standard postmortems with no questions about the death."

"Why was that second autopsy performed?"

"I don't know."

"The microphone, Mrs. Sloan," the judge reminds her, and Rosie realizes she's slumped back in her chair away from the mike. She straightens up again and repeats her answer. She looks over toward Quinn, but he's conferring with Bernie.

"Aren't second autopsies usually performed because there's some doubt about the results of the first one?"

"I guess so."

"Mrs. Sloan, who requested the second autopsy?"

"My father."

"Mrs. Sloan, your father was Dr. Thomas Nathan, wasn't he?"

"Yes." She's feeling very warm. What does he want with her father? He can't know, can he, how he grilled her about Abby's death? How he insisted on examining the body, how he wouldn't let Abby die?

"He was a rather well-known, highly regarded physician locally, wasn't he? Chief of medicine for several years at Bradford Hospital?"

"Yes."

"Your father told you why he wanted another autopsy done, didn't he?"

"I don't really remember. He was a doctor. He believed in second opinions, I guess that was why."

"Why did he want a second opinion?"

"The second one only confirmed the first."

"Mrs. Sloan, my question was, Why did he want a second opinion?"

140

"I don't know." She can't look at him, at that superior smile that he twists at her every time he asks one of his questions.

"Can you tell me how he reacted to the sudden death of Abigail Sloan?"

She knows she has to be careful. "He was upset."

"Of course. I'm sorry to have to go over this painful material with you. But tell me, was he supportive of you during the time immediately following her death?"

"Yes. Very."

"Supportive of both you and your husband?"

"Yes."

"If I told you that your father suspected foul play in your daughter's death, would that surprise you?"

Rosie's throat is so tight, there's so little air, she thinks she's going to black out.

"Mrs. Sloan, take a sip of this," Burden says, handing her a glass of water. She takes a sip, barely manages to swallow it, then rolls the side of the glass against her hot forehead for a second. "Mrs. Sloan," Burden says, returning to the previous unanswered question, "would it surprise you if I said your father suspected foul play in Abigail's death?"

"Yes."

Burden holds a paper that has been folded so only a scrawl of black ink shows out toward her. "Do you recognize this signature?"

She looks at it, but the whole page has gone blurry. She reaches into her skirt pocket and takes out the tissue she's been fingering on and off all morning, then tries to wipe the tears away with the ragged, grainy thing. Slowly, the letters become clearer. "It just says 'Tom.' "

"Is that how your father informally signed his name?"

Between colleagues, yes, of course. Small and neat. Most doctors would have had a barely legible T with a stretched-out top piece and nothing more. Her father has three easily distinguishable letters. And a line underneath it all. She's seen it a thousand times. Maybe ten thousand times. "Yes," she tells him.

"Your Honor, I ask that I might be allowed to enter this document into the proceedings."

"What is it, Mr. Burden?" Mannon asks, reaching his hand out for the paper as the attorney approaches.

"It's a copy of a memo sent to Dr. Silas Morgan, chief pathologist at Bradford Hospital, requesting an autopsy on the baby Abigail Sloan."

"Mr. Fisher, do you have any objections?" the judge asks.

"Your Honor," Ted says as Burden comes toward him with the document, "I fail to see any foundation for this item."

"I believe we're dealing with a pattern of abuse," Burden says, turning to address the judge.

"I'm going to allow it," Mannon declares.

Rosie's holding on to the sides of her witness enclosure, keeping herself upright when Burden holds out the paper to her, now fully unfolded. "Would you please look at the letterhead and tell me if you recognize the name."

She unwinds a hand from the wood and takes his offering. It's her father's memo paper, so she has no choice but to admit she does.

"Whose name is on that?"

"Dr. Thomas Nathan."

"Would you please read your father's memo aloud for us?"

She can't believe he's making her do this. The tears have started again. All she can do is shrug.

"Perhaps I can read it for you," he says, lifting it from her hands. " 'Dear Morgan. As we discussed, phone call, this morn, 12/17, re: Baby Sloan, please check for nasal contusions, pinpoint pulmonary hemorrhage.' "

It's what she's always suspected, but didn't know for sure. She's never seen this memo before. Never seen solid evidence that her father thought she had killed her daughter.

"Mrs. Sloan, do you know what those terms mean?" She nods. "Can you explain them to the court?"

"Nasal contusions," she says, pinching her nose lightly, then dropping her fingers suddenly, as she realizes what she's doing. "It means bruises to the nose."

"Pinpoint hemorrhaging?" he asks.

"I think that appears in cases of asphyxiation. But they didn't find that," she wails out at him. "The second autopsy was SIDS, too."

"Isn't it true that your father, a physician of considerable renown in the community, requested a second autopsy because he suspected Abigail had been murdered?"

"Objection, speculation, Your Honor."

"Overruled."

"Mrs. Sloan?"

"He never said that. He asked questions, but because he was the grandfather, he was in shock. He didn't want to believe she was dead. None of us did."

"Because it just didn't seem like she could die all on her own like that, did it?"

"Both autopsy reports say she did." She tries to look around him at Quinn, but her husband is bent forward, his face in his hands.

"But your own father, Mrs. Sloan, expressed suspicions about Abby's care?"

She nods. "You need to speak up, Mrs. Sloan, so that the stenographer can record your answers. Did your father express suspicions about your daughter's care?"

"Yes," she shouts at him.

"No more questions, Your Honor."

Rosie starts to stand up, but the judge stops her, reminds her that her own attorney may have questions for her. "I do, Your Honor," Ted says, and he comes to the stand, rests his arms upon the wood rail surrounding her, and smiles gently at her, not hurrying. "Mrs. Sloan," he finally says, "there were two autopsies done on your deceased daughter, is that correct?"

"Yes."

"Was there any difference in the findings of the two autopsy reports?"

"No."

"And what was the cause of death in each examination?"

"Your Honor," Burden protested, "we've been through all this before."

"Mr. Burden, you know as well as I do that he's entitled to reopen this."

"The cause of death, Mrs. Sloan?" Ted repeats.

"Sudden infant death," she says, and each word requires intense effort for her to form it for him. The sound of the pronouncement lingers, the way it used to when she'd lie awake back then and she'd feel it spring up, forcing itself upon her in the darkness.

"Do you know what SIDS is, Mrs. Sloan?"

"Yes."

"Can you give me a definition of that syndrome?"

"I don't know exactly, not scientifically, I mean."

"Do your best," he urges her.

"It's an unexpected death because there's no illness preceding it. It happens in very young babies, under a year, I think. And the baby's otherwise healthy. No other illness or injury shows up when they do an autopsy."

"Was there ever any official finding of wrongdoing in the case of Abigail Sloan's death?"

"No."

"Was there evidence of nasal contusions?"

"No."

"Was there evidence of pinpoint pulmonary hemorrhages?"

"No," Rosie says, shaking her head.

"Thank you, Mrs. Sloan," Ted says.

"Mr. Burden?" Mannon asks.

"Your Honor," he says, standing, "I have no more questions. The state rests."

"Mr. Fisher?"

"We rest, Your Honor, but may I have some time before summation?"

"Fifteen minutes," the judge says. "And then ten minutes each to sum up, not a minute more," he commands.

The second they're outside the courtroom door, Rosie asks Ted, "What's going to happen, what's he going to do?" She can hear the panic in her own voice, so she's not surprised when Ted insists they move down toward the storage area before she says anything else. "Tell me, Ted," she begs him when they're standing by the furnace once again.

"I can't say for sure, Rosie. I wish I'd seen that memo beforehand. Did you know it existed?"

"No. I didn't know my father hated me quite that much."

"Your father was upset, Rosie. He wanted to find cause, that's all."

She's got her hands twisted so tightly around each other, they ache. "I've paid and paid for the death of my first child and I never did anything except love her, Ted. I never hurt her." He puts a hand on her arm. She lets the silence sit around them momentarily before she continues. Then she asks him, "Can't you tell me what's going to happen to Jay?"

Attorney Fisher shakes his head a bit and seems to study the odd mixture of items—paper towels, paint cans, coffee, dried flowers, copier paper, brown wing-tipped shoes, and cans of minestrone soup—stored around them. "I don't know," he says. "But I'm sure Burden's going to request that you submit to a psychiatric evaluation. That I can almost promise."

She takes in a sharp, deep breath, and her shoulders rise way up. The word *submit* makes her see herself tied, spread-eagle, to a table.

"Hey," he says, touching her hand. "It's not so terrible. You might even like being able to talk to somebody about all this. You can vent some of your anger."

"Don't patronize me, Ted," she says. "Are they about to have me committed or something?"

"No, of course not. He'll ask you to have two or three sessions with a shrink. Over-the-counter, or whatever they call it."

"Outpatient?"

"Right. Like an office visit, that's all. It's a pro forma kind of a thing. Once there's an accusation of abuse, a judge starts to worry about covering his own butt. He has to make sure you're not secretly a psycho before he lets you have access to your kid again. The only problem you'll run into is if you refuse to do the evaluation. Judges, this one especially, place a high premium on cooperation. And it's tricky trying to refuse psychological evaluation—he might decide you're refusing because you're hiding something about your mental state."

"So all I have to do is shut up and be a good girl and let him take over my life, right?"

"Yeah, that's about the size of it. For now. And remember, this is temporary. Short term."

She's brought both her hands to her chest while he's saying this, and when she feels the wildness of her heartbeat, how out of bounds her blood has grown, she moves her hands away with such force, it is as though her hands are seeking to detach themselves from her body for a while. It's a few moments before she can speak again. "How can they be allowed to do this to me?"

"Rosie, let's concentrate on getting through today."

She turns her face from his because she's started to cry. Ted doesn't get it either, does he? she thinks, and she's furious with herself for thinking of him as an ally. He's part of the horrible system, too, isn't he? After this, he'll move on to something else, to Mr. and Mrs. Magnusen, probably, as soon as he walks out of here. Then he'll go home to his intact household. Maybe Ted thinks she did kill Abby and that the shrink's going to find out, yes, she is a psycho. Maybe he can't wait till she's carted away.

"As soon as the counseling stuff is done," Ted continues, "Mannon will set a new court date." She hears a shimmer, a wavering, in his voice that she knows is false cheer.

"All I wanted out of this was for Jason to be healthy again," Rosie says. "Why are you all against me?"

"Rosie, don't get paranoid now." He's put a hand on her shoulder, but she pulls away. "Look at me, Rosie." She's starting to cry again and she's rummaging in her purse for the packet of tissues she put in there. She wants to wipe the tears off her face. And then run. To the ladies' room for starters, then maybe all the way home. "Look at me, Rosie, please." She does. "I'm with you. I know you didn't do anything to either of your children. But the state's pushed this into the court for some reason, and we've got no choice but to deal with it. What I'm telling you is that the judge just has to cover his ass right now, that's all it is. You have to think of it as temporary."

"But my poor baby Jason is the one who's going to suffer." Now she's crying for real. And she's going to suffer. She's feeling it already, missing him. Her chest and her throat are so tight, there's only a fraction's worth of breathing space left for her.

"Think of it this way," Attorney Fisher says, "Jason's going to get to go on a vacation to his dad's house. You'll see him, he just won't be sleeping at your house. They'll have a great time together."

Rosie knows this is probably true. She just hadn't really accepted it would actually come to this. "You're right," she concedes. "I know he'll be okay with Quinn." She pulls another tissue out from under the thin plastic casing. She's not crying anymore so it's more just something to do. Something to twist besides her own aching hands. "Are we going to be able to get anything about the girlfriend not being there?"

Ted shakes his head firmly. "Go back in and sit down," he tells her, patting her arm. "I need two minutes to get my thoughts together. We're cool, Rosie, believe me."

She wants to believe him. Oh, so very badly, she does.

CHAPTER
SEVENTEEN

BURDEN GETS THROUGH HIS SUMMING UP IN well under his allotted ten minutes. Rosie wants to sink down through the floor. She hears him tick off her failings, counting them, as he so loves to do, by pressing one extended finger against another. "This chocolate she fed her child," Burden pronounces, then pauses, hands raised now, like the orchestra conductor he has become. Rosie sees the judge lean toward his words, anticipating, urging him onward, out of his pause. "This chocolate," he intones, "was willfully administered to bring harm upon an innocent, unsuspecting victim." He brings one hand to his throat as though he's gagging just thinking of it. "According to police reports," he tells the judge, "on one occasion, at the onset of apparent breathing problems, Mrs. Sloan summoned her husband to her home and then deliberately locked him and the emergency medical workers out of the house." The word *deliberately* is drawn out, musically trilled upon. Two of Burden's fingers are pressed down. "Mrs. Sloan locked out the very people who could have brought relief to her child. And why? To increase the look of the drama and the suffering. To increase the sympathy and attention she could get from those around her, particularly from her husband, from whom she had so recently separated. The police actually had to forcibly break the door down in order to gain access to her child." His words are punctuated by the forward thrust of his fist against an invisible barrier. The attorney presses his fingers back a third time and proclaims that Rosie presented symptoms to her doctor which couldn't be confirmed on examination, that she insisted on tests: "painful tests," he nearly bellows—to ease her own discomfort and anxiety—that she told people that she was glad her child was so sick, and that she was finally getting the attention she deserved as a result.

Rosie grabs for the yellow pencil which is lying on the table beside Ted's legal pad. *"Glad is not the same as relieved and I wasn't relieved,"* she writes. Her writing is so wildly loopy, she doesn't even know if he can read it.

He slips the pencil from her grip. *Relax*, he writes back. The letters are even and clear.

Burden has continued, of course. She's missed something. The stuff about how she kept asking for money from Quinn for all the procedures and how she never got a job. Never wanted a job. What did that have to do with any of this? Burden says each episode of illness was a premeditated attempt to lure her husband back. Each request for money a similar attempt. "And finally, Your Honor," the prosecutor says, his voice strong but strangely confidential in this vast room, "Mrs. Sloan has lifelong experience with medical terminology and procedures." Rosie has lost track of how many items he has counted upon his fingers, and she can't shake the feeling that it's important that she know. Were there six different ways in which she's behaved abominably? Seven? She starts trying to reconstruct the list in her head.

"In sum, Judge, we have a textbook case here of Munchausen's syndrome by proxy, a syndrome which is characterized by a parent with medical knowledge inducing illness in a child in order to gain attention for herself. Her doctor confirms that Jason's symptoms are unusual and that Mrs. Sloan demanded nonstandard aggressive and painful procedures for her child." The assistant attorney general has picked up the pace of his declarations. Rosie glances behind her at Quinn, but he's sitting with eyes closed, head tilted slightly back, hating her. Burden is still going on: "Mrs. Sloan's therapist confirms her dependency and need for attention, her interest in staying unemployed, her pleasure at seeing the child ill. Your Honor," he says, making it sound this time like he's pleading, "parents acting under Munchausen's syndrome are known to cause great pain and suffering in their children. And," he says, pausing, drawing his listeners toward him again, "they are known to cause the deaths of innocent children." He picks up his blue reference book again. " 'Victims of Munchausen's syndrome by proxy,'" he reads, " 'suffer a significant mortality.' Your Honor, that means they *die* in significant numbers." He closes the book so that it snaps loudly for all to hear. "There has already been one child death in the Sloan household, Your Honor. For that child, little Abigail Sloan, we, unfortunately, can do nothing. But for Jason Sloan, we still have a chance. Judge, we know about the chocolate in that first episode. What we don't know is what else she's forcing on this child. We cannot be too vigilant when it comes to protecting a two-year-old like Jason who is totally incapable of protecting himself. He cannot tell us what's really going on in that house. We *must* protect this child and remove him from Mrs. Sloan's care. Please, let us not have another innocent child's death on our hands."

Rosie has to cover her mouth to keep from having terrible noises escape. Ted strokes her arm. Not to comfort her, she knows, but to get her to behave. To shut up; to act nice. Dear God, she thinks, and pushes his hand away. Could she have done these things? Could she be this monster-mother and not know it?

"Attorney Fisher," she hears the judge's grumbly voice say, and the man next to her rises and steps forward to take his turn.

"Your Honor," Ted says, "Mrs. Sloan is a loving, caring mother. She has a child who is ill, and she has done her very best as a single mother to take care of him. Wouldn't any parent try to do everything possible to put an end to a child's suffering? Imagine a small child, your child, unable to catch his breath. Wouldn't you give anything, life itself, to save that child? This is all Mrs. Sloan has done. She has tried everything she can to create ease for this child. Of course she doesn't want to have to take away his playthings. Of course she doesn't want to have to spend vast amounts of money on things that won't necessarily do any good, but she will do those things in the hopes—even if farfetched hopes—that one of these things, the tests, the constant and thorough cleaning of her home, the removal of toys from Jason's room, will make this child well and comfortable and happy. Would you want a parent to stop hoping, to stop working for the health and well-being of her child? Of course not. Remember, Your Honor, Mrs. Sloan has suffered the tragic loss of her firstborn child. If this loss has made her slightly more vigilant and attentive than the average mother, isn't that entirely understandable?

"Judge Mannon, asthma is a terrible, terrible disease. Parents of asthmatic children rarely get to sleep through the night. They are always under the stress of not knowing when the next attack will come. But Mrs. Sloan has given unstintingly of herself, uncomplainingly, losing sleep, giving up a chance to reenter the job market, because she has done what a parent will and *must* do: try to get her sick child the best possible care available. She has done this, and nothing more and nothing less. She has taken him in the middle of the night to his doctor. She has followed the doctor's recommendations to the letter. If she has made mistakes, such as locking her husband out, it is because she was beside herself with fear for her child's life. Your Honor, Munchausen's syndrome sufferers don't care about their children, they're completely consumed with their own needs. That's not what we see here at all. Mrs. Sloan is a devoted, caring mother. Please don't make this little boy suffer any more than he already has by separating him from his mother."

When Ted turns around, he smiles at Rosie, and she's able to smile back. She feels so much better, she can't believe it. The whirling in her stomach has slowed—though not stopped—as though it were trying to pause and hear Ted's reasonable and calming words. It's all true what he's said, he's made Burden sound like a raving madman, just by contrast. Ted covers her hand when he reseats himself next to her. "We're okay," he whispers to her, and runs his hand over her back.

"Rebuttal, Mr. Burden?" Mannon asks.

"Your Honor," the attorney says, rising to his full impressive height and speaking more slowly than he has done through this entire proceeding, "I will only remind you that Munchausen victims suffer a high mortality rate. We must protect Jason Sloan and we must do it now."

"Mr. Amundsen," the judge says, and Jason's attorney rises. "Where do you come down on all this?"

"Your Honor, my findings are consistent with those of the state."

The judge is checking his watch again. "Given the seriousness of this issue, I'm going to rule on it right away," he announces.

Ted rises so suddenly from his chair, he nearly knocks it over. "Begging your pardon, Your Honor," he starts to say, but the judge silences him.

"Mr. Fisher, don't interrupt me." Ted sits again, and the smile is absolutely gone from his face. The whirling is back for Rosie; the violent, dizzying rush. She doesn't even know where it's centered. All over, all through her. It's in the room.

"I'm going to make a temporary ruling here, sixty days. There's clearly enough material here to warrant further investigation by the state and study on my part. Mrs. Sloan, given the nature of the accusations presented, I'm going to have to ask you to have an evaluation by a court-appointed psychiatrist. Do you have any problem with that?"

Ted whispers to her that she should stand. "No," she says, and the word is soft and strange, floating around her. Ted has already told her, she has no real choice.

"Very good, Mrs. Sloan. The attorneys will make those arrangements with the Department of Children and Families. You'll have the sixty days to complete that." Rosie is nodding. "In the meantime," he says, "I am ordering Jason placed in the care of his father, Quinn Sloan. His health is to be monitored regularly by a court-approved physician. Do the parties agree to have Dr. Linder continue with the child's care, to act as court physician?" Each of the lawyers rises and indicates his consent. "Our goal right now is to get Jason healthy again," the judge continues. "Once the psychological evaluation is complete, I will allow visitation in a state-supervised child-care center." Rosie can't really follow what he's saying because her head is so fogged up. "Mrs. Sloan, in order to make this phase of things work, you are to have no contact with your child during this period, do you understand that?"

No, she thinks. What is he talking about? "I need to see him," she tries to say, but the words mass incoherently upon her tongue.

Ted is standing now. "Your Honor, begging your pardon, this is certainly an unusual restriction you've placed upon my client, especially given the vague nature of the charges."

"Mr. Fisher, let me remind you that it is the sworn duty of the court to act in the best interests of the child. Erring on the side of caution is always warranted where children are concerned. If there is vagueness, as you say, we will move toward clarity. But until we have proof positive that it is safe to do otherwise and corroborative information from a mental health professional, I want this child to have no contact with his mother." His voice is tight with impatience. "Mrs. Sloan, I will repeat, you are to have no contact with your child during this evaluation period, do you understand?"

"No," Rosie says now. She stands. She's shaking, but she's standing.

"Mrs. Sloan, do you have a question about this ruling?" Mannon asks her.

"Yes." She doesn't know what the question is. She knows there's a question. There must be a hundred questions. "For sixty days I can't see him at all?" she finally manages to ask.

"Those are the conditions," he says flatly.

"Your Honor, may I have a word with my client?" Ted asks.

"Please do, Mr. Fisher."

Ted puts his arm around her, turns her so they face away from the judge, toward the back of the courtroom. "Rosie," he pleads with her, "just listen to him, don't argue with him, please, for Jason's sake."

She's grabbed hold of his arm. If he didn't have a jacket on, she'd surely draw blood, her fingers are arched so fiercely against his arm. "You didn't say I couldn't see him. He's too little to be without me for so long, Ted."

"Let it go now, Rosie. He's with Quinn—he'll be fine. Don't make it worse on yourself and Jason by arguing with the judge, okay? He could have said six months. He could have said eighteen months, Rosie, that's his prerogative. He still can say those things. He's being generous with the time, believe me. Go with what he says." The words come at her one at a time. Pellets. Stones. Rocks. Submit, bow down. Be nice. Are these choices? She nods once.

"Mrs. Sloan?" the judge says when she's turned back to face him. He's removed the half glasses. "Can you transfer Jason to your husband's care by eight o'clock this evening, or do you need Ms. Donovan to help you through that transition?"

"I can do it," Rosie declares. She wants that woman to stay far, far away.

"Good. Any other questions?" Mannon asks.

What she wants to ask is, How can you think I'm hurting my child? And then, Is it because it's true, have I been a monster, have I done terrible things to him?

"Mr. Sloan, do you understand the conditions?" the judge asks, moving on.

"Yes, sir." Quinn's voice sounds completely unfamiliar to Rosie.

"Mrs. Sloan, I must warn you that if you disobey this court order, I will have you held in contempt."

She can't form the words for an answer. She nods her head once.

"Mr. Fisher, I will be forced to confine your client if she violates this ruling. Understood?"

"Yes, sir."

"Gentlemen, thank you for your efficiency," Judge Mannon says.

"And you for yours," Burden declares, getting in, as is the habit of state attorneys, the true last words.

CHAPTER EIGHTEEN

ROSIE DOESN'T REMEMBER HOW SHE GOT from the courtroom to the parking lot. She can't remember if her shoes slipped along the corridor, if Ted was running next to her the whole time, or if he's only just come alongside her now. All she knows is that she needs to get to her car, to get to Jason.

Quinn's there, down at the other end of the parking lot, standing by her car. He heads toward Rosie and Ted moving so fast, his open topcoat lifts behind him like a hang glider. "Jesus, Fisher," he shouts when he's still thirty feet away. "You didn't say anything about Rosie not seeing him. Did you know, Rosie? Did he say anything to you?" Rosie shakes her head: there's no way she can speak yet.

"Quinn, I'm really sorry, I did what I could." Ted is extending his hands in a conciliatory gesture toward the other man.

"Don't give me that shit, Fisher," he says, plunging toward the attorney, thrusting the man's hands away. "You completely screwed this up. Why didn't you say something to me or to Rosie, that this might happen?"

"I swear, I had no idea it was coming."

"What the fuck kind of lawyer are you that you didn't know this could happen, that you didn't do something about it?" He brings his fist down against the roof of a blue Buick.

Rosie's begun to cry. Back inside the courthouse Ted said to her, "There's nothing we can do except follow the court orders."

"Look, Quinn," Ted says, his voice edgier than before, "this is a political thing. The papers have been dredging up all they can on a couple of abuse cases in the state where kids were returned to their homes and then died. Mannon probably saw this as an opportunity to become the new voice of the other side; the good guy stemming the tide of permissiveness or something."

"And why did you let him put her up there, open up all that autopsy stuff?" Quinn bellows at the attorney.

"I had no choice, Quinn. Abby's death is a matter of public record."

Quinn shakes his head.

"Why didn't you call witnesses? Why didn't you fight him?"

"I didn't want to give Burden any more of your life to shred."

Rosie finds her key, heads toward her own car, then fumbles with the lock. If she can just sit down, she thinks, she'll be okay. She'll be able to stop shaking. "I'm going," she shouts at the two men through the open window. "I want to have as much time with Jay as I can."

Quinn says, "Drive carefully," and something more that she misses over the sound of the engine starting up. It doesn't matter, she thinks. Nothing does.

ROSIE IS ROCKING JASON. NORMALLY HE wouldn't sit still for so long with her, but they sit now, waiting for Quinn in the darkening room, lulled, the two of them, into an almost trancelike state, their bodies drifting through space together. He knows, she thinks, though she hasn't told him, hasn't been able to find the words yet that would fix the image for his two-year-old mind and also not frighten him. I am leaving you, she is thinking, because that is what it will seem to him, she's sure of that.

She wants to hide him. She has imagined it: pushing him under a bed, a finger across her lips, urging him to silence.

She's gone over all the possibilities, real and otherwise, of how to conceal him: boxes, closets, basements, attics, airplanes, and trains. I'll go to jail, I don't care, she thinks, and for a few seconds—no longer than that—she feels victorious over them; over Ms. Donovan, Attorney Burden, and Judge Mannon; all of them, till she makes the sad final connection: In jail, she will not have Jay, either.

She has no fear for his safety. She knows that with his father Jason will be happy, safe, and loved. It's losing him that she cannot bear. What will she do with her days without him? What will he remember of her after sixty turns of the sun and moon? How much will he hate her for her desertion? How long will it take him to forgive her? *Will* he forgive her?

Quinn knocks. He doesn't use the doorbell, as though he knows instinctively not to shatter the quiet of their cocoon too jarringly. She rises, Jay still in her arms. When she opens the door, the baby turns his eyes back against her chest, against the assault of the porch light.

"I was thinking," Quinn says when he's stepped into the living room, "this probably wouldn't have happened if we hadn't split. They wouldn't have a case, would they?"

Though she hadn't thought of it before, she knows he's right. Her attorney was wrong, they shouldn't have emphasized the conflict between them. They should have come back together, united, shown the world that they were a team, even if they weren't.

"Jay," she says, talking over the ache in her face that has formed out of tears waiting to be allowed to flow, "you want to go sleep in Daddy's new house tonight?"

"Daddy's new house," he says, nodding, smiling, reaching for Quinn.

"Listen," Quinn says to her, "who's going to know if you stop by once in a while?"

"Are you serious?" she says to him. "You'd let me do that?"

He seems to hesitate for a moment, then says, "I know something about my child's best interest, I think. I don't want him to lose contact with you."

"What about the neighbors?"

"We'll be careful. Anyway, nobody there knows me or the situation. Come by at night. You can come through the sliders in the back. Maybe a couple times a week." She nods. It's not so bad now. She's going to see him. She kisses Jay.

"I love you, sweetpie," she whispers, her lips close by his cheek.

"I love *you*," he says exuberantly, then turns in Quinn's arms and lays his small fingers against his father's face. "I love *you*," he says. Quinn kisses the child's head. At least she can see him, she tells herself, taking a step back, beginning this new phase.

"His clothes and meds," Rosie says, handing Quinn the huge plastic bag that has been leaning up against the wall. "Call me if he needs more. He could grow and not fit any of these," she says, and the ache is there again, the tears clamoring to escape.

"We'll talk," Quinn says, and then they're gone.

ROSIE FEELS AS THOUGH SHE HAS TO BE careful how she schedules the visits with Jason that Quinn has offered her. She doesn't want to use them up too fast. A couple of times a week, he said. That works out to about every three days. She's told herself she ought to wait till Jason has been gone three days, but now, less than twenty-four hours since she let her child out of her arms, all she can think about is when she's going to see him again. Maybe if she sees him tonight, then she'll be more relaxed about waiting three days till the next visit, she rationalizes.

She dials Quinn's number. "Hello," a woman's voice says.

"Who's this?" Rosie asks, too startled to be polite. The woman doesn't answer right away. "Just let me speak to Quinn," Rosie says.

"He's not here right now. May I take a message?" Rosie's puzzled. She just assumed it was Diana, and that Quinn was hovering in the background, but maybe he's left Jason with a baby-sitter.

"Is this Diana?"

"Yes. Who's this?"

"Rosie Sloan. Where's Quinn?"

"At work. I'm sitting for Jason." Rosie feels like she can't get enough air, like somebody's sucked all the oxygen out of the room. Like how Jason must feel, she thinks. "Do you want to leave a message?" the voice at the other end asks.

"When's he due back?" Rosie manages to ask, though her voice is compressed into a thin remnant of itself.

"Just after midnight."

"Never mind, I'll call him at work," she says. Damn her, Rosie thinks, tears biting at her lower lids as she pushes the flash button and presses in the numbers for police headquarters.

"How can you leave Jason with her?" Rosie asks the instant she's got him on the phone.

"I needed a sitter, she said she'd do it."

"You're giving her *my* baby, Quinn. *I* can't have him but she can—do you know what that feels like?"

"Hey, I'm not the one who took Jason from you, remember. I'm not the bad guy here. I'm just trying to work it out for all of us. I'm operating at basic survival level right now."

"I don't want her with him."

"Listen, Rosie. I'll check the ads tonight when I get home, but if you want my honest opinion, he's better off with her than some nobody I could pick out of the classifieds. He knows her and he likes her."

"*I* don't know her."

"Well, then, meet her. Talk to her. She's doing us a huge favor, Rosie. She's working her regular job and this one, too, to help us out."

Right, Rosie thinks. The "work" she's doing is working her way into your life. "I wanted to see him tonight," she complains.

"We'll do it tomorrow night," he says, his voice becoming quieter, reminding her of the need for caution about their illegal arrangement.

"Okay," she says, and she's breathing real air again. Tomorrow's not so bad. Just one more night to get through. "How'd he do last night and today?" she asks him.

159

"He's good. He misses you and asks for you, but everything's fine."

Rosie is about to ask for details, to ask whether he slept well, what he ate, when Quinn says, "I gotta go."

She hears the click, the severing of their connection.

She's about to return the receiver to its place on the wall when she remembers what he said about how she should meet Diana. So meet her, he said. She punches in Quinn's home phone again before she can reconsider.

IT IS SO EARLY WHEN ROSIE DRIVES TO THE new Prospect Diner to meet Diana for breakfast the next morning, it is still dark outside. This is the only time—before work—that Diana can meet, and even so, it will have to be short, Diana has warned. Just as well, Rosie thinks, wondering why she's gotten herself into this. It will fill some of the time between now and seeing Jason, she tells herself.

Rosie picks out Diana the second she enters The Prospect. It is partly her youth but it is also partly that she's got her hands thrust deep in the pockets of her coat, burying herself in the folds of down, looking like she wished she could disappear. Rosie waves at her, trying to look like an ever-so-upbeat welcoming committee of one and catches her eye. The girl hesitates for a second but then walks over to Rosie's booth, approaching it more sideways than straight on, like she might change her mind and turn and run. But she does sit down. She even smiles, though that is truly fleeting.

"It was very nice of you to do this," Rosie says when Diana is seated opposite her. "I know it's hard." Rosie listens to herself gushing over this child-woman. She needs to tone it down.

Diana doesn't say anything, tacitly agreeing that she's mightily put out. She unzips her coat but doesn't take it off, perhaps, Rosie thinks, so she can flee quickly, if necessary. This girl-woman has perfect skin, firm as a baby's, and flushed in just the right places so she doesn't need any blusher. Her hands have found their way back into their pocket hiding places. Rosie wants to know exactly how old she is, how many years separate her and Quinn, but she knows it would be a mistake to ask.

A waiter dressed in black slacks, a white shirt, and a black bow tie that's badly tilted has suddenly appeared at their booth. "Welcome, ladies," he says, greeting them rather too exuberantly. "We've got a triple egg special this morning. Same price as the double," he says as he hands them their menus.

"I'll have two eggs over easy and toast," Rosie says, not even looking at the menu. "Unless you want more time," she says apologetically to Diana, who is still scanning the food list.

"Oh, no," the young woman says. "I can just order pancakes."

"And bacon?" the waiter asks.

"Sure," she says. "And coffee."

"You want the three eggs?" the waiter asks Rosie.

She turns down his offer of more cholesterol, but adds orange juice and coffee to her order.

"I don't know why I ordered such a big breakfast," Diana says when he's moved on. "Pancakes and bacon is ridiculous. I definitely don't need the calories. Usually, when I'm home, I just have coffee and toast. I shouldn't be having all this."

"But you're so thin, you don't need to be careful," Rosie says, gushing again, but it's true. She's one of those blonde waif types. Her puffy pink jacket dwarfs her and makes her body look like an afterthought to her clothing.

Diana shrugs. "Maybe. But it catches up for everybody, eventually. Sugar, flour, fat, maple syrup. Oh, my God, and bacon," she says with clear disgust with herself. "I can't believe I ordered bacon. That's so bad. I should have just had the coffee and toast." She's pulling the edge of the next napkin out through the opening of the metal dispenser.

"I figure in winter, anything's okay if it makes you feel better," Rosie assures her. "If bacon and maple syrup do it, great. With it being dark and cold so much of the time, I mean. I couldn't believe I had to drive here in the dark." Diana starts to nod, but it becomes a more ambiguous gesture, a mix of nod, shake, and shrug. Now that she's taken her hands out of her pockets, she's touched almost everything on the table; the cards encased in plastic that advertise wine and food, the napkin dispenser, the salt and pepper shakers, the silverware. She pulls a napkin partway out of the metal holder, then pushes it back in.

"Why'd you want to get together?" Diana asks suddenly.

The waiter reappears with their beverages.

Rosie sips her juice and looks at Diana. The younger woman has finally pulled a napkin all the way out of the dispenser and she's folding it into odd shapes, stroking it smooth after each new mutation. "So?" Diana asks again. "Why'd you ask me here?"

"To meet you, like I said on the phone. You're with Jason a lot. It seemed like we should know each other, not avoid each other." Diana nods. There's a wee hint of a smile. "So, tell me about yourself."

Diana shrugs. "I don't know what to tell."

"I could ask questions, then you could ask me questions, I guess."

"Sure," Diana agrees.

"Okay, what kind of work do you do?"

"I'm a teacher's aide. At Parkland School. In the special-ed classroom."

"Do you like it?" Rosie tears open a sugar packet and taps the contents into her cup.

She shrugs. "I liked it better last year, when I was in with the regular kindergarten. I liked that better."

"How old are the kids you have now?"

"All ages. Up through about twelve. But I like the little ones better. The younger the better for me."

"Like Jason," Rosie says.

"Yeah." Diana tilts her head to one side and smiles for an instant before her expression goes dark again. Like she's remembered that Rosie might not be too thrilled with her passion for Jason. "I might do nursery school next year if I can't get back into the kindergarten," she says solemnly.

The waiter has delivered their food. Rosie's pleased to see that her eggs are done just the way she likes them, so that when she cuts into the yolk it still runs, but not a lot. One side of the plate is mounded with hash browns, the other with very buttery toast. Diana spreads her scoop of butter out over her griddle cakes, then pours syrup over the top till it runs down and forms a sweet moat around them. She cuts a wedge out of her stack, then one by one, peels the different layers of pancake off the fork with her teeth.

"What kind of problems do the kids in your class have?" Rosie asks her as she sprinkles salt and pepper over her eggs.

"All different stuff. There's not enough money to separate out the different kinds of problems—you know, not enough money for as many classrooms as they really should have—so we have learning disabled, retarded, cerebral palsy, and physically handicapped all in one room. Of course, lots of them have more than one thing, so I guess it gets complicated how you *would* sort them if you could, but still, they shouldn't have physically challenged kids in with retarded ones." The young woman seems genuinely animated now.

"So you've got kids with some pretty serious problems in there?"

"Oh, yeah. Not custodial or anything, but heavy stuff."

"How do parents deal with that? I mean, asthma's hard enough," Rosie says as she spears some of her hash browns.

"You see a lot of different attitudes. Most of the parents, I'd say, they're more intense than parents of normal kids, more emotional, you know? I feel bad for them, what they have to deal with, but you can't let that kind of sympathy interfere. You have to get in there, tell them when they're on the wrong track, and sometimes—"

"Diana," Rosie breaks in, "did you call the Department of Children and Families about me?" This has only occurred to Rosie this second while she was watching Diana come alive talking about those other seemingly misguided parents.

"No." Rosie watches the color rise through Diana's face; the small pink cheek areas spread and darken. She's poking at the stack now, making row after orderly row of holes in the top pancake with the tines of the fork.

But it makes perfect sense to Rosie. It was the professional thing to do. Report an erring, intense, overly emotional parent.

"I think you did," Rosie insists. Diana shakes her head. Her fingers tighten around the fork and it sinks slowly deeper into the stack. Rosie speaks softly: "I know you did it, Diana."

The young woman pulls the fork out of the cake and points it at Rosie. "Stop it," she says.

"I'm not mad at you," Rosie tells her, gathering speed. "I'm not mad because I understand you were concerned about Jason." This part is a lie. Rosie's seething, and she's probably not hiding it very effectively, but she's going to keep on trying.

Diana is shaking her head. "You stop it or I'm getting up and leaving. I didn't do anything. I wouldn't've come here if I thought you were going to do this to me. I don't need this shit. Why would I report you? I didn't even ever meet you till today."

Rosie doesn't want to say, Because you're in love with Quinn. She's afraid that if she says it, Diana might say it's true. Instead, she says, "You knew *about* me. You knew I was married to Quinn. You wanted me out of his life. Out of his son's life."

"You're saying I did this out of jealousy or something?" She's pointing the fork at herself now.

Rosie nods. "Jason's with you now. He's *my* child and he's with you."

"Look, I didn't do this, okay? I'm sorry you can't see your child, but I didn't do it. I didn't call anybody."

"Yes, you did," Rosie says, leaning closer to her, jabbing the words right at her. Diana shakes her head. She's biting her lower lip. Rosie's sure that if she keeps the pressure on just a little longer, the girl will give it all up.

"You were worried about Jason, I know, and I'm glad of that." Diana's still shaking her head. "And probably everybody at work, all the teachers, kept telling you to do it, right?"

"Do what?" Diana says, and it's loud; a real outburst. People turn in their direction.

"Call the Department of Children and Families."

"I don't even know what that is."

Now Rosie's almost certain she's got to be lying. Wouldn't every special-ed teacher's aide know about that? "I can find out, even if you don't tell me," she says. This is a complete bluff. "The social worker told me if I suspect someone, and tell her, she'll confirm for me if that's the one who made the complaint. So I think I'll just mention your name, see how that flies."

"I'm getting out of here," Diana says, pushing herself out along the bench. She's pulling crumpled dollar bills out of her parka pocket. "You're sick, you know that?" she says, tossing the singles onto the table and heading out, straight out, much faster than she came in.

When she's gone, Rosie realizes that her heart's pounding and she's breathing like she just ran a mile. The girl hadn't given an inch, but Rosie had kept on, going at her with such force. How did she get so out of control? Maybe I am sick, she thinks. All the diner patrons have turned in their seats. How long have they been watching her and Diana? The place has gone so quiet, she can hear herself breathe. She lowers her head and tries to concentrate on her eggs and hash browns, but they float uneasily in the mist that rises up in her eyes. If she can act this strange, what else can she be doing that she shouldn't be doing?

CHAPTER NINETEEN

QUINN HAS HEARD, OF COURSE, ABOUT THE
episode at The Prospect Diner. Rosie doesn't much care just
now. She's got Jason on her lap and they're singing, "The Itsy
Bitsy Spider." She loves watching his little hands trying to
twist and turn the right way. She loves the way his voice war-
bles over the words. "Kisses?" she says to him at the end of the
song, and he lifts his head, puts his wet lips against her cheek,
then turns his face toward her so that she can bestow a kiss
upon him.

Rosie's car is parked a block down, and she's come in, as
Quinn advised, through the slider. Now he wants to extract
promises from her that she won't try to contact Diana anymore.
He says he has talked his friend out of getting an injunction
against his wife, but only if Rosie swears she won't try to contact her again.

"You're the one who told me to go meet her," she protests.

"*Meet her,* I said, not attack her."

"I told you, I'm sorry. This isn't the easiest arrangement
for me."

"I know that."

"Just tell her to cut up the strawberries before she gives them
to him. He could choke on those whole berries."

"Enough, Rosie," he warns.

"More spider, Mommy," Jason says, reaching for her hands,
touching his fingertips against her palm, and she is happy to

launch into the song once more, glad to be able to stop talking about Diana.

"I guess I should wash the dishes," Quinn says. "You got here before I had a chance to clean up." She nods. "So I can tell Diana you agree, right?"

"I'll leave her alone, Quinn. Just tell me when she's going to be here, and I won't even call."

"Good," he says, and starts toward the kitchen.

"Just you and me against the world now," she says to Jay when Quinn has passed out of sight, and like so many things these days, her own words bring tears to her eyes.

THE FOLLOWING AFTERNOON, WHEN ROSIE hears Quinn's voice on the phone, she knows something's wrong. "Rosie," he says, and it sounds distorted, not like her name at all. "Rosie, your lawyer wants to see us both in his office. He called me because he couldn't get through on your line."

"I was talking to Beth," she explains.

"Can she take Jason? He says I can't bring him to the office because you'll be there."

She almost says, *What about your girlfriend?* But catches herself, knowing that saying it would serve only one purpose—to anger Quinn. "I think she'll take him, but why do we have to do this?"

"He has new information from the judge, he says."

"And he wouldn't give it to you on the phone?"

"No."

"Quinn, that has to mean it's bad."

"I know. Call Beth. Let me know if she can't do it, otherwise I'll meet you at Ted's office in half an hour."

THEY HAVE TO WAIT FOR TED. ALICE, THE secretary he shares with the accountant and the psychologist, suggests they take seats out in the hallway. "Does he know we're here?" Quinn growls at her.

"I'm going to tell him right now," Alice says, her finger poised over a button.

"Does he have somebody else in there with him?"

"Yes, he does, but he's expecting you, so I'm sure he won't be long."

They move out into the hallway, and they both sit, but Quinn is up and moving within a few seconds. Rosie's just about to jump up herself when she sees Ted's office door open and the attorney emerge with another man. They're laughing together and Rosie finds that gratifying. How bad could it be, she thinks, if Ted's able to laugh?

"Come on in," he says to them when this last client has disappeared. He moves behind his desk, takes a seat. "Glad you could get here so quickly," he begins, not really even looking directly at either of them but more at the space between them, so Rosie knows it's going to be really bad. Neither of them has thought to slip out of their heavy coats. "So," Ted says, and then clears his throat, "the judge has issued an emergency order removing Jason from your care, Quinn, because there's evidence that you gave Rosie access to him in violation of the original order."

Rosie and Quinn stare at him in silence for a few beats of their hearts. "What do you mean?" Quinn finally asks. "Where does he go now?"

"Foster care," Ted says quietly.

"Jesus, Fisher, foster care?" He's gripping the arms of his chair.

"What if I deny I did it?" Rosie asks.

"You'll have to go into court and they'll ask you directly when you're under oath if you violated the judge's instructions. I don't know what evidence they've got, but they've got something. I also don't know whether you did this or not, but I can tell you that if you go into that courtroom and you perjure yourself and they can prove you did, frankly, I don't know when you'll see your child again."

"Damn it, Fisher, you never said they could put him in foster care."

"You never said you'd violate the order, now, did you?"

"Who knew?" Rosie says, turning to Quinn.

"Stop," he says quietly, though his eyes blaze out a clear warning.

"Did you tell Diana? Did you?"

"Rosie, stop," Quinn says, and this time she can feel the bitter edge of his anger reaching for her.

"Why? Let's stop playing games. I went over there, and it's obvious that Ted knows that. Did you tell Diana I was there?"

"It's not Diana."

"Ted," Rosie says, turning to the lawyer "it's Quinn's girl-friend who must have reported it. She's jealous, that's all."

"Jealousy's not a crime, Rosie," Ted says. "Her motivation doesn't matter. Disobeying a court order, on the other hand, *is* a crime: contempt of court. You're lucky Mannon isn't putting you summarily in jail."

"Tell him to put me in jail. That's what he said he'd do if I violated the order. I'm the one who committed the crime, so they should punish me, not Jay. They can't take it out on him, he's just a baby."

"Mannon warned you in court not to cross him. He warned you repeatedly." The attorney has stood up, distancing himself, Rosie knows, from her.

She stands, too, so she can meet his eyes. "Fine, I'll pay, but not my child."

"The court is doing what it thinks is best for your child."

"Bullshit," Quinn says, on his feet now, too. "You know it's bullshit, Fisher. They're going for maximum pain here, that's all."

"Wait," Rosie says, holding a hand between them as Quinn begins to close the distance. "What about Beth? My sister, Beth. She could take him." She looks over at Quinn. He's got his eyebrows raised, and he's nodding toward Fisher, con-firming the validity of her suggestion.

"Rosie, listen to me," Ted says, "Mannon's not going to let anyone you know have Jason anymore. As it is, only Quinn can have supervised visitation from now on. Limited visitation."

"What?" Rosie blurts out.

"How limited?" Quinn asks.

"Three, four times a week is typical. You'll have to set it up with the social worker."

"That's not enough," he says, rising out of his chair.

"Mannon kept the order to sixty days—all in all, he's been pretty lenient."

"Oh, Christ, Fisher, don't give me that patronizing shit." He heads toward the door. Rosie's just about to scream at him that he shouldn't be running out on this when he turns back toward them again. "Oh, Jesus," Quinn says. He hits himself in the forehead with the palm of his hand. "Oh, Jesus," he says, again, rubbing his forehead across his palm. "I don't know what I'm going to do." He takes a few disordered steps away, then stops. "I'm going to Beth's and I'm taking him," he announces.

"No," Ted says, raising a hand in warning. "Don't do that. You'll be arrested."

"I'll take him somewhere," he says, lunging forward, closing in on Ted, edging the lawyer back. "You've screwed this up so bad, I have to. I'm not giving my child up to the state." Quinn looks so huge and defiant, Rosie thinks he's going to knock Ted to the floor.

"Quinn, you know that's not going to work. You're a police officer. You know."

"Oh, shit." Quinn bays toward the ceiling. Then he's quiet for a while. When he speaks again, it's in a much softer, sadder voice. "Rosie," he says, reaching for her, one hand first, tentatively, pulling her to standing, then both hands on her shoulders, and he moves closer till he's against her stiff, resisting body, and she lets him stay. She leans her head against his chest, and she's thinking about their baby, about when he was born and how his tiny wail of complaint about being thrust into that cold and too-well-lit room made her and Quinn cry out, too, for love of him, for this baby they didn't even know yet, who had come to rescue them and make a family of them again. Quinn wraps his open coat around her, enclosing her, so they're both inside the heat of it, and he's swaying, almost rocking, riding out the pain, and they're moving together. "Jesus, Rosie," he says. She slides her arms around him.

"Guys," Ted says after a few moments. "They want the baby

this afternoon. If you want time with him, you probably should get moving. The judge gave permission for Rosie to be there for the transfer. I think I should be there, you know, as a witness, in case there's any questions that come up later about what went on." They still stand together, still moving slightly from side to side. "Come on," Ted urges, a hand on her shoulder.

WHAT CAN SHE SAY TO JASON? "WE HAVE TO do this, honey. Mommy loves you, Daddy loves you, but . . ." But what? "You have to go stay somewhere else for a few days." She won't say sixty days. He wouldn't comprehend that amount of time, anyway. May Donovan is waiting over by the door, Jason's suitcase next to her, her arms eager to lift him from her. Rosie kisses her child, her lips touching one cheek and then the other and he puts a hand on her face, exploring it, following out the shape of her nose, her cheeks, her mouth, laughing with thrilled delight when she makes a playful grab for his fingers with her teeth. "You'll be back with me soon," she says. "And Daddy will visit you whenever he can."

"Yes," Quinn says. "We'll do some special things, too." He leans toward his child and strokes his head.

"You'll have a good time," she says, and she has no idea what he's hearing. What he's thinking. He's holding a small racing car, running it across his hand. He lifts her hand, runs the car along her skin. "Vrum, vrum," he says, and smiles at her. She closes her hand around his, car and all, and everything fits, he's still that small.

"In sixty days he could be in the next size," she says to Ms. Donovan.

"If the foster mother needs more, she'll contact us," the social worker says. The foster mother? Rosie hadn't imagined a single entity, a foster mother, yet. The person who would care for him, make all the decisions from now on. How can she survive two months without seeing him? How can this be happening to her, to Jason? It's like she's in some crazy maze, took a wrong turn and can't get back out.

Everyone cries. Beth has to leave the room. Jason tries to

171

squirm out of May Donovan's arms as soon as he's handed over. "Time to go," she says, her voice star bright, and he squirms more fiercely against her. When she starts to walk toward the door he calls out for Rosie. And then for his father. Quinn is carrying the suitcase and the shopping bag. "Maaaaaa," Jason protests when Ms. Donovan opens the front door. "It's okay," Rosie lies to him. She follows them down to the car, as does Quinn, though she knows that she probably shouldn't, for she's sobbing and just making the poor baby's agony worse, but she can't let him go yet. After he's in the safety seat, May shuts the door without—of course—saying what Rosie always says, "Hands up, Jay." He's done it anyway; drawn his hands away from the danger of the slamming door, put them on top of his head. He's done it even though he's sobbing. Rosie puts her hands on the car, feeling for him right through the cold green metal. There are tears all over his face and his hands reach and reach and reach through the air toward her. "Don't worry about us," Ms. Donovan says, bright again, shining, as she opens the driver's side door.

CHAPTER
TWENTY

MAY DONOVAN ISN'T AT HER DESK WHEN
Protective Services opens in the morning. There's just a message machine with the social worker's patronizing voice admonishing the caller to "Listen carefully" as she details her working hours. The message lies—it says Ms. Donovan should be there, and she isn't. It says that the social worker will return calls in the order in which they're received. Rosie figures that's a lie, too. She redials every five minutes. She hasn't gotten out of bed, and she hasn't eaten breakfast. She's watched *Good Morning, America* and *The Today Show* and she's been channel-surfing through the audience-participation talk shows too long already. At ten-twenty, May finally answers her phone.

"I've got good news," May says, and Rosie's heart skips around excitedly for a couple of seconds, thinking she's going to say it's all been a terrible mistake and the investigation's been called off.

"What?" she says, her voice a breathy whisper.

"Jason's all settled in and he's very comfortable. I'm very, very happy with the setting."

Rosie can't speak. He's really not coming home, that's what May Donovan is telling her. They've really gone ahead and done this, taken him from her, given him to another woman, another family.

"We've got him with a super woman, a real dynamo, named

Monica Delano," Ms. Donovan announces, making it sound as though Rosie should be familiar with the name. "She's had a lot of foster kids, so I'm delighted he's with her."

"What if he stops breathing?" Rosie asks.

"Soon as I get off the phone with you, I'll get in touch with the doctor and set up a time when he can meet with Monica and go over all the procedures."

"Will he do that today?"

"Well," she says, a light gurgling laugh sound mixing in, "I can't say till I talk to him. I'm going to ask that he try to do it ASAP, but doctors are notoriously overbooked, as well you must know."

"If Jason has a breathing problem, he needs help immediately. Not three days from now."

"Monica has Dr. Linder's number, of course. She has all the medications you gave me and all those other papers. She and I have gone over everything you went over with me, so it's not like she's operating in a vacuum, Mrs. Sloan. Nine-one-one is just three key strokes away, remember. And she's got lots and lots of experience with sick kids, that's why I worked long and hard to get her for Jason."

May's voice has lifted up at the end of her little speech, a bit of boastful advertising of herself. Rosie knows she wants to be thanked, but Rosie won't do it. She hates this woman for coming after her and her child to begin with, and nothing she says is going to change that.

"He had a very nice breakfast," May says.

"Was he there overnight?"

"Oh, yes. And he slept just fine, too. No coughing, apparently."

"Maybe," Rosie says, defending herself, she knows, against this not so subtle implication that Jason is actually doing better without her, "this Monica just didn't hear him."

"If she didn't hear him, I would suspect it's because the coughing wasn't very bad."

"Mothers hear children before anyone else does, you know."

"That may be. In any case, he's doing very well. When I

stopped in this morning he was wolfing down his Frosted Flakes."

"Frosted Flakes? That's like ninety-five percent sugar. Why can't she give him Cheerios, they have almost no sugar?"

"I'll mention it to Monica."

Sure she'll mention it. She'll say, "The weirdo mother doesn't want him eating sugar cereals." Monica and May will laugh together. They'll laugh because they know it doesn't matter what Rosie wants anymore. "He's still my child," Rosie protests.

"Yes, he is," May says, though it has a patina of query to it. Rosie knows she's being humored, nothing more.

"What about Quinn's visits?"

"Well, he has to call the Court Services section; they act as liaison with the foster mother."

"My attorney said you would know."

"Maybe he meant I would know how to direct you."

"Quinn can't just call this woman, this Monica?"

"No. Mrs. Sloan, I'm going to have to hang up now because I've got a client here who needs my help."

I need your help, she wants to shout at her, but instead she says, "I need the information on this woman, the address, the telephone number."

"Mrs. Sloan, you aren't allowed contact with Jason, remember?" It's the patronizing voice again. The *listen carefully* words that she has on her message tape.

"But I can call and talk to Jason, can't I?"

"No."

"You're not serious? What can I do to him over the phone?" She's about to say, Even *you* can see I can't do anything through the telephone wires, but she holds back on the insult, knowing it will only make this woman feel morally superior to her. That it will be used as further evidence against her to the judge.

"The judge said *no contact*, Mrs. Sloan."

"But do you *know* that he meant no phone calls? What if I call *her*, this Monica? Can't I talk to her, ask her how my child is doing?"

"Once you have the number, yes. But you get that through Court Services, not me. Now, I really, really need to go. May I call you back, Mrs. Sloan?"

"Have you ever had a case like this before where a judge ordered no contact?"

"Mrs. Sloan, I suggest we stick to *this* case. There's nothing to be gained by looking at any other situations."

"What about precedent, isn't that important?"

"Precedent may not favor your position, Mrs. Sloan. Maybe you should discuss it with your attorney."

"Fine," Rosie agrees. "I'll do that."

"And, Mrs. Sloan?" the social worker says, "please, don't worry, he's absolutely, absolutely fine." She pronounces the second *absolutely* as though it has an inordinate number of syllables.

The effect is so cute, Rosie cringes. She slams the phone down and pushes herself out of bed. "What am I going to do?" she says aloud, her hands clasped together, her eyes turned upward.

The phone rings. It's Quinn. "Have you heard anything?" he asks. She tells him what she knows, how very little she knows. "He's with a family named Delano. The mother's name is Monica Delano. But Donovan won't give me the address or telephone number." Rosie pulls a phone book from her desk drawer and starts leafing through the D listing. "She's not in the book, Quinn. There's no Delanos."

"Try different spellings."

"How else could you spell it except D-e-l-a-n-o?"

"I don't know. D-I, maybe?"

Rosie turns the page. "Nothing."

"I'll figure out some way to get it. What town is she in?"

"I don't know."

"They'll have to give me the information for visitation; but who knows when they'll get around to telling me about that."

"You have to call the services part of the agency, Quinn."

"I did call, Rosie, I called first thing, but they won't tell me a goddamn thing. They said they have to negotiate with the foster family and, as of twenty minutes ago, they didn't even know who that was. They basically told me to stop calling them."

"Screw them. It's our child. He needs to see you, he must be scared out of his mind. He doesn't understand why he's where he is, why we deserted him. Call them back and tell them you know who the foster mother is and they should damn well get going on it."

"I'll do that, but you know that's not going to help, you know it has to be done in some time-honored, state-approved way, which sure as hell is going to involve that bitchy blonde woman and a lot of forms."

"Quinn, he could stop breathing while they fill out forms."

Quinn doesn't answer right away. "I know."

"What if this Delano woman just tells him to calm down when he has an attack? What if she doesn't want to be bothered going to the emergency room when it's dark or cold or raining? What if she thinks it's impolite to call doctors in the middle of the night? And let's be realistic, she's not his mother, she's just getting paid some allowance to take care of him. Acute illnesses are way above and beyond; she's not going to do it. Nobody but a parent would."

"Rosie, I don't know what to say. I feel like I'm going to collapse, I'm so shaky. I didn't sleep last night thinking about him. I just frankly don't know what to do next." She listens to his sigh, and then, to his silence. "Rosie," he says after a while, "would you go somewhere with me, have coffee or a drink? I need to get out of here for a while."

Rosie has a moment's panic, thinking May will call back and if she goes out she'll miss the call, but when she starts to answer, she says, "Sure," surprising herself. "We've got to work this out," she says, more to herself than to him. "We've got to have some approach because the state's just going to make him disappear out of our lives if we don't."

"You want to meet at Louie's for a drink?"

"No," she says. "We need lunch. We need focus. Meet me at The Prospect Diner in half an hour."

CHAPTER
TWENTY-ONE

QUINN ORDERS FOR THE TWO OF THEM. Steak sandwiches rare, sautéed onions, and chocolate milk shakes. He hasn't consulted her on the details, but he doesn't need to. Rare, onions, and chocolate are what she will want. The food comes fast and arrives hot. They are well into their sandwiches before either of them speaks again.

"What gets me," she says as she salts her french fries, "is how careful we were to protect him, how we screened every baby-sitter, how we interviewed all those day-care workers. And now he's with somebody we've never met, and he's with her twenty-four hours a day. We don't know where she lives or who lives there with her or what kind of hazards she's got in her house. She could have a cat or a bird or a rabbit that could be making him not be able to breathe. Anything could happen to him. She could leave him with some drunken nitwit if she wants to. She could leave him *alone*. How would we even know?" Her voice catches in her throat. Faster than lightning, she sees Jason dash into the street: nobody is holding his hand.

Quinn lowers his head, lets his eyes close for a few seconds. "I don't know," he says, drawing in a deep breath. He rubs the heel of his hand across the left side of his chest. "I've been thinking about Abby again," he says, shaking his head.

Rosie turns her eyes away, looking at the blackboard specials, reading about BLTs with Canadian bacon and Manhattan clam chowder. So she doesn't have to remember her firstborn lying lifeless in her crib. "You don't think I'm hurting Jay, do you?" she asks after she's read through the specials so many times she's pretty much got them memorized. "That prosecutor—or whatever he's called—he made it sound like I was poisoning him." She feels her face flush hot hearing the accusation again.

"No. Something's just got out of control."

"Yeah, caseworkers, lawyers, courts, judges," she enumerates slowly, making it sound sonorous as a litany. He nods, then sips his milk shake.

She remembers the stillness in the house after their baby died. As though everything—themselves included—were frozen in place around the moment when their infant ceased to breathe; frozen into a deadly tableau with her. She and Quinn didn't touch; didn't speak. And then the investigators barreled in, shattering the silence with their endless questions and accusations: their noise was unbearable. Then silence, again, an explosion of it, when suddenly the questions were finished.

"They can all go to hell, fucking with our lives this way," Quinn says, tossing the rest of his sandwich down on the plate. She watches the roll fall away, the different parts that had made up the whole drift from one another.

"So," he says after a few moments, "what do we do next?" He reassembles his sandwich, then pulls a napkin from the dispenser and wipes his hands.

She shrugs. "Maybe you could run a motor vehicles department check to try to get the address and telephone number." He nods, then glances around, checking, she knows, to see if anyone's heard her suggestion.

Rosie drags a french fry through the puddle of ketchup on her plate. She's thinking about Jay, about how he eats his french fries, how he sucks the whole length of them for the salt and ketchup, never really getting around to eating the potato part. She's remembering, too, how he sucked on the too-large strawberry Diana had given him; how easily he could have choked on it. She feels shivery, remembering it; remembering that strawberry that was big enough to stop

179

his breathing. "Did Diana give Jason his meals?" she asks suddenly.

He shrugs. "Yeah, I guess so." His response sounds unfinished, like he's asking her what exactly she really wants to know.

"Maybe she gave him something extra."

"What are you talking about?"

"Like the accusation against me. Maybe she gave him chocolate, like they said *I* did. She knew it would set him off. You're the one who said she knows all about allergies." Quinn shakes his head. Rosie leans closer, across the table. "Quinn, jealousy's incredibly evil."

Her husband pushes his milk shake aside. "Look, I know you hate her, but she's not evil. I don't believe she'd ever make him sick."

"Quinn, you're a cop. You know what people can do. Look at it like a police officer, not a lover, for a minute." The word makes her cheeks burn. "Face it, she had the wherewithal, the access to him, the knowledge about allergies."

He's still shaking his head. He hasn't said: She isn't my lover. "Rosie, this sounds nuts."

"Can you swear she wouldn't do it? Are you that sure? Do you know her well enough, do you know enough about her to know that she absolutely, positively couldn't have done it?"

He's silent for a few moments. "I don't know." She nods emphatically. "Maybe I didn't really spend that much time with her."

"And it was mostly in bed, wasn't it?"

He leans his head against his hand, like he's sheltering his eyes from the sun, or from what she's saying. When he looks up, he says, "The whole thing . . ." but doesn't finish the sentence. "I don't know." He's moving the straw around in the thick liquid. "I don't honestly think it's any more likely she did it than you did it. People get angry when they're jealous, but they don't hurt other people unless they're sick. I don't think you're sick, and I don't think she is, either."

This is a long speech for Quinn, a very long one. Rosie's caught off guard by it, distracted from the content.

"Do you think she blew the whistle on us, got word to the judge?"

"She says no. I'm choosing to believe her." Quinn turns sideways so he can see the clock high above the wall over the counter area. "I think I'll try the Court Services people again," he says, and slides out of the booth toward the back of the diner. There's a pay phone back there that he's already used once to try to make some inroads on the visitation question. Rosie's thinking about the time she was here with Diana. She wishes she'd thought to ask her then, "Did you slip chocolate to my child?" She could have surprised her with the accusation, caught her unaware. But the girl would have run, not answered that question, either. She remembers how Diana had slid back out of sight into the kitchen that night when she picked up Jay and the way she had seemed to want to dive into the pockets of that too-big parka. She's keeping close; keeping secretive.

Enough of that, Rosie thinks to herself. Why was she making so much of Diana? She didn't even have access to Jason anymore. Or did she? Rosie and Quinn couldn't see him, but there was nothing in the order that prevented anyone else from visiting him as far as she knew.

"I got the address," Quinn says, startling her. She hasn't seen him approach. He shows her a paper napkin on which he's scrawled an address and telephone number. At the bottom, it says *4:00*.

"You're going out there at four?"

"No, I'm supposed to call her then and set up the times. They said I can only go out there two days a week and the foster mother has to be present the entire time. I have to be supervised."

"You're kidding."

He shakes his head. "And it's to be at *her* convenience."

"Two days? He needs to see you more than that, Quinn."

"It doesn't matter what you or I think anymore. Not for at least two months, anyway."

At least? she thinks. It hadn't occurred to her that two months, horrible as that was, might not be the end of it. They would keep him after that, wouldn't they? They would say she

was mad, wouldn't they? No, she thinks, refusing to let her
mind settle on that, two months, that's all. "How long do you
get to be with him each time?"

"Two hours."

She's shaking her head. "Two months of this? Two months
of him being with a stranger twenty-four hours a day, and
seeing you, what is it? A total of eight hours a month?"

"Sixteen. I already did that multiplication."

"Sixteen. He's with her hundreds, maybe thousands of
hours. He's too young for this."

"They said in a month they could increase it if everybody's
willing."

"You mean if this foster mother condescends to give the seal
of approval?"

"I guess that's what it means."

Rosie picks up another fry and drags it through the ketchup.
Quinn's motioning to the waiter for a check when Rosie
remembers about Diana. "Quinn, listen, when you were on the
phone I was thinking about how anybody can go see Jason. I
mean we can't, but anybody else can, right?"

"So?"

"That means Diana can, too. I know you don't think she did
anything, but I'm not so convinced. Supposing she wanted to
get access to him, she could just go out there, and there'd be
nothing to stop her from seeing him. Taking him for a ride
somewhere." Quinn is looking at her, not saying anything.
"Feeding him something."

She sees the set of his jaw pulled so far forward that he looks
like an altogether different person. He isn't convinced of
Diana's innocence, Rosie can see that. "I want to call this
woman, tell her not to let Diana take him."

"Okay," he concedes. Rosie starts to slide out of the booth.
"Wait a second," he says, "how can she get the address when I
had so much trouble getting it?"

"If I call Court Services, they'll give me the number, won't
they, now that they have it?"

"I guess so."

"So, she just has to call and say she's me. Once she has the number, all she has to do is call this Mrs. Monica person or whatever her name is and ask if she can come over. Maybe she says she's his godmother or aunt or teacher. The foster mother will give her the address because there's no restriction keeping her from doing that. There's no restrictions on anybody except us."

"Okay, okay," he says, holding up his hands, trying to calm himself down, she knows. He looks straight at her as she stands up. "Maybe I'm not one hundred percent sure of her. Maybe we should do something about it."

Rosie lifts the scribbled-on napkin off the table. "I'm calling the foster mother. I'm telling her not to let Diana take him."

"Okay," he agrees. They head for the back of the diner; for the phone.

MONICA WON'T TALK TO ROSIE. COURT orders, she says. "Mrs. Sloan, I'm going to hang up now," the foster mother says, but there's a pause, no actual click.

"Wait," Rosie pleads with her not to end the call. "I know I'm not allowed to talk to *Jason*," Rosie tries again, but the woman cuts her off.

"That's not the way I understand it, Mrs. Sloan, and I got my explanation direct from Services. No contact with the mother, period."

"Damn her," Rosie says, covering the receiver with her hand.

"Let me talk to her," Quinn says, reaching for the phone.

"Mrs.—" he says, and he's obviously forgotten her name. "Yes, Monica. Right. We—I just had one question." He's nodding. She's got things she wants to say to him first. Boundaries to establish and rules to lay down and all that, Rosie figures. "There's just this one little thing you and I need to deal with up front," Quinn says. It's his cop voice, Rosie knows. That slow, sure style he uses when he's got people who are jazzed up over something and all out of focus. "Let me go over this one small item," he says. "Really?" he asks, and Rosie knows she's slowing down. "Here's the thing," he says. "I'm concerned that a Ms. Diana Messerly may come by asking to see Jason, and I want you to be clear on this one point, Monica. I don't want Jason to be released to her under any circumstances." A pause for her response. "Yes, ma'am. I appreciate that, Monica. I appreciate that very much. Do you have my telephone numbers? That's right. Let me give you my other number down at the police department," he says. Clever boy, Rosie thinks. Miss Monica should know who she's talking to. "Now, Monica, the court says I'm actually supposed to call you at four o'clock to set up our meetings. Do you want me to call back at that time?" He smiles. He's won her over. She's not making him call back. "That'd be fine," he says. "I understand. No, no, no. That makes complete sense to me, you've got no need to apologize. It's in both our interests, isn't it? Thank you for your help, Monica, and I'll see you at six-thirty." And then he hangs up.

"So?" Rosie asks, practically crawling up his chest.

"No problem. She wouldn't dream of handing a child over to a stranger, she said. She told me I'd have to come with photo identification before she'll even let *me* see Jay."

Rosie takes in a deep breath, puts her hand on Quinn's chest, patting it. "Good," she says.

"I'm going over there after he's had dinner." They're walking toward the front of the diner. "I feel better," he says. "She really sounded okay to me."

"She sounded obsessed with rules she didn't understand."

"Look, better she should be conservative about this stuff."

"I guess so," Rosie concedes. "I just wish there was a way to get him out of there." Quinn's quiet for the walk through the parking lot. Such a contrast to how he was with Monica. How he always is when he's being a cop. Probably the only time he's quiet is with her, Rosie thinks.

"You know," she says, an idea occurring to her just as they reach her car, "if Diana was doing something to make him sick and we could prove it, we'd probably have a good shot at getting him out of foster care."

"But you can't prove that."

She lets out a deep breath. "I don't know. Maybe if I knew what kinds of things she *might* be doing. I could figure out if she *was* doing it. I mean, if I just had more information, it might come together."

"What kind of information?"

"Medical. The kinds of things that might make him get sicker instead of better."

"Leave it alone, Rosie. She can't get to him anymore."

"I don't want him in foster care, Quinn. He doesn't understand why we deserted him. To him, it must seem like we didn't want him anymore. He probably thinks it's his fault. He must be terrified—he doesn't have any idea what's coming next. Shouldn't we be doing everything we can to shorten his time away from us?"

"What do you propose?" He's leaning up against her car.

"I'll start by going to see Greg Linder, asking him what he thinks she might have done."

"Rosie, don't lower yourself by going to him. You heard what he said in court—that you might have this syndrome. He's not on your side."

"He didn't want to say any of that, Quinn. You saw how reluctant he was, didn't you?" Quinn shrugs. "He got trapped, that's all. That's the game lawyers play: Trap and Twist. They trap you with your own words and then they twist those words into a noose around your neck. Isn't that what he did to me with those questions about Abby?" Quinn doesn't answer. "And Zoe. Zoe screwed us up, too, but she didn't mean to."

"Right. They all screwed us. My old man used to tell me, don't tell anybody anything, because in the end, they'll all turn it against you. That's why I didn't even want to get near that therapy. The whole thing was a mistake from day one."

"But the point is, Quinn, Zoe and Linder didn't mean to do us wrong. The lawyers just know how to work them that way. Linder really cares about Jason. If I go to him and tell him about Diana, show him how all that evidence in court they tried to put on me really applies to her . . ."

Quinn pushes himself off the car. "Does it?" he asks.

"I mean, it might," she says, amending her stand. "I just want more information. If there's any possibility it's Diana, we need to follow through, bring the information to the judge."

"Just leave me out of it," he says, and steps off toward his own car.

        ROSIE TAKES A CHANCE AND HEADS FOR LINder's office right from the diner. She figures if he's there, he'll fit her in somehow.

She's right. Marcy says he'll see her as soon as he's finished with his current patient. "I'll sneak you in," she whispers to Rosie.

There are two other small children in the outer office with their mothers. One of them is coughing fairly continuously as he plays with the plastic blocks, probably much more in need of Linder's time than she is. The other child is even younger than Jason, and she's sitting on her mother's lap. They're reading books together and the mother looks up toward Marcy's desk every few minutes, her weary look begging the receptionist to call her name. Rosie decides she'll tell Marcy to let the mothers and children go in before her, they've obviously been waiting a long time, but a few moments later, when "Mrs. Sloan," rings through the room, Rosie follows Marcy's lead toward the inner office without glancing back. This is for Jay, she thinks, not me, and he may be in more need of the doctor's help than those children out there.

"Rosie," he says, as soon as she's come through the door. He's gotten up from behind his desk and come over to meet her. "I know you probably hate me for what happened in court the other day. And I also know there's no way I can make it up to you." He holds his hands out toward her, palms up, as though he's making an offering of everything he has.

"I know how hard it is to be on that stand," she says.

"Come, sit down," he says, motioning toward one of the leather chairs in front of his desk. When she sits, he takes the other chair, the other patient chair, and they sit, side by side. "I know the outcome's awful for you." His gaze wanders over the books and papers on his desk.

"It is," she says, "but it's not just your testimony that did it."

"I made it worse, though. I know that. I've been going over and over it and I know I should have just said no every single time I said yes. I should have said *I* insisted on the tests." His fingers straightened a pile of three books, lining the bound edges up neatly.

"No, you shouldn't have, it wouldn't have rung true. He'd have made you look like a fool. A lying fool. But I don't actually think what you said mattered all that much. They knew about my first child, so I was doomed."

Greg nods, shifts his chair slightly, rolling it so he's facing her direction. "I'm sorry," he says. He holds his hand out and she takes it. He tightens his hold, pulling her hand gently toward his chest.

She feels her chair move slightly, the wheels bringing her just that little bit closer to him. "Things have really gotten screwed up, haven't they?" she asks. She's feeling slightly woozy, an odd mix of sweet and sad.

"Yes," he says. He leans his head forward and kisses her fingers. "We'll get it worked out because there's good stuff between us." She's thinking about touching his face, kissing him, just forgetting the idiot lawyers and judge, forgetting Marcy and those mothers and children out there, leaning toward him, but then she stops.

"I should tell you what I need because you've got a waiting room filled with kids out there—" she says, motioning back in that direction.

"Hey, the kids will be okay. The moms may not be, but the kids will be," he says, a flicker of a laugh mixed into his words. Yes, she thinks, like he said in court, with these childhood illnesses the emotional needs of the parents take center stage pretty often. He's been stroking her hand, but he stops. "I guess there's a time and place for everything, right?"

"I hope so," she says, her voice starting to disappear into a whisper.

"There will be," he assures her.

"Not now, though," she says, with more control. "I need your medical expertise on something right now."

"What is it?"

"I have an idea about what might be happening to Jay, why he's not getting better. I figure if I can go to the judge with

187

something that proves it's not me, he might let me have Jason back sooner than two months."

He sits back, but he still holds her hand between his own. "What do you think is happening?"

"I think the episodes might be set off by somebody who knows a lot about allergies. Somebody—not me—might be giving him something. Maybe chocolate, like the prosecutor said, maybe something else. Does that make sense? Could somebody give just the right thing to cause the kind of attacks he's had? Like, maybe somebody could doctor his medication or something?"

He closes his eyes for a moment, contemplating what she's proposed. "There are so many things that could set any given individual off—cleaning products, say, or strong perfume, but I can't honestly think of anything that would guarantee that kind of reaction."

"Chocolate?"

"Well, yes, maybe, but the attacks that came later weren't all that much like the first one, remember. If I had to testify as an expert, I'd say the subsequent episodes weren't chocolate induced. And there's the mechanics of it, how it would be done, and the motive, the why."

"The who and why I know. The who is Quinn's girlfriend. She feeds Jason sometimes. Maybe she gives him his medications, too. The why is that she wants to make me look like a bad mother and make Quinn hate me."

He stares at her, eyes narrowed on her face. "Is she like that?"

"If she did it, she's like that, right?"

"I guess so."

"If I can figure out how it might have been done, I can go to the court and show them it's not me, it's her."

Greg taps a finger against his lips. "Let me check some stuff out, talk to some people, and maybe I'll come up with something. Would she have access to a source of other medications?"

"I don't know."

"Does she work in a hospital or pharmacy?"

"No. But she might know somebody who does."

"Right, okay. Let me think on it. Anything else?" She shakes her head. "Let me get to my mothers for now," he says, standing. He leans over his desk and presses a button on the phone console. "Marcy, I'm ready for my next." And then to Rosie he says, "Take it easy, we'll figure it out." Their eyes catch for a moment and he smiles. "It'll work out," he says softly, just as a coughing child bounds through the door.

CHAPTER
TWENTY-TWO

Q UINN HAS PROMISED TO PHONE ROSIE AS soon as he's left Monica's house so he can tell her everything about his visit with their son. Rosie walks into the kitchen to check the clock on the wall oven. Again. Not even six-fifteen yet. He's probably still in his car, driving there. And he'll be there for two hours, visiting with Jay, and then another half hour to drive home. She looks at the clock, moving the minute hand around the dial in her mind. Nine o'clock. She can't stand here pacing out rooms for the next two and a half hours, she thinks. She's got to go out.

She doesn't think much about where she's going. Just drive, she tells herself, till she realizes she's heading north toward Bradford, toward where Monica lives. She knows the address. She's checked it on the street atlas. She's figured out the most direct route there and the circuitous back street ways, as well. She can see it clearly, the red circle she's made on the map that she's left back home. The bull's-eye that is Jason.

When she stops at a light, she realizes her heart's racing. What does she think she's doing? Was she going to circle the block, passing back and forth in front of Monica's house for the next two hours? Better she should have stayed home wearing out her carpeting. Now her windows are fogging up, closing her in. She rubs at the windshield with her hand, then turns right onto a side street, no longer heading toward the foster mother's territory. She pulls over and tells herself to calm down. She can hear her own breathing: she can hear the fear.

I've got no life, she thinks, starting to cry. She rests her head on the steering wheel. She shouldn't have driven up this way, she knows that. She searches in her purse for tissues, finds them, and wipes her eyes. After she takes a few deep breaths, she starts the car again. She'll go over to Home Depot, push a shopping cart around for a while and try to pretend that it's still important to her that she save pennies by buying giant supplies of light bulbs, nails, and ceramic tile.

HOME DEPOT TURNS OUT TO BE A BETTER solution than she anticipated. At first she just pushes the cart up and down the warehouse aisles and isn't really accomplishing anything more than she was by pacing out her living room, obsessing about courtrooms and foster mothers, but then she gets distracted by a display of new counters, faux-granite in blacks and whites and deep dark greens. She moves on to the faucets, the sinks, the shower enclosures. She reminds herself that she can't afford any of this, but she also reminds herself that this is a game; a fantasy trip that she needs to be playing. If I could, she says to herself, which faucet would I want? Which shower door?

It's in the wallpaper department that she runs into Megan, the woman she saw in Linder's office in the middle of the night. The one who held a redheaded daughter who was gasping for air. The night that Beth went with her and Jason. The night that Greg probably never got to sleep. The small blonde woman looks decidedly less bedraggled than she did the last time Rosie saw her as she explains that she's trying to "freshen up" a guest bath with new wallpaper. "Only trouble is that the fixtures are gray and the tile is mauve," she explains. "There's not many wallpapers in those colors, and for some reason, what there is tends to be huge prints. It's this tiny little room you can barely turn around in." She pantomimes her way through an amusing pirouette, hands held tightly across her narrow chest.

"Why don't you paint it?" Rosie suggests. "Do the walls in a light, soft gray and trim everything with the pink."

"I might have to," Megan says. "Except that I hate painting. I like putting up wallpaper."

"The usual bind," Rosie says, and they laugh.

"How are you doing with the asthma?" Megan asks as she slips a place marker into the sample book where silver and rose sheaves of wheat gleam off the page.

Rosie's tempted to run, but she puts her hands down flat on the Formica surface between them and says, "We're doing okay, hanging in there." She feels the tears struggling to surface, but she manages to keep them at bay. "Where's your daughter?" Rosie asks, trying to shift the talk from her child to the other woman's; to keep from having to explain what the state has declared about her.

"Tonight is Mommy's big, fun night out," Megan says, rolling her eyes. "I get a whole two hours every Thursday to catch up on errands."

"Lucky us," Rosie says, trying to commiserate.

"Oh," Megan says, flipping so quickly through wallpaper patterns now she can't possibly be seeing them. "You might be interested in our Cape Cod experience."

"Cape Cod?"

"Yeah. We took Christie there for a vacation and she started to really improve. After a week Joe went home—he had to get back to work—and I stayed on with her for two more weeks. She got better and better up there. We're thinking about moving there now."

"Seriously?" Rosie feels something terrible then, a sense of violent rage that's so fierce and directed so pointedly at Megan that it frightens her. Jealousy, she tells herself. She is overwhelmed by one thought only: Why is this woman's child getting better and not mine?

Megan sighs and her voice becomes much less bright; confidential: "I feel like my life breaks down into two parts—Before Asthma and After Asthma. There's nothing else. I live my whole life around this disease. Everything is because of it or in spite of it. Like it's the defining piece, you know what I mean?"

"Oh, yes." She most certainly does. The feeling of bitter envy is easing. She and Megan are fellow sufferers, she tells herself. She can learn from this woman. She can help her own child by listening to Megan.

"Well, I kind of know we shouldn't just rush up there—Joe likes his job. He's been teaching at this same school for six years now and he likes the people he works with. He's finally got the courses he wants to teach—an honors track and an AP. All my friends are here. All our family's in New York, so we'd be moving farther away from them, too, but if Christie's going to be healthy up there, I think we might do it." Now she's the one fighting tears. "To tell you the truth, I'm going crazy going back and forth on it."

"Has Christie been okay since you're back?"

Megan nods. "There's been no crises, no medication, no medical stuff at all, really."

"Maybe she just outgrew it, some kids do, you know. Maybe she'll be all right here, now."

"I know. I've thought about that, but true asthma doesn't usually work that way, especially when the patient is so young. And I've read up on it. Total environmental changes can make that kind of difference. And see, we're time-limited. If Joe's going to get a teaching job, he has to be willing to move at the start of the school year. We have to put the house on the market *now* to do that." She moves her hands as though she's juggling balls in front of her. "I don't know." She closes her wallpaper book. "I think we're going to do it. I want her healthy so badly, I can't take a chance on not doing it."

"I know what you're saying. It isn't rational, this mommy thing, is it?" Megan shakes her head. "Just hearing it's a possibility, I'm ready to pack up and go tonight," Rosie says, meaning it, absolutely, thinking for a moment of jumping back in the car, sneaking up on Monica's house, and stealing her child away.

"I worry it's not enough time yet, maybe it's just a short remission, you know?" Rosie nods. "We're papering the little bathroom because we're trying to spruce the house up before we put it on the market. The thing is, we've really decided," she says, pulling another wallpaper book from the slotted openings beneath the counter. "We put a bid in on a place up there and we're waiting to hear. Christie and I will probably move as soon as we can, then Joe will join us in the summer. I guess I was just saying it like we were undecided so I could go over my choices again."

"You have to go," Rosie confirms for her.

Megan nods and sighs. "I'll let you know where we end up. Maybe you can come visit, take the cure with us." She laughs lightly.

Rosie looks at her watch. She has nowhere she has to be for quite a while yet, but if she stays here with Megan, she'll start talking about how miserable she is. She'll become hysterical in the middle of Home Depot. Rosie wants to be able to go home, right now, pack Jason in the car and drive up to Cape Cod. That's all she can think about. Being able to hold him; put her arms around him and kiss him and take him to Cape Cod. Or to the supermarket. Or the park. To be with him again with nobody watching. "Good luck," Rosie says. "Gotta get back," she adds, pointing at her watch. Her legs don't feel all that sure about supporting her, so she lets the shopping cart take most of her weight as she moves away.

CHAPTER TWENTY-THREE

IT RAINS THAT FIRST WEEK JASON IS AWAY. The water comes down so steadily, lights are required in every room, and on every car. The sound of rain on the roofs and in the gutters is constant. She gets the name of the court-appointed shrink and sets up her three appointments starting ten days to the future, his first opening.

Rosie is learning to wait. To sit still. To rise from chairs slowly and walk from place to place at a steady, easy pace. There is nowhere to go yet. Beth says she should look for a job, and there have been moments when she supposes she is right. She tries to read—she's got a pile of novels she's taken out of the library, but she finds herself staring into space only a few pages into these stories.

Evenings, she watches TV in bed until she falls asleep, and both Quinn and Beth have said that is bound to make the nightmares worse, sleeping over the strange television noises. The nightmares are about Monica, or some stand-in for Monica because she has no idea what Monica looks like. This dream woman is different each time, but she always has Jason with her, and he's always gasping for breath.

Quinn has seen their son twice. He says Jason seems pretty happy, but that he's "clingy." He reports that Monica has two other foster children to care for plus two of her own, though they are older, the last of her batch, as he puts it. This gives

Rosie something brand new to worry about. She hadn't realized Monica would have so many distractions.

Quinn has given Rosie a police-style description of their son's new caretaker: "Five one, one hundred pounds, dark hair, dark eyes." It's not enough. Rosie can't pick her out in a crowd—not unless she's got Jason in tow. It occurs to Rosie that she could start hanging out in supermarkets near Monica's home, or even at the mall, waiting for her to come through with her foster children. Which two children's hands will she hold?

"Is the house clean?" Rosie asks Quinn during one of their phone calls.

"Clean enough," he tells her.

She wants to know if the electrical outlets are covered. If the knobs on the stove are beyond Jason's reach, if the cleaning products are locked away. Quinn says he'll check next time, but he forgets to do so. "I should be with Jason when I'm there, not poking under her sink," Quinn says, defending his failure.

"You want him alive, don't you?" she asks, and he agrees to check the next time he is at Monica's.

Between the second and the third visit, there are three full days, not two, to wade through. At night, the possibilities of danger rise up like ghosts through her sleep. Electrical cords dangle tantalizingly within reach. Unlocked doors beckon toward the outdoors, toward busy streets. Kitchen knives gleam.

Rosie has finished off the bottle of sherry in the pantry. There wasn't all that much in the bottle—just slightly over half. And she's thinking about getting another bottle, though so far, she's resisted. Beth comes by some evenings and makes her go somewhere—a movie one night, dinner another, but it does little to lift the pall.

After Quinn's third visit, instead of calling Rosie with his report, he shows up at her door with a pizza and beer. By the time he navigates from his car to her front door, the rain has nearly soaked the cardboard box. He's shaken up a little, he says, because Jason wouldn't let him go this time. He says he cried the other times when he left, but this time was very different. Worse. He screamed, Quinn reports as he puts the wet box down on the kitchen table. He covers his ears with his hands for a second at the memory.

"Like that first night, when the social worker came to take him?" Rosie asks.

"Much worse," he says. "And he was coughing. I thought he was going to have another attack. I can't stand this, not being able to do anything. It's driving me completely nuts."

"Call her," Rosie says, "make sure he's okay."

Quinn dials the number and Monica assures him that Jason was fine the minute he was out the door. "No breathing problems?" he asks. Monica says he's sleeping peacefully.

"Maybe she's not doing the right medication. That theophylline is tricky. If she's giving him extra, topping the spoon off, even, he could start wheezing," Rosie says when he hangs up.

"I went over it with her again and the stuff about getting the dose exactly right. She said Linder went over it with her, too, a couple of days ago when he checked Jay."

"He told me," she says.

"How did he think Jason seemed?"

"Okay. He said his lungs seemed, if anything, clearer." Quinn lifts his eyes toward her. She knows he's probably thinking about how if Jason's health is better when he's away from her, then maybe she did have something to do with the illness. Everybody thinks that. Sometimes she finds herself almost wishing he'd get a little worse to prove that it isn't her fault. She doesn't know what she should think or want anymore. Is there a way to win? Is it a game, a contest? Quinn and Rosie are pacing, searching out their own, separate patterns of thought.

"We should eat the pizza," Quinn suggests, stopping suddenly, lifting the lid, revealing a clam topping.

Rosie sits down at the kitchen table while Quinn collects plates, silverware, napkins, and glasses from around the kitchen. "I want to take him to Cape Cod, soon as we get him back," Rosie says.

Quinn brings over red pepper flakes and uses a knife to lift a piece of pizza onto each of their plates. Rosie doesn't think she can eat. She loves clam pizza, but she just doesn't think she can eat anything.

"I ran into Megan Moore. She has a child about Jason's age who has asthma," she tells him. "She took her daughter up to the Cape, for three weeks, and the kid didn't have any symptoms." Rosie uses a knife and fork to cut a small piece off her slice. Her token food. The mix of flavors of clam, tomato, and mozzarella on her tongue are startling. She's suddenly very hungry. She lifts the whole piece of thin-crusted pizza and brings it to her mouth. She can't eat it fast enough.

"What happened when she brought her kid back here?" Quinn asks.

Only the back end of the crust is left now. Rosie puts it down and wipes her mouth. "She was fine. It's only a couple of weeks, but she hasn't had to have any special care since."

"And do they know why?"

Rosie shakes her head. "I don't know. What's different up there? The salt in the air, maybe? The sea breeze? The moisture from the ocean? It could be one of those things, couldn't it?" Quinn shrugs. "The Moores don't seem to know exactly what it is, either. But they're moving there because they think it'll make a real difference for Christie. Megan said I can bring Jay up there, come for a visit, see how he does. And if it makes him better, I don't know, maybe I should move there, too."

Quinn is nodding. But she's thinking about how she's probably not going to be able to take Jason anywhere. How he's never coming back to live with her. And she's crying.

"Don't cry, Rosie," Quinn whispers to her, and Rosie doesn't know why, but that makes her cry all the more. "Rosie," he says. He steps over to her chair and holds an arm out toward her. She reaches for him, their arms linked along their length. "Come here," he says, bending his arm, drawing her toward him. She rises, letting him hold her, holding him, and he's kissing her mouth, both of them crying, both of them holding tight, and kissing more, and he's stroking her hair. She can barely breathe, remembering now, with these kisses, the shape of his mouth, the feel of his lips. She knows she shouldn't be doing this, but she doesn't pull away. She moves her hands over his chest, thinking about Greg and Quinn and what a mess she's making out of an already too messy situation. But, still, she lets Quinn hold her close and quiet. She needs shelter right now. "I have things I need to tell you," he says after a time.

"What things?" she asks, her head still lowered against his chest. They haven't looked at each other this whole time, they've only touched.

"You should know I'm off active duty. I'm on the desk." She pushes back a ways, back against the circle of his arms, so she can see him. "When you came in that day, I told you I was filling in, but it wasn't true. That's where I am now, doing dispatch up front or at the board, and that's where I've been for months."

"Why didn't you tell me?" They've stepped back from each other. Found their seats again. Their knives and forks. Their pizza.

"Because we weren't talking. I couldn't figure out how to say it. Every time I tried, it was harder." He shakes red pepper flakes out over his food.

"What happened?" She can still feel the warmth of his mouth over hers, and she needs to look away, to stop thinking about that.

"I was freezing on the job. I was a liability to everybody." He's moving the red pepper shaker back and forth along a short path.

"What do you mean?"

"Every time I went out, I don't know, I lost it, I couldn't take any action." He looks at her and she nods. He's started turning the shaker in a circle. "At first it was just big things, like if there was a threat, a show of weapons, that sort of thing. I'd back off, call in for help. I told myself I was just being cautious, following good procedure, but it wasn't that. I was scared, that's all, and I knew it." He's spinning it now, twisting the silver top round and round in place. "Then it started happening more and more and it was on less important stuff, even. I got so I didn't want to put my flashers on for speeders without calling in. I mean, I guess I'm exaggerating, I could still do idiot stuff like that, but I always felt this close to panic the whole time I was doing it." He holds his thumb and forefinger up, demonstrating the slim measure of comfort he'd had. "It got so I'd start to freak if I heard the radio crackle, you know, waiting to hear where they were dispatching me. Then it got so bad, it'd happen if I just had to get into the squad car." He's shaking his head.

"When did it start?"

"I don't know. A year and a half. Two years, maybe," he says, flatly.

"This has been going on for two years?" He nods. She's thinking about these two years. "Is that why you had an affair, did it have something to do with that?"

He looks up at her. "I wasn't having an affair."

"I mean, *we* weren't sleeping together. You weren't talking to me, you were keeping some sort of secret, Quinn."

"I wasn't sleeping with anybody, Rosie. This is the secret. *This.* What I've just told you."

"You should have said you weren't. I mean . . ." She's not really sure what she means. "In therapy, you said you were seeing a woman at work."

"No, I didn't."

"Yes, you did."

He shrugs. "I couldn't have said that because it wasn't true."

"I asked you, point blank, were you having an affair and you said this thing about 'there's this woman at work.' I remember the words, Quinn, believe me. And then you just drifted off, like you do. You didn't even finish the sentence." He smiles. "It's not exactly funny, Quinn."

"No, I know that. But I think I was talking about Francie, probably."

"Francie?" Francie O'Neil is twenty years older than Quinn, the great mother confessor to all the cops. "Then why didn't you say *Francie*? Why'd you say 'this woman I work with'?"

"Because I was talking to your therapist—Chloe, Zoe, whatever her name was. I think that maybe it was right after

Francie and I had a talk. She asked about you, I told her things were rocky and she had some stuff to say."

"What?"

"Just something about how you can tell a great love. A long-lasting one."

"How?" she asks, despite herself. She knows he's manipulating her, trying to change the subject.

"If you can still remember good stuff from the beginning, I think."

"What's the beginning worth if it falls apart after that?"

"I'm just telling you what she said. She says in really bad marriages, the people can't go back to the beginning and say, We were so in love, we were so attracted to each other. They look back to then and they think it was *always* awful and worthless. The ones who think it was so great once—intense was what she said. They're the ones who could be okay."

"We were intense," she says quietly.

"I know." She can see him swallowing; the effort of it. "I said to her, to Francie, what if you were only eighteen, what do you know when you're eighteen?"

"What'd she say?"

"She said that you know. She said, think back, if it still can make you feel good, and you wish it was like it was, like you want it back, then it was good."

She'd given up wanting it back. You can't be eighteen forever. This is life now, here, today. "Quinn, you should have said it was Francie, I thought you were talking about an affair."

"You cut me off, Rosie." She hears the other unspoken part: You always do.

"But I asked you," she says, her voice feathery, almost indistinct, but strangely her hand has tightened into a fist on the table.

"I guess I let you think it. It seemed easier, more convenient, maybe, I don't know. Maybe I thought my problem was worse than an affair." He's not looking at her, but going for the pepper shaker yet again.

"What? Having panic attacks at work was worse than infidelity, worse than screwing up everything we had?"

"I was having panic attacks about *living*," he says. He leans toward her. "Look, it's like I was in this dead state. And it kept getting worse, like it was a progressive paralysis. I felt like I was heading toward total immobility. When I realized what you thought, about an affair, I almost wished that's what it was. I wished I was capable of doing anything that bold. That would have been an incredible relief." He closes the cardboard box. More than half the pizza is still in there. He looks at her, his lips pressed together. "I shouldn't have let you be thinking that's what it was, I know. I'm sorry. I just kept hoping it would go away. I kept hoping I'd figure out how to start working again and that everything else would go back together. I've spent the last couple of months waiting for Pierce to call me in and sack me." He lifts the lid of the take-out box, stares at the pizza, then lets it close again. "I *wanted* to tell you." Again, he lifts the lid, lets it fall. "I figured when I finally got fired you were going to end up reading about it in the newspaper." His finger traces the letters on the box: BEST PIZZA. "Or maybe you'd run into one of the other guys or one of the wives and they'd tell you." He looks toward the front door. "That night Jay got sick when I called them to smash the front door?" He tilts his head in that direction and she nods. "I was afraid one of them was going to say something about it then." His eyes are still on the door. "I've been thinking about just taking off, getting the hell away, but I knew then I'd lose the insurance, all the medical stuff for Jay, so I put that out of my mind." He turns his gaze back toward her. "I've been thinking about a lot of really weird things lately."

"I'm sorry," she says, reaching for his hand. "Doesn't the police department pay for therapy in these cases, don't they want you to figure out what's causing it?"

"I know what's causing it."

"What?" she asks him, but she wished she hadn't. It's got to do with her, she knows. Her fault.

"I didn't know at first, but I thought about it so much, I think I do now. I think it's the Emerson baby."

"The one who died in the car?" He nods. "Did you tell Pierce that's what it was?"

"No. Why would he care? I had a scene that shook me up, but then I should have gotten over it. What they see is that I can't do cop stuff anymore. They don't care why. I had their therapy, those two sessions you always get after a high-stress scene."

"Two sessions isn't enough. You should have had more, and they should know that. This isn't the Dark Ages. When people get traumatized, they need help."

"Rosie, cops are supposed to be able to deal with dead people. I always did before." He sighs, looks away, shrugs. "Anyway," he says, turning back to face her, "I wanted you to know what was going on, finally."

She realizes she's feeling incredibly angry. She's angry at the police for dealing with him this way, for punishing, not helping him, and she's angry with him, too, for making her think it was an affair. But she's thinking, also, about how he's talking to her, like he used to, and she reaches for his hand, lets her fingers move over it briefly, remembering more, remembering what his touch was like, a sudden flare of heat, remembering them standing together moments before, kissing, and then she draws her hand back.

She also remembers the nightmares, how the accident was all he wanted to talk about day after day, well into the night, every night, going over the same details again and again. "I've got this freeze-frame in my head," he had told her. "It's like a color photo. The car goes up, and she's holding out both hands toward it. And I'm in the picture, holding her back," he says. "I'm standing there, doing nothing, just gaping at the flames." He'd covered his ears back then all the time, said the sound of the mother screaming for her baby was still out there. And he'd covered his ears tonight, too, hadn't he, when he'd talked about Jason's crying? Two years ago, Rosie had had to interrupt him, to physically shake him, to get him to understand that she was having labor contractions.

Once Jason was born, though, Quinn stopped talking about the accident. It was as though Jason had saved Quinn, brought him back from the edge. Becoming a family again seemed like a spiritual rebirth for both of them, and for Rosie it felt all the more intense for another child having died so close to the moment of Jason's birth. But now, now that Quinn had spoken of the accident for the first time since Jay's birth, she could see that that was exactly when *all* the talking slowed—not just the talk of the Emerson accident, but *all* of it. It had slowed and withered and finally died altogether. Like an old-fashioned LP record when the power is shut off.

There is silence again between them, here in the kitchen. He shrugs his shoulders. "I wanted to tell you," he says.

"I'm here," she says, sliding her hand along the table toward him. He reaches for her with an eagerness, a need that she had long ago come to believe she'd never see again in his eyes.

CHAPTER
TWENTY-FOUR

ROSIE'S GONE IN TO ATKINSON'S, THE LARG-
est store on Main Street, the one that has just about everything.
It's a stupid waste of time, she knows, but she can't bear being
alone in her empty house anymore. So she's here. In this store
that has everything she could need. Only it's not like she
needs anything, and even if she did, she doesn't have any
money.

She's told herself that being out in a public place is better
than being at home because she's less likely to start crying or
lapsing into one of her totally out-of-control screaming rages
against the judge. She's wandering here, not really taking in
what she's seeing, just shuffling through the departments till
she gets to the cosmetics, and there's something about those
perfect little boxes of color, two and three squares of bright
powder to a compact, all open, dozens of them gaping up at her
through the glass like that, that makes her hate the whole cosmetics industry for the way it manipulates women into wanting
what they don't need, and then just as quickly, she hates the
women, too, who buy it, who are so shallow as to put crayon
colors on their eyelids and worry about their looks instead of
their children. It's a fierce hate, more inflamed than what she
felt toward the judge when he said she couldn't see her child,
more intense than when he ordered Jason into foster care. God,
she wants to take a swing at them all, she's thinking, and then
she realizes that it—this terrible, bitter loathing—*is* for the

judge. For the way he has manipulated her, for the way he forced her into violating the order. ("Nobody made us violate that order, Rosie, we did it," Quinn keeps saying.) She's got to get out of here, this isn't helping. First, though, she has to fend off a saleswoman who is wearing perfectly applied makeup and one of those smocks that's supposed to make the sales of cosmetics seem equal to other uniformed professions, like nursing, and Rosie has to do the whole routine about how she's just looking, thank you. Time to go, she tells herself, refocusing, and as she turns, she sees a woman in a reddish pink parka leaning over another section of the cosmetic counter, deep in contemplation, maybe ten, twelve feet away. Rosie bends in that direction, trying to get a look at her face, but the other woman is turned so it's hard to tell if it's Diana, but the hair is the right color, the jacket, too, and then Rosie sees: She's got her hands thrust into those jacket pockets, just like Diana did at the diner. Rosie wants to pounce on her, throttle her, call her a bitch, right here, with everyone listening. She has to hold on to the edge of the counter for a second, just to ground herself, because she knows that if she does anything but walk away, the woman will get a court injunction against her. ("She isn't the one who turned you in, Rosie," Quinn still says.) And if Diana goes into court to complain about her, that will make the judge hate her more, Quinn tells her. It will give him more reason to pull back on his sympathy, and to widen the distance further between her and her child. ("Sympathy? What sympathy, Quinn? Did you actually think the man capable of sympathy?")

Rosie makes herself walk away from the girl, feeling the thunder of her heart in her chest as she goes. I'll go home, I'll have a drink, I'll be fine, she tells herself as she passes quickly through the housewares, the men's clothing, the handbags, and the shoes.

She looks over her shoulder, just as she gets to the women's clothing. She can't see all the way back to cosmetics, and certainly no one is lurking behind her, at least not anyone in an overstuffed fuchsia jacket. Diana wouldn't follow, though, would she? She'd turn and run in the other direction. This department is filled with customers. They must be giving something away, Rosie thinks, and starts to pull on her jacket and to prepare herself for the shock of cold air when she sees May Donovan emerging from the dressing room with an arm-load of clothing.

Rosie turns swiftly on her heels and out of the department. What a day, Rosie thinks. Caught between the two people I hate the most in the world. She dives for the door handle like it's a lifeline tossed out across the water. How unlucky can one person get? she asks herself. And then she wonders whether they really are the two people she hates the most. Maybe she hates Ted more, but no, that's not true, he's just a conduit, a go-between. He's actually protecting her interests in his own bumbling way. But Judge Mannon, on the other hand, she definitely despises more than either of those two women.

She can't take this anymore, this total loss of control—the courts call all the shots on her child's life, on her life, and Quinn's as well now. And now she's wondering if Diana's deliberately stalking her. She's sitting there in her car, clutching the steering wheel, and she can barely catch her breath. She knows she can't start getting paranoid, too, on top of everything else. She's just been unlucky today, that's all, she tells herself, trying to calm herself down. It's the world's worst coincidence that she ran into Diana, but that's all it is.

Rosie fits the key into the ignition, but her thinking gets sidetracked between there and actually turning the key. What if it's not a coincidence, their both being there, she's asking herself, and it's like somebody else has said it to her, somebody who's been watching this whole thing, maybe from the doorway, maybe from above or something, somebody who has got a much better perspective on the scene than she does. And she's wondering, Could they be in there together? Isn't it just too weird they'd both be there, separately? Isn't that even more of a coincidence than if they were together? And then she decides to sit there, to wait, to see, her car pointed toward the back door of Atkinson's. She's not sure what she's waiting for, but she's waiting.

An unlikely couple, May in her slim dress coat and Diana in her jeans and parka, they emerge from Atkinson's simultaneously. Rosie has on sunglasses—the parking lot, though it is night, is well lit—but just in case, she scrunches down as far as she can. Both the women carry shopping bags. Both of them enter the same white Toyota, May in the driver's seat, Diana as passenger. How can they know each other? Rosie wonders. Through court? No, Diana wasn't even in the courtroom. Maybe May questioned Diana and they got to be friends? No wonder that emergency order went through as fast, she's thinking. Diana knew exactly how to process it. She just trotted off to her little friend May and told her that Rosie was sneaking in to see Jason.

But they can't be friends, Rosie tries telling herself. They're so different, and there's at least ten years between them. At least. May has turned on the headlights and has started to pull away. They are friends, Rosie hears herself say. Or perhaps it is that other voice, the one with a longer view, a better perspective. They *are* friends.

BY THE TIME THE WHITE TOYOTA PULLS INTO Castleton, the old artists' summer community that's been turned into condominiums, Rosie has all but forgotten about the threatened injunction. She's keeping her distance from them, not all that concerned if she loses them—she's already decided that if she can't figure out where Diana lives this way, she'll find some other way to get the information tomorrow. Chances are, she can just look it up in the phone book. And if not, she figures with a little time and a little convincing, she can get it out of Quinn.

When May's car pulls over to the curb in front of number 36, Rosie drives on past at a steady pace. She wends her way back up through the condo community and out the central gate. She wants to give May and Diana a few moments to say goodbye and for the social worker to be well away from 36 before she returns, so she drives down to the nearby shopping center parking lot, where she turns around and then heads back to Castleton.

Quinn's friend opens the door to Rosie, but only for a second. She slams it hard, then leans her back up against it—Rosie can see the top of her head through the glass in the door. "Get out of here or I'm calling the police," Diana shouts at her, turning around only long enough to get this said.

"You better tell me how you know May Donovan first," Rosie says, and pounds her fist on the door.

"That's none of your business," the young woman retorts, and then there's a blow from the other side, down low. Diana has kicked the door.

"Yeah, maybe it's not my business, but the police might think it was their business. Let me in. Tell me the truth, before you bother getting them out here," Rosie implores the girl. There's no response, but Rosie can see that she's still there on the other side of the door, facing away again. Then Rosie sees the blonde head turn, hears one lock, then the other, being thrown, and the door is open once more. Diana has already taken off her puffy jacket, revealing a black ribbed knit shirt that clings along her rib cage, then disappears under a braided leather belt and into her low-slung pale blue jeans. She's tiny thin and her face has become splotchy red. "Quinn said you'd leave me alone," she protests.

"He didn't know that you knew Ms. Donovan."

"I swear to God I didn't think they'd take the baby from him," she says, her voice loud and unmodulated; a genuine outburst of panic.

"You need to tell me about it," Rosie says, stepping into the house without an invitation.

"I know," Diana says, and her wailed words echo jarringly through the nearly empty room. Diana motions for Rosie to sit on the one chair, and the younger woman sits on the floor opposite her, knees drawn up high. "How did you find out?"

"I saw you at Atkinson's together. Tell me how you know her."

Diana shrugs, then tightens her arms around her legs. "We're cousins," she says, not looking at Rosie, but off toward someplace where maybe she's hoping May is waiting to coach her through this interrogation. "I didn't know they'd take him

209

from Quinn, I swear I didn't," she reiterates, looking now at Rosie.

"You just knew they'd take him from me, right?"

"No, I didn't, I swear."

"You told her I went to see Jason, didn't you?"

"You violated a court order."

"But you started this whole thing, didn't you? You set that court order in motion. You called her, you made that first complaint against me and got the whole thing going." Rosie realizes she's digging her fingers into the corduroy of the upholstery.

"I just told her about it, that's all. *She* said I should do the complaint."

"What do you mean, you told her about it? Told her about what?"

"I gotta get some tissues," Diana says, rising up, crossing the room to the bathroom.

Rosie gets up from her chair and follows right behind her. She can see that there's no real escape route for Diana, but she needs to watch her, to be sure of holding her there, close by. "What did you tell her?" she asks as the girl stares into the mirror and dabs at her eyes.

"Just that Jason was asthmatic and wasn't getting better." She tosses the tissue into the toilet, then slowly pulls another out of the dispenser on the tank, then another, and a third.

"Lots of kids have asthma and don't improve, you know."

Rosie steps aside so Quinn's friend can come out of the bathroom and go back into the living space. They both sit again, but neither of them speaks till Diana says, "There was the thing about the chocolate. I told her how you started the first attack."

Rosie is suddenly aware of her own loud breathing. "That was an accident."

"But *I* didn't know if it was or not. And everybody, all the teachers at work, they all said it sounded suspicious, they were all pushing me to call. I'm telling you, it wasn't my idea. They said I had to *by law*. I wouldn't've even mentioned it to May if it was just me. And then I wanted to tell you that day in the diner, but I knew Quinn would hate me. I didn't want him to know what I'd done. He'd already told me there was no way it was you." She's wiping at her face now and then she puts her head down against her knees. When she looks up again, she asks, "Does he know?"

"No."

"I just wanted to run it by May, you know? She took it from there, she said Jason was really at risk. She told me about the Munchausen's thing. She made it sound like it could get completely out of control. Everybody, people at work especially, they all said, if you'd given him something once, you could do it other times. They kept saying how vulnerable he was. How maybe you were trying to punish Quinn. They talked about what *might* happen if I didn't do something about it." Her hands flutter in front of her for a moment. "They told me about all this really bad stuff they'd seen and they made me feel like it was all true." She shrugs again. "I really thought I had no choice but to do the complaint. May never said they'd put him in foster care. I feel so bad about that, I could die. And Quinn's going to hate me when he hears." She closes her eyes, moans, and lowers her head again.

Rosie's thinking, yes, of course he will, you stupid nitwit. She wants to say something about how ugly and dangerous jealousy is, about how transparent Diana's need to get rid of Rosie has been, but she wills herself into deep silence. She knows there are parts of this that mustn't be said yet. "So by the time it got to the Department of Children and Families it was exaggerated by what all these other people were adding to it, right?"

"Kind of, I guess."

"So what you ended up telling them wasn't even true."

"I just wanted him not to be sick," Diana insists. "I wanted somebody to make it right, that's all. I shouldn't have even told May. I'm sorry and I just wish . . ." The unfinished sentence drifts back and forth between them, waiting for one or the other of them to pick it up again. She's looking up at Rosie like she's begging for forgiveness, but it's enough, Rosie thinks, that she hasn't struck this girl or called the police.

"Did you feed him stuff to make him sick?"

"No," she shoots back with surprising fierceness. "I never hurt him."

Rosie nods. Maybe, maybe not, she's thinking. "You'll have to tell the judge this other stuff," Rosie says.

Diana's eyes narrow. "Why? It wasn't illegal. I really thought something might be wrong. I just wanted to protect Jason."

"But May Donovan is your cousin. That's not legal, is it, to report something through a relative?"

The young woman stares hard at her for a moment. "Why is that illegal?"

Rosie's taken aback by this response. It has to be illegal. May was acting on a relative's behalf. What was that phrase? Conflict of interest? Yes. May was acting on behalf of Diana's interests, and that meant she would be working to shore up the new threesome and get Rosie off the scene. "Does May know about you and Quinn?" she asks the girl. Diana nods. "So she knew you wanted to be with Quinn and get me out of the picture, right?"

"That wasn't why I did it." She's holding a hand out in protest. "Look, I didn't do anything wrong," Diana insists. "I'm sorry I screwed people up, but I didn't do anything wrong and neither did my cousin."

"What did you think was going to happen to Jason and me by starting this?"

"I don't know. Maybe I didn't think it through, okay? But I was worried about Jason. I didn't know you. I thought he was in danger. That's what everybody kept telling me." She pats tears away from her cheeks.

"But now you know that wasn't true, right?"

"The whole thing got out of hand," she says. "And like I said, I'm sorry."

The way Rosie's figuring now, if she tells Ted how it all started—how she's got proof now that the complaint was motivated by jealousy, even if it's not strictly speaking illegal, maybe he'll get the whole thing reversed. "Will you tell my lawyer that you're the one who filed the complaint and that you don't think it's true anymore?" Rosie feels herself avoiding the word *lie*. She doesn't want Diana to panic and refuse to go forward with this.

Diana lowers her legs and crosses them in front of her. "If you want me to."

"I definitely want you to," she says. "Would you withdraw the complaint?" The girl nods. "Good." Rosie searches through her woven bag for a pen, then rips a deposit slip out of her checkbook and writes out Ted's full name and address. "He's in the book. Call him tomorrow by nine o'clock and tell him all this, how it's not true and you're sorry you filed it and want to withdraw it, okay?" Diana nods as she takes the paper from Rosie's hand. Rosie feels downright good now, finally. And her breathing doesn't even hurt anymore.

CHAPTER
TWENTY-FIVE

IT TURNS OUT THAT ROSIE IS WRONG ABOUT everything getting miraculously fixed up by Diana's confession. The younger woman did, as Rosie had directed her, call Ted the following morning and deliver her statement, which, according to his report, was fully punctuated by sobs. But according to her lawyer, that disclosure wasn't going to change anything.

"But she told you she lied to DCF, didn't she?"

"She didn't put it quite like that. She said she misrepresented the situation because she was being very heavily influenced by others. She never said anything about lying. In fact, it sounded to me like she was reading a script. I'd be willing to bet she got advice from somebody as to how to phrase her little confession so that it couldn't get her into any trouble."

"Do you think she got advice from the social worker?"

"Maybe. But it really doesn't matter who it was, I don't think."

"But that's all euphemisms. She's still saying she lied."

"Let me put it to you this way, Rosie. Even if she says she lied and that every word out of her mouth when she first filed that report was false, it wouldn't help you."

"How can that be?" Rosie wails at him. "It *has* to help, Ted, the woman says she made it all up. She says she got pressured into making the complaint. It wasn't done freely. Doesn't that make it a fraud or something?"

"No. It makes it a mistake on her part. An overreaction, that's all."

"But didn't she tell you she was willing to withdraw the whole complaint?"

"Yes, and that won't change anything, either. The judge's decision to remove Jason from your care wasn't based on Diana's complaint at all. It was based on evidence the state found when they acted on her complaint."

"But if she lied . . . ," Rosie persists.

"Rosie, I'm telling you that her complaint *isn't relevant.* Her state of mind and her veracity are *not* in question. Nothing whatsoever about her is in question. The unfortunate truth is that *you* are the one now under the microscope. The judge doesn't care who set this in motion. He's watching *you.* So I'd advise that you behave yourself. No more violations of his orders. Concentrate on not crossing him and forget this girl, please. Stop wasting energy on her."

"But if a lie started it all . . ."

"Rosie," he says, his voice sharp as a slap across the phone line. "You're not listening to me. You mustn't lose your focus here. You need to be clear on what you're dealing with. The only thing that matters right now is that the judge has decided you have to go ahead with a psychiatric evaluation and abide by his rulings. Do you understand?" He spaces these last few words out.

No, she thinks. This is completely screwed up. He's telling her to keep her mouth shut. Act like it didn't happen. Pretend she doesn't care if she can't see her child.

"Does Quinn know his girlfriend started this whole thing?"

"I told him," Rosie says. She wishes now she hadn't been so eager, hadn't sounded quite so full of victory.

"How'd he deal with it?"

"He was crushed, I think. He said it had really already been over between them, but it was a difficult blow, anyway, knowing how she lied to him. Then I ended up getting really depressed over *his* loss. I mean, we're losing everything; everything in our lives is falling apart, piece by piece. What's going to be left us when this is all over?"

"Don't be discouraged," Ted tells her, but rather than sounding like encouragement, the phrase has the heft of a warning. Discouraged is just one more thing she can't be anymore. It doesn't fit the required set of public behaviors she's allowed now that her life has been surrendered to the powers of the court. She's got to wear heels and a skirt and act upbeat.

"I *am* discouraged," she says. "Mortally discouraged."

"Don't be," he reiterates, and she hopes maybe he'll go on, that he'll finish the sentence, that he really meant to say, Don't be discouraged, be hopeful because . . . But he doesn't elaborate; there is no because. "Take care," he says, and it is another of his admonitions. She wants to say, You know, I still don't think I understand the playing rules, but he's gone. The dial tone has returned.

CHAPTER
TWENTY-SIX

ROSIE IS DRINKING YET ANOTHER CUP OF coffee and going through the help-wanted ads two days later. She has to do something—all she's been thinking about is what Jay's doing from one minute to the next. Whether Monica has let him have his blanket when he gets stressed. Whether he's still waiting for her, looking up at every sound he hears at the front door, his small heart beating faster in anticipation, then halting dead in his chest at the realization that she isn't coming. Did he hate her now? Does a two-year-old hate and blame? What about all the stress this put him under? Didn't stress increase the likelihood of an asthmatic attack? Maybe she could get Greg to send a letter to the judge about that.

So she diverts herself now, circling the one possibility in the classifieds—the least awful choice in a long list of awful choices. It's for a real estate agency that Rosie figures must be falling apart because their ad says "experience is nice but not necessary." The idea of having to sell anything makes her slightly ill, but she finds herself strangely drawn by that one word: *nice*. She has imagined for herself an office of women, chairs pulled together in a close circle, talking not about how to exploit their clients but how to make them comfortable. A sort of real estate/therapy crossover for those with high anxiety levels around major life changes. She's circled nothing else—all the other ads insist that experience is necessary. She is *x*ing out an ad for a "super aggressive closer" in tele-sales when the phone rings.

"Monica just called me," Quinn informs her. Rosie can hear the distress in his voice. "She wants to switch the time for my visit with Jay."

"Why?"

"Linder wants to pick him up, and that's the only time he has—this afternoon. He's taking him for a checkup."

"But I thought she wasn't supposed to let him go with anyone."

"That's what I said, but she says the court ordered the checkups, which is true. And that the court approved Linder, which is also true. She says all she promised was that she wouldn't release him to a *stranger*." He speaks the word with clear distaste for the woman he is quoting.

Rosie crumples the bottom portion of the classified page in her hand. "I can't take it anymore, Quinn. We're nothing in this arrangement."

"We're less than nothing, Rosie. And we're dealing with this woman who's obviously getting her thrills out of controlling us. And now she's lecturing me: When I told her I was pissed that she was canceling me—and I didn't use that word, believe me—I got all this crap from her about how police officers ought to know that court orders have to be followed to the letter."

"Quinn, what if she's just a loon, a power freak?"

"I don't know, I really don't." She has a flash of him as he was in court, head lowered to his hands, despairing.

"We've got to get him out of there, Quinn. You're a cop, do something."

"A judge is bigger than a cop, Rosie. We've got to work with what we've got. We're going to have to work with Monica, not the judge, to get the best deal we can for Jason. Like all I can think about right now is how he'll go nuts when he sees Linder come through the door."

Rosie imagines Jason and Greg Linder facing each other in Monica Delano's living room. She remembers how he held the child's hand, stroked his back. "Quinn, he'll be all right with

218

Greg. Jay likes him. And it might not be so bad for him to get away from that house and be with somebody he's comfortable with for a couple of hours. I'm not saying it isn't horrible that we have no say in our child's life anymore, but Jay'll be all right with this today, anyway."

"I hope you're right."

"But, Quinn, how come Greg isn't just going to the house the way he did the last time, did she say?"

"Yeah. I asked. She said Linder needs to bring him into the office to do the complete physical that the court requires."

"And he's going over there to pick him up? That seems a bit much."

"She doesn't have a car so he's apparently doing this as a great favor to her. She said she wasn't going to turn down free help."

"She doesn't have a car?" Rosie feels that surge of panic that's become so familiar over the last few weeks she could map its twisted route of pain on an anatomy chart. "What if Jason needs emergency treatment? How's she going to get him to the hospital? Quinn, I can't believe this, the court placed him with somebody who can't even get to the hospital?"

"I assume she'll call a taxi."

"She's not going to want to spend that kind of money. She told you, she's all into free help."

"I'll tell her if he's ever sick she should call a taxi and we'll reimburse her. Or, I could tell her just call me. That's free."

"You know she won't do that. That'd violate her complicated visitation rules."

"Well, I'll tell her to call Emergency Medical Service, then, nine-one-one."

"This is so bad. She's got so many reasons not to be dealing with the asthma, I can't believe it. This is so irresponsible of the judge. Look, I'm going to hang up and call my lawyer."

"Wait a second," he says. "Don't hang up."

"What?"

"That Cape Cod stuff?"

She feels her stomach do a weird sort of spin. What if he says he's not going to let her take Jay up there? That he's going to make it a requirement of their separation that she stay here? Though what does it matter? she realizes. Going to Cape Cod, even having Jay with her, all that's just fantasy land now. "What?" she asks him.

"This kid, the Moore kid? Is she out of Linder's care now?"

"I don't know."

"Does she see him at all? What did the mother say about that?"

"I don't know any specific details. Why?"

"Last night I was going over all the differences, trying to figure out what it could be. You know, between here and there. Salt air, all the things you mentioned. All of it was stuff that's there, on Cape Cod, but not here, right?"

"Right."

She hears him draw in a deep breath. "Rosie, what if it wasn't something on the Cape that did it? What if it was getting away from something here that caused the change? I mean, what if it was having a vacation from Greg Linder?" he asks, his voice noticeably slowed. "What if he's not such a great doctor?" Her heart's beating so fast, she can't figure out how to breathe. "Could he be incompetent?" Quinn asks. "I mean, you know about credentials and what to look for with doctors. You're the one who looked into it."

She doesn't think she's going to be able to speak. To tell him.

"You think he's all right?" Quinn asks.

"Maybe we should check out his credentials," she finally manages to say.

Quinn is silent. Then he asks, "You've already done that, haven't you?"

"Yes and no," she says. Her voice is wobbly, exposed. She feels downright chilly. "He was recommended by the emergency room doctor who knew his work. You only check the credentials when you don't have a medical referral." She knows she's covering for what she's failed to do, but her explanation does have some truth to it. Her father always said that the best recommendation comes from another doctor. Especially if he's sending you to someone he'd use for his own family. Hadn't that ER doctor said that, "I'd use him"? Weren't those his words? Couldn't she rely on that?

"Rosie, how do we check him out?"

"I'll do it, don't worry." She stands up, like she wants him to know the conversation is finished. She's not sure why she doesn't want him poking around, but she doesn't. She's twisting the telephone cord all around her fingers. If there's something to be found, she wants to get at it first, present it to him, not the other way around. "Look, he's fine, I'm sure. Megan would have said if there were problems." She doesn't really believe that. What basis would Megan Moore have for evaluating a doctor's competence?

"Maybe Megan hasn't put it all together yet."

"I told you, this other doctor was totally confident in him."

"But if you're still seeing him—socially, I mean—you shouldn't be the one checking him out, should you?"

"Oh, come on, Quinn. Is that what this is about? Are we back to jealousy as a governing life force?"

"No. That's not what this is about. It's about Jason."

"Right." She punches at the air. The cord twisted over her hand looks like a strange weapon, a soft variant on brass knuckles.

"Well, maybe it is partly about that. I mean . . ." There's a drift, a long space in his explanation. She tries to pull the cord off her fingers, to free her hand and not pull the receiver out from where it's resting between her shoulder and her ear. "All that stuff I said about him, that's beside the point," he tells her, his voice shadowy, like it's gotten waylaid inside the phone. "I want to try. You and me, Rosie. All these twists and turns we've taken lately, I want to talk about them like we did the other night. Like we used to." His voice has a different sound to it now, and it reminds her of something else, but it's a foggy, partial memory, like a face she can't quite put a name to. "I mean," he continues, but then drifts again. The silence doesn't bother her this time. She likes it, closes her eyes the better to feel it. She'll wait. Then suddenly he says, "Oh, hell," breaking off his own thoughts, jarring her the way a mild earthquake might, rumbling and shifting under her feet, throwing her off

221

balance. "I can't talk about this on the phone," he declares. "Just do this thing with Linder, take care of it. But do it fast, okay?"

"I will," she says, steadying herself with a hand on the kitchen table.

ROSIE KNOWS EXACTLY WHERE THE REFER-ence work is that she needs to check. She doesn't even have to speak to a librarian. It's easy except for that moment when she slides the book off the gray metal shelving and imagines the entry for Gregory Linder missing from the page, a large white blank area gaping up at her instead. She slides the book back without opening it and walks then, through the aisles between the tall gray shelving, gathering her resolve. She stops in front of the book once more, slips it forward, opens it right there on the shelf, not giving herself time to change her mind while she carries it to a carrel. She forces her hand to turn the pages, to come to it, Gregory Linder's name. It's all there, his name, his medical school, his internship and residency, his certification. She's almost surprised. Silly thing, she reprimands herself, I've let Quinn confuse me. But it's here. And it's enough. Even her father would have considered it enough.

She closes the huge volume so that it makes that wonderful muffled slap, as though everything between the covers is being sucked back and reabsorbed; readied for the next person.

This new information coupled with the ER doctor's recommendation would be enough for anybody, she thinks, but she'll go on to the hospital anyway. So she'll have just that much more to show Quinn. So she can say, See, I've got good instincts about this stuff.

At the hospital, she is surprised by how uncomfortable she feels pushing open the door at the end of the corridor leading to the personnel office. This is such a public declaration of her mistrust, she really doesn't want to go any further. And besides, she's satisfied with what she's got. It's just Quinn who won't be.

Why didn't she just telephone? She feels like she's skulking along the walls, wishing she were in disguise, praying that

Greg won't come bounding around a corner. She looks over her shoulder when she hears footsteps. It's not him. But of course he won't be here in the middle of the afternoon, she assures herself. He's in his office, examining patients.

She pauses outside the door of the personnel office. She could just turn around, she tells herself, but no, Quinn will want to know what she's done. She's got to do it. She pushes on through the door, up to the long counter that separates her from huge stacks of files. "May I help you?" an angular-faced woman whose head is crowned with flowing brown hair asks her.

Rosie's words stumble over one another, trying not to be said: "I'd like, I mean, if a person needed to know about a doctor . . ."

The woman stares at her, then her face softens and she tries to translate. "You want a recommendation for a physician? You go the the central administration office for that. I can give you directions to there, or you can call. I can give you the number."

"No," Rosie says. "I want to check on a doctor's credentials." She sighs. She's done it. All that's left is to say his name.

"He's affiliated with this hospital?" Rosie says he is. "Then what I can give you is our fact sheet," she says. Rosie nods. "The doctor's name?" she asks.

Rosie pronounces it carefully. It takes a long time to say it. Has she dragged it out? Said it too loudly? But no one else is near enough to have heard. Will this personnel worker tell the others who work at those desks? Will she tell him, Greg Linder, himself?

The woman types into her keyboard and almost immediately a printer begins to chatter away. "Just one minute," the woman tells her, then stands, her hand poised to receive the paper as it emerges from the machine.

The information on this single sheet is very much like that in the reference work in the library, though it is slightly more detailed. There are more abbreviations and more locations listed than the other source revealed.

"Is that going to be sufficient?" the woman asks.

"Probably," Rosie tells her, still looking it over. "Can you tell me if there are letters of support from when he applied for affiliation here?"

"Oh, yes, there always are."

"Could I see copies of those?"

"No, ma'am. The fact sheet is all we give out unless you have written permission from the doctor."

Enough, she tells herself. We're filling time so we don't go too nuts about what's happening to Jason. But like Quinn said, what we really need to do is work with Monica to improve Jay's situation. And, she tells herself, I need to learn how to get on with things. She will go back over the want ads, she tells herself. She will be less judgmental about how hideous they all seem. She will call the "experience nice but not necessary" real estate woman.

And once she's out in the hospital parking lot, out in the air (escaped, like a criminal, from the scene of her crime), she starts thinking she should call Greg and apologize. Or, no, not apologize, because really, she can't even mention this, but she could move decisively away from it. She could ask him, Shall we have coffee? She can close the distance again. Yes, she'll go over to his office. She catches herself—is she just avoiding this whole job business, the getting on with life that she was just two seconds ago saying she had to attend to? Maybe. But reconciling with Greg was part of getting on with it, too, wasn't it? I'll call him, she decides with determination. Maybe he didn't have anybody coming in for that last appointment, that consultation slot. And I'll start again, she thinks.

As she gets into her car, she remembers suddenly about Jay's afternoon schedule. Greg is picking him up at Monica's. Probably using his consultation appointment time to do so. Her heart has started beating fast, faster. So if she went over to his office, to see Greg, she could also see Jason, she realizes. If he's examining Jason, she could see him. Be with him. She can barely catch her breath. Would that be against the order? She decides not to think about that. If anyone questions it, she'll say she went to see Linder. She'll say she forgot—hadn't *known* (she might get away with that)—that Jay was with him. She looks at her watch: one o'clock. Yes, if push comes to shove, she will say that she thought the checkup was at one o'clock. They won't be able to prove that Quinn told her it was around the time of his visitation. There's nothing they can prove. I can see my baby, she thinks, tears of relief flooding her eyes as she turns the key in the ignition.

CHAPTER
TWENTY-SEVEN

GREG LINDER'S OFFICE IS LOCKED. ROSIE knocks, but no one answers. She'll wait. She paces the corridor for a while, then goes back down the stairs to the parking lot, scanning for him. She walks down to the lot entrance, watching the street, trying to decide which direction he'll be coming from. Then she goes back upstairs, does some more pacing, some sitting, cross-legged, for a while on the blue commercial carpet whose pattern of interlocking diamonds she has plenty of time to analyze. Then more pacing. Another trip to the parking lot.

She'll call his answering service, she decides, then walks to the next building, to The Coffee Stop, where she's hoping they'll let her use the phone.

The thin waiter who begrudgingly allows her access to the telephone behind the counter ("You sure it's local?") is the same one who served them when she and Greg came here together. The phone rings many times. She waits—endlessly, it seems—watching the waiters hustle from one table to the next. Finally, just as she is about to give up, her call is answered. "Dr. Linder's answering service," a bored female voice chimes at her.

"I need to reach him," Rosie says.

"Is this an emergency?"

"Not exactly," Rosie says, and winces at her mistake. She

will be relegated to priority two, she knows, even if she now claims to actually have an emergency.

"May I have your name and number, please?"

Rosie recites her home number to the woman but explains that she's not actually at that number at the moment, but that it's very important that she reach the doctor. She asks for the number where he can be reached so she can call him directly.

"He's on an emergency right now," the woman says.

"An emergency?" Rosie repeats. The woman's words have made her feel dizzy. She's curled uncomfortably over the phone, trying to keep out of the way of the waiters who need to work around her.

"Yes, ma'am. Can you tell me the nature of your problem?"

"He's supposed to be giving my son an exam and he's not in his office. I'm concerned."

The woman clears her throat. "He canceled his afternoons because of this emergency. You didn't get a call canceling your appointment?" The empty sound of boredom again.

He canceled his appointments because of Jason, she thinks, because Jason is having a crisis. "Is he at the hospital?" Rosie asks.

"He's not seeing patients this afternoon, ma'am. I'm sorry for the inconvenience, but you can call his office first thing in the morning and reschedule, if you like. I am sorry you didn't get a call."

She wasn't going to be able to make this woman understand. "Is he at the hospital, Bradford Hospital?" The black-clad waiters' bottoms graze hers as they pass behind her. Rosie squeezes herself tighter against the counter.

"If you want, I'll have him call you when he calls in, but I'm sorry, I'm not at liberty to give out any more information."

Rosie puts her finger on the disconnect button. The sound of the dial tone is refreshing, almost as though it can erase the unpleasant talk of the last few minutes. She finds the number for the hospital and dials that. She knows, from all the years in her father's house, how these things work. If she says she is a patient looking for Dr. Linder, she will be referred back to his answering service. No point in pursuing him that way. She has to *be* his answering service or his office manager to expect any kind of result. A woman with a cheerful, ready-to-please voice answers and asks how she might direct Rosie's call. "This is Dr. Greg Linder's office, can you page him, please?"

"One moment, please," she's told. Much better, Rosie thinks.

She hangs on, holding so long, that her waiter is trying to catch her eye, presumably to tell her that she has to get off the phone, but she turns away from his stare, unwilling to receive his message. The hospital voice comes back. "He's not answering his page," the woman chirrups at Rosie.

"Would you mind trying again?" Rosie asks, and she's left hanging once more. He could be in the bathroom, she tells herself, or doing a procedure, though she knows the nurses are supposed to answer a page for a doctor who is tied up in a medical emergency. One of the waiters puts a piece of chocolate cake down next to her. Another says, "Excuse me," and motions for her to step aside so that he can get some coffee beans out of a drawer she's obstructing. Now she's blocking the cake. "It's a medical emergency," she tries explaining to the first waiter, but he's moved out of earshot. Life and death, she will say to them, if she must. "He's still not answering," the telephone voice tells her.

"Can you let me have admissions?" she asks, and she's duly transferred.

"Admissions," the next voice announces.

"This is Dr. Linder's office, can you tell me if he's admitted a Jason Sloan yet?"

There's a pause and then a sure, brisk, "No, I show no one by that name."

Hearing that, Rosie feels relieved. Jason hasn't had to be admitted to the hospital. Linder's emergency had to have involved someone else. But then where exactly is Jason now? "Could he be in the emergency room and not show on your record?" Rosie asks.

"Oh, yes. ER isn't counted as an admission. That I can't help you with. Shall I transfer you?"

The first waiter, the one who granted phone use, has thrust

his wrist at Rosie and he points at his watch, clicking a finger-nail over its crystal. She has no idea when she started these calls, so she has no idea how long she's been on. But she does know he wants her out of there. She nods at him. "Yes," she tells the woman at the other end of the phone connection. The waiter leans on his elbow on the counter next to the phone, staring at her. "It's life and death," she says to him, covering the phone.

"It better be," he says. "We don't have room back here for you to be tying up that phone like this."

She's connected with ER while he speaks. "Do you have a Jason Sloan signed in this afternoon?" she asks. The waiter has stood up and gone down to the other end of the service area.

There's a pause and Rosie hears, "No one by that name."

If she hangs up the phone, she knows that guy will never let her pick it up again. But she's run out of ideas for now, so she lowers the receiver—slowly, though, because she's hoping for inspiration before she has to actually surrender the phone once and for all. When she has settled the telephone back in its cradle, she comes out from behind the counter. "Thanks," she says to the waiter as she passes him.

"No problem," the guy says, but he's rolling his eyes. "Is he-she-whoever going to live?" he asks as Rosie walks past him.

"I don't know yet," she says.

SHE HAS TO LOOK FOR ANOTHER PHONE, SHE tells herself once she's gotten back into her car. She'll go to the mall and make some more calls there. She'll call Quinn and get him to call Monica. Or maybe she should just go home so she can get a call from Linder in case he's trying to reach her. She could call his service again, see if they'll tell her if he's gotten the message yet. Then she realizes she's at the intersection where she can go left, to the mall, or right, toward Monica's house. She's really close to Monica's. Maybe Linder's brought Jay back there by now, she thinks, and turns the steering wheel decisively right. And if he has, maybe she'll get a glimpse of him, maybe he'll be in the living room, just visible in the crack Monica will open in the door.

Rosie is shaking when she pulls up in front of the house.

CHAPTER
TWENTY-EIGHT

ROSIE GETS HER FIRST VIEW OF JASON'S foster mother—or a woman she assumes to be his foster mother—as she peers out at Rosie through one of the two long side windows next to the front door. She's a tiny creature, no taller than a twelve-year-old, and she has jet black hair that spills down over her shoulders and back and nearly across her face as well, in tight curls. The woman surprises Rosie by opening the door wide to her.

"Yes?" the woman asks, and Rosie understands that she has no idea who it is that's standing on her front stoop. Rosie also sees how easy it might be: her hands can take hold of the narrow shoulders and shake and twist till the tiny woman's knees give, till she capitulates and is down on the floor. Taking Jason will be simple, then.

But no, she won't touch this woman. She mustn't give her cause to call the police. Perhaps she can lie her way through to the interior of this house and to Jason. She'll say she's doing a survey on something to do with children. Eating preferences? Bedtimes? She'll ask if she can come in for a minute and run a few questions by her. If only she'd thought to bring a folder or a clipboard; something official looking. Rosie puts her hands into the pockets of her jacket—a desperate, fumbling grasp at old shopping lists and tissues. Nothing there to lend credibility.

The woman in the doorway lifts her eyebrows, urging her caller to get on with whatever she has come here seeking.

Rosie, lifting her empty hands as though surrendering, simply says, "I'm Jason's mother. Are you Monica?" What other real choices has she with this woman?

"Yes," she says, but Rosie sees that Monica's startled by her revelation, that she pulls back slowly on the door, drawing it toward her as though it were a stiff curtain that she might magically wrap around herself and thereby disappear. "You're not supposed to be here," Monica declares. But she hasn't slammed the door between them. She hasn't even tried to close it. Monica looks up into her eyes and Rosie sees the elaborate pattern of sun lines that crisscross her face.

"I'm not here to see Jason," Rosie says. "I just wanted to put a face to the person Jason's with, to see you, and I thought if you and I"—she gestures between them, trying to link them— "if we could see each other, we'd both be more comfortable. You know, to see we're just people. Just moms," she adds quickly. She's afraid to stop talking, afraid that if there's space between her words, Monica will fill it in with a refusal; the thunk of a door pulled forever shut. "I wanted to see you," Rosie continues, her voice going shaky on her. And then she's thinking again about pushing the door open, forcing it out of Monica's grasp. She's such a small woman, and if Rosie's read the facial lines correctly, much older than she. She could easily overpower Monica if she wanted to. She hasn't seen her baby in over a week.

Monica's nodding. The dark curls bounce around her shoulders as she moves her head. "Everybody thinks I'm the wicked stepmother or something," she says, and smiles at her own joke, even laughs, and Rosie's reluctantly drawn along into the smile. "Is it the hair?" Monica asks, but doesn't wait for an answer. "Somebody once told me I've got too much hair for my body. That I looked like something out of mythology." She shakes her head, contemplating it. "Which I guess means I look like a witch, or whatever they called those things. You think it's the hair?" she asks.

"Oh, no," Rosie assures her. "You've got fabulous hair."

"Too curly this time, though," Monica says, pulling at one of the strands. "Too much of the perm stuff or maybe it's too

232

long or something." Monica lets go of the curl and it springs back to its shorter length. "I like it softer than this, like the way it gets four weeks after I get it done," she says, sinking her hands into the mass of it at the back of her head, then lifting, stretching, fluffing. "A friend of mine who used to work in a shop a long, long time ago comes to the house and does it for a really great price." She stops and looks at Rosie like she's said too much already; remembered suddenly who she's talking to. She's nervous now, Rosie thinks with a feeling of triumph. "Anyway," Monica says, her tone more distant so that Rosie knows there's not going to be any more girl-talk about permanent waves, "Jason's not here."

So that's it, Rosie thinks. That's why she hasn't slammed the door in my face or called the police. Jason's not here, so she has no fear of me. I have nothing to gain by forcing my way past her, and she knows it. Rosie has to think of where to begin again. "My husband told me that Jason was having a checkup this afternoon. Is that where he is?"

"Yes. Like I told your husband. With Dr. Linder."

"I tried to reach the doctor," Rosie says, "and his office told me he had an emergency. I was worried that it was something that had happened with Jason."

"I seriously doubt that," Monica says. "People don't have emergencies when they're with their doctors." She laughs for a second, then seems to think better of it and realigns herself squarely in front of her home.

"Shouldn't they have been back by now?" Rosie inquires of her.

"Don't ask *me*. I don't have any idea how long it takes. There's tests, isn't there? I don't second-guess experts, if you know what I mean. But look, I know how you feel, having somebody else taking care of your child. But you can trust me—I have my own natural kids. I've got five of my own, two grandchildren, and one on the way, and I don't treat yours any different than those flesh-and-blood ones, believe me, and they're all, every last one of them, fine and healthy."

Now Rosie really wants to shake her, this little bit of a woman. She wants to say, You can't know. Nobody's taken one of your children away from you, have they? But she says nothing. She waits through Monica's explanations of her expertise. The list of her children's accomplishments, the details of her licensing, her selection four years ago by the local newspaper as Mom of the Year. She's stopped using the door as a shield. It stands open; discarded, beside her. "I've had twelve foster kids, counting Jason, and I've never lost a one," she crows.

"Have you ever had one with asthma?" Rosie feels the razor edge in her voice—the one she'd wanted to keep hidden— surfacing.

"Not asthma, no. But sicknesses. Different sicknesses. I've dealt with lots and lots of doctors. Lots and lots of sicknesses, believe me. Injuries too. Disabilities."

Rosie's been trying to get her breathing even and slow again. She knows she needs to talk, not attack. "I didn't realize you had that much experience. What you're telling me definitely makes me feel a lot better," Rosie says, deciding to lay it on, sugar and syrup and honey all in one sticky scoopful, blanketing the sarcasm so heavily she doesn't think it'll work its way back up through to the surface. Monica's gaze widens. She likes the praise, if that's what it can be called. As long as Monica likes it, Rosie thinks, she'll lay on some more: "Most women, once their kids are big like yours, they'd never volunteer for more of them."

"Nope, but I love it," Monica croons.

"I'm very comforted knowing that you've got this kind of background, that you're so caring and dedicated."

Monica fills her lungs with air, swelling herself up the way small birds do when they're preening.

And then Rosie realizes nothing's going to happen here. Nothing at all. How can it? Jason's not here. The only chance she has of seeing him is to plop herself down on the front steps and wait. Wait even if Monica asks her to leave. Wait even if the police arrive to question her recalcitrance.

"But you shouldn't come by here," the foster mom reminds her. "It's not allowed."

"I know. And I know I put you on the spot. I'm sorry."

"It's okay," Monica says, shrugging. "It doesn't matter, with him being gone anyway. But I'm wasting oil, keeping the door open, I should go."

"Sorry," Rosie says. "But thanks for talking to me." She holds out her hand and Monica grasps it, her hand small as a child's within Rosie's. Monica nods, but she looks over her shoulder like she's wondering if she has enough food in the kitchen to invite Rosie for some kind of repast. "Could you call me when Jason gets back?" Rosie asks.

Monica draws her hand back. "I'm not supposed to."

Rosie nods. "I appreciate everything you've done for him, really," she says. "How about my husband? Could you call him?" Monica's doing that wide-eyed thing again. "How about if I tell Quinn to call you in an hour?"

"Make it two," Monica says. She looks away. Rosie can see there's more she's thinking about telling.

"Why so long?" Rosie asks.

"To make sure he's back."

Monica's not looking at her, still. What's she keeping back, what doesn't she want read off her eyes? "That's longer than a physical, much longer," Rosie observes.

"He said he might take him out for a bite to eat. A field trip, he called it."

"Who said that? Dr. Linder?"

"Yes," Monica says, still not really looking at her.

"Did he say where?"

"No. I just mentioned it because they might not be back in an hour, and I didn't want you worrying if he still wasn't back when Mr. Sloan called."

"Thanks," Rosie says. Is this progress? Monica has confided something about the details of Jason's whereabouts, yes, but she's also let him go off on this totally open-ended visit when he should have been with Quinn. She wants to say, Don't let him go with anybody else, okay, Monica, I don't want him in other people's cars. "Did he have Jason in a car seat?" she asks, thinking, why would he, he doesn't have any children of his own. How often does he drive his patients around? Surely not often enough to equip his car with a safety seat.

"I didn't look, but he must, isn't it the law?"

"People break the little laws like that in their cars and in their homes every day, don't they?"

"Don't ask *me*," Monica says, but Rosie knows she gets the point about the illegal hairdresser.

"I don't want him in cars without safety seats," Rosie says, thinking her newly established moral superiority will get this demand met.

Monica doesn't say anything, doesn't nod. Rosie knows what she's thinking. She's thinking how she's in charge now and considering what Rosie's accused of, she has nerve to be talking about car seats. Rosie reaches into her pocket again for one of those mangled tissues. She tries to unwind it, to spread it wide, to make it look like she's going to blow her nose, not dab at tears, but the tissue disintegrates as she tries to stretch it over her face. "Thanks, Monica," Rosie says, waving the remains of the tissue at her in farewell as she backs down the steps.

CHAPTER
TWENTY-NINE

THE PHONE BEGINS RINGING WHEN ROSIE IS standing outside her new front door, trying to figure out which pocket she dropped her keys into when she got out of her car. By the time she gets the door open and runs toward the kitchen, the sound is gone. Quinn's probably trying to reach her. She takes the stairs two at a time, heads right for her bedroom; for the handwritten phone directory she keeps in the nightstand. He doesn't answer. She tries him at the station house, but he's already left for the day. Betty Margolis answers with a bright-toned, "And how may I direct your call?" better suited to a department store than to a police station. "You call him more now than you did when you two were together, don't you?" she comments, laughing, when Rosie identifies herself and asks for Quinn.

"Is that your business?" Rosie snaps at her.

"I meant it as a joke," Betty insists.

"I didn't think it was funny."

"I'm sorry, Rosie."

"Right." Rosie's already regretting her harsh tone. Betty's one of the cops Rosie has always liked. "Look, Betty, I'm sorry," she says. "I'm just feeling jumpy tonight."

"No problem," Betty says. "I wasn't thinking, you're right."

"Could you just leave him a message that says I'm looking for him?"

"No problem," Betty repeats before she cuts the connection.

Rosie's been trying not to tell people about what's going on, trying to avoid them pitying or judging or despising her once they knew she'd been accused of harming her child. *Not* telling them, that was what was getting in the way, probably, making her seem so harsh. The complicated ways she had to avoid that center from which all the tension flowed. But she just couldn't stop now, fill them all in, ask them for their support. What if they didn't give it? What if they blamed her, too? She just couldn't risk that right now.

She's got to focus on the important stuff. Like getting hold of Quinn so that he can call Monica. She dials his apartment again—still nothing. So where the hell is he? She checks the time. Dinner, probably, though he shouldn't have just gone off without saying where. If he's worried about Jason—which he damn well should be—then he should be here, right this minute, following up on everything they talked about earlier.

She's standing over the phone, waiting for it to ring, shifting back and forth from one foot to the other, starting to feel like a fool: She's staring at a stupid telephone, talking to it, willing it to ring. She looks at the kitchen clock again. "You've got to call Monica," she admonishes the absent Quinn. Her stomach has started growling just as angrily at her as she's been growling at Quinn. She definitely should be eating something, she knows that, but she can't.

In the high cabinet over their refrigerator, she finds Quinn's brandy bottle. She fills a juice glass halfway up and drinks it off, her brain fooled by the container it's in, she figures when she realizes how very quickly she's dispensed with it. Eat, she instructs herself, and maybe it's the brandy, but the only thing that really appeals and seems simple enough to prepare is cornflakes. She shakes cereal into a bowl, pours on milk, serves herself up another glass of "juice," carries it all upstairs with her, and turns on the bath. She draws the flakes through the milk, moving the spoon in continuous curving motions all around the bowl, an almost mesmerizing routine that she can barely stop in order to eat. When she's finished the flakes, milk, and brandy and her tub is filled, she picks up the plastic purple bubble-bath container shaped like a pudgy, benevolent dinosaur, and pours a lot of its contents into the tub. She takes off her clothes, dropping them into a pile at her feet, steps into the burning hot water, easing herself down inch by inch and settles in. She thinks she'll probably hear the phone. She thinks she will if she can get herself to concentrate on it, but she's drifting already, the heat and water doing strange but welcome things to her brain. And then too, she's not really used to brandy, she thinks as she watches her arms float in front of her and she lets go for the first time all week.

IT TURNS OUT SHE ACTUALLY CAN HEAR THE phone, but not till it's rung a couple of times. Not till she's been startled awake. Might she have drowned if she'd slept much longer? She remembers the story of Mark Twain finding his grown daughter slipped beneath the surface of the bathtub water. The water's gone cold and her limbs are stiff, she discovers, as she tries to push herself to standing. She's still listening and it's still ringing, but it can't go on forever. She pulls a towel from the rack and wraps it around herself. The phone has stopped and there's a cold stillness in the room. In the whole house. She'll have to get dried off, into her pajamas, and then she'll try Quinn again. It must be about time to call Monica, surely. If she can't reach Quinn, she'll call the woman herself. She'll be sweet as she can, and she'll get through to her. She won't ask for much, just, Is he back yet? No, she'll say, "Is he *home* yet?" That way, she'll put Monica at ease, acknowledge that Monica's the one in charge, that Jason lives with her now. Temporarily. Rosie's willing to say even that word: *home*. If she can. She'll try.

"MONICA," ROSIE SAYS, AND SHE WONDERS IF the foster mother can hear the brandy in her voice. She ought to have made herself a cup of coffee before she dialed this number.

"He's not here."

Rosie sits up straighter. She had been settled comfortably into bed, propped up by several pillows, but she's at full attention now. "It's getting kind of late, isn't it?" Rosie asks, hoping that phrasing her concern as a question will force Monica, as a mother, to agree with her; to do something about it.

"The doctor's keeping him overnight."

"What?" The word explodes against the telephone.

"And I'm not supposed to be talking to you."

"Is he sick? Is he hospitalizing him?"

"He's just having him sleep at his house. Good-bye, Mrs. Sloan."

"At least give me his number," Rosie demands, but the dial tone is her only answer.

I don't need her, Rosie thinks. I've got his number. It's on a paper somewhere in her purse, she knows. She heads down to the kitchen where she's left her bag and starts riffling through its contents, but everything's falling back down on her hands. She can't see a thing, and finally she just turns the bag upside down and lets it all tumble out onto the floor. She begins searching through all the scraps of paper: last week's shopping list, the directions to the courthouse, a receipt from the toy store, Greg Linder's telephone number. "Ha!" she says aloud. "I don't need you after all, Monica."

She dials his number and it rings for a long time. "Come on," she coaxes him, and then, finally, there is a connect.

"Dr. Linder," his resonant voice sings forth.

"What are you doing with my child?" Rosie snaps at him.

"Rosie? I've been trying you for hours. Don't you have an answering machine?"

"What are you talking about?"

"I've been calling you since this afternoon."

"That was you calling? Look, is Jason okay? Why do you have him?"

"Yes, that was me calling. And Jason is fine. I've got him here, at my apartment. I got this maniac idea that if I kept him, I could sneak you in to see him, but then I couldn't get hold of you. This is the modern age, Rosie, you need an answering machine."

"He's all right?"

"Yes, and look, I know you've been worried about him—Monica told me. I'm sorry I upset you. My intentions were completely the opposite. I guess it was a stupid idea because obviously I made things worse, not better, for you. But believe me, I've been trying to reach you. You want to see him?"

"Of course I do. Are you kidding?"

"Well, I know when you and Quinn tried this, it backfired."

"True, but there was a spy in our midst back then. I defi-nitely want to see him."

"Okay, then."

"If I come there I can see him, right?"

"That's the whole idea."

She pulls one of the white kitchen chairs away from the table and sits down—she has to, her legs feel like they can't hold her up anymore. "You are so wonderful I can't believe it."

"I am completely out of my mind is what I am."

"Yes, thank goodness."

"So, before I chicken out and have second thoughts about violating a court order, why don't you get over here?"

"I'll be there as fast as my little car will carry me."

"Hey, I didn't mean that. He's here all night, so you don't need to rush. You can stay as long as you like as far as I'm concerned. Just promise me you'll drive slowly and carefully, okay?"

"Yes, sir."

"And I assume you're not going to tell anybody about this because I figure my medical license is on the line if anybody finds out."

"Of course I won't tell anybody. I'm not an idiot. You know, I've seen what people do with this kind of information."

"I suppose you have."

"*You* haven't told anybody, right?" she asks him.

"Of course not."

"I *will* tell Quinn, but not tonight. Maybe tomorrow."

"Don't even tell Quinn."

"Why not?"

"Because it'll put him under unnecessary pressure; moral

241

pressure. He's a cop and he's going to be thinking about the right thing to do. He's going to have one of those personal slash professional quandaries. He doesn't need that right now and I, personally, don't need to be worrying if he's going to do the straight-and-narrow and rat on me."

"He wouldn't."

"Maybe I'm being overly cautious, but I like it that way. It *is* my career, my livelihood, on the line here. And like I said, Rosie, he's a cop. And he can't be a witness against you if he really has no knowledge of it having happened."

"All right," she concedes. She's certainly not going to waste time arguing with him about it now. She'll go see Jason and she'll deal with the Quinn part later. "Can I talk to Jay for a second?"

"Just get yourself over here. I've put him down to sleep so if I wake him now, he's going to be too groggy to understand it's you on the phone anyway. You can wake him up when you get here."

"You are divine," she says.

"But not so heavenly that I don't have a real world address, so let me give you directions."

"Oh, yes," she agrees. And she's laughing. Like everything's over, done, and solved.

CHAPTER THIRTY

SHE'S SO GLAD TO SEE GREG, TO HAVE HIM put his arms around her. There's such a sense of relief in it, of having arrived, finally, that she could almost forget why she's come this far, riding through three towns over roads she doesn't know, winding her way along darkened streets (hasn't anybody told them about streetlights in this part of the world?) to get to this place. "Come," he says, "sit down with me, relax for a few minutes." He cocks a thumb over his shoulder toward the living room.

She laughs. "There's no way I can relax, Greg," she says, brushing aside his suggestion with a back-and-forth motion of her hand.

"Let me get you a drink, then."

She shakes her head. "No, thanks."

"Come on," he urges. "As a physician, I'm prescribing it. We need to get your stress level down."

"Okay. A little one, after I see Jason." She can barely stand still. She's shifting around, ready to take off in whatever direction he points her.

"Hang on," he advises, holding up a hand. "Let me give you my professional thinking on this first: I'm recommending we let him sleep a little longer on the chance that he'll wake on his own at the end of one of his natural sleep cycles. If we artificially wake him—"

"Wait a minute," she breaks in, "on the telephone you said I could wake him."

"Yes, I know I did and in fact you probably will *have* to, but I'm just saying that if we wait a little bit longer there's a chance, and I admit it's not that great, but there is that chance that he'll wake on his own. If you wake him, he's likely to retreat back into sleep—you know what babies are like at this age when you wake them. And physically it's better to let him alone, too. Jolting him could set off another breathing episode."

Rosie nods. "Could I just look at him?"

He smiles at her. "If you promise me you won't go past the doorway, because I know how tempting it'll be once you're in the room."

"Okay. Just at the door," she agrees.

He leads her down the corridor to the bedrooms. "I put the mattress on the floor," he whispers as they approach the door. "I didn't know if he slept in a bed yet and the last thing I wanted was for him to fall."

"I don't have him in a bed. I've still got him in a crib, and Quinn told me that Monica does, too."

"That's what I thought." He opens the door slowly, letting the light from the hallway lend the darkened room a pale yellowy glow. She pieces the view together—there is the rounded curve of his bottom, the hands tucked beneath his face, the small shape of him curled like a nautilus beneath a blanket. She leans in, trying to catch sight of the rise and fall of his back, to follow his breathing, but Greg holds her arm, anchoring her firmly in place. She squints her eyes and stretches her hand out so it seems as though she can slide it along his body and touch his dark hair. Her palm is hot and achy with the pseudo-touch. Linder tugs lightly at her arm and she backs out of the doorway. "He's okay?" Her whisper feels rough inside her throat. Without thinking, she touches Linder's face. It's a trade-off, it feels like, for not having her hand against Jay's warm skin.

When Greg has closed the door, he strokes the back of two fingers gently over her cheekbone and, still whispering, says,

"Don't worry. He's fine, but he's exhausted by all the changes we've put him through."

"That the state has put him through, you mean."

"Yes, that's what I mean. Rosie, I'm going to try to take him as often as I can; as often as I can get Monica to agree to it."

"She'll give you a hard time about that."

"No, I don't think so. She didn't fight me at all today on it. I think she's very happy to have somebody step in and give her a break." Linder has taken a seat on one end of the couch and motions for her to join him.

"But what if she starts farming him out to anybody who comes along with an offer?" Rosie starts to slide her shoes off. She's going to be here for a while, it looks like.

"You mean somebody else besides me? Some friend of hers or something?" Rosie nods. "She likes me because I'm court appointed," he reminds her. "And I'll make sure she knows I'm available whenever she wants a few hours off. That'll kind of forestall her even thinking about calling anybody else."

"How often can you do that? I mean, you've got your practice and . . ."

He's shaking his head. "I'll work it out. I'll have her take a taxi up to the office, if it comes to that. Look, it's important. I can shift patients around if I have to for the next couple of weeks. And I'll try to set times up in advance with her. Then you'll know ahead, too, and you'll be able to see him during the day and not have to wait out his sleep cycles like this."

She reaches toward him, across the expanse of sofa. "Thank you," she says. He nods as he takes her hand.

"Please, Rosie, get an answering machine so we can be in touch on this?"

"Tomorrow. As soon as Caldor opens." He smiles. "Jay could sleep on like this till morning, couldn't he?" she asks, slipping her hand away from his.

"He could, I guess, but eventually we'll wake him." Greg stands up, adjusts the collar of his knit shirt. "So, what would you like? Wine? Sherry? Something fiercer? Dr. Linder always likes to provide choices with his prescriptions. We specialize in custom-design drugs, here."

"Whatever you recommend. You're the doctor."

He pours them each a glass of wine. She doesn't quite catch the name of it, but it's an after-dinner rather than a table wine, and he serves it up in small, almost miniature stemware. The drink is a little sweet, and a hint of orange finds its way over her tongue. "It makes my head spin," she tells him after several sips.

"That's a good sign. It means you're ready to relax. If you didn't feel it, you'd be too far gone already and I'd have to start worrying."

She laughs and slides into the feel of the laugh, a lovely release, a melting. "Are we talking medically here?" she asks.

"Absolutely. The ability to relax can be measured in sighs, smiles, and laughter. Those are all textbook physiological signs that a physician will look for when he's evaluating stress."

"And your diagnosis, Doctor?" Each of them has an arm stretched along the back of the couch, and as they lean toward one another, their fingers slide closer, approaching, but not yet meeting.

He narrows his eyes slightly and studies her. "I'd say you're stressed, but not hopelessly so."

"Ah, that's good to know, though I'm not sure that's a very trustworthy diagnosis. I certainly feel hopelessly stressed. I know I look it. I can't believe how deep the furrows under my eyes are getting."

He slides his arm farther along the couch back till his hand reaches, then covers hers. His fingers keep going, moving ever so slowly down the length of her forearm. "You don't have furrows under your eyes. You look beautiful."

"I didn't mean it like that," she says, embarrassed that she sounded like she wanted his compliments.

"Hush," he says. "Don't interrupt the learned doctor's diagnosis." She laughs, softly, and he joins in. "Can I get you a refill?" he asks, and she lets him lift the glass out of her hand.

She can't believe she's downed a drink this fast. She sits up tall, pulling herself back to where she's supposed to be. She can't forget about Jason. "None for me. I'll just finish what's left in there," she says, pointing to the minuscule quantity in the curve of her cordial glass.

"I'm just freshening it," he says, refilling hers and his in rapid sequence, then returning it to her. "Doctor's orders, remember. To my best patient," he says as he brings his glass to ring against hers.

She giggles. "If I'm high, am I still classified as a good patient?"

"Not good, my dear. The best. Capital letters. The Best."

"Seriously," she says, sipping the golden liquid. "Are there really good patients and bad patients? Do doctors keep these lists of traits or something that they look for in their ideal patients?"

At first he only smiles and takes a seat beside her. "Seriously?" he asks after a few moments. She nods. "Yes, there are good and bad ones, but it's a personal thing. Different, I suspect, for every doctor. Some of them hate the scared or squeamish patients or the ones who don't follow directions to the letter. Those kinds of things don't usually bother me. What does bother me are the ones who want a quick fix. They come in, they tell you their symptoms, and they want you to cure them on the spot and be done with it. Not everything, not asthma, certainly, can be dealt with in a ten-minute office visit, but you can't tell them that."

"If that's your definition, maybe you shouldn't be counting me in with the good patients. When I come in with Jay, all I want is for you to make him better, period. Sort of, 'Hey, Doc, let's get it right this time, please.' "

"Of course you do. We all want that same outcome, we all want Jason better, and we want him better now. But that's not really what I meant. You at least understand that if I don't find the perfect fix the first time out, it's because there is no such thing, but that I'm bringing my expertise and training and my personal way of thinking to the problem. You understand that there is problem solving to be done, not just a yes-or-no answer, because every single patient brings a whole set of unique life issues to his doctor that must be addressed in order to deliver the finest care. I mean, if it were as simple as my so-called bad patients wish it were, we wouldn't need physicians, would we? We could issue everybody their own reference books and let them read up on it—or CD-ROMs, maybe, let them push a button and get the answer with sound and visuals. And I'll tell you something—you know which patients are absolutely the worst?" She shakes her head. "The ones who if you say you have to check further into something, say, 'Don't you know that already?' " He looks at her for a moment and laughs gently. "Wow," he says. "I'm really ranting, aren't I? Maybe this *should* be the last drink. Sorry about that. I do have this problem separating my personal and professional lives, don't I? I am sorry."

"No, no, don't be sorry. I think this is really interesting— maybe because I witnessed my father agonizing over these exact same things, but I do think it's fascinating. I'm wondering, though, if maybe what you prefer is simply a more educated patient, one who understands that looking something up isn't a sign of ignorance."

"That could be. But you've mentioned your father and you've reminded me that you're a physician's daughter. That makes a big difference, too."

"Right. You get to see firsthand how a doctor agonizes over each patient. You develop a different level of understanding."

Greg nods. "True enough."

"I assume your father suffered along with each of his patients?"

"Oh, Lord, yes. He took every patient as seriously as if they were part of his own family. He became part of their families. My mother had to compete with his practice, big time. And we kids did, too. We could never count on him being around for family events. Not even the big holiday gatherings, recitals, or graduations. If a patient needed him, he was gone."

"Did your father live to see you become a doctor?"

He's silent for a moment. "He's not dead, Rosie."

"Oh? You use the past tense when you talk about him. Is he retired?"

"Well, I wouldn't use such a delicate word, actually. He was forced out. By one of those other kinds of patients."

"Sued, you mean?"

"Yes, ma'am. And worse. Criminal charges that were outrageous, but which eventually he lost."

"Criminal?"

"Negligent homicide."

"A medical situation?"

"Yes." He runs his hand across his mouth. "A medical situation of the most volatile sort. He lost a baby in delivery. It happens, of course. Not every baby can be born live and healthy, even under the best of circumstances. But parents, in their grief, always need someone to blame."

"I would have liked that luxury with Abby."

"I know. It's very natural. Juries look for scapegoats, too," he tells her. "It's really part of their job description. They're being asked, Who should be punished for this? and the doctor is the obvious answer almost every time. Let's face it: there's a basic human need to find a cause for every effect. My father was doomed from the moment he stood accused. And he lost everything—the right to practice, his income, and all his savings. He kept pumping money into legal counsel till he had nothing left—his personal form of catharsis, I guess. But that was almost ten years ago," he says with a dismissive hand gesture. "Now he lies on the couch and watches the talk shows. I got him a recliner last year so at least he'd be semi-upright. I don't know why I thought that was so important, but he never uses it, anyway. He lies there like a sick, dying man watching the talk shows, like he's in some kind of trance and the TV is just background noise. Do you know that there are talk shows on almost continuously through the day if you search enough for them? And believe me, he searches. He scans those channels with a vengeance. It's his whole meaning now. His only exercise, too." Greg pantomimes holding a remote control, aiming and firing repeatedly in front of himself. "I think he wants to find victims who are worse off than himself." He looks at her for a moment. "You know, I don't think I want to talk about this anymore." He stands up. "There are a lot of litigious morons out there, and it gets worse every day with

249

this *Court TV* and *People's Court*. He doesn't watch that stuff, by the way."

"I don't think I ever will, either."

"No, I suppose you've had enough of the real stuff, too." He pours himself another drink, points the bottle toward her, but she covers the small circular opening of her glass with two fingers. Greg puts the bottle back down on the mantel.

"Rosie?" he says, posing it as a question or a beckoning, perhaps. "You can stay the night if you want. See him in the morning. I'd like it if you would."

She smiles at him. "I don't think so. Not tonight. I should see him and go home, I think."

"Rosie," he says again.

She waits. Her name hangs between them like an invocation of a distant presence. She's thinking maybe she should just put her drink down and forget relaxing or whatever this is and get clearheaded again, but there's no coffee table, no obvious place she could put the wine to rest. She feels flustered; pressured, though he has given her more than adequate space. "How are we going to know if Jason wakes up if we're out here?" she asks him, shifting the focus.

"We'll hear him. He'll call out."

"He doesn't usually call for me in the middle of the night. He's a good sleeper if he isn't having breathing problems. I think he's more likely to turn over and go back to sleep."

"Rosie?" he asks again, this time leaning slightly toward her as he speaks her name. When she doesn't answer he says, "You're backing off, aren't you?"

She shrugs. "I don't know what I'm doing. I'm waiting to see Jason right now. Maybe I just can't deal with two things at once," she says, and her hand flutters around her face. "I know I'm being inarticulate, but alcohol does that to me."

"You've had all of two drops, I think," he says, eyeing her glass.

"You've refilled this twice," she points out, lifting it for him to see.

"Three thimblefuls," he estimates.

"And I had some before, too," she confesses.

"Ah-ha. I'll accept that as cause." He looks at her and smiles. "But I guess in any case, *I* should back off?"

"I'm just trying to keep my brain focused and you're making it harder in every way, I'd say." She smiles at him.

"At least I'm having an effect on you, still."

"Oh, that you are, Dr. Linder, I promise you that," she says, and she takes another sip of wine. "And this, too," she adds, raising the glass.

He sits again, leaving more breathing space between them now. "It's because of what happened in court, isn't it? I blew it then, didn't I?"

"No, I told you, I don't blame you for that."

"Right. You didn't blame me, but you can't have been happy."

"I wasn't happy with anything that went on in that courtroom."

He nods. "If I hadn't been called to the stand, there wouldn't be this divide between us now." He moves his hand along the leather welting toward her, but only just so far, then he slides his fingers back along the curved seam. Forward again and back. Both their eyes follow the slow movement.

"It's not just that."

"I've done something more? What? Tell me," he says, looking up, his eyes exploring her face.

"No, not you, that's not what I meant. It's me. It's where my life is. It's this mess with Jay. Give me time, Greg."

He nods. "I feel a little . . . panicky." He speaks slowly: "I don't want to lose what we had." He starts to say something more, but stops.

"What?" she asks, reaching her hand toward him, along the same seam.

"I was falling in love with you," he says, turning his eyes full on her. She feels herself blush under his gaze. "I don't want to lose that." He shakes his head. "I want us to get back to that." He leans closer, his eyes so much darker now. "I was falling in love with you."

She closes her eyes for a second, she's not sure why, trying to think, maybe, or clear her brain. Trying not to look at his eyes and his lips, not to want them, or even have to consider them, and then he's kissing her, and she's aware of the shape of his lips—so different from Quinn's—on hers, and thinking, We were falling in love. She wants to be closer now, right now, but she's still got this ridiculous glass in her hand and she's holding it near their faces, almost like a torch, like she's lighting up their kiss. When they part, she sees that he, too, still holds a glass. "Yes," he says, as he lifts the glass from her hand, and she nods, not sure what she's agreeing to, only knowing that it wouldn't be so very bad to agree with him.

"Jason?" she says, speaking her child's name as a funny sort of question that starts to get lost in the intricate puzzle that is his reaching for her.

"Later. Soon," he says. The darkness in his voice now has such a presence, she can almost grab hold of it. "Ah," he murmurs, his hand open and soft against her cheek.

An electronic noise, jarring and amplified, and so close, it almost seems to rise out of his body, startles her, and she pulls abruptly away from him. "Damn," he says, reaching for the phone, which sits upon the long console table behind the couch. His hand rests on the receiver, but he doesn't lift it. "I won't answer it," he says, drawing his hand back.

"Yes, you will," she says. It isn't a criticism, merely an observation.

He nods, picks it up.

"Dr. Linder," he says. Then, after a pause, "Did they give you the child's chart readings? The last dosage? Good," he says, writing the information down on a pad that bears advertising for one of Jason's current prescription medications. "Give me their number. No, I'll call directly on this one. We've got potential trouble here."

He doesn't even put the receiver back, just pushes the flash button, gets himself a clear line. "Sorry," he says to her, holding the receiver away from his ear, shaking it, thereby placing the blame, she supposes, on that instrument. "I need to face the truth. There is no personal life in medicine."

"It's okay," she says, smoothing her sweater across her hips.

"Mrs. Patterson?" he asks a moment later into the phone.

What's he planning to do about Jay? Rosie wonders. Maybe he's forgotten that the child is even here. She mouths Jason's name at Greg and points down toward that corridor, but he's too involved with his patient to even notice she's there anymore. Let him forget about it, then, she decides, the thought clear as a revelation.

Let him go ahead and agree to meet the family at his office and then she'll have to be the one to stay with Jason. Or better yet, she'll take him back to her house. He'll have to agree. This family—Patterson, was it?—they'll already be on their way to his office by the time she and Greg finish arguing about what to do with Jason. By then it'll be too late. He'll have to go out there himself—he wouldn't dream of leaving them out there, waiting in the dark and cold for him. He'll *have* to let Jason go with her. And she'll say to him: No one will know. Come by in the morning and pick him up. No one will know. It can work, she tells herself, heading for the bedroom hallway. She'll wrap Jay up in that blanket he's under, maybe grab another if she can find one, and take him home. She fumbles with the doorknob to her child's room, opens the door, and flips on the light. He doesn't stir. "Jay, baby," she says, kneeling at his side, her voice low, not meant to be overheard. Her heart's beating like mad. She wants to scoop him up into her arms. Gently, she reminds herself. No jolts. "Jay?" she asks, not touching him, even yet. There's no response. Toddlers sleep so deeply, she knows there's no way he's going to respond to his name being spoken so softly. She'll have to lift him up. Getting him into a car seat when he's this zonked isn't going to be easy, she knows.

She pulls back the blanket, and for a moment she almost thinks it isn't him. His face looks swollen, damp, but it is him. Or maybe a sick version of him. His eyes open for just the briefest moment, but they don't focus, just close back down again. She kisses his forehead, but he's not warm. He's been sleeping soundly, that's all it is, she tells herself. The sheet is soaked under his face; he must have been breathing through his mouth and drooled across it. She pulls him onto her lap, and there's no resistance. He's limp, and she sees, as his head slides

253

back, that his eyes aren't even fully closed, they're maybe three-quarters closed. She shakes him gently, carefully, but his shoulders only sag in her hands. "Jay," she says, her voice louder, intended to pierce through the sleep. "Jay," she says, and this doesn't look like sleep, not even like deep sleep. His breathing is slow and quiet, but not like when he has an attack. The smell of his breath is all wrong, like something burnt. What's wrong with him? Is this some kind of coma? Has he had a seizure or something? "Jason," she says sharply, and when he doesn't even flinch, she clutches him to her, the panic so fierce it feels like her body is about to be pulled in a hundred different directions. "Greg," she screams. A piercing sound, but Jason doesn't move. She repeats her call, even more strident this time. Jason's mouth drops open wider.

"What?" Linder asks. He's next to her.

"What the hell's wrong with him, Greg?"

"He's sleeping, Rosie. Put him back down, please." He has his hands over hers and he's trying to get her to move Jay back off her lap, back onto the mattress.

"There's something wrong with him," she insists, but she's letting him guide her arms forward. When Jason is settled back on his makeshift bed, he lifts her arms away from the child, pulls the blanket back over him, and then tries to get her to rise up from the floor.

"There's nothing wrong with him but exhaustion," he says.

"That's not just sleep, is it?"

"What isn't?" he asks her, his voice at whisper level now. He's holding her hand, trying to get her to move out of the room, but she wants to stay. "I'll talk to you out there," he says, indicating the corridor with a tilt of his head.

"We should take him to the hospital," Rosie pleads.

Linder doesn't speak till they're in the hall. Then he says, "Rosie, if you take him to the hospital, I'm the one who's going to examine him, right?"

She shrugs. "I don't know."

"Well, I am. And I already told you what's up with him."

"I can't wake him, Greg, he's not responding to anything. Not to my shouting, not to my shaking." She's pulled her arms out of his hold and she's gesturing back toward Jason's sleeping place. "I'll take him back to my house while you go see these other patients," she says, but she plans to go directly to the hospital. It isn't far from here. She can be there in ten minutes. They'll take care of him.

"I'm not going to the office. The Patterson child is okay. They were just concerned. They had questions. I handled it all over the phone." Greg has taken hold of her arm again. "Your little boy is trying to recuperate from extreme exhaustion due to physical and emotional upheaval. We're not moving him. We're letting sleep do a natural cure on him. Shouting and shaking will push him deeper right now, Rosie. That's what we want to avoid. And anyway, *you* certainly can't go to the hospital."

"Why not?"

"Because you'd be violating your court order in a public place. Once the judge got wind of that, he'd put your little boy under lock and key. No more foster home, then, Rosie—he'll put Jason in an institution. Or, alternatively, he'll put you in jail and you won't be able to see him that way, either. Judges are notorious for equating disregard of their authority with irrationality and insanity. He'll decide you do fit into that Munchausen profile, after all. You'll be digging yourself into a very deep grave that way. Right now you need to stay calm. Besides, you can see him here almost any day."

She feels a chill go up her back. His tone has been gentle—confidential, really—and with a pang of sadness, maybe, but what he's saying is just plain frightening. What's left now? Be a good girl, a quiet girl, and step back, let her child be pushed and pulled yet some more by a judge and a social worker?

Linder has led her back to the living room now, though it's been awkward, jolting—she's held back every step of the way. "Rosie," Greg says, "now that you've seen Jason, you should go home. You need sleep just as much as your child does." He has her jacket in his hand and he holds it open for her, waiting for her to put her arms into it.

"Are you sure he's okay?"

"Absolutely." She slips her arms into the jacket and he

255

adjusts it lightly over her shoulders. "Though I'm not so sure about you anymore. What did I say earlier? That you were stressed but not hopelessly so?"

"Something like that."

"Well, I think you just went over the top. I don't think I could manage to get any laughs or smiles out of you anymore tonight. Your shoulders are so tight, they scare me."

"He doesn't look like himself, Greg."

"Nobody looks the same when they're sound asleep, you know that."

"But I know what he looks like asleep. This is different."

"Precisely. This is exhaustion. You know, you *do* have a tendency to overreact to his symptoms. I mean, what that DCF worker said in court about your responses to this disease— none of that was really all that far off the mark."

She'd been buttoning her jacket, but now she stops. "You never said that before."

"Right now you're exhausted, and the stress and, of course, the alcohol are all going to exacerbate your reactions." He nods at her, agreeing with himself because she obviously won't. Has she overreacted? Has she brought this whole hideous situation down on herself by having maternal instincts that were totally out of whack?

"So do you think you can drive yourself home, or should I call a cab?"

"I can drive," she says, though she isn't quite sure this is true. She just wants to get out of here; to get away from him and his lack of sympathy, fast. She lifts her purse off the chair she'd dropped it onto earlier, and he reaches out toward her to embrace her, to make his recently spoken words grow foggy and indistinct, she knows. She steps back, beyond his touch.

"I'm sorry," he says, stepping back himself. "That phone call wrecked everything, didn't it?"

"It wasn't the phone call. It was my child." She's struggling with the lock on his front door and he reaches around her, turning the bolt, pulling it exactly the right way, his arm against her arm, his breath in her hair. She pushes the door forward as it opens, steps through and turns, backing down the stairs. "Call me in the morning and tell me how he is, okay?"

"Of course. As soon as he's awake."

"Thanks," she says. She takes the path to the car on the run, though once she's in the driver's seat, she realizes she has no idea what she's thanked him for, and no idea where it is she's running to.

CHAPTER
THIRTY-ONE

SHE HAS TO PUSH ON THE BELL AT QUINN'S house for forever. Maybe she'll have to get the police to break his door down the way he did the night Jay was sick. It's not that big a place, why can't he hear her? "Because he's gone to sleep, you fool," she says aloud to herself. She has no idea what time it is, but she knows it's late. There's hardly a light on in the whole condo complex.

Finally, finally, she hears his footsteps behind the door. "Rosie," he says when he opens the door. "I called you a hundred times tonight, there was no answer. Are you all right?"

"I'm fine," she says, coming through the door, "but I think something strange is going on with Linder."

"What are you talking about—the credentials didn't check out?"

"No, they did." For a moment she can hear Linder's voice as though he's right there, whispering the words in her ear: *Don't even tell Quinn.* "He told me not to tell you," she says before she has a chance to pay heed to the remembered warning.

"Wait, what are we talking about here, Rosie?" He puts his hand to his forehead and rubs it. "I just woke up, you need to start over, tell me what's happening." He sits down on the arm of the love seat and motions for Rosie to sit somewhere, but she's too jumpy to light.

Rosie takes a deep breath. She's not sure where the story begins. Or what the story even is. She just knows there's some-

258

thing out of whack, something that needs telling. "Linder took Jay back to his house after he examined him. Monica told him he could keep him overnight."

"What? Where does she get off doing that?" He's got both hands on the couch arm, like he's going to push himself sky high any second.

"The court made her his temporary parent, so I guess she can do that; let him sleep at somebody else's house." Quinn is shaking his head. "The point is, Linder called me and told me I could come over and see Jay. He said he was putting himself on the line by doing that, by letting me violate the court order, which he was. He said not to tell anybody, which was totally logical under the circumstances, and I said I'd only mention it to you, but he said not to tell you, either."

"He knows I'm a cop, right?"

She's nodding. "He said it'd put you in conflict, because you'd feel like as a cop you had to report it."

"Right. So he made it seem like he was doing me a favor, having you keep it a secret from me?"

She considers this for a moment. "I guess you could say that. But he's right, isn't he? Now that I have told you, you want to report him, don't you?"

"No, I'm not turning you in."

"And he said if you didn't know about it, you couldn't be a witness against me."

"Husbands can't be compelled to testify against their wives, Rosie."

Of course. She'd forgotten that. Had Greg also? "None of that's important right now. Here's the thing: I really got nervous when I saw Jay. He didn't look right to me."

"Didn't look right how?"

She can picture his damp little face, the open, dry mouth. "I'm not sure, but maybe like he was in a coma, almost."

"Jesus, Rosie, a coma?"

"Well, I don't know because I've never really seen anybody in a coma, and I'm not a doctor. Maybe I was over-reacting. Linder said I was, that Jay was just sleeping very deeply, that he was exhausted. Maybe he's right, but when I said we should take him to the hospital, he said there was no point to that because he'd be the one examining him there, too."

"That time we had him at the hospital, remember you told the nurse he wasn't breathing right then? You got all panicky, but he was okay, remember?"

He doesn't believe her. He thinks she's a hysteric, doesn't he. "So maybe it wasn't a coma."

"Is there a reason, something that would cause a coma?"

"I don't know. That's what makes it scary. But you're right, I'm probably wrong about it."

"I didn't say you were wrong."

Yes, you did, she thinks. "I'm probably stressed and exhausted," she says, repeating Linder's diagnosis, "but maybe it was some complication of asthma, or maybe," she says, the thought coming into view as an all too vivid photograph of the foster mother bending over, administering to her child, "maybe Monica screwed up the dosage and he's taking too much."

"Then why doesn't Linder pick up on that?"

"I don't know," she says, her voice sharper now, angry. She really doesn't know anything anymore.

"Or maybe, like I said yesterday, Linder's incompetent." Rosie shrugs. "Would taking too much of one of his medications make him go into a coma?"

"How would I know?"

"Don't you usually look all that stuff up in the library? You always have a handle on all this medical stuff, Rosie."

"I don't this time, Quinn." She's got her hands clenched together in front of her, trying to keep from flying completely apart. "Look, for all I know, Linder's drugging him with something." She feels faint now, hearing these words that she hadn't wanted to let come together into a thought. She bites down on the side of her index finger. It doesn't stop the tears from starting up in her eyes.

"No," Quinn says, shaking his head, and she feels relieved. Quinn doesn't think Linder would do it. "He has no reason to do that," he says, and she nods, grateful for his easy dismissal of that possibility. "But how come another doctor at the hospital wouldn't be the one to examine him?"

"I don't know, he didn't say."

"But why didn't you just ask him that? Or why didn't you insist on another doctor? Or a second opinion, whatever it's called."

Because, she thinks, remembering it, the way he said it, it seemed like a given: If they went to the hospital Linder would be the examining physician. "It didn't occur to me to question it. Greg Linder is Jason's physician. And you have to trust your doctor or you're nowhere." She gives these words the sound of absolute conviction, but she doesn't believe them. She's spent a lifetime holding fast to her physician father's rules: *Get a second opinion. No one is infallible. Don't put yourself or your family in jeopardy because you're afraid (embarrassed, too lazy*—there were lots of variants on this one) *to challenge a doctor's opinion. Or, because you're attracted to him?* Her father hadn't mentioned that one. All right, so she needed a clearer head about her child's illness. And, okay, Quinn had been right, she shouldn't have been mucking it up with non-medical stuff like kisses, or wine, or even restaurant dining, for God's sake.

"I think I should go out there," Quinn says. "I'm going to put some clothes on."

He's already started up the staircase of the duplex but she's right behind him when she begs, "Please, Quinn, don't do that. He said I was reacting all out of proportion. Maybe I was." She hasn't mentioned the brandy and the wine, that they may have contributed to this exaggerated state of mind. "If you go stomping over there to have a confrontation with him, it's going to be obvious I violated his trust and told you all this." She's holding on to the stair railing, almost pulling at it, as if she could draw him over to her side of the issue that way. "If it turns out there's nothing wrong with Jay, he'll never let me back over there to see him, because he won't trust me anymore."

"And if there is something wrong with Jay?"

"I know we need to do something, I'm not denying that. I

just don't know if it's this, rushing over there in the middle of the night."

Quinn's sigh is long and weary sounding. "Okay. You have a better suggestion?"

She shakes her head. "That's what we need to think about."

He runs his hand back through his hair. "I can't take it if anything happens to Jay," he says, his voice cracking. He lowers himself down to sit on one of the steps and puts his head into his hands. She sits beside him, stroking his arm, then she brings her face into the space between his shoulder and neck. She wants to say, "It'll be be okay, Quinn," but she can't. She wants him to say it to her, too. She slides her arms around him and they each hold on tight to the other.

CHAPTER
THIRTY-TWO

"**Y**OU SHOULD LIE DOWN," QUINN SAYS, and he motions with a tilt of his head, toward the upstairs.

They both go up to the bedroom and they stretch out, side by side, but not touching, on his bed. "You get some sleep," Quinn says, and then they both close their eyes.

The first time she wakes, she sees that he has turned on his side toward her, and that he is awake. "Sleep," he says to her, and she closes her eyes again.

The second time she wakes, he says, "There's one more thing I need to tell you about the Emerson baby."

Has he been awake this whole time, watching her as she sleeps? He's turned on his back and his eyes scan the ceiling. She pushes herself up on one elbow. "What?" she asks softly.

He reaches behind him, adjusting the pillow against the wall and then he pushes himself up with both hands so he can lean against it, but he still doesn't speak. Rosie knows all the details, anyway. Everybody in town does, all the gory particulars were examined day after day on TV, in the paper. A media field day. And he told her, day after day, about it. The husband, the driver, was killed instantly. In the passenger seat, the mother, nine months pregnant, was screaming, "My baby, save my baby," and Quinn practically ripped the door off the car and pulled her out. But then she'd kept screaming, witnesses said. And he said so, too. She'd been there on the grassy verge, screaming, one hand on her big belly, one hand pointing

263

toward the blue Chevy, screaming, "My baby, save my baby." It wasn't till afterward, when the car blew up, that he found out about the thirteen-month-old in the backseat. "It wasn't your fault, Quinn," she says, finally.

"Then why does it haunt me, Rosie? Why, when I finally sleep, do I see her face and that look of horror? Why do I still hear her screams? It feels like I can't ever do enough penance for her pain. I held her there, at the side of the road. She watched that car blow with the baby inside."

Rosie's sitting now, too. "Quinn, you have to tell yourself that you saved that woman. That you saved her unborn child. That baby's fine and healthy now. Okay, you didn't save the other child, but you aren't Superman. You aren't Jesus Christ. If you hadn't been there, the other two would have died as well. And you know, you didn't cause that car crash. And it's the car crash that killed that child, Quinn, not you."

"I know." She sees him wince, hears a sharp intake of his breath. He's seeing it again, hearing it, she knows. "I've tried telling myself all that stuff, but it doesn't help. It's more powerful than I am. It's got me sitting behind a desk now, answering telephones. I can't even ride in a squad car." He stops and his body shudders. She knows there's more. She waits, listening to the only sound; the sound of his breathing. "I know we've been over all that before. The one thing we haven't talked about is that I think it's what wrecked us. I mean, I couldn't let you touch me." She closes her eyes. "I couldn't let you like me."

"You should have told me," she whispers.

He shakes his head. "I couldn't. I wanted you to hate me; I needed to make my pain as fierce as hers."

"Oh, Quinn," she says, then slowly brings a hand to his shoulder, to the spot where she had brought her face to rest a few hours earlier. Why hadn't she guessed this? Helped him?

"And it's made all this stuff with Jay much worse."

"How did it make that worse?"

He taps the side of his fist against his lips. "Because I kept thinking I deserved to have a sick child. That it was meant to be. I thought of it as part of my punishment. I even figured I deserved to have the state take him from us." He covers his face with his hands for a moment, then says, "Rosie, I wanted the pain." His voice breaks and he closes his eyes. "And I'm a selfish bastard. I wanted the court to punish me. That's why I didn't fight enough for him."

"Quinn, the court isn't doing this for your peace of mind. They're after me in this. And you didn't make things any worse for Jay, you just made it harder on yourself, that's all." She moves next to him, facing him, but his eyes aren't on her. They're tracing the shape of the room, fleeing out through the windows.

"I don't know if that's true. I felt so numb, so passive. I should have fought it more. I should have come out more fiercely on your side or something. *Something*," he says, pounding a fist against his thigh. "Rosie, you have to believe me when I tell you I never wanted Jason to die for that baby. I didn't even want him to be sick, but it was all so confused"—he moves his hand in a circular motion, as though he's stirring a distasteful brew—"Jay and that baby. It started to feel like what was happening to him was meant to be and that I shouldn't and couldn't do anything about my own suffering. But I know I could have done more for *him*. I could have been there with you—this whole thing scares the hell out of me. I mean, it's like I was sacrificing my child to the state for my own peace. Forgive me," he begs her. His whole upper body is shaking and she knows he's trying to hold back tears.

"Quinn, you didn't do anything wrong, not with that baby and not with Jay." She strokes his face along the jawline, her hand pricked by the nearly day-old beard. "You were just one of the victims of an accident. And now you and I, we're victims, together, of what's happening to Jay. So there's nothing to forgive." She kisses his mouth and she tastes his tears. When he slips his arm around her, it is not so much an embrace as an acknowledgment of her presence. He doesn't try to draw her against himself.

Through the rest of the dark morning they lie side by side; closer than they have been in months, or perhaps longer.

265

Occasionally either or both of them sleeps, lightly, floating away from, not into, their troubles. When either of them awakens, it doesn't feel shocking to realize where they are, or how they are both there in that same space together, on his rumpled bed. In sleep, they do touch, for in turning toward and away, the limbs of one can't avoid grazing the other's.

When she sees light coming through the window, she kisses his mouth again and whispers his name. Then she says, "I'm going to call Linder now." He opens his eyes and nods, as though he has heard her right through his sleep.

She sits at the edge of the bed, prepared to wait through many unanswered rings until she wakes him, but the phone is picked up almost immediately. "I was just about to call you," Linder tells her when he answers.

"How's Jason?"

"He's great. He ate a huge breakfast and he's raring to go. I'm telling you, the curative effects of a long sleep are astounding."

"You think he's all better?"

"Absolutely. He's terrific."

"Can I talk to him?"

"Hang on," he says, and then a moment later, "here he is. Say hello to your mom," she hears him coach from the sidelines.

"Jay, it's Mommy. Did you eat your breakfast, sweet boy?"

"Tell her what you had for breakfast, Jason," she hears Greg say.

She can hear his breathing, separate from Greg's presence. At least she knows he's there still, breathing still. "Did you have cereal?" she asks him.

"Tell her Cheerios," Greg prompts. "Tell your mom about the Cheerios."

"Jay?" she asks. "Jay, say hello, honey." She waits. "Jason, say hello."

"Rosie," Linder says directly into the phone, "he's playing dumb right now. Does he even understand about telephones yet?"

"Oh, I don't know. I guess he doesn't. He always asks to talk on the phone, but it's mostly really listening that he ends up doing."

"Well, that's definitely what's happening today," Greg observes.

"When can I see him?"

"When I work it out with Monica. I'll call you later."

"You're sure he's all right, Greg?"

"Absolutely. Now stop worrying. But I've got to run. I've got a million things to do before I get out of here and of course I've got this extra stop with having to take your child over to Monica's. So you're going to have to hang up. When I'm running late, I always drive way, way above the speed limit. I'm bad that way. And I don't want to do that with your child in the car, if you know what I mean." There's a deliberateness in the last few words that startles her.

Did she know what he meant? Why did that sound like a threat to her? And why did he keep saying 'your child'? "He better be all right," she says. It's almost a question, just slightly sharper.

"Oh, I agree with you, absolutely. Talk to you soon," he says, and hangs up.

Quinn has sat up on the bed. "Something's wrong, isn't it?"

"I couldn't tell."

"Did Jay say anything?"

"No. But he almost never does on the phone. Sometimes he just tries to lick the receiver."

"Could you even tell if he was there?"

"He's there and he's breathing. I don't think Linder was faking that. Everything seems completely okay. I probably shouldn't have gotten off on that 'he better be all right' business. I don't know why, but I started to get spooked by what he was saying. Like he was, I don't know, threatening me."

"What kind of threat did he make?"

"I'm not even sure it *was* a threat. He just said he had to hang up so he didn't speed with Jay in the car."

"There's something wrong if he's threatening you, Rosie."

"But that's the thing, I don't even really know if it's a threat." She's buttoning and unbuttoning a button on her shirt.

"It's the sort of thing you might say to be funny. You know"—and here she imitates his deeper voice—" 'You better let me hang up so I don't drive too fast.' "

"We've got to find out more about him. Can you get more on him?"

"I can try. I can go back to the hospital, see what I can dig up."

"Okay. Call me at work the second you finish there." He's sitting on the bed, rubbing his forehead with his hand. "What's this creep doing?" he asks as he gets up off the bed. Halfway across the room, he stops and turns back toward her. "Screw work," he says. "They can get a temp to answer their stupid phone. I'm calling in sick and we're doing this together."

CHAPTER
THIRTY-THREE

BREAKFAST AT THE NEW DINER IS A JOKE. Both Rosie and Quinn order black coffee in the hopes that it will make them alert in spite of their sleepless night. She breaks her doughnut into at least a dozen pieces, leaving it scattered like a small unsolved jigsaw puzzle on her plate. He stabs his fork at the yolks of his sunny-side-up eggs, then dips a slice of toast into the yellow puddle. Two bites of that, and he's had enough. Both of them keep checking the clock. There's no point in going over to the hospital till there's actually somebody in the personnel office. More black coffee. He tries calling Monica to check on Jason, but the child has not been delivered to her yet.

They check the clock. Their watches. More black coffee. And finally, on the third call, Monica reports that, yes, Jason has arrived. "How is he?" Rosie asks Quinn as soon as he gets back to their booth.

"She says he's okay, but not great. He's coughing."

"What?" The coffee cup slips in her hands and she barely manages to lower it to the saucer without dumping all the liquid onto the table. "What did Linder tell her to do about it?"

"I asked her, but I didn't get an answer."

"What do you mean?"

"I mean she changed the subject. She asked me if I was aware that you'd gone over to the doctor's house and forced your way in to see Jason."

"What? He called *me*," she says, pointing a finger at herself. "He asked me to come over there. Anyway, how could I force my way in? He's bigger than I am, she knows that."

"He told her you sweet-talked your way in the door, then when he took an emergency phone call, you sneaked off and grabbed Jason and started to leave the house with him."

"Oh, no."

"Is that what happened?"

Rosie can't say anything at first. "I did go into the room where Jay was sleeping when Linder was on the phone, but he was going to let me see him anyway."

"Did you go over to Monica's in the afternoon?"

It seems like a month ago to Rosie. She can't believe it was only yesterday. "Yes," she says, watching Quinn nod as he contemplates all the gaps she's left in her version of what's happened.

"She says you talked your way into her house so you probably did the same thing to him. She says it's obvious that you would have tried to take Jason if you'd found him at her house, so she believes you grabbed him at Linder's."

Rosie's shaking her head. "Why is he doing this?"

"I don't know. You said he didn't want you telling anybody, but now he's the one who's telling Monica. That doesn't make sense."

"You think I'm lying, don't you?"

"I think I really don't understand." He's holding his fork between his thumb and forefinger, shaking it so it bounces like mad.

"Okay, Quinn," she says, raising up both hands, palms out. "You just go on to work and turn me in, or whatever it is you want to do, okay?"

"Rosie," he says, dropping the fork, catching hold of her hands. "I believe you. I believe you absolutely. But I'm scared. I'm scared because I think we're up against something really bad right now. I think Linder might be trying to get you put in jail." He's whispering and he's pulling her hands closer to him.

"What are you talking about?"

"Linder told Monica that he thinks you slipped Jay something while he was on the phone. That he'd been fine up to that point, but a couple of hours later, he had an attack. A completely unexplained attack."

"Oh, no, Quinn. Oh my God, our poor little baby." She pulls back from his hold and one of her hands smacks into her water glass, sending it flying across the table and onto the floor.

"Rosie, listen to me, follow this, please." She's grabbing napkins out of the dispenser, mopping up the mess on the table and her lap. A waiter whisks the glass away with one hand and with the other uses an enormous sponge to remove the water from the floor. "Rosie," Quinn repeats, "Monica told me I can't see Jay unless he's better and if he isn't, that the doctor is going to want to examine him again." Rosie nods. "I said I didn't trust his judgment and that I wanted another doctor, and she said I should be more worried about my wife seeing my child." Rosie goes for some more napkins and Quinn stops her hand. "Rosie, look at me." She lets him keep a hold on her hand and turns her eyes back toward him. "We've got to figure out what he's up to."

"He's making our baby sick, Quinn. It's simple. We've got to get Jay out of his care."

"Maybe there's another explanation. Maybe Linder really believes what he's saying. Maybe he really, honestly thinks you're making Jason sick."

"Then why would he say I forced my way in there?"

"Maybe Monica's the one who's changing it. Maybe all he said—or meant—was that you went into Jason's room when he was on the telephone."

"I should have insisted on going to the hospital and . . ." She stops. She's going over their conversation of the evening before, yet again.

"What?" Quinn says, asking for the rest of her unfinished thought.

"Wait a minute. Last night he was threatening me, too. He told me that if I went to the hospital with Jay, they'd report me to the court and Jay would be institutionalized. Now, how would the hospital staff even know I wasn't supposed to be with Jay or that there was a court case?"

"They'd know if he told them."

"Right, but that's the only way. He definitely didn't want me going to the hospital. He was trying his damnedest to scare me off it. Quinn, we need to get to the court, have them get another doctor. We need an injunction or whatever it is they do."

"We don't have enough to make the court even listen to us, let alone intervene." He lets go of her hands. "The court will believe *him* if he tells this story about you going over there. You're the one under suspicion, not him."

"Then we need to go over and talk to Monica, convince her."

"That's a lost cause. She loves Linder. She calls him The Doctor, and the way she says it, I swear, she sees it all lit up in neon. He's got her in love with him. And she told me, she'll call the police the second she sees you or even hears your voice on the phone. She may call them on me if I come too openly to your defense."

Rosie shakes her head. She's thinking about Linder, all that business about how he was in love with her. How he kept her in the living room, away from Jay, with seductive words and touches. She closes her eyes to try to lock it out. When she looks at Quinn again she asks him, "Why do we care if she calls the police? You know everybody on the force."

"Not on the Bradford force. And they're legally obligated to notify the court of violations. They will. They won't have my conflicts, they'll just pick up the phone and report your violations."

"Okay, you're the cop. What do we do?"

"We go to the hospital, just like we planned, and we check deeper. We get something the court *will* look at."

"And if we don't find it?"

He shakes his head. "I don't know yet." He takes out his wallet and motions to a waiter for the check.

CHAPTER
THIRTY-FOUR

"**N**o," THE WOMAN IN PERSONNEL TELLS Rosie, "we never release that information. I told you yesterday, the fact sheet is all we give out. We have to protect our employees. I mean, if you worked here, you wouldn't want just anybody walking in, looking at your references, would you?"

Rosie hates it when people phrase their questions so that you're almost forced to agree with them. "I wouldn't care," Rosie says, hearing the belligerence in her voice. "And it seems to me, the only person who would care is somebody who's covering something up."

The woman frowns at her. "Privacy's a very important issue these days and we take it very seriously." The woman holds a folder with green and yellow stickers on it against her chest like a shield.

"What about if there's an emergency?" Rosie asks.

The woman shrugs. "There aren't any exceptions."

Quinn leans forward, his hand sliding across the counter toward the woman. "My son is very, very ill, and I think it's because his doctor is incompetent. He's two years old, and I feel helpless. I'm watching him get sicker every day."

Rosie can see the hesitation in the woman's face. The militant frown is gone. She's weakening, Rosie thinks. "There's nothing to keep you from changing doctors. Upstairs," she suggests, a thumb lifted toward the ceiling, "in the information

273

office, they'll give you the name of another specialist. That's what I'd do."

"We've thought about that," Rosie says, trying to keep her tone easy and respectful. "But it's more complicated than that," Rosie says, but she can't continue. She doesn't want to have to explain that she's been declared incompetent. "I want to keep this doctor from ever having access to my child, like if he's admitted to the hospital, or the emergency room."

"Or access to another child," Quinn adds, but Rosie wishes he hadn't. This might be overkill. It might make the personnel woman think they're out for vengeance; for wholesale ruination of a career.

"The only way you can get to those documents is with a court order. That's the only way." She's tightening back up, just like Rosie feared.

"Everything's so completely screwed up," Rosie says. "He can see our baby anytime he wants, and we can't. The court thinks I'm making him sick, but I'm not. If the doctor keeps being able to see him, I'm afraid—oh, God, I'm so afraid." She covers her mouth with her hand. She's not going to say it. Quinn has put his hands on her shoulders while she's talking. Okay, now I've done it, said that about the court, she thinks. She's going to dismiss us because I'm a crazed hysteric.

"You know," the woman says, putting the folder down, "even if I had the authority to hand the files over, you wouldn't find anything much in them. I mean, if you're thinking the recommendations will say he was incompetent someplace else, forget it. If he got written up that way, Bradford Hospital wouldn't have hired him. We wouldn't have even called him for an interview. And anyway, in this business, you never see that kind of stuff in the files. All these doctors," she says, motioning behind her toward the stacks of files, "they all got their recommendations from other doctors. They went to the guys who were their colleagues and friends. So there's never anything negative in any one of those files. Take it from me: doctors don't bad-mouth each other. Just try complaining to one of them about another one of them, and you'll see how they close ranks around each other." Rosie's thinking about how wrong this woman is, for she can remember how her father would catalog the faults of other physicians. "They *know* who's good, who's bad," the woman continues, "and they wouldn't send their own families to their best friends, but they'll send you and me, returning favors, jumping through hoops." Did her father do that? Did he bad-mouth his colleagues at home, then cozy up with them at hospital staff meetings? "I can promise you that every last one of those recommendations in there will say something positive," the woman concludes.

"But you check on their background, don't you?" Rosie asks.

"Transcripts, training background, that sort of thing?" Rosie nods. "Yes, that would all be in there."

"And if there were any criminal charges, that would show up, too, wouldn't it?"

"Yes, and we wouldn't hire them. But you know, criminal charges aren't usually brought against doctors for medical *procedures*. People sue doctors all the time, but they don't charge them with *crimes*, per se. There was a big case last year—not here. A patient died because of a really, really stupid mistake. A doctor—a seasoned, experienced doctor, not some kid—mistook a dialysis tube for a feeding tube and killed his patient by having feeding solution put into her dialysis catheter. That doctor had criminal charges brought against him—but not homicide—just reckless endangerment or something. And that was an outrageous mistake, a mistake you or I, untrained people, would never have made. Not unless we were impaired, maybe. You know, drunk or on drugs. But this time the prosecutors just couldn't look the other way, it was so extreme. So maybe he partied before he came on duty." She looks straight at Rosie. "They're not gods," she pronounces, and nods her head, emphasizing her sureness about this diagnosis. "But now I'm off on my favorite hobby horse," she says, her voice lighter. "Sorry about that. I guess I just don't like privilege, and freedom from prosecution seems a bit too privileged to me."

"Why is it that doctors don't ever get charged?" Rosie asks.

"What the doctors will tell you is that if they were open to charges of homicide, nobody would ever be a doctor again. They'd all be afraid to make any decisions or do any surgery. They'd certainly be afraid to take any risks or try anything experimental or unusual. Me, I say they should be afraid."

She glances around, checking to see if any of her fellow employees are in earshot, then she laughs softly. "Of course if anybody here heard me talking this anti-doctor talk like this, I'd be fired in a minute," she says, much more quietly.

"At least somebody here is being careful about who gets hired," Rosie is quick to say.

"Oh, I wish," she says, straightening a pile of papers on the counter. "All I do in this office is send out forms and log them in when they're returned and keep guard like this. For which I am sorry," she adds, picking up her folder again, and then several others. "And I'm sorry I can't help you more. Have you tried the medical societies? That's what you should do next. They keep records of complaints, you know, like a medical Better Business Bureau."

"Thanks," Quinn says.

"I hope your boy gets better."

"Thanks," Rosie says.

"And if it's any help, I've never heard anything negative about your doctor. Linder it was, right?"

"Yes," Rosie says. "And it helps."

"SHE ENDED UP BEING PRETTY DECENT," Rosie comments as they're exiting the building.

"So what?" Quinn says, striding ahead of her, then turning around to sum up. "We didn't get anything."

"So we'll try the medical society, like she said."

"And they'll say the same thing. They'll say they have to protect privacy, that if we want to file a complaint, they'll be happy to accept it. What do you think a medical society is? It's a group of doctors. Isn't that the ultimate fraternal organization?" Rosie has to practically run to keep pace with him in the parking lot. When they reach her car, she slings her woven bag against it. "There *has* to be some way to get something. We have to try, Quinn."

"I know," he says, pacing a path back and forth across the front end of the car. "I just want somebody to tell me why it's so damned complicated to get a check on a doctor."

"Maybe this is the wrong way to approach it. Maybe we should be talking to other patients, not these organizations. Like that woman Megan, the one who's moving to Cape Cod. I could call her, ask her if she had some gripe with him. Then maybe we can tell the judge about her, too."

"One person with a gripe about a doctor isn't going to be enough to get a judge to bar Linder as the doctor."

"Well, then we need more names. There's power in numbers, isn't there?"

"Yes, but where exactly are you planning on getting those names?"

Rosie shrugs. "Maybe Megan knows somebody else who used him. Maybe that person knows another person."

"That's not going to go anywhere."

She's still got hold of her purse by the end of its strap and she shakes it so it strikes the ground, sending loose gravel flying. "You got a better idea?"

"No," he admits, shaking his head.

"So we do what we can, Quinn." She slides the bag back onto her shoulder.

He runs his fingers through his dark hair. "Jesus, Rosie," he says, "I've got that same feeling now, that panic." He's got his hand over his chest, rubbing at it, rubbing at some pain. "That thing I told you about when I can't get into the squad car."

"Quinn, listen to me," she says, putting her hand over his. "Doing this stuff might save Jay. Standing here doesn't. You see that, don't you?"

"Yeah. Of course."

"You drive," she says, moving over to the passenger door, reaching into her bag for her keys and tossing them to him. His hand is at shoulder height when he catches the keys. She waits for his hand to move, but for a moment, he's absolutely motionless, hand still raised. She's got her fingers hooked into the metal trim along the door and they're starting to ache.

And then his hand comes back down. "Let's do it," he says, putting the key into the door lock of her car. She takes hold of the door handle and slides in next to him.

THEY MAKE ONLY ONE STOP—A PHARMACY, where Rosie asks to use a phone book and successfully retrieves the Moores' address. Then they move on to Megan's house. "I just hope she isn't off looking at properties on Cape Cod," Rosie says as they head up the front pathway. Rosie leans into the bell. And then she leans again. She's reaching for the knocker when Megan opens the door, coffee cup in her hand, her pink chenille robe falling partly open over her tartan plaid flannel pajamas. "Oh, hi," she says, one hand over the front of her robe, like she could hide it that way. "A friend drove Christie to day care, so I'm getting kind of a late start this morning, sorry."

Rosie introduces Quinn to Megan and they shake hands. "I don't want to bother you, but we wondered if you could talk a little about Linder with us."

"Dr. Linder? I guess so. You want to come in, have some coffee?" As they enter the house, Megan gestures toward the packing boxes whose corrugated flaps reach upward in mock supplication and the general disarray that makes the house look as though it's been thoroughly ransacked. "Just don't look at me or the house," she earnestly requests, as though such total blindness were actually possible.

"So you're definitely moving?"

"Oh, yeah. It's sad, leaving everybody, but I think you do what you have to do for your kids, if you know what I mean."

Rosie says she does. When she and Quinn have taken seats at the kitchen table, she asks the woman, "Do you still think Cape Cod was what made the difference for Christie?"

"What do you mean?"

"I mean the change in Christie's health. You think it was Cape Cod that did it?"

"Well, yeah. I mean I'm making this move and all." Megan glances around the kitchen. The counters are covered with utensils, cookware, spice jars, and packaged foods. "It's always harder than you think it's going to be to organize it and pack it all up," she observes. "You two want coffee?"

They both say they do, then Quinn asks, "Did it ever occur to you that something else besides Cape Cod might be making your daughter get better?"

"Well, we thought about all kinds of things, but the cause and effect seemed pretty obvious." She locates two mugs, pours the coffee, and brings it over to the table. "Sugar and milk," she says, pushing stoneware containers and spoons over toward them.

"What about Dr. Linder?"

"You mean did I ask him what he thought about the move?"

"No, I mean, did you ever think it might be him?" Rosie asks.

Megan narrows her eyes and looks first at Rosie, then at Quinn. "Meaning what?"

"Did you ever think he was causing, or at least not curing whatever it was that was wrong with Christie?"

"Well, no, I don't think so. I mean I wanted him to make her all better and he didn't, but that's what everybody wants for their child. But I'm realistic, too. Medicine is really complicated, especially asthma. I mean they don't know that much about it, do they?"

"But she got better when she stopped seeing him," Rosie says, trying to push Megan back to that thought.

"Yeah, but not right away. Not till we'd been on the Cape for a while." She stops speaking and looks at them through narrowed eyes. "What are you trying to say?"

"We think he's making *our* child sicker and we're trying to find out if anybody else thinks something like that is happening to their kids."

"Jesus," she says, putting her hand over the top of her coffee mug. "Why would he do that?"

"We don't know," Quinn says.

"No," Megan insists, shaking her head. "He was so good with Christie, it was like he really loved her. And he gave us all kinds of information, like articles and charts and medication information because he wanted us to really understand the disease. He wasn't always pushing to get to the next patient. I really liked him." She laughs. "My husband started teasing me about him because I talked about him so much, said all this stuff about how great he was, you know?" She looks at Rosie and says in a somewhat quieter voice, "He's attractive, isn't he?"

"Oh, yes," Rosie agrees.

"But I told my husband, it's not that. I mean, it's not that Dr. Linder's attractive. It's that your child's almost dead one minute and fine the next, and he's the one who saved her. I mean, you can't help liking somebody who does that, can you?"

Rosie says she knows what Megan means.

"I felt really bad not going back," Megan continues. "But once she was better my husband said he didn't see the point of spending all that money on the visits, and I kind of had to agree. I kept meaning to call him, to explain, but you know how it is. It's kind of embarrassing, even if you've got a good reason, when you stop seeing a doctor. But I would have gone back if she hadn't gotten better." She pauses for a moment. "No," she says, shaking her head. "I don't think you're right. He wouldn't do that kind of thing."

"Do you know anybody else who uses him?"

She thinks for a moment. "Emily Porter. I met her going into his office one time when I was going out. We graduated from high school together. She's got an infant with asthma."

"We'd like to talk to her, too, about Linder. Do you happen to have her number?"

"She's over on Barlow Mountain," Megan says, lifting a phone book off the top of one of her packing boxes.

"I DIDN'T LIKE HIM SO I DIDN'T KEEP USING him, that's all," Emily Porter says pointedly. She's a small woman, so full of energy, she doesn't seem to be able to stay still. One minute she's bouncing her baby on her knee, the next she's swinging her along the floor through her legs. The tiny child laughs and begs for more with her eyes. And somehow the mother manages to talk through it all.

"Why not?" Quinn asks.

"He's just not what I want in a doctor. When I go to a doctor, I don't go for small talk, I go to hear what's wrong and how to make it better. I hate the ones who feel compelled to do comedy routines while they're examining you. Why do they think I'd want to laugh when I'm nauseated or in pain? I'm into firm personal boundaries, so I hate that kind of stuff."

"Was Linder into that, comedy routines?" Rosie prods her.

"Well, no, not the comedy stuff, but I was just using that as an example of how they can invade your space inappropriately. My problem with Linder was that he was too heavy into explanations. Over coffee, no less, a whole hour of it, one time. Too much protesting, you know what I mean? I kept thinking he was trying to show how much better he was than my last doctor. 'See how I bend over for you?' Like that. Exactly the kind of stuff that makes me uncomfortable. It's embarrassing is what it is. It was like he was doing an advertisement for his dedication all the time, you know what I mean?"

Rosie thought maybe she did. "So you stopped taking your daughter to him?"

"Yes."

"Because of that? Because he was too much of a self-promoter?" Quinn asks her. His voice sounds resigned, Rosie notices, like he's just repeating unimportant information. Probably he's thinking, as she is, that if they want to make any headway, they're going to need the name of another patient. Emily has nothing concrete for them.

"Yeah. That stuff's important to me. You end up not trusting people like that, so if you've got a kid with asthma, which is potentially one of these forever things, I figure you should find a good match. Doctor-to-patient match, I mean."

"But you didn't think he was incompetent, or anything like that, right?" Rosie asks, still hoping.

"No." She's holding her baby over her head, then bringing her down so the child's belly bumps her forehead. Baby Suzanne is squealing with delight each time they make contact.

"Is Suzanne still being treated for asthma?"

"Yes."

281

"Would you say she's a lot better now that she's with another doctor?" Rosie asks.

"About the same, actually," Emily says just before she rubs noses with her daughter. "Asthma sucks, don't you think?"

"Yeah," Quinn says. "It sure as hell does." He looks over at Rosie. Each of them can read the discouragement in the other's eyes. There's nothing to be learned here. Rosie stands up, and Quinn follows her lead.

"Though my doctor, this new doctor, says that if they start out this early, like Suzanne, they can outgrow it. Which is pretty much the opposite of what Linder said. So then, what do you believe? I mean, is this new doctor just trying to get me to be less totally stressed over it, or is he really right and Linder's wrong? That's what bothers me about this illness. How are parents supposed to know what to do?"

"I guess we could read stuff. Research it ourselves," Rosie suggests.

"Yeah, sure, and you don't think there'd be even more opinions that way? The truth is, they don't know and we don't know, right?"

"I guess that's true," Rosie admits. "Are there other things they disagreed on, these two doctors?"

"Probably." She considers for a moment. Suzanne is left to sit quietly on her mother's lap for this brief time. She seems perfectly content to do so—she barely moves. "They do different medications. One medication is the same, but completely different dosages, and one is just a different drug altogether. And my new doctor says it's dangerous to take aspirin if you have asthma."

"Linder prescribed aspirin?" Jason wasn't ever given aspirin.

"Well, not straight aspirin, but the antihistamine he gave Suzanne had some in it. The antihistamine he had in his office—maybe you got it, too."

Rosie nods. Jason takes an antihistamine Linder initially handed to her. Safer than trusting a pharmacy, he had said. "Did Suzanne have a bad reaction from it or anything like that?"

"No. I think she only took it once before I changed doctors."

"Did you file a complaint against him?"

"No. Why would I?"

"Because he prescribed something he shouldn't have."

"Well, maybe we're using the wrong words here. He didn't *prescribe* it, he handed it to me. You know, like samples; free, in the office. And I think it was just an over-the-counter thing, anyway."

"Did you tell Linder you were upset with him?"

"No. I don't even use him anymore."

"But he gave your child dangerous medication."

"It depends on which doctor you believe, doesn't it? I mean, it's like when you go to a new hairdresser, you know? The new one says, 'Who cut your hair last? Boy, did she ever botch it.' They always put down the last one so they look better, don't they? Maybe that's all the second doctor was doing, marking out his territory."

"Can you give me the name of your new doctor?"

She hesitates. "Look, he's going to hate me if he thinks I've ratted on him."

"But you haven't ratted on *him*. It's Linder we want something on."

"Yeah, but he's not going to want anybody to know that he said something to me about Linder. That was off the record."

"Did he say that, that it was off the record?"

"I don't remember." She's started bouncing Suzanne on her knee again. "I *think* he said that. Look, I need him on my side for the long haul."

"Okay, so what if I call and all I ask is his opinion of giving aspirin to kids with asthma but I don't say anything about Linder or you?"

"He'll know it's me that told you."

"I'm only asking because our child's in real trouble," Rosie pleads.

"It's okay," Quinn interjects, holding up a hand to call a halt to Rosie's interrogation. "Let's not make Emily upset."

Rosie turns to look at him. To glare at him. She was making headway, she thinks. Why is he making her back off this way? "Come on, Rosie," he says. "She gave us enough of her time."

283

"Sure," Rosie says, though she's ready to pinch him.

Quinn is already standing at the door. "Come on, Rosie," he says.

"Wait a sec," Rosie hears Emily say behind her. "Maybe it's not such a big deal. I guess it's not such a big deal just to tell you his name." Emily's rocking Suzanne in her arms and the baby's eyes are starting to close, just a little bit at a time. "It's Dr. Brian Blake."

"Thanks," Rosie says, her voice only a whisper. She wants to put her arms around this woman and hug her, but she doesn't want to crowd her, to push through what she probably thinks of as her personal boundaries, to do what she objected to in Greg Linder. And then an idea occurs to her, that maybe personal boundaries were being pushed in a very specific way. "Did he ever say he thought he might be falling in love with you?" Rosie feels her own face color to say this. She hopes Quinn is looking at Emily, not her.

"God help us," Emily protests. "No."

Rosie's relieved about that. The hour of coffee is standard, but the rest, thankfully, wasn't.

"Do you know anybody else who uses Linder?" Quinn asks.

"I might. I go to this support group for families of asthmatics and there's one woman there who I think used Linder for a while, but I don't know if she still does. She might have something to tell you." She steps back into the room and uses her free hand to pick up a pencil and a used envelope from the shelf where the family mail has accumulated. She moves the sleeping baby up against her chest so she can write the name and number down, and Rosie holds the envelope against the shelf so Emily can perform this feat with one hand.

"This means a lot to us," Rosie tells her as she slides the paper into her pocket.

"SUPPORT GROUPS COULD BE JUST THE THING, Quinn," Rosie tells him once they're back in the car. "We can check where he used to practice. I think it's somewhere in Pennsylvania. We can see if there's a support group there, talk to people, get some more dope on him." She's feeling excited now, like there's a route leading somewhere real.

"Pennsylvania's a big state, Rosie."

"Well, I know that, but probably we can figure out where he practiced by checking an old licensing book or something."

"Rosie, we need a plan, we can't just ride around all day like this. We need to get to that judge by this afternoon, not next week. Every time that doctor has Jay in his care, our child's at risk."

And then she's seeing him again, that sad, distorted face that wasn't quite Jay. It was weird, this search they were on. It was for him, but it made her almost forget him, too. She looks at the dashboard clock. "It's ten-forty already. When is Linder supposed to come by and see him?"

"I don't know. Monica said this afternoon. All I know is we can't keep drinking coffee and lounging around with these people."

"I don't exactly think of what we've been doing as lounging, Quinn."

"Well, maybe that's the wrong word for it, but we've got to put a little faster spin on these encounters or we're going to risk losing Jay for the night again."

"I don't want that to happen, but I also think you can overdo in the other direction. You were ready to rush out of Emily's place without getting anything from her, and you can't do that, either."

"I wanted you to stop pushing her so hard, that's all. As soon as we said we were leaving, she gave up the doctor."

Rosie has to admit this *is* what happened. "Did you do that, trying to get me to leave, on purpose?"

"That's a time-honored police trick."

"It came in handy," she admits.

"I sometimes do," he says, smiling.

THEY REACH AMY CICCOLLI, THE SUPPORT group member Emily put them onto, on their first call. They're trying to save time now, so they're using the telephone instead of driving all over town. Amy says she likes Linder and that she still takes her child to him. But her child has not improved at all. She admits that she and her husband have talked about changing doctors, but never very seriously. "Changing doctors is really tricky," she explains. "I don't want to insult him. And besides, asthma is so weird. I think it takes time to see real improvement. We need to give it more time and obviously he knows more about it than we do."

"Nothing conclusive there," Rosie comments to Quinn after that phone call.

Dr. Blake, when he finally calls back, says that aspirin should never be given to asthmatics because it can actually cause a bronchial reaction in some patients. "How bad a reaction?" Rosie asks him.

"Mind you," he says, "it may have no effect on some people. On others, it could be very serious. Shock, respiratory failure." The words send a chill through Rosie. "It's sometimes given by accident when a patient isn't even aware that he's asthmatic. Or if someone is having coughing problems or symptoms that seem coldlike or allergic, a patient may buy an over-the-counter antihistamine. Those antihistamines vary tremendously in their ingredients and strength, but they can be deadly if they're taken in combination with certain other drugs or if there's an underlying condition in the patient, like asthma. In my opinion," he says, "no antihistamine should be sold without a prescription. Not one of them. And for this very reason."

Rosie wants to hang up, to go find Jason now, to check his breathing, his heart rate, but she needs more information from this man. "Would all doctors be aware of this problem?" Rosie asks him.

"They should be. But remember, patients don't always tell doctors everything they're taking. Doctors can't read minds."

"Have you ever heard of a doctor who deliberately gave an asthmatic patient aspirin?" she asks, careful not to mention Linder or Emily.

Blake doesn't answer right away. "The only way I'd know something like that for sure was if I saw it happen," he says in a decidedly more subdued tone.

"And have you ever seen it?"

"No, of course not."

"Have you ever heard of it?" She knows she's beginning to tread on ground that she promised she would stay away from.

"That would be hearsay," he tells her after a pause. "And absolutely inadmissible in court."

"I didn't say anything about court," she reminds him. He knows that she's tracking a specific doctor, probably knows exactly who. And he's telling her, she's quite sure, that he'll be of no help to her if she tries to take legal action against him. "Let's just suppose you had heard of such an incident. Would you speak to the doctor about the error?"

"I don't do hypothetical situations, Ms.—"

"Sloan," Rosie reminds him.

"Ms. Sloan, I have an office full of patients, so please excuse me," he says, and cuts their connection. It's just like the woman in personnel said, the doctors close ranks around themselves. They cut off the outsider.

Quinn has another idea: "What do you think about calling around to pharmacies?"

"To what end?"

"I don't know, exactly. Maybe we could figure out which one he buys his drugs at, see if maybe we can get some information on this antihistamine."

"Good thinking," Rosie says, reaching for the phone directory. She lifts it toward her, but then doesn't open it. "Doctors don't order the bulk of their drugs from pharmacies. They go directly to the manufacturers. They have sales representatives who come around and take orders."

"Then let's call the drug company."

"Yeah, fine, but what drug company is it?"

"What about the bottle, doesn't it say on that?"

"They were those little pills, remember? The ones that we ground up with the food. We had them in samples, the individual packages. And I gave all of them to Monica. But wait, I might have one in my purse, I threw a couple in there in case we were away from home at dinnertime." She grabs for the woven bag, and with one firm shake toward the floor, dumps the contents. With a flattened hand, she spreads the contents out across the rug. "Ah," she says, holding up a foil wrapper. "No pills, but I do have an empty wrapper." She opens the folds of the crumpled packet. "Mannerling," she reads. "They're in Westover, New Jersey."

Quinn is already dialing directory assistance, and a moment later, Rosie is saying hello to someone in a pharmaceutical company, her voice brimming with forced cheer. "This is Dr. Greg Linder's office in Bradford, Connecticut. May I speak to his sales representative, please?"

"All of our reps are in their territories this week," a woman tells her. "Let me connect you with one of our sales managers."

"Don't push too hard," Quinn advises while Rosie hangs on the line, listening to country-western music.

"I'll be cool, don't worry." She holds the receiver away from her ear and makes faces at it. "They need a musical adviser at this place," she comments. And then she's speaking again to New Jersey: "Yes, well, we've had a break-in here, and we're trying to determine what drugs were taken. Do you have a record of recent samples and orders the doctor has taken so we can give an accurate report to the police?"

"The police are asking for that kind of detail?" the man at the other end asks.

"Well," Rosie says, "I think they want to make sure they know exactly what controlled substances have gone missing, but I think they want to be aware of the other stuff in case they find a cache of it somewhere."

"Give me a second, let me get your records," he says. "Here you go," the man says, and a moment later he reads off a list of medications. "Wait a minute," Rosie says, stopping him at the name of the foil-wrapped antihistamine. "That's an aspirin combo, isn't it? We've got an asthmatic practice here, that's got to be an error."

"Well," he considers, "if he's got a general allergy practice, he'd be using that for some of his non-asthmatics."

"He has very few children who aren't asthmatic."

"Is this a pediatric practice?"

"Yes."

"Hmm. Then I don't know why he has so much of this on his regular order. This isn't a pediatric drug. In fact, it doesn't even come in suspension or syrup. There is no pediatric form because of all the problems with aspirin and young children and Reyes syndrome."

"And you also didn't mention any antihistamine that's specific for asthma."

"Just a second, let me go back a screen. No, I don't show anything else."

"One last thing," Rosie says. "Can you refresh my memory on our rep's name? The police want that, too." He spells the name out for her. "I'm really sorry, but they'll probably be calling you, too, double-checking what I tell them, making sure this wasn't an inside job. Maybe they suspect me, I don't know."

"Jeez, the world is getting so weird."

"You know it," Rosie agrees.

"What?" Quinn says when she's barely put the receiver back to rest in its cradle. Rosie explains all that he hasn't heard. "That doesn't get us anywhere," he declares.

"Yes, it does," she insists. "Linder's got a stockpile of the wrong drug. He doesn't even order an appropriate one."

"He just gets the right one somewhere else."

"Okay, I'll grant that, but he still has this one that's bad for asthmatics. And Linder specifically told me that he prefers this preparation. He said kids get turned off by all those sugared spoon concoctions and that crumbling this one into food is much safer and sounder."

"But that's what you've always said, too. You hate those baby Tylenols because of that. You're the one who told me never to give them to Jay because if I did he'd start to think of medication as being like candy."

"Right, because then they might seek it out and overdose."

"Exactly."

"Yes, and that's why when Linder explained it to me, it seemed perfectly reasonable."

"But maybe it is. Maybe Linder's right to prefer an adult medication to those grape juice syrups."

"No, this guy just told me, it's not recommended for children. And he's a representative of the manufacturer, an official spokesperson."

"You said he was a salesman."

"Sales manager."

"Right. But not an official spokesman of the company. And not a scientist."

"Stop talking like a cop, Quinn."

He nods. "It's just that I've been in a courtroom. I know what this is worth. Especially when it's gotten under false pretense. Remember, you lied to this guy about who you were."

She knows he's right. But what was she supposed to do, just ask him to tell tales on one of his steady customers? "Look, Quinn," she says, "Linder's poisoning these kids. Not strychnine or arsenic, but he's giving them the wrong medication. A parent could make a mistake, give a child like Jason a baby aspirin or two. Sometimes nothing happens. Sometimes they get sicker. Sometimes, maybe they could even die, but it's going to look like an asthma death when it happens. Compromised breathing, whatever. Quinn, maybe Jay doesn't even have asthma. Maybe he's just having a reaction to aspirin."

"Do you think aspirin could cause what you saw last night? It was like a coma, you said."

"I don't know. Maybe that's something else. If he screws around with one drug, maybe he screws around with two or three."

Quinn's rubbing his hand over his chest. "Okay," he says, "let's keep going."

"I'm calling Pennsylvania."

"Pennsylvania? Where, exactly, Rosie?"

"A medical society in Pennsylvania, I don't know."

They follow a trail through the telephone bureaucracy of the State of Pennsylvania, through the health services departments. One agency recommends another and that one, another, till eventually a woman with a West Indian accent tells her that they've reached the state office that fields complaints about physicians. "I think you might have to go back three or four years to find anything on him," Rosie tells her. This time there's no country-western music. No music at all. The woman has put the phone down on her desk while she does her search, and Rosie can hear the voices of her office mates, some occasional laughter, and the clicking of keyboards.

"Yes," the woman says when she returns to the phone. "There have been some filings against him. A little packet of them, and all within a few days of each other." Like people got together and talked about it, Rosie thinks. A bunch of mothers giving each other courage.

"What are the charges?"

"Let me see. This one looks like inappropriate procedures, oh, and the second is exactly the same. The last is the same with 'intent' added to it."

"What does that mean?"

"It means somebody thought he was making his mistakes on purpose, madam."

"I see." Rosie's been standing this whole time, winding the long telephone cord around her hand. This pronouncement makes her feel kind of woozy. She reaches a hand out toward the wall for support, and Quinn slides a chair over to her. "Did the agency follow up on these complaints?" she asks as she sits down.

"No. There were no investigations in these cases and no rulings. But you should understand, that's a fairly common outcome."

"But why wasn't there follow-up? Were the charges withdrawn or something?"

"No. If they were withdrawn, these records wouldn't be here. There was no investigation because he closed his practice. That settles a case pronto, madam."

"You're kidding?"

"Oh, no, madam."

"But he's practicing here, in Connecticut."

"Well, that's pretty common, too. Medical licensing is done by states and each one is different. And anyway, these aren't criminal charges, these are consumer complaints. We keep a record so that people who are looking for doctors can check out backgrounds and make decisions about which doctors to use. It's a community service, that's all."

"Could you give me the names of the people who filed those complaints?" Rosie asks, though she knows she's not going to get them.

"Oh, no, madam, that's confidential. For that you need to have the doctor sign a release form."

"What about the specifics of the claim—the inappropriate procedure, can you tell me what that was?"

"No, madam. You need the release for that, too. Would you like me to send one to you?"

"No, I think this is enough for now, thank you."

"WHAT TIME IS IT?" ROSIE ASKS AFTER SHE'S told Quinn the details.

"One-thirty."

"Looks to me, the way those claims were all filed within a few days of each other, that maybe a support group got together and decided to put some pressure on him. And that it worked," Rosie concludes.

"Yeah, well, sort of. It sent him into another state to keep doing what he was doing. Now he just does 'improper procedures' or whatever, on *my* child." Quinn shakes his head. "I'm calling the foster mother," he says, lifting the phone from the wall and pressing in a set of numbers. "Monica, this is Quinn Sloan. I'm coming by to see my son," he announces a few seconds later, in what Rosie thinks of as his power voice. Rosie reads the tightening of his eyes and the forward thrust of his jaw and knows that Monica has told him that Jay's already gone. "No, he's supposed to be with *me* this afternoon." He taps his fist several times against his chest. "Now you listen to me, you have no right to pass him off to this man this way." And then it is obvious from the way he turns his eyes suddenly toward Rosie that Monica has hung up on him. "Damn," he says, and slams the phone back up against its wall base. "We need to see a judge," Quinn proclaims. "Call your lawyer."

* * *

IT IS WELL INTO THE AFTERNOON, GROWING dark, in fact, before Ted is finished in court and can see them. They have waited in the attorney's outer office for nearly two hours, against the notion that he might have finished in court earlier. He seats himself in his desk chair and pushes against his desktop, sliding the chair back into a reclining position that Rosie thinks would be vastly more appropriate in front of a TV. Quinn tells him all that they have found: the dissatisfied patients, the strange drug order, the file of charges in the Pennsylvania office.

"All doctors have charges filed against them. These are meaningless now because no action was taken on them."

"Not all doctors move into another state. He ran," Rosie points out.

"Coincidence."

"It's not coincidence."

Ted's feet have found their way up onto his desk. "I'll tell you what he's going to say. He'll say he was planning to move anyway." Rosie and Quinn exchange a look. Rosie can see in the narrowed glare of his eyes that he's just as frustrated by Ted's dismissal of their evidence as she is. "What you have is of no more value than a collection of rumors."

"What about this business with the aspirin?" she asks him.

"Will this sales manager testify in court?"

"Why do we need him? Why can't we just get a fax of Linder's drug order?"

"A fax is not a court document. An original is. But we have no right to that. You can try to get the drug company to send it, but I suspect they won't feel much sympathy for your case after you tricked them into talking this afternoon. If Linder gets wind of that, by the way, he can charge you with harassment, and that's just going to make you look bad in court."

"These other mothers . . ."

"You haven't told me anything that sounds like they even suspect him of anything. They sound like they wish medicine were a more reliable science, that's all. That they wish they didn't have sick kids. The real question is, will these mothers be willing to come into court? Will they testify against Linder?

293

You said one of them didn't change doctors because she was afraid of hurting Linder's feelings. You don't honestly think she'll go before a judge and make an accusation against the man, do you?"

"No, I guess not."

"But together," Quinn says. "All this stuff together has weight, doesn't it? There's a leaning toward suspicion at least. Some buildup of evidence."

Ted takes his feet off the desk, lets the chair rise back to upright. "Quinn, you're a police officer, I assume you've been in a courtroom before—before all this business with your son started." Quinn nods. "Then you can answer that question yourself."

"Yeah, I can," he admits. "It's worth shit."

"Exactly."

"It's my child," he reminds the lawyer.

"If you want, we can still try. I'm willing to work on it and go to the judge, but I just want you to know you shouldn't expect to get an action against this guy for all your time and money. If trying is going to ease your pain, though, I will help you," he says, picking up a pen and sliding his yellow pad closer. "You want to try for a release from Linder to get the Pennsylvania records? Maybe we can get to the drug records that way, too."

Quinn and Rosie exchange looks. "Yeah, I think so," he says. "Otherwise we've got nothing."

"What if he won't give it to us?" Rosie asks.

"Then I can go to the judge and say he refused. That's going to look bad all on its own. Maybe even worse." He nods, slides partway back down on his chair. "Try going back to these other patients of his, see if they're willing to give depositions. Chances are they thought about what they told you and decided they've already said too much. But there's always a chance one of them will have the opposite reaction. Maybe they've been thinking for a long time that something's off about him and haven't wanted to admit it to themselves, but now that they hear somebody else voicing concerns, what's been bothering them seems to be more defined. Sometimes that makes people open up. It's a long shot, but it might work. Remind them that other people are seeing problems with him. Tell them about the other stuff you've found—the drugs, the charges. Who knows? Maybe we'll get lucky."

"How long is this going to take?"

"Well, let's see. We need to get the release letter typed up, send it registered to him, and give him forty-eight hours to respond. Then we have to Fed Ex stuff back and forth with Pennsylvania. Another two days. If these women are willing to give depositions, we have to get them in with a court stenographer." He's writing this down as he speaks. "Middle of next week at best, I'd say. Not that we could get on the judge's calendar much before that, anyway."

"Why can't you hand-deliver the letter to him, send somebody out to Pennsylvania?"

"I can, but he still gets his forty-eight hours and he can stall the court beyond that with a well-turned phrase. And don't forget, hand-delivering something, especially long distances like that, is a hell of a lot more expensive than the U.S. Postal Service or Fed Ex."

"Screw the expense," Quinn says, looking at Rosie for backup.

Rosie nods in confirmation.

"We'll spend a little more, then, do things in the fastest way, if you prefer."

"Yes, of course we prefer that," Quinn says, his hands closing tightly over the arms of his chair.

"Quinn, let me be frank here. I'll go after all this stuff, but I actually think it's the wrong way to go. I think right now you shouldn't push the judge on this at all, but you should wait out the time he asked you to. I know how these cases go. The judge will probably feel that we're wasting his time bringing in this vague stuff and that's not the mood we want to put him in. We want him to think you follow directions to the letter. That's what judges like."

Rosie is shaking her head. "No," she says. "I'm not sitting this out. I'll get another lawyer if you prefer, but I am not sitting this out."

Ted brings his chair upright once more. "I said I'd do it. I just had that brief obligation there to let you have the full picture, not lead you on about what to expect from all this."

"Fine," Quinn says. "We expect nothing."

"No, that's not true," Rosie says, "I expect to get my child back."

QUINN AND ROSIE GO TO THE RUSTY NAIL. It's the closest restaurant to Ted's office. "We can't be thinking at our best if we haven't eaten all day," Quinn points out, though he sounds as though he's reading from a technical manual when he says it. Rosie's got this jumpy feeling, not just in her stomach, but her whole body now. Maybe it's hunger or maybe she's coming down with something. Her fingers are tingling, too. I can't get sick, she tells herself. I have got to stay together for Jay, she thinks as she scans the menu.

The room is fairly quiet mid-week like this, with only two other tables occupied. At one of them there is a family with a toddler who is waving a french fry around in each hand, and Rosie's missing Jay so badly, her chest starts to hurt and her hands are tingling worse than ever. She feels so trapped. Is she ever going to be able to sit someplace and live her life with her child, watch him eat his fries? She can't do that anymore, the way these people can. The way the ones out in Pennsylvania can, now that they've scared Linder off. Why can't that happen here? Why can't we get lucky that way? she's thinking when Quinn asks her if she wants coffee.

"You know, Quinn," she says when their beverages arrive, "Linder has been scared into running before. He ran when things got hot for him in Pennsylvania. What if we scare him again?"

Quinn shakes his head and says, "Don't even think about it, Rosie." He takes another sip of his coffee, then asks, "How?"

"We've got the names of a bunch of people who don't think all that highly of him. At least two of those women, Megan and Emily, left his practice."

"Yeah, but Megan left because her child got better, not because she had questions about his competence."

"Yes, but he doesn't know that. They never explained to him why they left. He just knows they're not bringing their children to him anymore. And we've got the name of this agency in Pennsylvania. We also have the name of the drug salesman he orders his aspirin compounds from. Suppose we called him up and read him a list with all those names on it. That might start him thinking we were onto him. He'll understand the connections. Maybe he'll think we have more than we do. Maybe it'll be enough to make him decide to leave town."

"It's not a good idea, Rosie."

"Why not?"

"You heard what Ted said. He said we've already screwed things up with going to the drug company and lying. And we don't know what Linder would do. He's got access to Jay."

"And that's what we're trying to stop, Quinn. Do we have some other route we could maybe follow on this?"

"We can wait till we get this put together the right way. In the court."

"That's next week, Quinn." She reaches for her purse with one hand, for the check with the other. "You want to split this?" she asks, waving the check at him.

"Whatever."

"Quinn, I saw Jay last night. I saw how he looked—we're losing him. Aspirin can kill asthmatics. I can't wait till next week."

"No," he says, turning his coffee cup in slow circles round the saucer. "We can't wait."

LINDER DOESN'T ANSWER HIS PHONE, SO ROSIE reads the names very slowly—to assure absolute clarity— onto his tape: "Megan Moore, Emily Porter, Amy Ciccolli, the Pennsylvania Public Health Department, Division of Consumer Complaints Against Licensed Health Practitioners, and Michael DeMarco of Mannerling Pharmaceuticals.

"Now he can listen to it in his leisure time," Rosie says, pleased with her dramatic rendering. "And really think about it. He can't hang up on it in the middle."

"He can push the stop button on his tape."

"True. But he won't do that till he's figured out if there's some explicit threat at the end."

And then they wait. He'll call, she knows it. He'll call and he'll demand to know what she knows. What she meant. She'll try and deflect him. "Me?" she'll say. "What list? You sound upset. Are you upset?" She'll deny she was the caller, and she'll concentrate on trying to gauge how frightened he is.

An hour passes, and there is no call.

Rosie starts thinking how, if Linder's really scared, he might just run out immediately and leave Jason alone in his house. Or worse? Could he do something worse? Could he do something to Jay? They should have waited till he returned Jay to Monica. "Maybe we should have waited," she says to Quinn.

"Don't do this to me," Quinn complains. "You lose your courage now, we're down the tube."

"I was just thinking, what if he takes it out on Jason?"

"Oh, Christ, Rosie. You chose to ignore that before." He lowers his head to his hands.

Rosie's pacing out the room. "I am such an idiot," she says, screaming it at the walls. "Why am I so impulsive? Why didn't we listen to Ted? Why didn't you stop me, Quinn? Didn't you think about this, about how he'd do something to Jason? Why didn't you stop me?"

Quinn has stood up and he walks toward her, reaching for her, but she jumps away from him. "Rosie," he says, using his power voice again. "It's done. Now we have to wait and see what happens. It's all done."

"I'll kill myself," she says, head back, hands clasped together in front of her, suppliant.

"Rosie," he says, grabbing for her now, putting his arms around her and trying to hold her. She fights him for a few seconds, but then lets go, collapsing against him and their sobs play awkward counterpoint each against the other.

When the phone rings, they nearly explode out of their embrace and run toward the kitchen. On the way, Rosie manages to retrieve a tissue from her pocket and to wipe at her tears. Before she lifts the receiver, she takes in a couple of deep breaths.

"Rosie? Hi, it's me, Greg," Linder says, his voice light and friendly. "I hope you weren't worried about where we were."

"No," she says, her voice shaking.

"Here's what's happening. We just took a few turns on the merry-go-round up at the mall and Jay loved it. He's fine, by the way. Did I tell you that? He is much, much better."

"Then why do you have him?" she asks with a great deal more ferocity than she'd intended.

"Excuse me?" he says after a moment's pause.

"I mean Quinn was supposed to have him this afternoon."

"Wait a minute, Rosie, we had an arrangement. I was going to try to get him here so you could see him. This was not easy. Are you telling me that seeing him is no longer important to you?"

"No, it's still important." Yes, of course it is. And that *is* what he'd promised, she reminds herself. God, this was so confusing.

"Well, then, do you want to come over?"

"Yes, yes I do. I'll be there as soon as I can."

"Did he mention the call?" Quinn asks the moment she's broken the connection.

"No. He just got home, I think."

"So maybe he didn't listen to his messages."

"I don't know. I guess anything's possible. But it's kind of creepy, isn't it? I was expecting him to rant and rave at me, but he was downright charming."

"Maybe those names don't really mean anything to him, maybe we're on the wrong track. Or maybe he didn't recognize your voice? Is that possible? You didn't say who it was."

"I'm going to assume it's that he hasn't checked the machine. Look, I should get going. I want to see Jay," she says, looking around for her purse.

"It's too neat, Rosie. He's up to something."

"What?"

"I don't know. Some kind of trap. Maybe I should go with you."

"You know he won't let me in if you're there."

Quinn shakes his head. "Take my service revolver."

"Oh, sure, and your bulletproof vest?"

"Don't joke like that, Rosie. If you have the gun, he won't do anything."

"People who carry guns get killed by them, Quinn, remember? You're the one who always said that, you know."

"Okay, okay, don't take it. But promise me this, don't push him. We've pushed him enough with that list. He may be listening to it even as you drive over there. He may yet get worked up to a rage by the time you get there."

"Fine." She's striding toward the door.

"And this time, if Jason doesn't look right, you should insist on going to the hospital, okay?"

"I will." She stops, her hand on the doorknob. "Which should I do, Officer? Back off or insist?"

"Insist," he says. She nods. "And don't forget to lie and cheat and to beat the hell out of him if you need to."

"That's what I thought," she says.

"And call the station house if you have to."

"Okay."

"I'll go back to my place. Call me the second you get out of there. Go to a pay phone, okay?" She nods. "Two hours is all I'm giving you," he says.

CHAPTER THIRTY-FIVE

SHE KNOWS THAT SHE SHOULD JUST STAND there patiently now that she's rung Linder's bell, not push, but she can't: she's banging on his door. Of course she should be calmer than this, but she's thinking he's in there, listening to that message tape and she wants him to stop. She wants to distract him from that, get him over here, to the door. Why doesn't he answer? Her fist comes down even harder against the door. This isn't rational, she tries reminding herself, but then she thinks, why should it have to be?

Because it matters, she counsels herself as she waits, shifting from one foot to the other, going down the two steps in front of his condo, then back up, taking a break from pounding because her hands have started to hurt.

And then he opens the door. "Oh, hi," he says. He's holding a glass of amber liquid in his hand. He shakes it slightly, and the ice cubes chatter against the glass. "A drink for you?" he asks as he motions for her to come inside.

"No," she says. "I just want to see Jason. That's all."

"Really?" he asks. "I thought you might have something else in mind."

He's heard the tape, she thinks. "I came over to see Jay," she says, reminding him, for he's started walking in the other direction, away from the bedrooms, toward the bottle of bourbon and the ice cubes. She won't even go in that direction, she thinks. She'll stay right here, by the door.

"You know, I don't think you're being completely forthright with me." She doesn't answer. "Sit down for a minute."

"Just let me see Jay." And then she jumps, startled by the doorbell sounding right behind her.

"Goodness," he says, dragging mock surprise through his words. "Who could that be at this hour? Could it be that you roused the neighbors with your battering against my house?"

"If you heard it, why didn't you answer?" she asks him as he makes his way toward the door. She has to step aside so he can take hold of the knob. Then she's thinking, she's not going to stand around waiting for him to make small talk with whoever's out there, she's going to see Jason while she has the chance, and she makes a dash down toward that part of the house.

She pushes the door open to the room where he'd been last night and tries to find the light, running her hand over the wall where it ought to be. Just as her fingers find the tiny projection and push it up, someone grabs her arm. "Leave me alone," she warns, not even turning to look at him while she tries to pull away. She can see Jay over there, under that same blanket.

"Calm down," a voice says to her, and it's not Greg's. She turns and sees that a police officer holds her, and that another officer, a woman with long blonde hair, is right behind him. "Let's go back in the living room for a minute," the officer says to Rosie. She stares at him for a moment, sees the absolute blueness of his eyes, and she sees what she used to see in Quinn's policeman's eyes: pure conviction and assurance. There's no point in fighting him, she knows. Linder has somehow managed to summon this heavy artillery.

"Are you Mrs. Sloan?" the officer asks her once they're back in the other part of the house.

"Yes. He called you, didn't he? He told you I was coming here, right?"

"I'm Officer Spinelli," he says, ignoring her question and cocking his thumb toward his name tag. "This here is Officer Smith and she's going to need to do a quick search on you," he says as the female officer begins to pat her down.

"Do you know that you're in violation of a court order?" Spinelli asks.

She looks at Linder. "He asked me to come here." Linder says nothing. "Tell them," she says.

"I've told them the truth already."

"He set me up. He told me to come over."

"Even if he did ask you, ma'am, you'd be in violation, either way. You're not allowed to have any contact with that child."

"My child is ill and he needs to go to a hospital."

"Well, that may be, ma'am, but, number one, you are not a doctor, and number two, Judge Mannon has said you may not come near that child. The police have to enforce what the court decrees. If it weren't so, the system wouldn't work. Now, do you understand what I am telling you?"

"Yes, I do, but I'm telling you that *this* doctor is not taking care of him, he's making him sicker. And Jason's not even supposed to be here, he's supposed to be with his foster mother, Monica Delano."

The officer looks at Linder. "What about that, Doctor?"

"His foster mother is Monica Delano, but she has given me permission to have the child stay overnight with me here."

"We'll need to check that."

"Fine. I'll give you her telephone number."

"Marie?" the officer says to the other cop. "Dial her up, will you?"

"The phone's in here," Linder says, showing her the way to the kitchen.

"My husband's on the Eastleigh force," Rosie says, reaching for any information that might help.

"Well, we'll talk to them. Eastleigh, I mean, but right now we have to address this problem. Dr. Linder says you've been harassing him. Is that true?"

"No, sir. He's been making my child ill, giving him the wrong medication."

"You were in court on this matter of the child's illness already, weren't you?" he asks, and she realizes that he's working from the assumption that she's a madwoman. A child abuser. The court says she is, so of course he believes that.

"Did you call Dr. Linder on the phone tonight and threaten him?"

"No, I did not." This isn't even a real lie. She read a list, that's all. She didn't threaten.

"He says you've been calling and threatening him. He says that you called him and said you were coming here tonight and taking the child away from him and that you had a gun."

"What?" she says, and even laughs at how close this came to being true. "That's totally ridiculous. I don't even own a gun."

"Your husband does, though, if he's an officer. Do you know where his service revolver is kept?"

"No."

"You don't? Now I am truly surprised to hear that."

"All right, I do know where he keeps it, but his gun doesn't have anything to do with this. I didn't threaten Dr. Linder and I didn't say I was coming over here with a gun."

"Did you call him?"

"No."

"Did you leave any messages on his machine?" She hesitates for a moment. Linder wouldn't have saved that message, it was too incriminating.

"No."

"Well, that's definitely interesting because he's got what sounds like your voice on a tape that he has already played for us. He says you've been calling and hanging up repeatedly, and we can get the phone company to tell us where those calls originated, just for verification, if we need to."

"Then you better check and see if he called *me*, because I'm telling you, he invited me over here," she says, trying to distract him from the tape and her lies about it.

"And I explained, that doesn't matter. You're still in violation."

Linder and Smith have returned to the room. "The foster mother gives permission," the officer reports.

"Ma'am, you're going to need to come down to the station so we can settle this court-order business."

She sighs, lifting her shoulders high—perhaps it is a gesture of resignation—as she does so.

"Do you want to press charges, sir?" the officer asks Linder.

"Yes, I definitely do. I tried to be patient with this woman but things have really gotten out of control. There have been constant phone calls, then she started showing up at the door—in the middle of the night, sometimes, shouting stuff at me, demanding to see the child. The neighbors are complaining about it, too." He shakes his head.

"Lies," Rosie says.

"You want to charge her with harassment?"

"Assault, too. She kicked me when I opened the door."

"I didn't," Rosie insists, not believing he's said this. She starts toward him—she's not sure why, maybe to press her face up against his, maybe to say, I thought you were falling in love with me, but Spinelli has his hand on her shoulder, silently cautioning her to stay where she is.

"Is there some federal charge, too, like misuse of the communication lines?"

"I'll look into it, sir."

"Okay, ma'am, you'll have to go with us," Smith tells her.

"Can you let me see my child first?"

"Ma'am, that would be a clear violation of the court order, I can't let you do that. And I'm sorry, but I'm going to need to cuff you," Spinelli says as he snaps the metal around her wrist. "Sorry about that, but I think you're a little agitated."

"Of course I'm agitated," she says, "I'm being falsely charged."

"I've got you on that tape," Linder says.

"You bastard," she hisses at him. "If anything happens to Jay, you're dead."

"This is what she's been doing, these kinds of threats, in the middle of the night," Linder says.

Officer Smith is tugging just firmly enough on the handcuff so that it hurts her wristbone. "Let's go, ma'am," she says.

"You'll need to come down to the station house, Doctor. I'm sorry about that, but if you want to press charges, that's the way it's done."

Linder nods. "That's a small price to pay to have this settled, to be able to get a night's sleep again."

"Who's going to stay with Jay? He's going to leave him alone," she says, almost wailing it, really, as they go out the door.

CHAPTER
THIRTY-SIX

"**P**LEASE, MRS. SLOAN, DON'T CALL THE
doctor again and don't under any circumstances go over there.
You don't want to make it worse," Spinelli says to her after
Quinn arrives to retrieve her from the station. Once they really
see that he's a fellow blue, the rhetoric of rights and charges
and violations eases a bit, but she can tell, they haven't really
figured out who to believe yet. They're a little like the doctors,
she thinks, the way they close rank around their own. But they
were also making painfully clear the limits of their protective
power. If Linder is adamant about pressing charges, they tell
her, there's nothing they can do about it. Still, even that observation gives her some hope. They have said, "if he is
adamant," implying, perhaps, that if he is not completely
immovable, they might use some skills of persuasion to get
him to reconsider.

"You could file your own charges," Spinelli suggests. "I
mean, it can't hurt, I wouldn't think. And then sometimes that
makes the other guy think twice, drop his charges. Especially
when he starts to add up how much it's all going to cost him in
time and money."

"What I need is to prevent him from having Jay in his care,"
she tries to get them to understand.

That's a different matter, they tell her. "You have a lawyer
for that?" Spinelli asks.

She says she does.

"Is he any good?"

Rosie almost says, He was recommended by someone I trust, when she catches herself and merely shrugs. "How would we know?" You certainly can't tell with doctors, she's thinking.

Spinelli shakes his head. "I don't know. Sometimes it seems to me like the less they promise you, the more you can trust them." By that criterion Ted would be a good lawyer—he's told them the case is virtually hopeless. But of what help is their good lawyer if he can't provide them with a way out?

"Some lawyers," Spinelli is saying, "start talking about their rates before they talk about your issues. I don't like that. Those ones are out there to rack up the hourly fees, that's all. Does he seem like that?"

Rosie looks at Quinn. "No," he says. "He seems decent."

"That's all you can hope for," the policeman observes.

Quinn drives her back to Linder's house so she can pick up her car. It is still the middle of the night. "Are you sure you'll be okay with the driving? You're shaking," Quinn says when he sees her whole upper body seeming to vibrate.

"It's nothing," she says. "Just a giant shiver. It's from being here in front of his house, knowing he's probably watching me. And also being this close to Jay but not being able to see him."

Quinn taps the steering wheel with the side of his fist a couple of times. "I don't know what this guy is, what he wants."

"You knew from the beginning he was up to something, didn't you?"

"No," he says. "I was jealous, like you said, and that was all. I didn't have the vaguest idea about anything being wrong with him. You believe in doctors, you know what I mean?"

She nods. "Look," she says after a while, "thanks for bailing me out tonight."

"There wasn't any bail," he points out.

"Well, not technically. But you know what I mean. Thanks for coming to get me and all."

He nods. "I'm going to follow you home." He pushes aside a pamphlet entitled "So Your Child Has Asthma" so that he can see the clock on his dashboard. "One-forty A.M., give or take. This clock never was very accurate."

"What's a couple of minutes this time of night, anyway?" she asks, pulling her keys out of her jacket pocket.

"Drive slowly, you're tired," he warns her. "Don't worry about me, I'll be following no matter what speed you go. Get some sleep and call when you wake up, and we'll try to figure out what's next, okay?"

"What's next is calling Ted, I guess."

"Probably," he agrees.

"Then some waiting and praying," she adds as she leaves his car.

SURPRISINGLY, SHE SLEEPS TILL NEARLY EIGHT o'clock. But the instant she is awake, she is very wide awake. Quinn doesn't answer his phone. Maybe he's in the shower. Maybe he'll answer in five minutes.

She doesn't want to wait. She dials Monica's number. "It's Rosie Sloan, Monica, please don't hang up." The foster mother doesn't say anything, but she doesn't hang up, either. Rosie takes in a deep breath. "Monica, does Jason really seem all right to you?"

"He's *got* asthma," she says, as though Rosie is a slow child who must have everything explained to her many times over.

"But does he seem much sicker than when he first came to you?"

"No. Dr. Linder says he's much better."

"When should Quinn come by today?" she asks, careful to phrase it as a given that Quinn will be coming by and that only the specific time needs to be negotiated.

"He's got him for the day again. The doctor, I mean."

"Why?" Rosie asks, and it feels like groups of tiny creatures are dancing up and down in her abdomen, banging against all her organs.

"He wants to have him checked with another doctor. To fine-tune the medication, he said." The abdominal creatures have gone nearly mad with frenzy. And her hands are tingling so badly, she can barely continue to hold the phone.

"Do you have the other doctor's name?"

"No, I didn't ask."

"Would you call Quinn when Jason gets back? Just so he knows Jason's safe and sound?"

"If it's not too late."

"Even if it's late," Rosie says, and hangs up before Monica can offer more protest.

CHAPTER
THIRTY-SEVEN

NO ANSWER AT QUINN'S NUMBER STILL. NO answer at Linder's.

She tries the doctor's answering service. "I think I have an appointment for my daughter today at ten-fifteen, but I just wanted to double-check the time," Rosie tells the woman who answers.

"We're canceling all his appointments for today, ma'am, sorry about that."

"Why are you canceling?"

"The doctor's got an emergency."

"All day? Oh, no," she says, deliberately putting a bit of a catch into her voice. "My child's really not doing well. Her congestion's awful."

"I'll be happy to give you the number of the doctor who's covering for him," she says, her voice rising, waiting for Rosie's answer.

"Yes," Rosie says, rather pleased with herself for getting a lead on where Linder might be taking Jay. "Is there some kind of problem developing? This is the second time he's canceled me recently," she tries, fishing for information.

"Well, I'm sorry about that, ma'am, but we are just the answering service here."

"Oh, yes, I didn't mean to imply it was your fault. I was just worried about the doctor."

"I wouldn't know any details, ma'am."

"Right. Okay, then, I guess you should just let me have that other doctor's name."

The woman reads it out, letters and numbers coming at Rosie so fast, she can barely take it down. "And your name?" the service woman asks.

"Jones," Rosie says, wincing at her own ineptness in giving such a common name. "My daughter's name is Amanda."

"He said he'd fax me his appointments in a couple of minutes, so I'll take you off the list once it gets here. That'll save me one call, anyway. If you want to reschedule, you can call me back later this morning."

Rosie thanks the woman, hangs up, and checks the time on her clock radio. Chances are if she tried this other number she's just written down—this doctor who's covering for Linder— she wouldn't get him this early anyway, she'd get only his answering service and they wouldn't be able to tell her when or even if Dr. Linder was bringing in a patient for consultation. No point in bothering with that yet, she decides. She's got a much more promising route to follow: the woman at the answering service has as good as told her where she could find Linder right now if only she can move fast enough. If he's faxing his appointments in to his service, that has to mean he's gone to his office to get the appointment book.

Rosie is already pulling her nightgown over her head, grabbing for yesterday's slacks and shirt from where she tossed them across the chair the night before, then she's racing through the house, grabbing for her purse and keys. In the car, at the first light, she runs her fingers through her hair. She doesn't check her own image in the rearview mirror because she doesn't want to know how bad it is. And it occurs to her that she should have called Quinn, but too late now, she thinks. He'd only tell her she shouldn't be doing this. The police said it right in front of him: *Don't call Linder again* (which, she'd already tried to do) and *don't go to his house.* Did it help that this wasn't his house, but his office that she was heading toward? No, of course it didn't, she knows that.

Driving out of Eastleigh in rush hour is easy, she quickly realizes. Nobody seems to be heading north, everybody's coming the other way, out of Bradford. But southbound traffic is an uninterrupted, unmoving line that she hopes somewhere, well north of here, Linder is caught in, trying to get from his house to his office.

He said he'd fax me his appointments in a couple of minutes, the woman had said. What if he was already at the office when he called her? Maybe by a *few* minutes he meant only two. Maybe all he'd needed to do was make a copy of his appointments on one office machine and then transmit the fax and by now he was already finished. Gone out of there. Destination unknown.

But if he is still there and she shows up? Then what? He'll call the police, that's for certain. That'll be the end of it, she thinks. They'll probably jail her this time. She's violated their precious order *and* she's been warned by the police to keep her distance from Linder.

She has to block Linder *today*, any way she can. Her child could die while they figured out with their slow-as-molasses approach to problem solving when they could schedule a new hearing.

She's driving too fast when she pulls into the parking lot, and she has to hit the brake so hard, her car goes into a spin and she barely manages to stop before hitting a black Honda. His car. She can't believe it. His car, she thinks. He's still here. And the creatures in her abdomen have started cavorting again. Silently, she warns them to hush.

She takes the elevator to the second floor and then covers the corridor down to his suite on the run. The door is closed, but when she turns the knob, it gives under her hand. She makes her way through the empty waiting room, moving slowly, being as quiet as she can, rolling on the balls of her feet, as though trying to touch the floor as little as possible. She leans forward as she goes, hoping to see him before he sees her, trying to catch a glimpse of him before her footsteps give her away, on past Marcy's unoccupied station, till she reaches the doorway to his office.

And he is there, very close by, really, though with his back to her, and totally unaware of her presence. Drawers are pulled open everywhere. He's lifting books from the shelves next to his desk, loading them into a cardboard box. Behind him, in the small examining room, she sees the shape that must surely be her child on the examining table, the same white blanket tossed over his body as on the previous two nights. "I've come for Jason," she says, startling Linder so thoroughly, he drops the heavy text he's holding.

"I'll just call the police," he says, moving toward the desk. "I'll remind them to bring their steel bracelets because you're so agitated. Was that the word they used? Yes, I think so. Agitated."

"They won't come this time," she says, wishing it were true.

He laughs, the light, breathy noise of someone finding amusement in a cleverly turned phrase. "Why's that?" His hand has started to lift the receiver already.

"Because the judge has ruled against you," she says, reaching for a lie so large, the words arrive wrapped in an aura; a pulsing, purplish halo of light. It makes her face beat hot in response.

He puts the phone back down and turns to face her more directly, folding his hands in front of himself. She's shaken him: his fingers are moving, wandering one over the other.

"The three women in Pennsylvania—Reddington, Pennsylvania," she clarifies with emphasis, reaching for the name of the town out of the health official's ramblings. "Do you remember them?" she asks, though she doesn't wait for an answer from him. She knows she must keep talking, to prod at his anxiety and keep him from making the call. "They've given depositions." She's nodding, making it real. Yes, it has already happened, she tells herself. Her stomach is calm now, resilient, a firm, springboard from which this information can be launched. It is an easy series of lies. All she has to do is pretend that the best of all possible outcomes has already occurred. That all that she has hoped for has come to pass. "And your patients here: the Ciccollis, the Porters, and the Moores. We have depositions from them, too. The judge knows now that you've made those children ill. He knows that there's a pattern. And that it's been done with intent," she says, each word of her last phrase pronounced so slowly, the letters seem to rise individually from her lips.

She glances over at Jason, but for only a second. She needs to keep her eyes on Linder. Jason hasn't moved, though maybe that's just as well. If he were to roll over, he could go right off the edge of the high table.

"You're deluded," he says. "You can't honestly believe I made Jason ill, can you?" He extends a hand over in the child's direction, but Rosie doesn't take the bait and turn toward her child again. She knows that Linder's trying to distract her.

"Yes, I think you made him ill."

"Now, wait a minute," he says, "did I come tackle you and your healthy child on the street or something? Did I force you in some way into becoming my patient? No, you came to me, with a child with breathing difficulties. Because you wanted me to pass a magic wand over him and make it all go away. That's what *you* wanted. That's what parents always want. Make it all go away." He says these last words in a child's singsong whine. "You don't want doctors, you want shamans and priests—no, you want gods. Don't you think that's asking a bit much?" The whine is gone. Now the words are strong; combative.

"We want you to be honest and caring, that's all."

He laughs. "Right. As long as it works. As long as we cure you, right? As long as the coughing stops. As long as the baby's born A-one, perfect in every way. And anything short of perfection is our fault, isn't it? I told you what they did to my father—they crucified him because a baby died. Because he couldn't bring a child back from the dead. I swore I wouldn't let my patients get that kind of power over me ever, raking me over the legal coals, placing blame and fault." He's got both hands on the desk, leaning forward, shouting all of it at her.

She remembers then what the woman in the personnel office said to her: criminal charges are never brought against physicians unless there is overwhelming evidence of wrongdoing. "You know he botched that delivery," she says, hurling the words at him. "He *killed* a child. There were no birth defects involved, no accidents, and you know that. I checked on it."

She's shaking, this lie is so bald, but as she speaks it, he stiffens, and she knows her guess is right on target. His father killed a newborn through some terrible act—omission or commission, she can't say which, but she's sure it's one of those. "If a doctor is at fault, he should be blamed," she declares.

"Every single one of you sought me out, dragging an already sick child behind. But every single one of you loved it when that shot of adrenaline worked its magic, didn't you? Are you going to tell me you didn't get a rush watching your baby come back from the brink like that—you loved it, right? Right? Answer me," he shouts at her when she doesn't respond. He pounds his fist against the desk.

"I wanted my child healthy, that's all. Of course I was glad he was better."

He nods and runs his tongue across his lips. "Glad, yes, you certainly were. I told you, you were a very good patient. Good medicine is a two-way street, you know, just like a marriage. But you were good at it. You practically knelt at my feet, you loved it so much, didn't you? Answer me," he bellows at her again.

"Yes," she says, and she almost gags over this horrid truth. What he's saying is true—she would have done any-thing for him in those moments. Knelt before him? Yes. Groveled and crawled to hear her child breathe evenly? Of course. But she can't deal with that now. She has to think about Jay, nothing else.

"Because a *recovered* child is so much better than just a plain healthy one, isn't he? You had a very sick child and I'm the one who made him better, remember that. I never made *anyone* ill," he insists.

"Then why does my child lie there like that if he's okay?" She still hasn't seen Jason move. She's not close enough to tell if he's even breathing.

"Because he's got asthma and because he's sedated."

"Sedated?" Now she's the one shouting. "Why the hell is a two-year-old sedated? You're slowing down his breathing that way, you're—"

"Who is the doctor here, Rosie?" he interrupts. "Jason's

316

sleep has been badly compromised lately. He's been under tremendous stress. You know all the reasons why he would benefit from sedation, surely." He takes a seat at his desk. "Do you know what we need in this country?" She's so taken aback by this non sequitur, she can't respond. "We need to educate people about the medical profession. People don't understand what we do, how much time and thought it takes to plan out a program of care. They want their medication and that's all. They come in to a medical practice, they come for a visit, and then they take their prescriptions and run. That's their real magic, you know—the medication—and they have no use for us till those meds run out. They'd rather have all their conversations with their pharmacists, not their doctors, because they can do *that* for free. But don't you think a doctor should be able to keep a few patients long enough to build up a practice? If they want magic, they can get magic right here, that's fine with me. It's what kept you coming back, isn't it?" he asks, pointing at her, but beyond her, too, over her shoulder, to some unseen assemblage of other parents and patients. "It's not such a bad way to make a living, actually," he adds, almost brightly, as though this is the clincher line to a clever speech he's just delivered.

"That's why you gave them aspirin, isn't it?" He grasps the arms of his desk chair. She sees his hands working at the leather. "So they'd have to come back. You created symptoms, didn't you? So you could save them, have us fall at your feet, beg you to cure our children."

"What are you talking about? All I'm saying is I'm good at what I do. I know asthma. I know how to help children and their mothers."

"The antihistamine with aspirin, Greg. It's not even a pediatric drug. It induces asthmatic symptoms. You gave it to your patients so they'd continue to have symptoms. Why? So you could keep pulling them back from near death? So you could look like a goddamn hero?"

"Rosie, I'm afraid you're in over your head here, medically speaking. You know what your problem is? You were cursed by being born into a physician's family, and believe me, I

317

understand that perfectly. You confuse yourself with your father, don't you? But you have to remember, he was the doctor, not you. I really shouldn't have to stoop to explaining these things to you, but yes, I use some nonstandard procedures. I've had very good luck with them. If doctors never tried anything new, we'd never defeat any disease, would we?" He leans forward, resting his arms, one atop the other, on the desk.

"Children aren't supposed to take aspirin at all, Greg. There are all kinds of possible complications. Every parent knows the potential deadly combination of aspirin and viral illness."

"As far as I know, we weren't talking about viral illnesses, were we? I deal with asthma and allergy. Stop presuming to know more about this than I do." He hammers the desk with his fist again.

"You made my child's bronchial system nearly go into arrest."

"Rosie, all drugs have side effects. You ought to look in the *Physician's Desk Reference*." He pulls a large red volume from the shelf. "There isn't a drug listed in here that doesn't have at least twenty possible side effects. Should we stop administering all these drugs that have other possible positive effects? And, let me point out, there are side effects to every food you ingest. Should you stop eating? I don't think so."

"You're just trying to confuse the issues. None of this matters. What matters is that you deliberately gave this drug to my child, knowing that it would bring on breathing difficulties. Tell me why. So I'd sleep with you? Was that it?" She sees a smile pass across his lips, then disappear. "Tell me, which turned you on more, my total fear and helplessness when Jay couldn't catch his breath, or the longing looks I gave you after he came back? Which turn-on was better for you? My pain or my pleasure, Doctor? I want to know exactly what it was that made you put my child's life in danger."

"Don't exaggerate. His life was never in danger. I'm the doctor here. I know what I'm doing," he says, stepping from behind his desk. "I know how to control dosage. I never put him at any real risk."

"I'm taking Jason now," she says. She walks over to the examining table, lifts the blanket, and Linder hasn't moved to stop her. Rosie brings her face down to Jason's. He's breathing, but it's a shallow sound, and just like the other night, he doesn't rouse at all when she calls his name. She looks over at Linder. "You said he was all right. You said you took him on the merry-go-round. Monica said he was all right."

"He was. It wears off," he says. "It's just to relax him."

"What did you give him?"

Linder reaches into his pocket and takes out a container of medication and hands it to her. "A compound with phenobarbital." She sees it has Jason's name on it. "In the good old days they used phenobarbital routinely in combo in asthma meds, you know. It cuts down on that shakiness you always hated that they get after the adrenaline." He closes her hands around the container. "But he could overdose if you gave him too much, couldn't he?"

"I never gave him that drug."

"Really? That's strange because this bottle has his name on it." He pulls the container from her hand, grasping it by the very edges of the cap and the bottom only. She tries to grab for it, but he holds it aloft. "There's such a tiny dose specified here, I'm not even sure it'd have an effect, frankly," he says. "But you know what? There's much more than that missing from the bottle, isn't there, Rosie?" he asks, holding it toward the light, examining it. Her hands grab high at the air, but his reach well exceeds hers. "Why did you give him so much, Rosie? And when did you do it?"

He backs away from her, hand still above his head and sets the bottle on the highest shelf, then gives it a flick so that it skitters backward where even he wouldn't be able to get to it again without standing on a chair.

"Listen to me," he says, turning back around to face her. "I'm leaving so I'm not going to bother you anymore. We both need to get out from under this"—he circles a hand, searching for the right phrase—"cloud of suspicion?" He raises his eyebrows questioningly. "We need to get on with our lives, you and I. So let me put it to you this way. You leave me alone, and

319

I'll leave you alone. I'll toss that bottle in the river. That way we'll both get a fresh start, all right?"

"Sure," she says, knowing there's no point in arguing with him.

"I'm going to need to keep Jason with me for a couple of days. Just to insure some lead time out of this town."

"No way," she says, standing in front of her child, her hand behind her, against the table.

"Relax, it's just for a couple of days. We'll make a little deal here—you don't call the police and I don't forget what the right dosages are for Jason's medication. Then you sit tight and I'll call you, tell you where you can pick him up. There won't be anything in his system by that time. In fact, he'll be ready to ride the old merry-go-round again if you feel like going to the mall," he says, his tone as light as though he's talking about a weekend stay in the countryside. "I don't think you'll have any trouble with breathing problems after that. You'll be able to forget all this happened."

She starts to gather Jason into her arms.

"I can't let you take him."

"You can't stop me."

"That's not really true, Rosie. I've got the weight and strength if you want to go one-on-one on this."

He grabs hold of one of her wrists and twists her arm behind her back so that she has to let go of Jay and go where Linder now directs her, over to the other side of the room.

"The police already know everything. It's too late for this."

"What they know is that you're deranged and that you caused this illness by overmedicating your child. Jason's condition right now will only reinforce that idea. I've reported how you keep breaking into my home. I'll just add that I think you've been slipping him all kinds of things he shouldn't have. Your prints are all over that pheno and all the other drugs you held in my office. All the ones that in excess can cause some pretty terrible symptoms. And if I tell the police that I was desperate, that the only way I could think of to save him was to get him out of this town, away from you, for a day or two, they'll go with it. And so let me make this really clear," he growls as he pulls up sharply on her twisted arm, "if you do call the police, when and if you find Jason, he may have so much medication in him that he'll be in cardiac arrest or lapsed into a genuine coma. This isn't one, by the way, it is, truly, just sleep—medicated sleep, of course. Oh, and I did mention all those possible side effects way back when I first prescribed all his medications, right?" She's having trouble catching her breath. "The court thinks you're an abusive mother. They think you've got a psychological disorder. Rosie, they think you're a crazy Munchausen mom with one dead child already. And by the way, thank you for telling me that sweet secret about baby number one. Little Miss May Donovan was beside herself with joy when she heard about Abigail. And all that stuff about your Daddy second-guessing everything you ever did. All that *made her case*," he whispers in her ear, "as I'm sure you'll agree."

Rosie wants to push the bastard away, to bite and kick him, but he's got so much pressure on her arm, the slightest move she makes is agonizing. "The judge knows about you, Dr. Linder," she manages to say.

"What? Those depositions you talked about?" He's leaning against her, his mouth close against her hair. "And what were those patients' names in Pennsylvania, pray tell?"

She's never known the names, of course. "I don't remember," she says.

"Because you don't have them. Because I haven't signed a release yet. I only got it last night—and it was very nice of your attorney to tip me off that way. Those names aren't public information, but privileged information. There was never any finding of fault, so no one—*no one*—has the right to get those names until I say so. Which, I might add, I have no intention of ever doing."

"Your patients here gave depositions," she protests.

He shakes his head back and forth and though he's behind her, he's so close, she can see the motion easily. "No way: Amy Ciccolli? She's a rabbit. I know who the skittish ones are, the ones who'll back down. She got so hysterical when I resuscitated her child, I had to hold her in my arms and stroke her for ten minutes to calm her down, stroke her foolish head. She wouldn't let go of me. She couldn't do anything on her own. Believe me, I'm a careful man, Rosie. I'm very, very good at this. I know Ciccolli wouldn't have given you a deposition. None of them have, none of them will."

"What about me? Didn't you think I was skittish?"

He shrugs. "When you first came in you were."

"And the others were, too, you're right. Because they were terrified for their children's well-being, just like I was. But now that I've made it clear to them what's been going on, they're not nervous anymore. They're angry. They're furious. And now they've given me depositions, so believe it, Greg." Maybe she's being too confrontational, she thinks, suddenly scared of winding him up tighter than he already is, but he's hesitated just the slightest, not shot back a hard answer this time, and he's even eased up momentarily on her arm. Then he twists again.

"I don't think so," he says. "Did you tell them that you've been accused of abuse? I think that might get them to reconsider. Have they discussed it with their husbands? Husbands don't like to make waves, you know. They always think the mothers overreact to illnesses, anyway. Husbands are always taking me aside and confiding that they think their wives have lost perspective on the illness. Or that they're too overprotective of their children. The husbands aren't home all day listening to the wheezing, and they're usually not the ones who lie half-awake through the night listening, growing more and more weary. So it never seems so bad to them. It seems like there's lots of exaggeration. The husbands will think the women are overreacting yet again. They'll see you as an extreme version of their own wives. They'll say, 'Calm down or you'll lose it altogether like Rosie Sloan. No wonder her husband left her.' Think about it: Why would they be supportive of somebody the courts have virtually declared insane? Gee whiz, but life's unfair, ain't it, Rosie?" he observes, pulling up again on her arm.

"And you know something, none of this would have happened if your husband hadn't picked up that little teeny-bopper of his—what was her name? Diana? She's the one who screwed it all up by going to DCF. Poor misguided thing, she thought she was getting at you by calling them in. Once she started that up, though, I *had* to shift the balance a bit toward you. And then you—you wanted to start poking. 'What could somebody be giving him?' you asked me." He laughs. "Damned if I know, right?" She's trying to look behind her, to see if Jason's still all right, but Linder's completely blocking her view.

"I couldn't have them checking my credentials, you can see that, can't you? And I honestly thought there would just be a little reprimand to you, a slap on the hand, a bunch of home visits. And maybe that's all it would have been if you hadn't fought that social worker so much and gotten on her bad side. I told you to be nice, but she told me you were really bitchy to her. Was it worth it?" His lips are so close to her neck, she feels his breath. "Anyway, I am sorry it went so far—court, foster care, and all that. But we can blame Diana for it all, I think. If it hadn't been for that girl, I'd have had Jason all recovered by now. You'd have told everybody in town what a splendid job I'd done. That's worth a few more paying customers." He looks around the room. "I wanted to take more of this stuff with me. It's expensive enough to have to start over without having to buy all your equipment new."

"If you run, they'll know you're guilty."

"Of what?"

"Of making Jason ill. Of making other children ill."

"I really was falling in love with you, you know," he says, letting go of her arm, trying to turn her around to face him.

"I believed you," she says, letting him hold her. She doesn't know what she's going to do next. What he's going to do next. "I did like it when you saved him. And it got better—better every time," she says, struggling to come up with something to appease him and calm him down. "So why did you turn against me?" she asks him, touching his face. "We would have been good together." Her own words make her dizzy.

He laughs. "Don't try to con me," he says.

"But you should go now," she advises him, whispering it, making it into a confidence shared. "You should get out now while you can, get a head start on the police, at least. Quinn called them, they'll be here any second," she lies. "Please, for me, save yourself."

"I don't think so. Quinn doesn't believe you. He thinks you're a hysteric." He looks at her and she sees how firmly his eyes have fixed her. When he draws her closer against his body, she tries not to resist. "Did you and I ever kiss?" he asks. "I can't say I remember."

"Did you love me at all?" she asks, forcing herself to speak the words.

"I don't think I know whether I did or not. Things got derailed too early." She watches his mouth move toward hers, and she wants to let him kiss her, knows it would be best, but her body disobeys her and she leans away, evading his mouth. He lets go of her, pushing her from him so that she stumbles for a moment, nearly falling. When she regains her balance, she backs away from him, toward one of the open drawers in the examining area.

She can see the silvery instruments lined up in their molded trays. What she learned, years ago, from her father's warning lectures is how very sharp they are, how they're designed to make fast, clean, razor thin entries through the skin. If they're properly maintained, her father had told her, they need very little pressure. Which is why she had to be sure to stay away, far away from these. Her hand reaches in and grabs an instrument. She holds the scalpel up in front of her, the blade tilted firmly in his direction. "I'm taking Jason," she says.

"Don't be silly. Give that to me," he says, closing the distance between them.

"You stay back." She slashes at the air between them with the knife.

He takes two more steps toward her and she takes a step back. He laughs. "You're not going to be very effective as a fighter if you're going to retreat, are you?"

His hand flies out suddenly toward hers and she knows, she has known, that he's going to go for her wrist. She pulls up her hand, simultaneously turning the knife down sharply so that his hand contacts the blade as he reaches for her.

"Yow," he howls, and pulls back a step. It takes a moment, but then the blood is flowing fast and bitter red against the whiteness of the side of his hand. He moves toward the sink, pulling a wad of paper towels from the dispenser, holding them with his good hand against his bad one. Rosie watches the towels turn red. Her stomach is swirling. She hadn't expected the wound to be so long. She cannot remember the knife entering his flesh. It will need stitches, many of them. "I don't want to hurt you," she says, "but I will if you don't let me out of here."

"Give me that goddamn towel," he shouts at her, motioning toward a pile of terry cloth hand towels on the cabinet next to her. The blood has soaked through the paper towels and is dripping freely into the sink.

She picks up two towels and tosses them toward him. They land at his feet and he stoops to pick them up. With her hip, she pushes the drawer of instruments soundly closed along its metal tracks, then leans back against it. In the distance she hears sirens. "I told you," she says, pointing the tip of the scalpel toward the window, toward the sound, hoping it's really coming here, for her, that Quinn has figured out she needs them. "You better go now. I won't tell them I even saw you."

"Maybe I *was* falling in love," he says as he wraps the towel tightly around his hand. She shakes her head. He stares at her, seems about to say something, but the siren is getting closer. He backs away, eyes firmly on her, stops to lift his sport coat off the desk and put it atop one of the cardboard boxes. When he tries to pick up the box, he winces, drops the box back down the few inches he's lifted it, and clutches his injured hand. All he takes with him as he goes out the door is the sport coat, draped over his bandaged hand.

Rosie goes to the window and scans the street below, but there are no police cars speeding toward this spot. "Come on," she shouts at the sirens. She crosses to the other side of the room, positions his desk chair next to the shelves, climbs up on it, sinking down into the leather, and retrieves the bottle of medication he's stowed up there. She drops the bottle into the pocket of her jeans.

Next, she walks over to the examining table where her child is lying. "Hi, sweetpie," she says, and strokes the hair from his forehead. He opens his eyes, seems unfocused at first, and then smiles and reaches his arms up toward her. As she lifts him, he slides his hands around her neck, then puts his head back down to sleep on her shoulder.

In the elevator he's alert enough to reach his hand toward the bank of buttons. "Pussy buddy?" he asks, and Rosie brings him close enough so that his finger can touch the L button and light it up. When the elevator doors open, Quinn is coming through the front door.

"Are you both okay?" he asks her.

"Yes," she says. "But we need to get him to the hospital to make sure. Did you see Linder leave?"

"No, I just got here. Is he gone?" She nods. "How gone?"

"I don't know yet. Gone to a doctor or hospital, I think. He needs to get stitches fast."

"How badly did you hurt him?"

"Just enough, I think." Quinn holds the front door open so they can pass through. "How did you know I was here?"

"I didn't. You weren't home, so I just went looking. I figured you went after Jason. I tried Linder's house first, then here."

"And you called the police?"

"No," he says, and she realizes the sirens have stopped.

"I heard sirens. Weren't there sirens before?"

"Well, this *is* a city. You could probably hear them a couple times an hour here." He lifts Jason from her arms and carries him to the car. "Emily Porter called me. She said she couldn't sleep at all last night and she wants to talk to you about some things she left out."

"Are you kidding me?"

"Nope."

"She didn't get more specific than that?"

"Well, she said you asked her if Linder ever told her he thought he was falling in love with her."

"And?"

"She said she's not sure why you asked that, but if he said it to anybody else, she'll make a statement and, I quote, 'Get the filthy con.' "

"Well, hallelujah," she proclaims, laughing. "So maybe we're okay, Quinn?"

"We're okay," he says, putting his arms around both of them. Rosie feels Jason's hands slide over her neck. She feels the pat-pat-pat of his tiny hand just at the top of her back, sees that his other hand pats Quinn in precisely the same place.

"We're all going to be okay now, Jay," she whispers to him.

Sylvie, a twenty-one-year-old mother afflicted with attention deficit disorder, swears that she left her six-week-old baby girl alone for only five minutes. But in those five minutes Sylvie's life is shattered.

For her baby has vanished.

Suddenly the desperate young mother finds herself in a terrifying trap. No one will help her get her baby back, because no one believes she was kidnapped. Sylvie realizes she alone must solve this crime—or lose her baby forever.

SLEEP, BABY, SLEEP

by Jessica Auerbach
Author of *Catch Your Breath*

"This gripping story of a young mother searching for her kidnapped baby could have been lifted from recent headlines. . . . Told with edgy intensity."
—*Publishers Weekly*